13-05-22

The Holding

By Lynda Faye Schmidt

Liz,

   Thank you so much for being an
advanced reader for The Holding, for
supporting me so beautifully on my
author journey, and for being a
steadfast friend. I appreciate you
immensely and I feel blessed that
you were brought into my life.
I pray our bond will remain
strong, no matter where life
takes us. I pray for you, too,
as you grieve your own loss,
of the holding,
         Much love,
                          LF Schmidt

The Holding

First published in 2022 by

Halifax, NS, Canada
www.ocpublishing.ca

Cover design by David W. Edelstein
Original cover photo by Danielle O'Brien
Interior book design by Grace Laemmler

ISBN - 978-1-989833-16-2 (Paperback)
ISBN - 978-1-989833-17-9 (eBook)

DISCLAIMER
This novel is based on true events. While people, places, and events
may closely resemble real life, it is a fiction. Written from the author's
perspective, the lines between imagination and reality have been
intentionally blurred to honour the authenticity of the author's emotional
experiences while respecting the anonymity of the real-life people that
her characters portray or are inspired by. The author in no way attempts
to tell someone else's story or version of truth, simply her own.

The Holding *is dedicated with love, devotion, respect, and limitless gratitude to my father, Kenneth William Smith, 1938–2000.*

Reviews for *The Holding* (prequel to *The Healing*)

"*The Holding* evidences Lynda Faye Schmidt's growth as a writer. Through her protagonist, Cate, she makes herself completely vulnerable by sharing the harrowing physical, emotional, and spiritual challenges she has faced. Her deeply intimate relationship with her earthly father, is equalled by her relationship to her God and Father and her love of both shines from the pages. Having recently suffered personal loss, I found the ending extremely poignant and I cried shamelessly."

— Elizabeth Kingsman, daughter, wife, mother, Christian

"*The Holding* took me on an emotional journey. I could relate to Cate's challenges and rallied with her as she found the inner strength to endure life's tribulations."

— Michelle Jones

"Had me captured from the first page to the last."

— Linda Smith

Reviews for *The Healing*

"Lynda Faye Schmidt has expertly written a story about inner freedom, self-love, and the quest for meaning amidst the vicissitudes of life… A rare literary gift for fans of deeply moving and emotionally captivating tales."

—Jane Riley, reviewer for The Book Commentary

"Plot-wise, *The Healing* is an immensely entertaining, feel-good novel…the storyline truly waxes in emotions… If you are charmed by stories like *Eat, Pray, Love*, *The Healing* is the book for you."

— Vincent Dublado, reviewer for Readers' Favorite

"*The Healing* details a woman's journey in finding herself and overcoming past traumas. Written as a fiction but based on Lynda's real-life experiences, *The Healing* is a very personal exploration of what it means to be well, to live your authentic purpose, and how to transform challenges into growth."

— Kara McDuffee, My Question Life Blog

Chapter 1

"*H*ELLO? ANYBODY THERE?" WILLIAM yells. He peers through the shaded glass, one hand over his eyes, the other banging on the thick steel door. He wipes the sweat along his hairline with the back of his sleeve, then turns to his wife. "Hang in there, Donna."

"I feel like I'm going to faint," Donna says. Her knees buckle. Blood gushes out between her legs, forming a crimson pool at her feet, just as the lights in the hospital flicker on and the night watchman appears. William steadies his wife, his arm around her waist.

"Hurry up then," William says to the watchman when he opens the door. "I was about ready to smash the window. Where the hell is the on-call doctor?"

"I'll call," the watchman says. He presses a button on his walkie-talkie. "Looks like we've got an emergency situation here," he says. He tucks the walkie-talkie back into its holster and walks around to help William support Donna. "There's a wheelchair just over there," he says, pointing with his head down the hallway to the left.

William and the watchman guide Donna to the chair and lower her onto it, the watchman's bulkiness in sharp contrast to William's slight stature.

"Is my baby going to be alright?" Donna says, her voice barely a whisper. Her head falls to her chest.

"Christ, I think she just fainted," William says.

"Well, don't just stand around gawking," says a nurse, who has appeared out of nowhere. "Let's get her to an examining room."

The nurse grabs the wheelchair and William follows her as she walks down the corridor at a stiff clip. The name tag on her massive bosom says Nurse Peever.

"Is she going to be okay, Nurse?" William asks.

"It's hard to say," she answers. "I'll be sure to send for you once the doctor has a chance to examine your wife and get her stable."

Nurse Peever steers Donna down the hallway, leaving William to find his way to the waiting room. The sleepy town has a population of less than two thousand, more like a village really, and the only hospital is so trifling it is more like a clinic. At this hour it is silent, completely deserted, with no sign of anyone, not even a janitor.

The waiting room is as he remembers. A massive wood-panelled box television set is in the corner. A motley selection of chairs that look like donations from the thrift store line the wall, and the single coffee table is laden with magazines and newspapers. William looks at his watch. It is just after four in the morning, and he is exhausted. He plunks down on a tattered, green suede recliner with a broken knob.

The drama has been distracting, and now, alone with his thoughts, the worry sets in. William realizes how little he knows of the secret rituals of childbirth. He pushes his dangling cowlick from his high forehead, takes off his glasses, and closes his eyes. He attempts to convince himself that everything is going to be okay.

Donna has come around to find she is no longer in a wheelchair but on an examining table with her legs splayed, feet draped over two metal footholds. She looks around the room, then voices her first thought, despite her mental fog. "Is my baby okay?" She cringes. With each contraction her abdomen feels as though all the muscles are tearing away from her skin.

"Oh, thank goodness, you've come to," Nurse Peever says. "I'm sure your baby's just fine." She pauses from wiping up the dried blood caked to Donna's thighs. "You seem to have stopped bleeding, that's a good sign. We need to stop your contractions. If you continue to labour and the baby is born now, by the size of you I'd reckon the baby might not survive."

"What?" Donna gasps. "How do we stop them?" Her hands move protectively to cradle the cantaloupe-sized bump of her belly.

"Just try your best to stay calm," Nurse Peever says. "Take some deep breaths. The doctor will be here any minute."

As if on cue, a young man dressed in powder-blue scrubs appears in the doorway, already snapping on a pair of rubber gloves.

"Hello, Dr. Crenshaw," says the nurse.

"Nurse Peever," he replies. "So, what do we have here?" His voice is muffled by his face mask.

Donna tries to overhear as the doctor, who looks to be fresh out of medical school, discusses the situation with the nurse, but they've lowered their voices and she is unable to make out anything. After a few minutes, the doctor approaches her bedside.

"Mrs. Henderson," Dr. Crenshaw says, looking at the chart that Nurse Peever had only just begun to fill in. "I'm going to check your vitals and the baby's too, but I think it's only fair to warn you that judging by the amount of blood you've lost, you're likely hemorrhaging. We might have to perform an emergency Caesarean section."

"A C-section?" Donna strokes her belly. "I was so hoping I could have this baby naturally, like I did with my son. I don't understand, everything went so easy with him."

"Each pregnancy is different," Dr. Crenshaw says. "But let's not jump to any conclusions until I conduct my exam."

The doctor proceeds with his examination.

"Well, Mrs. Henderson, it seems both you and the baby are stable." He tosses his gloves into a waste can. "The hemorrhaging appears to have stopped and the baby's heartbeat is in a normal range, but your contractions are getting closer and more intense. A Caesarean won't be necessary, your baby is coming soon."

Labour progresses quickly and at 5:15 a.m. a tiny baby girl arrives into the world, red-skinned and wrinkled. Nurse Peever takes her in her large hands and wipes the fluids from her face with a cloth. The baby lets go a loud, healthy cry.

"Is it okay?" Donna asks weakly, her face drawn. "Is it a boy or a girl?"

"Your baby girl is going to be just fine," Nurse Peever proclaims. The baby is so small, her body rests easily in the palm of the nurse's hand. Her scrawny arms and legs dangle awkwardly over the sides. "She's premature, but not as small as I imagined she'd be. Still, I've got to take her to the infant

ICU immediately." She bundles up the baby in a pink blanket with practiced efficiency. "I'll let your husband know the good news and be back to check on you soon."

Nurse Peever finds William pacing the hallway outside the waiting room. She leads him down the hospital corridors to the ICU. There is only one clear, plastic crib. William moves up close to the glass window. His baby girl is squalling, her face as red as a ripe beet. Her tiny arms flail about, naked and exposed, having escaped the swaddling of receiving blankets. Plastic oxygen tubing trails from each nostril.

"She looks so frail, more like a doll," William says, choking on tears. "How long does she have to stay in this incubator?"

"It's too early to tell," says Nurse Peever. "But I've been at this work a long time and I think she'll be out of here sooner than later."

William places his hand on the window and stares at his little girl. Something switches inside his heart as a fierce protectiveness is ignited. "Daddy's here," he whispers, fogging up the glass.

"Let me take you to see your wife now," Nurse Peever says, interrupting the tender moment. She leads William by the arm down the hall.

Donna has been moved from the delivery room to a four-bed maternity ward. The other three beds are empty, the sheets pulled tight with the corners tucked in military precision.

"I'll leave you two alone," Nurse Peever says, closing the door behind her.

William strides over to the bed where Donna is recovering. Her dark auburn curls are wet with sweat, she's as pale as a pitcher of skim milk and can hardly keep her eyes open.

"It's so good to see you," Donna says to William, wiping a tear from her eye and blowing her nose. "They had to take our baby girl to the ICU."

"I know, I just saw her," William says.

"She's such a tiny little thing," Donna says, a tremor in her voice. She looks about to burst into tears. "She's like a new baby bird, just hatched from the egg. You know she fit in the palm of the nurse's hand?"

"Nurse Peever is the size of brick house," William says with a chuckle. "A baby elephant would look small in her hands. But I saw on her card, she weighs five pounds, one ounce. That's not so small."

"Do you think so?" Donna asks, her lip quivering.

"I do," William says. "Try not to worry so much; it won't do any good, and besides, any daughter of yours has to be feisty, I'm thinking. I've got a full day's work on my desk so I'm going to go check in on our little girl one more time and then head on home."

"You're leaving? So soon?" Donna's mouth curls into a frown. "Don't you think we should at least decide on a name for her first?"

"Yeah, I guess so," William agrees, stuffing his hands into his trouser pockets. "We thought we still had lots of time to talk about it, didn't we? How about Elizabeth or Beatrice, after one of our mothers?"

"Those names are so old-fashioned," Donna says. "What do you think of Sandra-Lee?"

"Sounds like a southerner or a character in a movie," William says. "What about Kate, after your friend?"

"Oh, I love that! I've missed Kate so much since she moved to Australia last year. Maybe we could spell it with a *C*? I've always thought that was a pretty spelling." Donna gives him a big smile and he kisses her goodbye.

William leaves the hospital and locates his 1957 Chevrolet in the empty hospital parking lot and climbs in. The car is nine years old now, but still in pretty good shape. He notes a layer of dusty grime has accumulated on the windows, a perpetual occurrence in the Canadian prairies in spring. It irks him to no end, but there's nothing to be done about it. He starts the car and turns on the windshield wipers while pressing the handle for a squirt of windshield fluid, then eases the car into drive. He turns out of the parking lot and onto the narrow street. In no time at all he's pulling into the alleyway behind their home.

The house is small, one side of a duplex, conservatively constructed with plain eggshell-white stucco and coal-grey wood trim around the windows and doors. The gunmetal-grey shingles on the slanting roof gleam in the early morning sunrise.

William walks through the back door into the coat room, takes off his shoes, and hangs his windbreaker on a hook. In the kitchen his mother, who loves to fuss over her beloved first-born son, is bustling about.

"Oh William, thank goodness. I've been beside myself waiting. It's been hours since you tore out of here like a fox stealing a hen from the barn! How are Donna and the baby?" Elizabeth absent-mindedly pats down her silver-blue hair, tucking a wayward home-permed curl behind her ear.

"We have a baby girl, Mother," William says. "She's a tiny little thing, being so early. She has to be in an incubator and—"

"What?" Elizabeth interrupts. "A baby girl? I never would have thought Donna would deliver so early. An incubator? That sounds serious. For the life of me—"

"Please, Mother," William interrupts. "It's because she's so small and frail. She's on oxygen, because her lungs are underdeveloped. It all happened so fast, I'm still in a bit of a daze, to be honest."

"Well, alright then, I'll put some bread in the toaster oven, baked it fresh just yesterday mind you," Elizabeth says with a quick peck on his cheek. "Go ahead and sit. A hearty breakfast should help clear your head."

"Thank you," William says as he washes up at the sink. "Is Michael up yet?"

"Oh, that dear boy, what an angel, but yes, he does like to get up early, which is a good thing as I see it. He ate of all of his breakfast for me and was so nice and tidy. He was a big boy and even used the toilet after. Mark my words, I'll have that boy trained before his mother gets home from the hospital. I'm sure it will make Donna's life much easier, and really, I can't fathom why she has waited so long to try, he's just such a cooperative little man. Anyway, he's busy playing in his pen, I just checked in on him a few minutes ago and he's happy as a bug, so don't you worry, just sit and relax."

William lets out a weary sigh and drops onto a kitchen chair. Elizabeth passes him a steaming cup of hot, black coffee, then rushes to fetch the newspaper from the front porch. She peeks in on her grandson on the way back to the kitchen, queen of killing two birds with one stone. She efficiently slathers the toast with butter and honey and serves it up with a bowl of shredded wheat smothered with thick cream and brown sugar. She wipes her hands on her apron and lowers her petite frame down in a chair across the table.

"Now, what's this you said about an incubator?" Elizabeth asks without preamble. "And did you choose a name for her? Do you think she looks like a Henderson or a Dietrich?"

William nearly chokes on a mouthful of cereal as he swallows the urge to laugh. He finishes chewing and swallowing before he answers.

"I don't know the first thing about the incubator business," William says. "But we did choose to name her Cate, after Donna's friend. You remember her from our wedding, I'm sure. As to who she looks like, I think it's too soon to tell."

"Well, I suppose you have a point," Elizabeth says. "Although Michael is such a Henderson through and through, with your startling, dark blue eyes and hair as platinum as yours was at his age."

"You'll be seeing her yourself soon enough," William says. "Maybe you'll be able to tell who she looks like. As for me, I need to get a move on to work." He pushes back his chair and gets up to leave. "Where's Dad?"

"Oh, you know him, always has to be busy at something. He's down in the basement, figuring out how to install a proper cellar for you."

"That's kind of him," William says. "I'll go give my teeth a quick brush, then head off." He sets his dishes in the sink, gives his mother a brief hug, then checks in on Michael, still content in his playpen. He lifts him up in the air and Michael squeals, a huge smile on his chubby face.

"Goodbye, son," William says as he gives Michael's hair a ruffle. He sets him back down. "Be a good boy for your grandma now."

William stops by the hospital after work, as promised, and finds his wife in a jovial mood.

"It's good to see you smiling," he says as he comes around the side of the bed. He kisses Donna on the forehead. "I stopped by the ICU and I could swear Cate is looking stronger already."

"Yes, she's a spirited one," Donna says. "I just wish she didn't need to be in that incubator. It looks so sterile. I'd do anything to hold her, and I'm so disappointed I can't breastfeed her. But at least my prayers were answered and I didn't need a C-section."

"Did the doctor say when the two of you will be discharged?"

"Actually, yes. Dr. Crenshaw said I can go home after a week, just like I did with Michael. He's not as sure about Cate. He said it will depend on how fast her lungs develop and how quickly she can put on more weight. But as I said earlier, William, that little girl is a feisty one. I'm sure she'll be ready to come home soon."

A week later Donna's prediction comes true and both mother and daughter are discharged from the hospital. Donna puts Cate on an intense feeding schedule, and she gains an entire pound. It's almost hard to imagine how scrawny she'd looked at birth.

By sixteen months, Cate bears no resemblance to the tiny preemie who entered the world. Her crown of fine hair is blonde like William's and curly like Donna's. She has an outgoing personality, an advanced vocabulary, and a quick-to-smile disposition that wins over everyone who meets her within minutes.

Donna is hanging laundry on the clothesline in the backyard on a warm summer morning when the phone rings.

"Mommy will be right back," she says to Cate and Michael as she drops a shirt back in the laundry basket. "You two stay put."

"Okay," Michael says. He and Cate are sitting on a blanket in the sun, and he is pretending to read to his sister from a book he is holding upside down.

When Donna returns ten minutes later, Michael is bent over a raspberry bush in deep concentration and Cate is nowhere to be seen.

"Michael, where's your sister? I told you both to stay put."

"Sorry, Mommy." Michael looks around, bewildered. "She was right there when I saw this ladybug." He points to the spotted insect perched on a jagged green leaf.

"Well, she can't have gone far. She doesn't know how to walk without holding someone's hand. You go look behind the sandbox and I'll check over by the shed."

Donna's heart starts to beat faster as it quickly becomes clear that Cate is not in their yard. She tries not to panic, but her voice goes up an octave when she runs over to Michael, who has become distracted by one of his construction trucks in the sandbox.

"Michael Henderson, put that crane down this instant!" Donna says, more firmly than she means to. "Your sister is missing and we have to find her. Come with me and we'll go look out front."

Donna lifts Michael up onto her hip and walks to the front of the house. It is a quiet side street with little traffic, but Donna is terrified. She imagines her daughter lying on the asphalt, having been hit by a car.

After scouring the block, Donna runs with Michael back to the house. She dials William at work.

"William, I don't know how it happened. She was right there and now I can't find her and, and…"

"Whoa, slow down. Can't find who?"

"Cate," Donna says, biting her trembling lip, hardly able to hold the phone steady. "I was hanging up laundry when the phone rang. When I came back outside, she was gone."

"Cate? How can that be? She can't take two steps without falling over." He is already getting up from his desk, fetching his keys from the drawer.

"William, I'm so petrified," Donna says, sounding slightly hysterical. "What if she's been kidnapped?"

"God, don't even say that out loud," William says, the words coming out harsh. "Stay put, look in the house in case she went back in. I'm on my way."

William drives like a bat out of hell, his foot pushing the accelerator down hard, but when he thinks of his little girl wandering the streets alone, he fights to keep to the speed limit. The short drive feels like a million years. He pulls into the alley and honks the horn to let Donna know he's there.

"Any luck?" William asks as he jumps from the car and slams the door.

"No, nothing," Donna says, through a river of tears. Even Michael looks stricken, his hand in a fierce grip in Donna's and his eyes darting left to right.

"She's got to be somewhere close by, we're just not looking in the right place," William says, trying to sound reassuring. "You know how she loves to hide in tiny spaces. But whatever the case, seems she's got her balance and is walking on her own."

William turns to look down the street and sees Cate walking toward them, one hand held by an older man. William recognizes him, maybe from the curling club, but he doesn't recall his name.

"Cate!" William runs toward her, Donna following behind more slowly with young Michael in tow.

"Daddy, I watting!" Cate holds out a dripping cone, a moustache of ice cream across her upper lip.

"I'm sorry," the stranger says. "I tried to get her back to you right away, but I didn't know where you lived and—"

"Never mind," William says, his shoulders slumped with relief. "The important thing is she's home. But where did you find her, and how did you find us?" William hugs Cate closer.

"Just a few blocks away. She didn't seem to have a clue where she lived, but she took my hand and led me to the park," he says, pointing in the direction of the playground. "I had no idea we were so close to her house until just now when she called out to you. I was just praying I wouldn't have to take her down to the police station."

"Well, thank goodness. The important thing is she's safe," William says.

"Yes, thank you so much." Donna reaches for Cate and pulls her in close.

"I'm sorry for causing so much worry," the man says.

William's gaze softens and he unclenches his teeth. "It wasn't your fault," he says. "Thank you for bringing her home. You look so familiar. What did you say your name was?"

"Oh, I'm Carl. My wife and I play bridge at the community centre sometimes, and I think I've seen you two there a couple of times. I'm so grateful I noticed Cate wandering around. I knew she must be lost and thought I'd buy her a cone from the ice cream truck while we figured out where she lived."

"We are grateful too. We can't thank you enough."

William turns to Donna and scoops up his ice cream–covered daughter and hugs her tight. "Don't you ever wander off like that again, you hear me?" he says, his eyes moist with tears. He tries to sound strict, but his heart is too full of gratitude that nothing terrible happened. He shudders.

"I sowwee Daddee," Cate says as she buries her head into William's shoulder.

"It's okay, Caty-bug. I'm just so happy you're okay."

A few days later, William is wakened at five a.m. by Cate calling out for him, her early morning habit of late.

"Daddeee, Daddee…"

"I'm coming, I'm coming," William says as he scuffles down the hallway in his chocolate-brown velveteen slippers. He lifts Cate out of her crib and throws her in the air to make her giggle, then sets her down.

"Good morning, Dad," Michael says from the doorway, sleepy-eyed in his wrinkled-up Snoopy pajamas.

"Good morning, son. I guess your sister has everyone but your mother wide awake. Shall we all go get some breakfast?"

"Okay," Michael says.

"I hungwey!" Cate concurs.

The three of them plod down the hall, Cate holding firmly onto her father's hand. When they get to the kitchen, she slips her hand free, runs to the pantry, and stands on her tiptoes. She reaches for the Cheerios box on the middle shelf, and almost topples over.

"Hold on a cotton-picking minute," William says, busy putting on the kettle for a cup of instant coffee.

"Otay, Daddy, but den some Teerios pease?"

"I wish your mother would reorganize this pantry like I suggested, so you can reach the cereal shelf," William mumbles under his breath as he grabs the cereal box.

"Uh-huh," Cate says. "Teerios, Teerios, yeah, yeah."

William's grin breaks into a laugh. He can't help but be amused by his daughter's spunk. He sets her in her high chair and fastens the strap, then helps Michael into his booster seat and pours them both heaping bowls of cereal.

He stirs some sugar and milk into his coffee, the strong aroma seeping into his still foggy, half-asleep state.

"Joose pease?" Cate calls out.

"Can I have some toast with peanut butter too?" Michael asks.

"Yes, okay, both of you, just let me get in a sip of my coffee first. And Michael, the correct way to ask for something is to say 'may I,' not 'can I.'"

"Daddy eat ceeweel?" Cate says, holding out her sticky hand full of Cheerios.

"Thank you for the offer, Caty-bug, but Daddy likes Shredded Wheat, remember?"

"Wheaties, Wheaties, yeah, yeah," Cate sings.

The three fall into a comfortable silence. William reads the morning paper while the children gobble up their breakfast. When everyone is finished, William gathers up their dirty dishes, scrapes the soggy scraps into the garbage can, and sets the dishes in the sink.

"So, what are the three of you going to be up to today?" William asks.

"Mommy said last night we are going for groceries this morning, and I have playschool after lunch," Michael says.

"Hmm, sounds like a pretty busy day," William replies. "Are you going to be a big boy and help your mom at the store?" Turning toward Cate he adds, "And Caty-bug, I don't want to hear any stories of you wandering off on your mother. You stick by her, right?"

"Stay wif Mommy, yeah, yeah, yeah!" Cate sings.

"That's a good girl." William smiles. "And what are you going to do at playschool today, Michael?"

"I don't know," Michael says, his face in serious contemplation. "Missus Patterson always has different stations for us to play at, but I hope she puts boats in the water table. I love boats! And, I want to play with Jeffrey, but not Craig. I hate Craig!"

A stern look crosses William's brow and the slight crow's feet around his eyes crinkle up at the corners.

"Hate is a very strong word, Michael, and I don't want to hear you using it, all right?"

"But Daddy, I do hate Craig. He's a mean boy. He always takes my toys away from me."

"Mean or not, that's no reason for you to be the same," William instructs. "Two wrongs don't make a right. I'm not saying you have to play with him or anything, I'm just telling you I don't want to hear you using that word."

"Okay, Daddy, I won't say hate no more."

"Anymore," William corrects. The jovial mood in the kitchen has shifted.

"I best go get ready for work," William says. He lifts Cate down from her high chair.

"No! No, Daddy!!" Cate pleads, throwing herself against his leg.

"Now Cate, you know Daddy has to go to work. But if you two rascals promise to be good while I go get ready, I'll let you watch some television."

William walks into the living room and switches the television on, then turns the channel to the Access Network.

"Maybe *Sesame Street* or *Mr. Dressup* is on," William adds.

Michael and Cate whoop with delight. Donna hardly ever lets them watch TV in the morning, except for Saturday morning cartoons. They scamper over and climb into William's recliner to nestle in beside one another before he can change his mind.

"Wake up, sleepyhead," William whispers in Donna's ear.

"Is it morning already?" Donna asks, groggy-eyed and unable to read the bedside clock without her glasses. She stretches her arms out in front of her and arches her back like a cat.

"It's only six o'clock, but Cate woke me and Michael at five again this morning," William says, already making his way across the hall to the bathroom to shave.

"Where are the kids?" Donna goes to the closet and pulls her terry housecoat off the hanger, then follows her husband to the washroom.

"They're fine, I told them they could watch a little TV."

"William, I must have told you a million times if I told you once, they're not allowed to watch television on the weekdays."

"A million, eh?" William says, lathering thick shaving cream over his square jaw. "I suppose you should be the one getting up with them when Cate starts hollering at five o'clock every morning then. On my time, it's my rules. And a little TV never hurt anybody."

"That's not fair," Donna says, her cheeks reddening. "I didn't hear her or I would have gladly gotten up!" She unrolls a few squares of toilet paper and flushes, then pushes in beside William to wash her hands.

"Look, Donna, if you don't like it, I'm sorry, but you've got to learn to let go of some control once in a while," William says, getting frustrated.

"You wouldn't say that if it was one of your rules I was breaking." Donna pauses and looks to the ceiling as she dries her hands on the towel. "Like how about if Cate or Michael forgets their manners and don't say thank you when the baker at Klassen's offers them a cookie? It's only a little word, never hurt anyone. So, I guess I won't bother to correct them? Or better yet, what if Michael doesn't help clean up from the craft activity after Sunday school again, shall I not bother to reinforce that rule either?"

William finishes swishing the hair stubble from the edges of the sink before he replies. "What the hell, Donna, do as you like. You always do anyway."

Just then there is a loud crash from the end of the hallway. Donna bolts to investigate, tying her robe. She rushes into the living room only to see two suspicious-looking faces feigning innocence and a jar of Grandma Elizabeth's crab-apple jelly shattered all over the hardwood.

"Okay, what's going on here, which one of you was into the jam?" Donna asks, her hands on her wide hips.

"I did, Mommy. I sowee," Cate confesses as big tears of remorse slip down her chubby cheeks.

"It's okay." Donna sighs. "Everybody has accidents. I'm glad you admitted to it, but you know you aren't supposed to go into the fridge by yourself. Now both of you stay in Daddy's chair so I can get this cleaned up and nobody gets hurt. I don't want you to get a piece of glass stuck in your foot."

As Donna is sweeping up the mess, William walks onto the scene of the crime looking calm and handsome in his charcoal-grey suit and tie. He surveys the damage but doesn't say a thing. He blows the kids a kiss and says goodbye, making an obvious effort to avoid Donna, then steps gingerly around the broken glass in his pathway, through the kitchen, and out the back door, letting the screen door slam shut.

Later that day, Cate develops a fever. Donna would rather not pack her up and take her out to the pharmacy to purchase children's aspirin, so she calls William at work.

"Hi, William, I hope I'm not interrupting anything important," she says, twirling the phone cord nervously between her slim fingers.

"I just got out of a meeting, so it's not a big deal," William answers, although he sounds distracted. "What's up?"

"Cate came down with a fever this afternoon, while Michael was at school," Donna says. "Sharon picked the boys up, but I never thought to ask her to pick up some baby aspirin. I just checked her temperature. It's ninety-eight. I hate to have to disturb her, she's all conked out, so I thought maybe you could leave a few minutes early to get to the pharmacy before it closes."

"Jeez, Donna, weren't you just at the store this morning?"

"Well, yes, but I didn't know we were out of children's aspirin. Is it really that big of a deal?"

"It's not that I mind picking up aspirin so much, and you know I'd do anything for Caty, it's that the pharmacy closes at five," William says. "You know I don't like to leave work before then. But I guess I can leave a bit early this one time. Let's just not get into the habit of this, Donna. I wish you would just take my advice and keep a list on the fridge to keep track of things as they run out and save us this hassle."

"Yes, dear," Donna mumbles, and sighs. "I'll get right on that."

As he walks into the house, William is greeted by the tantalizing aroma of meatloaf and mashed potatoes. He gives Donna a stiff peck on the cheek, then takes the bottle of liquid children's aspirin out of the brown paper bag, grabs a spoon from the drawer, and makes his way to Cate's room.

Cate is curled up on her side in her crib in a restless sleep. Her face is flushed and her fine curls are stuck to her head, the sweet smell of baby powder emanating from her moist skin. William's frustration with Donna melts away, replaced with love and concern for his little girl. He reaches into Cate's crib and tucks a lock of hair behind her ear.

"Wake up, Caty-bug. Daddy's home. I brought some medicine that's going to help you get better."

Cate opens her red-rimmed, runny eyes and peers at William.

"I seepy," Cate says.

"I know, sweetheart. Just swallow this down and you can go right back to sleep."

William holds Cate's head up to take the spoonful of medicine. When she lays her head back on the pillow and closes her eyes, he traces butterfly kisses across her cheek, one of their secret rituals. She is already asleep when William tiptoes out of the room.

Cate's fever has her waking up in the middle of the night, crying out, "Daddy." She sounds so forlorn. William gets up and rushes in to comfort her. He swaddles her in her favourite blanket, cuddles her to his chest, and rocks her.

"Hush little Caty-bug, don't you cry," he sings to the tune of "Hush Little Baby."

Cate smiles in her half-sleep, looking as content as a caterpillar in her cocoon, like she is in the safest place in the world.

"That's my girl," William croons. "Daddy's always gonna be here to take care of you."

Chapter 2

"*D*O IT AGAIN!" CATE says, entranced by the magic powers of her babysitter's teenage grandson. Now that Michael is in kindergarten, Donna has taken a job in the Sears department store. While her mother's at work, Cate is being minded by an older woman down the street.

"What, this little trick?" the woman's grandson asks, producing a quarter from behind Cate's ear.

"How do you do that?" Cate asks as she claps her hands together with delight.

"A magician never tells his secrets," he says. He closes then opens his hand, the quarter vanished once again. "That's part of the code."

"I can keep secrets," Cate insists, even though she is horrible at it. She remembers the time Michael told her not to tell their parents about their fight, when their mother was out selling encyclopedias door-to-door in their neighbourhood, and how she told her mother every detail as soon as she got home. She remembers telling her mom about the surprise birthday cake in the freezer. But those were accidents.

"Well, if you're sure…," he says. His voice trails off, as if he isn't certain.

"I'm sure," Cate says, crossing her heart. "I want to be a magician too."

"All right then, but my magician's book of secrets is downstairs," he says.

"Okay." Cate puts her small hand in his and follows him down the dark stairwell to the basement.

It smells musty. There is a furnace and water heater in the corner to the right, an old sink and washer-dryer. "My book of secrets is in here," the boy says, leading her to a room on the left. From the doorway Cate sees a single bed covered in a dark blue bedspread, a tall wardrobe against the wall, and a checkered shag area rug on the cement floor.

"Where's your magician's book?" Cate asks.

"I keep it under my pillow," the Magician answers. He winks, his dark eyes almost black.

Cate feels the energy in the room shift. A prickly sensation runs down her spine and a sick feeling rises in her belly.

"We need to lock the door, to keep our secrets safe," the Magician says with a finger to his thin lips. He closes and then locks the door. He takes Cate by the hand and leads her to the bed. He pats the spot beside him. "Come, sit down."

"Um, uh, I, I don't want to. It's more fun to watch magic than to be a magician, I think."

"That's not true," the Magician says. "We're both gonna have fun." He starts to unzip his jeans.

"Don't you need your book of tricks?" Cate leans over and lifts the pillow, but there is nothing there.

"I'm gonna show you an amazing trick that we don't need a book for. I'm gonna show you how you can make something grow with only a few strokes of your hand."

"I, I don't want to learn that trick," Cate says, her heart pounding. She has no idea what he's talking about, but she knows what's tucked away in his underpants, behind the zipper. "I want to go now." Cate gets up off the bed, but the Magician pushes her back down.

"That's not how it works," he says, his voice raspy. "Once you say you're going to keep a secret, you have to follow through."

As he talks, he lowers his jeans to the ground. He takes off his white underwear and kicks them aside, then climbs onto the bed beside Cate. He takes her hand and places it on his already hardening penis. Cate is horrified to discover hair, as dark as the hair on his head, growing in a thick thatch below. Her brother's privates are bald, just like hers. It makes the Magician's privates seem even more ugly and sinister.

"It's okay, don't worry," he says.

"I'm scared," Cate says, her voice barely a whisper.

"You can cover your eyes with your other hand, if you want," the Magician says.

Cate covers her eyes, but the sounds the Magician makes terrify her. She bites her bottom lip and tries to drown out the noise by singing a song in her head.

After a few minutes she smells something salty and feels something sticky on her hand, but she doesn't dare take her other hand off her eyes. She stifles back a sob and then hears the Magician get up.

"You can open your eyes now," the Magician says. "I've got more magic tricks to show you, another day. Here, wipe your hands and we'll go back upstairs." He hands Cate a tissue. "And remember, don't tell anyone. This is our little secret."

"I won't, I promise," Cate says in a small, scared voice she barely recognizes as her own. She wipes away the stickiness, but the smell still burns in her nostrils.

"That's a good girl. 'Cause if you tell anyone, anyone at all, I'll have to kill you." The Magician draws a line across his neck with his hand, making a slicing motion, and sticks out his tongue.

Donna picks up Cate from the sitter's later that afternoon. Cate can't bring herself to look her mother in the eye. She hops in the back seat of the car and stares out the window. Donna is preoccupied. She doesn't notice her daughter's uncharacteristic silence. She drives to Michael's school and pulls over at the curb to wait.

After a few minutes, Michael runs up, out of breath. He slides onto the seat beside Cate and tosses his backpack at his feet.

"How was school?" Donna asks, already starting up the car.

"Fine," Michael says.

"That's good. I have a few errands to run, but you two can stay in the car together, I won't be long."

Donna parks the car in the shade of a tree, rolls down the window a crack, and locks the door before dashing off to the pharmacy. Michael retrieves his comic book from his backpack and starts to read. Cate stares down at her hands. She can still smell a horrible odour and she stifles a gasp.

"Are you okay, Sis?" Michael asks.

"Yeah, sure," Cate says. She tucks her hands under her legs.

"Well, you sound funny. Are you sure you aren't getting sick?"

The idea of being sick sounds like a good way to avoid going back to her sitter's.

"Now that you say it, I do feel like I might be getting a cold."

Cate manages to avoid going back to her sitter's for a few days, feigning a cold with dry coughs here and there, but finally Donna insists she can't miss another day's work.

"Mommy, please," Cate says. "I, I don't feel well. I just want to stay home with you."

"I know you do," Donna says, taking Cate by the arm and leading her to the car. "I'd love to stay home too, but Mommy has to work. Money doesn't grow on trees, you know."

Cate resigns herself to her fate. She wishes she was in school, like Michael. With a heaviness that seeps into her bones, she crawls into the back seat. She pulls her knees up to her chest. *I guess I am a bad girl,* she thinks to herself, *too curious for my own good, just like the Magician said.*

Cate is always on pins and needles when she's at the sitter's during Donna's shifts at Sears. Sometimes the Magician isn't there. Other times he leaves her alone. He acts like nothing has changed, doing his old tricks with the quarter. But sometimes he forces her downstairs to his room, and with each visit, the Magician becomes more emboldened.

Cate learns how to be a magician of sorts after all. She disappears inside herself the moment her abuser reaches for her hand. As she walks down the stairs, she counts backward from ten. When they arrive in his room, she pretends she is an astronaut in a rocket ship that is blasting into outer space. In reality, her spirit hovers somewhere near the ceiling while her body endures the abuse. Sometimes Jesus appears in Cate's imagination, a gentle-looking man, like the pictures she's seen in Sunday school. He takes Cate by the hand and they dance together in a flower garden, their heads tilted back in joyful laughter. Sometimes God visits her as a wise old man with a white beard. He holds her face in his hands when she looks down at what the Magician is doing to her and turns her gaze away. Sometimes she imagines she is home, with her father, who holds her in his strong, loving hands, keeping her safe—her place of refuge.

When the Magician finishes using her, he provides the tissues necessary to clean up the evidence. He tells her to get dressed and instructs her to line her panties with extra tissue. Before they go back upstairs, Cate puts her helmet and space suit in her imaginary closet. She puts on her happy face and smiles for the world as she walks back up the stairs and emerges from the dark.

She surprises herself, to discover she is able to keep secrets after all. As soon as she gets home, she locks herself in the bathroom. She scrubs at her body with soap and a nail brush until her skin is raw. She scrubs her soiled panties then hides them in her closet to dry before tossing them in the laundry. She feels like she would die if anyone knew how dirty she was. Especially her father. She locks away her secrets in the back of her mind and buries the key.

Chapter 3

IT'S THE SUMMER OF 1972 and Cate is six years old. William comes home from work with a skip in his step, hardly able to contain his news until dinner.

"I accepted a new job," he says as soon as everyone is seated around the table. "The company is offering me a big raise to take over the manager position of their accounting department in Lethbridge. They're expecting me to start there in August."

"Lethbridge?" says Donna. "Isn't that in southern Alberta?"

"Yes, it is. I know it will be a big transition for everyone, but the pay is such a huge increase, you won't have to work part-time anymore."

"Hooray!" Cate says, her face glowing. She feels lighter, just at the thought of the move, of her mother not having to work, of not ever going to a sitter's. "I can hardly wait!"

"How far away is Lethbridge?" Michael asks. "Will I still get to play with Jeffrey?"

"Sorry, son, no chance of that." William cuts a slice of roast beef and dips it in gravy. "Lethbridge is a good six hours' drive from here. But don't worry, you're such a great kid, you'll have a new best friend in no time."

"I'll really miss Jeffrey. But I suppose you're right. And of course, Cate is my best friend of all." Michael turns to his sister, sitting beside him, and smiles.

"I think we should have a special dinner this Sunday to celebrate," Donna says. "I'll make your favourite, William. Lemon meringue pie."

It's the first Saturday morning after the big move into their brand new house in a development still under construction in the southwest corner of Lethbridge. It is a stand-alone, single-family house with beige siding and a small verandah in front. The yard is still nothing but dirt, piled high in mounds here and there.

Donna has been a little overwhelmed with the long list of things to do. There are still cardboard boxes scattered across the kitchen floor with newsprint spilling out, the dishes tucked inside. Donna has picked up mini cartons of cereal, paper plates, and plastic cutlery until she gets the kitchen in order.

"Hooray!" Cate says, when she spies the row of cereal boxes lined up on the kitchen counter. "I just love Frosted Flakes. Thanks, Mom!"

Cate cuts around the perforated edges of a cereal box with a plastic knife. She pulls back the flaps and pours in milk, then digs in with her spoon.

"You and your sweet tooth," Donna says. "But don't get used to eating sugared cereal. This is a special move-in treat and then it's back to wholesome cereals without added sugar."

"That's right," William says. He looks up from his newspaper. "When you're all done, I think you're old enough for me to take the training wheels off your bicycle. What do you think, Cate? Do you want to give riding two wheels a try?"

"Two wheels?" Cate says. She starts to panic at the idea. "I don't think I'm ready yet, Daddy. Besides, Mommy said I have chores to do this morning."

"Oh, that's all right, darling," Donna says, oblivious to Cate's distress. She has started wiping down the inside of a cupboard. "You go on ahead with your father. Michael can help me out in here."

"Let's get a move on then," William says as he gets up from the table. "Go change out of your pajamas into some old scrubby jeans and meet me outside after you brush your teeth."

Cate changes into her Lee jeans, hand-me-downs from Michael. She brushes her teeth and puts on her sneakers, all the while her heart sinking. She goes outside and shuffles over to where William is just unscrewing the last bolt from her training wheels.

"Hey, there's my girl!" William dusts his hands off on his trousers and walks over to Cate. "Are you ready?"

"Yes, Daddy." Cate does her best to calm her nerves and sound confident.

"You can do this, Caty-bug," William says two hours later, his voice steady. "You have to get the wheels going just a little bit faster to stay up. That's all you need to do, just go a bit faster."

Cate crashes once again into the hard, cold gravel of the alley. Tears trickle down her dusty cheeks, making wet streaks. William runs over to her.

"It's no big deal, Caty, just a few scrapes; they'll heal up in no time."

"I'm sorry, Daddy. I'm trying my hardest." Cate gets up and brushes her hands on her jeans.

"It's okay, I know you are," William says gently. He helps her get up, and once she is seated firmly, he holds her bicycle steady by the handlebars. He looks her in the eye. "Stop that crying, wipe those tears away, and pull your chin up. You can do this, I know you can. Just because some things don't come easy, doesn't mean you should give up."

After an entire morning of stubborn effort, William's plan achieves a modicum of success. Cate manages to ride without training wheels for a few solid seconds before she falls over.

It takes a lot of Saturdays, but finally, Cate figures it out. She appreciates the freedom she feels on two wheels. Despite the scrapes and bruises, she is grateful for her father's determination and that he refused to give up on her.

"I'm home!" William calls out one afternoon, a week before the start of school. "Donna, can you gather up the kids?"

Donna finds Michael and Cate in Michael's room, pretending they are detectives. Cate has a notepad and pencil and is writing down clues.

"C'mon, you two. Daddy's home and he's got a surprise. Michael, take off that cumbersome ol' trench coat of your father's, and both of you go take a seat on the couch in the living room."

Donna's excited energy captivates the children and they quickly do as they are told.

"I wonder what it could be?" Cate says, wiggling side to side with a huge grin on her face.

William enters the room holding a black ball of fur in his hands.

"Ta-da!" he says as he sets the puppy on the wood floor. "Mommy and I decided to buy you two a puppy to help you adjust to the move. I know it's been hard on you both, but especially you, Michael."

"Seriously?" Michael jumps down from the couch and runs over to pet her. "It's ours, to keep?"

"She sure is," William says, a huge grin on his face. "What do you say?"

"I've always wanted a puppy," Michael says. "Thank you, Dad! And I'm gonna help take care of her too."

"Me too," Cate says, running over to join in. "Aw, she's so cute! Oh, she just licked me!" Cate squeals.

"That means she likes you," Donna says. "I suppose we need to come up with a name for her. Any ideas?"

"How about Snoopy?" Michael asks.

"Snoopy is a great name, but I think it's for boy dogs," William says.

"How about Fluffy?" Cate asks, stroking the puppy's soft fur as the dog wags her little tail.

"Naw, that's not a real name," Michael says. "Do they list dog names in the encyclopedia?"

"No, I'm afraid not," Donna says. "But what do you think about Trixie? One of my school friends when I was around your age had the sweetest dog, a golden retriever, and that was her name."

"Trixie?" Michael says. "I think that's a great name!"

"It's settled then," William announces. "Trixie Henderson, welcome to the family."

On the first day of school, Cate is so excited she can hardly hold her hands still enough to button up the new powder-blue cotton dress Donna purchased for her the week before.

Mrs. Cunningham, Cate's teacher, is an ageing spinster without much of an imagination or tolerance for anything outside the box. Cate enters the classroom and looks around at the rows of desks, wondering which one she should claim, when Mrs. Cunningham takes her by the arm.

"Why don't you sit here, across from Cindy?" the teacher says in her loud, authoritarian voice. "She's another chubby one, just like you."

Cate is mortified. Her cheeks redden as she slides into her assigned desk. She hadn't realized she was chubby.

"Hi, my name's Cate," she says to Cindy, who looks equally embarrassed, her fair, freckled cheeks turning bright red to match her fiery ginger-coloured hair.

It isn't a great start for either of them, but once Mrs. Cunningham distributes their new spelling and phonics workbooks and their first selection for the daily home reading program, Cate flips through the fresh, stiff pages with delight, her embarrassment all but forgotten. She has already begun learning to read and write, with Michael's help.

On the way home from school, Cate sees Cindy walking just a few feet ahead of her and runs over to join her. She discovers that Cindy lives across the street and a few houses up from her, and they walk and talk all the way home. They quickly become the best of friends.

In early November, William announces at the dinner table that he is going to flood the backyard to make a skating rink.

"Can I come out and help you?" Michael asks.

"Me too!" Cate says, always an echo of her big brother.

"Okay," William says, pushing his cowlick absently from his brow. "But I must warn you, it's darn cold out. It takes a while, so you'll need to be patient."

Michael and Cate nod their heads in agreement. As soon as they finish dinner they jump down from the table in excitement. They head into the mud room to get dressed. Michael has a new snowsuit from Sears, still store-stiff, and Cate has his old, gently worn one. They put on brightly coloured scarves, hats, and mittens, all hand-knitted by Grandma Henderson. William puts on his heavy parka and pulls the hood up over his ball cap, then slides on his sheepskin-lined, suede leather gloves.

"Let's get a move on, then," William says.

"How do you make the yard flood?" Cate asks as she plods down the cement steps in her heavy boots.

"It's easy enough," William explains. "You just turn on the water from the faucet inside the house, connect the garden hose, and let the water run out until the yard is covered evenly."

"But how does the water turn to ice?" Cate wonders aloud.

"Water turns to ice because of the cold," Michael says. "We don't have to do anything but wait. I learned in science, when the temperature drops below zero, water will change from a liquid to a solid, right, Dad?"

"That's right, son," William says with pride in his voice.

"I hope I'm as smart as you someday," Cate says, a little jealous of her brother's superior knowledge.

"Don't worry," Michael says. "I'm good at science, but you're good with words. And besides, you'll learn all about solids and liquids when you're in grade three."

"Why don't you two fetch the garden hose from the shed while I go down to the cellar and turn the water valve on?" William says.

Michael and Cate crunch across the thin layer of snow that has accumulated on the frozen grass, giggling as they race the short distance across the yard to the shed. Cate is about to slide the door open when Michael stops her.

"Wait a minute!" Michael says with a conspiratorial whisper. "What if there's a scary monster in there?"

"Ha, ha, very funny!" Cate laughs. "Everyone knows there's no such thing as monsters."

"I'm not kidding!" Michael says, in his most serious voice.

Cate is pretty sure her brother is teasing, but not totally. "You're j-just trying to scare me," she says.

"Well, I guess we won't know for sure until we open it, right?" Michael says while slowly creaking the shed door open.

"Daddy! Daddy!" Cate screams. She bolts to her father, who has just come back outside. "Michael said there's a monster in the shed!"

"Whoa there!" William says. "What's this nonsense?" William picks up Cate and holds her close, rubbing her back. "You know better than that, Cate. There's no such thing as monsters. And Michael, that's not very nice to scare your little sister like that. She's only six, after all. Now you apologize to your sister and let's get to work."

"I'm sorry," Michael says.

"That's okay," Cate says, forgiving him instantly.

Flooding the yard turns out to be less exciting than Cate and Michael had anticipated. They watch as William holds the hose and a stream of water flows out to cover the ground. It's been at least ten minutes, and there is still only a small patch of ice forming.

"You guys can take turns holding the hose," William says. "Girls first, okay?"

Cate grabs the hose with mitten-clad hands. It is heavier than she thought and the hose suddenly jerks upwards and out of her hands, spraying William in the face.

"Sorry, Daddy!" Cate cries out.

"That's okay, it was an accident," William assures her as he wipes his face with the back of his coat sleeve. "Here, let me help you."

William leans over and grasps Cate's hands underneath his own, helping her to direct the water properly. Cate sighs and cuddles in closer until it's Michael's turn.

"I love you, Daddy," Cate says, her words coming out in puffs of condensed air.

William squeezes Cate's hand in a way that says "I love you" as clearly as anything he could say.

A few weeks before Christmas, Mrs. Cunningham decides it is prudent to inform her grade one classroom that Santa Claus is a fabrication.

"But, Mrs. Cunningham, my mother just told me last night that Santa is real," Cindy says, speaking with her hand in the air but before Mrs. Cunningham has given her permission.

"I don't believe I called your name," Mrs. Cunningham replies. "But to address your comment, all I can say is your mother is a liar. Most adults in our society have agreed to pass on this ridiculous story of Santa, but as an educator of truth, I can't tolerate such foolishness."

Cate, who just posted her letter to Santa in the mail, is grief-stricken, but she decides misery loves company. When her cousins arrive the day after school gets out, Cate shares the shattering news with her cousin Sarah, who is two years younger than her.

"You're lying," Sarah cries out, then runs into the kitchen to tell the adults, who are sitting around the table playing cards.

"Cate, did you tell Sarah there is no Santa Claus?" William asks, in front of the whole extended family.

"Yes, I did," Cate admits, her lower lip out. "Mrs. Cunningham said it was foolishness."

"I can't believe you, of all people, would be so mean-spirited," William says. "I'm beyond disappointed."

"I'm sorry, Daddy, and you too, Sarah," Cate says as she bursts into tears. "I felt bad as soon as I said it, but I can't take it back."

"That's right, you can't. And that's a good life lesson for you," William says. "Now off you go to your room to think about it by yourself for a while."

Cate runs down the hall and throws herself onto her bed. She sobs into her pillow at the unfairness of it all. Eventually she calms down and her sobs trickle off to sniffles. She hears her cousins playing together in Michael's room across the hall and feels even more wronged and sorry for herself. She knows what she did was mean and spiteful. Worst of all, ruining it for Sarah didn't make her own stolen magic any easier to bear.

That night when William comes into Cate's room to say good night, he leans in close and whispers in her ear.

"Did you learn your lesson?"

"Yes, Daddy, I did," Cate whispers back. "Next time I'm going to think before I speak."

"That's my Caty-bug. Now off you go to sleep. Tomorrow's a new day."

It's Michael's turn to be the Christmas elf, so on Christmas morning he gets the privilege of passing out the stockings. It is a Dietrich tradition that everyone has to wait until all the stockings are distributed before they look inside.

Cate is beside herself with excitement, impatient to see if Santa brought her the Barbie shoes and accessories she asked for in her letter. She remembers Santa isn't real, that it's her mom and dad who fill her stocking, but that makes her even more hopeful.

When Michael passes the last stocking out, Cate wastes no time dumping the contents of her stocking onto the floor in front of her. There, amongst the mandarin orange, candy cane, and yo-yo, is the package she's been dreaming of: rows and rows of different-coloured Barbie shoes all contained neatly inside the plastic wrapping. Cate jumps up and whoops in delight.

"I got them, I got them," Cate sings out as she runs around the living room doing a happy dance. She asks her mother for a pair of scissors and skips back to her spot on the carpet, ready to open her prized gift, only to discover the package missing. She feels like her heart is going to break and wonders if she dreamed the whole thing.

"Look everyone," her cousin Amanda says, holding up the missing package. "Santa brought me Barbie shoes."

Cate looks over, devastated.

"I think you made a mistake," Cate says, standing up. "Those were my gift from Santa."

Amanda refuses to admit she stole them. The girls start to fight. Soon the adults get involved.

"The only fair thing to do is to split them fifty-fifty," Donna says.

Cate is outraged at the injustice. Once again, she learns that sometimes life just isn't fair.

⁓

Spring arrives in Southern Alberta like a lion, the winds roaring. At first the wind bites ice-cold, but then it shifts warm, the infamous chinooks. The snow hasn't melted completely, and there are giant slushy puddles in the backyard.

Dressed for fun in slick raincoats and black rubber boots, Cate and Michael are having a contest with Cindy over who can make the puddle water splash further with a swift stomp of their foot when William comes out the back door.

"How about getting a jump on baseball season and throwing the ball around a bit?" William asks.

"Really?" Michael asks, obviously delighted at the prospect.

"That sounds like fun," Cindy says, a gleam in her eye. "I've never played baseball before."

"Isn't it too cold out to play ball?" Cate says. She's certain that baseball will be another one of those things she's not good at.

"Naw," William insists, rubbing his hands up and down his slacks, in seeming contradiction.

Cate looks around at all of the puddles and patches of snow in the alley, then down at her clumsy rubber boots. She can already imagine herself dripping wet, muddy, cold, and miserable.

"But," Cate persists, "what if we slip and fall?"

"If it's too cold and muddy, you don't have to play," William says. "Michael, Cindy, and I can play without you easy enough."

Michael stares down at his feet, not saying anything. Cindy looks over at her friend with a shrug of her shoulders. Cate doesn't want to be left out.

"No, I guess you're right," Cate says. "What's a little cold and mud anyway?"

"Okay, good, that's the attitude!" William says with a smile. "I'll go get our gear from the crawl space."

Moments later William sprints over, an extra oomph in his step, carrying the baseball bat under his arm and holding a glove in each hand with the ball nestled in one glove.

"So, who wants to batter up?" William asks.

"I do!" Michael says.

"Okay, Michael, you head on over to the end of the alley there by Martha."

Martha is the name William gave the abandoned and battered old VW that has been parked by their shed since they moved in. Donna has been reminding him every day to get it towed, but he hasn't gotten around to it.

"You can be the catcher, Cate," William says as he tosses Cate one of the kid-sized gloves. "Go crouch behind your brother. I'll be the pitcher, and Cindy you can go stand over by the tire I set on the lawn to be our first base, all right?"

Michael manages to make a few really good connections with the bat. Cindy turns out to be a natural at the game, with a strong arm. Cate doesn't manage to catch one ball, although she comes close once, the ball skimming the rim of her glove before bouncing onto the gravel and rolling into a puddle.

"How on God's green earth did you miss that one?" William asks in an impatient tone. "The ball practically jumped right into your lap!"

"I'm sorry, Daddy, I'm trying."

"I know you are. Are you willing to keep at it a bit longer, or are you ready to call it quits for today?"

"Nooo,…I, I…" Cate bites her lip and looks over at Cindy. "I don't want to give up, Daddy. It's hard for me, but I'll keep trying."

"I have an idea, Dad," Michael says. "Why don't we change positions, let me be catcher for a bit so Cindy and Cate can try to hit the ball?"

"Yeah, okay, that's a good idea." William's voice is softer, calmer.

Unfortunately, the change-up does little to improve the situation. Cate has as much difficulty hitting the ball as catching it. When yet another ball lands in a puddle after Cate fails to make contact, William throws down his mitt and stomps over to where Cate stands.

"Are those eyes in your head or just holes?" William says, his voice rising. "Can't you see the ball?"

Without waiting for an answer, he moves behind Cate and grabs her hands firmly, repositioning them on the bat. As soon as his hand touches her skin, it's as though something inside him softens.

"I'm going to help you. Okay, son, you be the pitcher and give it your best."

Cate misses. William picks up the filthy ball and throws it back to Michael.

"Hold on a minute, son." William positions Cate's hands, feet, even her knees, trying to induce the proper stance, but Cate can't relax. Tears streak through her mud-crusted cheeks.

"I, I'm sorry, Daddy, it's like my hands and eyes can't talk to one another," Cate says.

"It's okay," William says, wiping the tears from her cheeks. "The important thing is you tried. Baseball isn't everything. I'm sure you'll find a sport you like, eventually." William stands up, hands on his hips. "I guess that's it for today. Thanks for being such good sports."

"I should be going home now anyway," Cindy says. "Do you want to play tomorrow?"

"Okay," Cate says.

Michael picks up the bat, the ball, and the gloves and sets them on the back step. He takes a seat on the cement step and pats the spot beside him.

"C'mon over here, Sis."

Cate shuffles down the alley, sloshing puddles with her boots, and plunks down beside her brother with a sigh.

"It's okay," Michael says. He gives her a hug.

But Cate doesn't feel okay. She doesn't understand why she can't catch a ball or hit one with a bat. She wishes she wasn't so clumsy and uncoordinated and says a little prayer under her breath.

She and Michael remove their boots in the mud room and hang their coats to dry. They walk through to the living room, where Donna is curled up on the couch with a *Reader's Digest* on her lap.

"How did the baseball game go?" Donna asks.

"It was awful," Cate says.

"Awful? What do you mean?"

"I'm terrible at baseball," Cate says, the words catching in her throat. "I tried my best, but I didn't catch the ball even once. I think Dad's disappointed with me."

"You weren't that bad," Michael says.

"Yes, you know I was."

"Well, baseball isn't for everyone, Cate," Donna says matter-of-factly. "Try not to worry about it too much. And I'm certain your father isn't disappointed. You know he thinks you're the bee's knees."

"Bee's knees?" Cate says. "What does that mean?"

"It means you are perfect in your dad's eyes. Now, why don't you two play while I get the potatoes on for dinner?" Donna suggests.

Cate's disappointment and sadness melt away like a Popsicle on a hot, sunny day. She and Michael play Hansel and Gretel. Cate is the evil witch, hiding out in her sugar-candy house behind William's recliner, waiting for unsuspecting children. Her dolls, the poor children who reach their untimely fates, are stacked in a heap in the oven, underneath William's chair. Michael is the hero woodsman who captures the evil witch and makes her recite the spell to bring the doll-children back to life. Afterwards they race Michael's Hot Wheels down the hallway, then tidy them up and sprawl out on the living room carpet in front of the television and settle in to watch *Escape to Witch Mountain*.

"Whatcha watching?" William asks cheerfully when he walks into the living room a little while later.

"Walt Disney," Michael answers.

"Our favourite show," William says with a smile. He sits down in his recliner to join the kids until dinner.

The "to be continued" announcement comes on the screen just as Donna pops her head into the living room.

"Dinner's ready. Everybody, go on now and wash up."

On the way to the bathroom Michael turns to Cate and William. "Maxwell Smart secret agent handshake?"

William laughs and the three of them perform their handshake ritual. William's smile reaches right up to his eyes. Cate is certain the stickiness from the baseball game has all been forgotten.

William pushes back his chair from the table and goes to where Donna is stacking the dirty plates. He sets them down and sweeps her into his arms.

"You really outdid yourself today," William says. "Why don't you go and lie down for a rest or read your book while I clean up?"

"William, that's so sweet of you!" Donna says, shocked at the rare offer. "But I can manage this. Why don't you go and enjoy some time with the kids or watch some sports on television? It is your day off after all."

"No, I insist. In fact, when I'm done cleaning, I'll get Michael and Cate started on their bedtime routines and then I'll come give you a nice back massage. How does that sound?"

"That sounds absolutely wonderful!" Donna says, a glow in her cheeks.

Once the kitchen is spic and span, William shoos Michael and Cate to their rooms. Cate picks out her pajamas and heads into the steamy bathroom. She hears William whistling a happy tune and then sees him slip into her parents' bedroom. She hears the click of the lock. She wonders, not for the first time, why they lock the door sometimes. It makes her think of how the Magician locked the door. She shudders, but then she remembers, the Magician is far away and can't hurt her anymore. And she knows with absolute certainty that her father would never hurt her mother, or anyone, like that.

Cate is towelling off when William opens the door to his room and turns around quietly. His cowlick is dangling in the wrong direction and his shirttail is untucked. He has a huge grin on his face.

"Are you all finished your bath?" William asks.

"Yep, I just need to brush my teeth," Cate says.

"Well, it's Michael's turn for his bath, so go on and get into your jammies and you can brush your teeth later when he's done."

As Cate is pulling on her pajama bottoms, Donna comes into her room. She is looking all smiles too. Cate feels comforted that both her mother and father are happy.

"Did you enjoy your massage?" Cate asks innocently.

"Yes, it was fine," Donna says with a blush. "I just remembered, though, I put in a load of laundry before dinner. I best go and put it in the dryer."

"Would you like me to read from *Charlotte's Web*?" William asks from the doorway as Cate brushes her shoulder-length hair in front of her vanity mirror.

"Yes, please, Daddy. I love it when you read to me."

Cate crawls under the cozy covers and snuggles up to her dad. The light from her bedside lamp bathes everything in a soft glow. She is drifting off when William closes the book.

"One more chapter, please, Daddy," Cate says with a yawn.

"You're already half-asleep, Caty-bug. How about if I just read two more pages?"

Cate falls asleep before he finishes the last page, a peaceful smile on her face.

Cate is almost blinded as she squints up into the sky, trying to determine what time of day it is. She saw someone on *Bonanza* use that trick, but all she knows of how to tell time is by the growling in her stomach. It's long past lunch, but hours until dinnertime. She puts away her skipping rope and goes into the house.

The kitchen is a chaotic mess. William has pulled all of the dark cupboard doors off but hasn't finished sanding them. They are still laid out on the basement floor, and William has gone into work, leaving gaping holes where the cupboards are supposed to be. Donna is on her hands and knees on the floor, scouring away at the grout with a scowl on her face.

"Can I have a snack, please?" Cate asks.

"Really, Cate?" Donna looks at Cate like she's just asked the most ridiculous question ever. "Can't you see I'm busy? If you're hungry, it's your own darn fault. I told you at lunch to eat all of your tuna sandwich, but you stubbornly refused, so you can darn well just wait until dinner. Maybe you'll make a better choice next time."

Cate is a bit taken aback. Her mother hardly ever uses the word *darn*. Cate mulls on her mother's advice but doesn't imagine she will make a better choice the next time, because she dislikes tuna sandwiches. She chooses to keep that information to herself and disappears into her room. She tries to distract herself from her hunger pains by reciting one of her favourite poems by A. A. Milne over in her head. She giggles, picturing tubby Winnie the Pooh enjoying a big jar of honey. She decides to read one of the adventures of her favourite character and his friends in the hundred acre wood. She is deep into the story of the blustery day when William peeks his head in the door.

"Hi, Daddy!" Cate says with surprise. "I thought you had to work."

"Well, I do, but it's such a gorgeous day and to be honest, I couldn't concentrate so I decided to leave early. It is Sunday after all, and my stack of paperwork will still be there when I go in tomorrow." William scratches his stubbly chin. "I really should go deal with those cupboards, but I need some fresh air to clear my mind. Would you like to go for a walk with me, over to the pond?"

"I would love to, Daddy!" Cate is thrilled with the turn of events. She inserts her bookmark and sets her book on her nightstand.

"Where's your brother?" William asks. "He might want to come along too."

"He's over at his friend Terrance's house."

"Oh well. Your mother's lying down with a headache, so I guess it's just the two of us."

"Okay, Daddy, I'll go get my sneakers."

Cate ties her shoes in record time. She finds William in the kitchen putting homemade oatmeal cookies into an old yogurt container and pouring milk into a thermos. He tosses the snack into Cate's school backpack in the mud room and slides into his shoes.

"Do you mind carrying our snack for us?" William asks.

"Sure, Daddy, no problem." Cate beams, proud to be helpful.

William grabs Trixie's leash and whistles. The dog appears from under the back porch and barks, her tail wagging.

"Want to go for a walk, girl?" William says.

Trixie barks again and wags her tail with greater enthusiasm. The three of them head out in the direction of the pond.

"Check out that bird," William says in a whisper. "It's almost completely camouflaged."

"What does camouflage mean?" Cate asks.

"That's when an animal blends into the surrounding habitat."

"What's a habitat?"

"It's just a fancy word for house."

"I like fancy words." Cate takes her father's hand and they continue exploring in the brush. Trixie stops to sniff something, then dashes off to chase a squirrel, her forgotten leash dangling from William's pocket.

When they arrive at the pond Cate sits down on a patch of soft green grass, takes off her backpack, and retrieves the thermos and yogurt container.

"These cookies are just so yummy!" Cate says. "I count six; that means we get three each!"

"You get top marks for your math," William says with a laugh and a wink. "Just don't tell your mother. You know she doesn't like us eating unhealthy snacks, especially this close to dinner."

"Brownie's honour!" Cate mimics her father's wink and makes a salute with her hand to her brow.

After their snack and rest, Cate is ready to investigate. She looks under rocks, hoping to discover some pond creature or other. Frogs are her current obsession.

"I found one!" William whispers, pointing through a tangle of bulrushes he has pulled apart. Cate joins him as quickly and quietly as she can and hunkers down to peer in. There is a frog squatting on a smooth rock just on the edge of the water. He isn't much to look at, a dull brown with stripes down his back and big round eyes that look surprised. He seems oblivious to his intruders and stays put, making loud croaking noises. Trixie comes crashing onto the scene and the frog jumps into the pond and disappears in the murky water.

"Daddy, can I have a pet frog if I can catch one? I'll look after him all by myself and feed him and everything."

"I don't think your mother would appreciate a frog in the house any more than she appreciated the ants and worms you brought home earlier this spring," William says as he ruffles her hair and tucks a ringlet behind her ear. "I don't imagine you'd be able to catch one anyhow. They're darn slippery, you know. Besides, they belong out here in nature, not trapped in a jar or a box. You've got Trixie to play with."

At the sound of her name, Trixie bounds over and licks Cate's cheek with her slobbery tongue.

"Well, we best get a move on, it's almost four thirty," William says, squinting down at his watch.

"Do we have to?"

"I'm afraid so." William sounds equally disappointed. "But hey, pretty soon it will be summer holidays. Maybe I can take a week off work and we can go camping as a family. How does that sound?"

Cate thinks spending a whole week in nature with her father, with all of her family, sounds as sweet as the taste of sugar.

Chapter 4

*I*N GRADE THREE, CATE'S life takes off in even more positive directions: her teacher, Ms. MacDonald, is young and enthusiastic, fresh out of teacher's college; she makes a new friend, Kimi, who has just moved to town from the Indian reserve outside of Pincher Creek; and she's developed her first crush on a boy named Clarence, with big brown eyes and a similar love for reading. Ms. MacDonald is an aspiring writer and engages the class in creative writing lessons that spark Cate's vivid imagination.

One Saturday morning not long after school starts, Cate is sitting at the kitchen table, scribbling away on a pad of foolscap with her freshly sharpened yellow school pencil while her mother is baking, the sweet smell of cinnamon rolls permeating the air.

"What's captured your attention?" Donna asks.

"I'm writing my first chapter book," Cate says, not bothering to look up.

"Chapter book, eh?" William says as he walks into the kitchen to fill a glass of water from the tap. He peers over Cate's shoulder. "That sounds pretty ambitious for a girl your age. What's it about?"

"Kimi was telling me some exciting stories about her ancestors, and I decided I want to write a story about an Indian princess who can talk to God," Cate says, her face lighting up.

"Is Kimi a new friend?" Donna asks. "I don't remember you mentioning her before."

"Yeah. I've never met anyone like her. She knows so much about nature, and she tells such wonderful stories."

"Well, it's nice to hear you're making new friends," says William. "Does Cindy like Kimi too?"

"No," Cate says with a sigh. "Cindy said some pretty mean stuff. She said all Indians are lazy and they drink too much."

"Unfortunately, there are a lot of people around here who are prejudiced," Donna says. "But I'm glad you know better than to judge someone because of the colour of their skin or their culture."

"You and Daddy have always told me it's who you are inside that matters," Cate says. "If you don't mind, though, I'm at a good part and I don't want to forget what I was going to write next."

William laughs. "All right then, I guess we've been told. Good luck, Caty-bug. I hope you'll let your ol' dad read it when you're done."

"Sure, Daddy, you can be the first one."

Cate is still at it a few hours later when Donna starts to prepare lunch.

"Your arm's going to fall right off if you keep writing at that pace," says Donna.

"That's silly," says Cate, but she isn't so sure.

"I'm not being literal," Donna says, seeing Cate's uncertain expression. "It's wonderful that you've found something you love to do, but you need to have a balance of activities. Go on now and find your father and brother, I think they're out in the backyard, or perhaps in the basement, and then all three of you wash up for lunch."

"Okay." Cate takes her pencil and paper to her room and tucks her writing safely away in the top drawer of her dresser before going off in search of her father and brother.

After lunch she wants to get back to writing her story, but Donna insists she get some fresh air and exercise. Michael and William head out to the backyard to rake fallen leaves and till the garden, but Cate has no interest in joining them.

"Can I go over to Kimi's to play?" Cate asks.

"How far away does she live?" says Donna.

"Not far, just a few blocks down the alley. I can ride my bike."

"Okay," Donna says as she dries the last of the lunch dishes. "But be sure to come back in time for dinner, if not before."

Cate puts on her new watch so she won't lose track of time. She finds her bicycle leaning against the side of the house and pedals down the alley.

"God is a mountain, God is a tree," Cate sings a song she makes up along the way.

When she sees the brightly painted red fence that stands out amongst all the brown and grey of the neighbourhood, she hops off her bike, lays it on the ground, and opens the back gate.

Kimi's yard is bursting with clutter. There is a huge garden, although most of the vegetables are picked over and finished for the season. Sunflowers that are beginning to dry out climb the side wall, a wheelbarrow stands abandoned, and there are dream catchers and wind chimes dangling from under the covered patio that runs along the back of the house, in front of their kitchen. Cate walks along the stone path and rings the bell at the back door.

"Cate, how nice to see you, come on in," says Kimi's mother.

"Can Kimi come outside to play?" Cate asks.

"She's in her room reading, if you want to go on in and ask her yourself."

Cate walks down the narrow hall to Kimi's room and enters with a knock. Kimi is lying on her bright yellow bedspread, a book in hand.

"Cate!" Kimi says and sets her book aside. "Come on in."

The girls decide they want to go on an adventure to Riverstone Pond. Cate is pretty sure her parents wouldn't approve of her going without an adult, but when Kimi tells her mom their plans, she gives them permission.

Kimi knows the sounds of different birds. She even knows the names of most species in their area. Cate is wonderstruck by how much knowledge her friend has and follows her with excitement as they explore through needle-and-thread grass, silver sagebrush, and bulrushes.

"This is a crocus," Kimi says, parting a thick sheaf of grass to reveal a patch of the purple-petalled flowers. "They have a spice called saffron in their stigma."

"What's a stigma?" asks Cate.

"It's those dark, powdery-looking things in the centre."

The girls continue on their trek. Kimi shows Cate a Baird's sparrow nest. They are careful not to disturb it. They take a break to sit on a rock at the edge of the pond.

"I'm writing a story about an Indian princess," says Cate. "She's beautiful, just like you."

"Beauty is of your spirit," Kimi says. "Only those with a pure heart can see it."

Just then a red-tailed hawk appears in the blue sky overhead.

"Look up," Kimi says in a whisper, her finger to her lips. "That hawk is a very lucky sign."

Cate is mesmerized by the broad span of the bird's wings.

"Wow!" she whispers back. "Why is it lucky?"

"According to my people, the person the red-tailed hawk flies beside is a Seer," Kimi says.

"What is a Seer?" Cate is still staring up at the hawk that is hovering gracefully nearby.

"Someone who can see into the future."

"That's so exciting," says Cate, a little louder than she intends. The hawk flies off, but Cate's skin still has goosebumps. She turns and looks into Kimi's intense yet soft milky-brown eyes. "I bet you're a Seer, Kimi. Can you tell me my future?"

"I'm too young to be a Seer," says Kimi with a smile. "But I know you have a good heart and you are my best friend."

The next week Cate comes bursting through the back door after school.

"Mom! You'll never guess what Ms. MacDonald has organized for my class!" She rummages in her backpack and hands Donna a crumpled-up letter.

"Hmm, looks like a permission form for a field trip," Donna says.

"Not just any field trip, Mom." Cate does a little jig and twirls herself around. "We're going to Head-Smashed-In Buffalo Jump. It's a sacred Indian burial ground!"

"That certainly does sound exciting," says Donna as she scans the form. "It says you're going on the twenty-first, that's only a week from now."

"I know, I can hardly wait!"

Cate wakes up early on the big day to make sure she has everything ready. She's already gone over the list of things to bring three times and has everything stowed in her backpack, except her packed lunch, which is in the fridge. She's laid out jeans and a T-shirt, plus her zippered sweatshirt in case it is chilly, and will grab her windbreaker and hat when she heads out the door.

Cindy stops by to walk with her to school, as usual. She's not nearly as taken with the field trip.

"I don't know why you're dying to see some old bones," says Cindy as they walk along, hand-in-hand down the alley. "It sounds kind of gross to me."

"They're not just any old bones," Cate says. "They're thousands-of-years-old bones, skeletons from way back when the Plains people used to hunt bison for their food. They used every part of the animal, you know. The skins for clothes and the blood too."

"That's totally gross," Cindy says with a shudder. "And besides, long bus rides are so boring. I hate having to sit still for so long."

"I won't be bored," Cate says. "I brought my book, *The Lion, the Witch and the Wardrobe*. It's very exciting."

"That doesn't sound very fun to me," says Cindy. "Are you going to sit with me on the bus?"

"Oh, gee, I'm sorry, Cindy, but Kimi already asked me, on the day Ms. MacDonald told us about the field trip."

"I don't know what you see in her," says Cindy with a scowl. "We used to have so much fun together before she moved here."

"You're still my best friend too," says Cate, with a squeeze of Cindy's hand. "Maybe you can ask your mom if you can come over to my house to play after school?"

The children all chatter at once as Ms. MacDonald gets everyone loaded up onto the big yellow school bus. Cate and Kimi find a seat near the back of the bus and put their backpacks on the floor at their feet. Kimi is telling Cate a creation story about a trickster who can change shape from a person to a wolf, when Cindy looks over from her seat across the aisle.

"I hope you don't hurt yourself, walking on all those old bones," Cindy says to Kimi. She pulls on the corners of her eyes to make them slant. "Me Indian, me love old buffalo bones," Cindy says.

"That's not nice," Cate says, glaring at Cindy.

"So, what?" Cindy says. She sticks out her tongue. "You two book-nerds deserve one another. Besides, Clarence has agreed to be my buddy today."

As if on cue, Clarence walks onto the bus and makes his way to sit beside Cindy. Cate can hardly believe Cindy is betraying her, after she confided in her that she was in love with him.

Cindy looks around to make sure Ms. MacDonald isn't looking and sticks out her tongue again. She makes a show of taking Clarence's hand in hers.

"Just ignore her," Kimi says in a whisper. "Don't let her spoil our fun, we've both been looking forward to this day all week."

"Yeah, you're right," Cate says.

Cate can't help but feel a deep pain in her chest and a sense of foreboding. Still, the forty-five-minute bus ride flies by for her and Kimi. When the bus pulls into the drop-off zone, Ms. MacDonald stands at the front of the bus and reviews the safety rules.

"The first thing on our agenda is a theatre presentation in the Interpretative Centre," Ms. MacDonald says. "Then you will have half an hour before lunch to explore the exhibits in your pairs. Please make sure to stick together. I will blow my whistle when it's time for lunch. After lunch, we will take a hike along the lower trail. Any questions?"

A dozen hands pop up. Ms. MacDonald answers a few questions, then directs the children to form a line and leads them into the building.

Cate and Kimi are walking together during the hike of the lower trail. They are looking up at the cliff, fascinated by the tumulus that towers in the sky above them, when Cindy sticks her foot out to trip Kimi.

"Oops, sorry," Cindy says as Kimi falls to the ground, scraping her hands in the gravel. "It was an accident."

There is a wave of nervous laughter among the children standing close by. Cate helps Kimi up and she dusts off her pants. Kimi doesn't reply but Cate is furious. She knows it wasn't an accident.

"That wasn't nice," Cate says. "I still want to be friends, but not if you're going to be mean to Kimi."

"Who says I want to be friends with an Indian-lover?" Cindy says.

"Excuse me?" says Ms. MacDonald, who has materialized out of nowhere, holding onto Clarence's hand. Cindy glares over at him and he casts his eyes to the ground.

"I won't have anyone in my classroom using such disrespectful language," Ms. MacDonald says. "Cindy, I want you to say you're sorry, and when we get back to the school you are going to be staying after the bell."

"I'm sorry," Cindy says, not looking Kimi in the eye.

Cate isn't sure if her friend is truly sorry or just upset because she's in trouble. She hopes they can all move on and be friends, but she has a heavy feeling in the pit of her stomach. She chooses to ignore it.

Cindy appears to get over her initial dislike of Kimi, or if not, she at least keeps her feelings to herself. Clarence moves away and Cate's crush is transferred to another boy in her class, blonde-haired, blue-eyed Murray. They exchange love notes and chase one another out in the field at recess. Cate feels content with her social life and loves school.

She finishes writing her chapter book. She weaves a trickster wolf into her story of the princess who can talk to God. As she's writing about the wolf, she thinks of the Magician, whose abuse still lingers in her frequent nightmares.

"I loved your story," William says, returning Cate's notebook to her. "I must admit, I was surprised by your wolf character. He was so scary and realistic."

"Yeah, well, I have a good imagination," Cate says, uncomfortable. "I decided to make the bad guy a wolf like in *Red Riding Hood* and *The Three Little Pigs*. And Kimi told me that creation stories often have tricksters who can transform from people to animals."

"Well, I don't know much about writing stories," says William, "but I think your story is a huge accomplishment. Are you going to let Ms. MacDonald read it?"

"Yeah, she said she'd love to read it," Cate says. "I just wanted you to be the first."

"I'm so proud of you, Caty-bug. Who knows, maybe you'll be a famous writer some day."

A few weeks later Cate comes home from school and disappears into her room without a word or stopping by the kitchen for a snack, totally out of character. Donna knocks gently on her door.

"May I come in?" Donna asks.

"Yeah, I guess so," Cate says, her voice sullen.

"What's wrong?" Donna takes a seat on Cate's bed and rubs her shoulder. She can see that Cate has been crying.

"Nothing," Cate says, with a sigh.

"Now, Cate. You don't have to tell me, but don't say nothing when it's clear something is wrong."

"Okay, you're right, I am upset," Cate says, fresh tears springing forth. "But I don't want to talk about it right now."

"Okay, darling. I'll give you some quiet time, but if you change your mind, I'll just be in the living room reading my book."

When her mother leaves, Cate gets out her new diary, a gift from her parents for her ninth birthday.

April 15, 1975
Dear Diary,

Today Ms. MacDonald gave me back my chapter book. She said she liked it, a lot. But then, on the last page, she wrote me a note. It said she was concerned, that the wolf sounded so real. She asked me if there might be someone in my life who was a shape-changer, like the wolf. She asked if someone was hurting me. She asked me if I'd like to talk with her, or the school counsellor. I'm so ashamed. I don't want to talk to her or anybody else. I don't think I'll ever write another story again. I don't know what to do. I'm scared she will tell my parents. I think I'll die if they ever find out the truth.

Cate closes her diary, locks it with the key, and returns it to her nightstand. She crawls under her sheets and falls asleep. She dreams of wolves and magicians and dark, musty basements.

Chapter 5

*W*ILLIAM BOOKS A SITE at Clear Lake campground, in Manitoba, where his family used to go camping when he was a kid. He's excited to share his childhood refuge with his family and goes big with the purchase of a used tent trailer for their week-long summer vacation.

An enthusiastic energy charges the air as the Henderson family works together to get ready on the day before their departure. Donna is in charge of the menus, and she takes Cate with her to purchase all their groceries.

"Can we get these to roast on the fire?" Cate asks, holding up a jumbo bag of marshmallows.

"Sure, why not, we're on holidays after all," says Donna.

Cate tosses the marshmallows into the cart, along with the other tempting assortment of unusual treats like Tang drink crystals, Jiffy popcorn, and Cheezies.

Cate gets up early the next day. She wakes up Michael, then goes into her parents' room.

"Time to get up, sleepyheads."

"Ugh, what time is it?" Donna asks, as Cate jumps into their bed between them.

"It's not quite six," Cate says, glancing over at the clock radio. "But Daddy said we should head out early to get a jump on traffic."

"That's true," William says. He gives Cate's crazy slept-on hair a ruffle. "I'm so happy to see you taking such a keen interest, Caty-bug." William stretches and throws off the sheets. "Off you go, then. Go get dressed and your mom and I will be out to join you shortly."

After a quick breakfast, William loads the last few items into the trailer. In the trunk of their car he stores the cooler with the packed lunch Donna put together the night before. He hitches the trailer to their faded gold Chevy Impala, then calls out for Trixie. Michael and Cate hop into the back seat, loaded down with their backpacks stuffed full with things to keep them entertained for the long drive. Cate has placed a pillow for herself on the floor, giving up the entire back seat for her brother.

Cate reads her new Nancy Drew book and plays with her Barbies while Michael reads comics and does word puzzles. They play I Spy together and sing songs like "The Quartermaster's Store." They each have a bag of penny candy that they bought with the quarter Donna gave them. Cate savours the sweet tangy flavours of Mojos and blue whale gummies while Michael crunches on potato chips. Trixie jumps from the floor to the seat and back again, sniffing for crumbs.

After lunch at a roadside turnout, Cate changes places with Michael and curls into a ball on the back seat. She conks out for the rest of the journey.

It's late afternoon when William pulls up to the campground registration hut. He fills in the paperwork and pays the deposit, then drives down the gravel road to the spot they are assigned, the number 37 painted in green on a short wooden post at the entrance, peeling and faded from the sun.

Their site has a large clearing nestled amongst aspen trees, a fire pit with a rusted metal grate, and a wooden picnic table.

"Why don't you two take Trixie and go for a little explore around the area while we set up camp?" William says.

"Just make sure you don't go too far and get lost," says Donna. "And I don't want you to go to the lake by yourselves either. And don't talk to strangers."

"Okay," the children say in unison, both excited for an adventure. Michael takes hold of Cate's hand after he clips on Trixie's leash.

Michael and Cate explore the dense aspen forest surrounding their campground. Trixie pulls on her lead to investigate all the dank, stinky smells.

"I think we've been gone quite a while," says Cate, after only half an hour or so. "Maybe we should head back?"

"It will take Mom and Dad a long time to get everything done," says Michael. "We'll just be in the way. I think we should keep looking for a playground. I'm sure I saw a symbol with a swing on the map at the entrance."

"Okay." Cate is already completely lost, with no idea which direction their spot is in, but she trusts her brother.

Michael leads the way and soon, sure enough, he finds the playground. Beside it is a public bathroom, a small wading pool, two vending machines, and a nine-hole mini golf.

"Wow, this is so great!" says Cate. "I'm glad you convinced me to keep going."

Michael ties Trixie's leash to a rung on the bicycle stand and tells her to lie down. Cate runs over to the merry-go-round. "Will you come twirl me, Michael?"

Michael spins the merry-go-round as fast as he can, then jumps on to join his sister. They jump off and dizzy-walk, then fall into the soft grass, laughing. On black-tire swings they pump their legs to soar high into the blue sky dotted with clouds. They whiz down the slide that gleams silver in the sun. They climb the monkey bars, their hands already beginning to callous as they hang from the metal bars.

"The sun is getting lower," Michael says. He looks up at the sky, the clouds a soft pastel pink. "We better get a move on."

They fetch Trixie, who has fallen asleep on the warm asphalt. Michael follows all the landmarks he noticed on the way and soon they are back at their campsite.

Donna is pinning a plastic tablecloth to the picnic table and William is shaving tree branches with his jackknife to make roasting sticks.

"Finally, you're back," Donna says, dropping her clip and rushing over to give them both hugs. "I was worried sick."

"I told you not to worry, that they'd be fine," William says. He sets down the pile of sticks and tosses another log on the already flaming fire. "Let's cook up some wieners, I'm starved."

After eating fire-roasted hot dogs smothered in ketchup, mustard, and relish, Donna gets out the bag of marshmallows. The grey-black sky is illuminated by their fire, the only light until the next campsite. They tell stories and sing songs, smacking now and then at the pesky mosquitos that have come out in full force.

"My goodness, William, it's ten o'clock," Donna says with a gasp, squinting with her flashlight at her watch. "We better get these two in their pajamas and off to bed if we're going to get up early and go down to the lake for our fishing excursion."

Cozied up in bed beside her brother, Cate falls asleep to the rhythmic chirping of crickets, her heart full up and overflowing with happiness.

The sun shining in through the thin canvas of the tent trailer wakes Cate up early. She shakes Michael's shoulder, but he swats at her like a fly. She looks over at her parents' bed. They are both fast asleep, tucked in their sleeping bags. Cate takes off her pajama bottoms and pulls on her jeans. Trixie looks up and wags her tail, thump, thump on the floor.

"C'mon, girl," Cate whispers. She grabs her diary and a pencil, then slips quietly outside. She finds a spot to crouch behind a bush and does a little shake, having forgotten the toilet paper inside the trailer. Trixie scampers off into the bush to do her business and returns looking for a treat. Cate washes her hands at the outdoor tap, ice-cold, and dries them on her jeans. She fishes out a Milk-Bone from a plastic container.

"Sit girl, shake a paw," Cate says, then gives Trixie her reward.

Cate picks up her diary and plops down in a lawn chair next to the fire pit, all traces of their cozy fire turned to ash. Trixie lays down on the ground beside Cate's feet.

July 25, 1976
Dear Diary,

I feel so lucky. I'm so happy to be camping with my family. Yesterday I had so much fun playing with Michael. He's such a great big brother. He's my best friend. Hot dogs roasted on an open fire taste so much better than when Mom boils them in a pot on the stove. I kept burning my marshmallows, letting my stick get too close to the fire, but Daddy took over for me and they turned out golden brown and crispy on the outside and soft and melty on the inside. They were so delicious. I sat on Daddy's lap and we cuddled up while Mommy told us stories from when she was a little girl on the farm.

I've never slept in a tent trailer before, with trees all around me, under a big night sky. I thought it would be scary, but it wasn't at all, it was peaceful. I felt like a caterpillar must feel, all cozy in my own sleeping bag cocoon.

I'm really excited to go fishing today. Daddy said Grandpa taught him how to fish when he was around my age, and he's going to show me how. I hope it isn't hard for me to learn, like riding my bike, or worse, playing baseball.

After a breakfast of slightly burnt toast that Donna prepares on the Coleman gas stove and eggs fried in a skillet over the open fire, Donna washes the dishes while William sorts out the fishing tackle. Everyone helps to carry their gear down to the lake, where William rents a small motorboat from the vendor. Cate does a little dance on the dock.

"I've never been in a boat before," Cate says. "I'm so excited!"

"Me too," says Michael. "I love boats."

"Well, climb on in then," William says, reaching for Michael's hand to help him in, then Cate's. He hands them both a life jacket. William starts the engine and steers the boat away from the dock and out onto the open water.

"I don't know how much things have changed since I was here last," William says, "or if I even remember the way, but I'm going to try and find Dad's old favourite fishing spot." He gets out his map and looks it over, then turns the boat sharply to the right.

William navigates the boat into a somewhat secluded clearing. There is a small waterfall nearby that makes a tranquil backdrop, but the lake's crystal-clear, blue-grey water is perfectly still. William shows Cate and Michael how to thread worms onto hooks and cast their lines into the water while Donna reads her book, looking up once in a while to watch.

The art of casting a line turns out to be more difficult than Cate anticipated, but instead of pushing her, William does it for her and she just holds onto the rod, waiting for a pull. William has told them they need to be as quiet and still as they can, so the fish don't sense there are intruders. The silence feels peaceful to Cate, not boring at all, like Cindy warned her it would be. Cate is off in her own world when she feels a tiny tug.

"Daddy, I feel something!" Cate says in an excited whisper.

"Let me take a look, Caty-bug." William sets his own fishing rod on the bottom of the boat and steps toward the side. He peers into the lake.

"I can't see anything, are you sure?"

"I'm pretty sure," Cate says, her excitement mounting. "Come and hold my rod and see."

William steps behind Cate and wraps his arms around her, then places his hands over hers to take hold of the rod.

"Yep, you've caught something, that's for sure. I'll help you reel it in."

He shows Cate how to turn the handle slowly.

"Look, it's splashing, trying to get away," Michael says, pointing at the commotion.

Even Donna seems spellbound.

"Steady, Caty-bug, steady," William says. Soon the line is reeled in close enough for them to see the silver gleam of fish scales. "Pull her in now."

With William's help, Cate brings in her first catch. It plops onto the floor of the boat and writhes.

"It looks so sad. What kind of fish is it, Daddy?"

"That's a pickerel. The tastiest fish of all. Although looking at him, he can't be more than six inches, just enough for a small snack, I reckon."

"I don't want to eat him. Can we just set him free, back in the water?"

"Now, Cate, don't be silly and sentimental," William says with a wave of his hand. He's already pulled the hook out of its mouth and is getting out the cooler of ice. "We eat fish, just like we eat cows and chickens. It's the cycle of life, Cate, nothing to be sad about."

Cate knows what her dad says is true, but her heart feels heavy nonetheless. She decides she doesn't want to fish anymore.

"I think I'll take a rest and read with Mommy now," Cate says, deflated.

William turns away to help Michael bait his hook again. They manage to haul in three more decent-sized pickerel and one jackfish that he does throw back in, saying they are the rats of the lake and taste nasty.

An entire morning out on the lake has everyone tired and ready for lunch. They return the boat and haul their cooler full of fish back to their campsite. William starts up the fire, guts and cleans the fish, and tosses them in a pan with salt and butter. Cate picks at her food. The fish does taste delicious, but she keeps seeing the sad look in the eyes of the fish she caught, and each bite seems to catch in her throat.

Chapter 6

CATE WAKES UP EARLY and gets ready for her first day of grade five. She puts on her panties and stands in front of her dresser mirror, looking at her body that has begun to change. She can see the tiny buds of breasts swelling. Her nipples are larger too. She squeezes her arms tight against her sides to form a slight cleavage and imagines having ample breasts, like her mom.

A couple of weeks into the new school year, the doorbell rings just as Cate is tidying up her breakfast dishes. Michael answers.

"Hi, Cindy, you're here early," Michael says. "I'll let Cate know you're here, come on in."

En route to school, Cate asks, "So, how come you were so early today?"

"Well, actually, I have a big favour to ask," Cindy says.

"Sure, what is it?"

"It's about my math homework. I tried to do the problems on my own, but I just couldn't seem to figure out which step to do first. Can we stop at the school playground so you can help me finish?"

"Sure, no problem," Cate says, having completed her homework easily.

"I don't want you to help me, exactly," Cindy says as the girls sit down at one of the lunch tables and Cindy retrieves her math scribbler from her backpack. "We don't have time, and it's all just too confusing. I was hoping you would just give me the right answers. I can copy yours if you have your math book with you."

"You mean you want me to let you cheat off me?" Cate asks.

"Well, yes, but only just this one time," Cindy says. "I'll get into so much trouble if I show up without my homework completed again. But if you help me out, just this once, I promise I won't ask again. Maybe you can come over after school and teach me, properly."

Cate doesn't feel good about cheating, but she doesn't want her friend to get into trouble and she doesn't want to deal with Cindy being upset with her again.

"Okay," Cate says. "But just this once."

Cate goes over to Cindy's house to play after school, and somehow the homework remains forgotten as the two girls become engrossed in setting up a pretend veterinary office. Cindy wants to be a vet when she grows up, and it's one of their favourite games.

The next morning, Cindy shows up at Cate's house early again. Cate feels heavy. She knows what's coming next, and her stomach lurches with unease.

"Can I copy your homework again?" Cindy asks on the walk to school.

"You promised me," Cate says. "You said you would only ask once."

"I know," Cindy says, looking down at her feet. "But I forgot all about it until this morning."

"I'm sorry," Cate says. "I don't want you to get into trouble, but cheating doesn't feel good. If you want my help, we can work on it together when we get to school. Maybe Mrs. Wright will be in early and we can ask her to help too."

"You're such a scaredy-cat," Cindy says with a scowl. "I thought you were my best friend."

Cindy runs off, leaving Cate with a heavy heart.

Mrs. Wright is teaching the class about poetry in English and Cate is excited. One of the assignments is to choose three of the six forms that Mrs. Wright has taught them, and Cate can hardly decide which three. She easily composes a haiku about an eagle and a limerick about frogs, but when she tries to write a blank verse, she finds the precise metre of iambic pentameter a challenge. She stays after school for extra help. She ends up writing a poem about love that Mrs. Wright reads to the class as an example.

When I feel Daddy's hands holding me tight,
When Mommy says everything is alright,
When my brother protects me from my fears,
That's when I know how it feels to be loved.
When I hear an eagle high in the sky,
When God is there with me when I cry,
When I dance with Jesus in a garden,
That's when I know how it feels to be loved.

Cate is a little embarrassed, but mostly thrilled.

"I loved your poem so much," Kimi says on the way home from school. "I found that poetry unit really hard, but not you."

"Thank you. I've always liked reading poetry, but I never wrote many poems before, and only ones that rhyme."

"I suppose we all like different things," Kimi says. "Which reminds me, do you want to join me on a hike in the gully down by the train yard this weekend? I want to look for some new rocks for my collection."

"I would love to. I'll ask my mom tonight at dinner and let you know tomorrow."

With Donna's permission, Cate picks up Kimi at her house the next Saturday morning, and they ride their bikes across town, to the Canadian Pacific train yard. They set their bikes down in the tall grass and make their way down the steep decline to the gully. There is a trickle of a creek, an offshoot of the Old Man River, that gurgles through the rocks. Kimi stops once in a while to examine a rock but tosses most of them back. She only wants rocks with an unusual shape or colour for her collection.

Cate isn't much into rocks, but she enjoys just being with Kimi out in the fresh air. She knows that soon it will be too cold to enjoy weekend excursions like these. As she walks along in comfortable silence, she daydreams about the main character in the book she's reading. *Little Women* is set in the mid 1800s. She wonders what the gully might have looked like back then, before the settlers arrived on the prairies. She is thinking about the feisty Jo March, when she hears a familiar screech in the sky.

"Hey, Kimi," Cate whispers to her friend a few feet in front of her. "Look up!"

A red-tailed hawk soars above them.

"I wonder if that's the same hawk we saw by the pond a while back?" Cate says.

"Maybe," Kimi says. "It might have a nest somewhere nearby."

The girls sit down quietly on the ground to watch.

"I remember you telling me that the person the hawk flies beside is a Seer. You said you were too young to be a Seer, but maybe you're old enough now?"

"Maybe," Kimi says. She shudders.

"What's wrong?"

"Nothing," Kimi says. "I just had a strange feeling come over me, that's all. I think maybe we should leave."

Cate gets a chill. The energy from her friend feels like a dark foreboding.

A week later, the most popular boy in the class asks Cate if she wants to go to the gully with him. Cate wants to go, even though she doesn't know him very well.

"Can Kimi come too?" Cate asks.

"Sure, why not?" Tim says. "I'll invite Derek. It can be a double date."

Cate feels excited and nervous. Her first date.

The next Saturday Cate picks up Kimi and they ride their bikes to the gully. Kimi spots Tim and Derek sitting by the train tracks.

"Hi, Cate, hi, Kimi," the boys call out in unison as they get up and brush off their pants. "Follow us, we have a fort set up, just a few minutes from here."

Cate looks over at Kimi. She looks as nervous as Cate feels. The girls hold hands and follow the boys through the tall brown grass and bulrushes. Soon they see what Tim has called a fort, a rudimentary construction of old, tattered, faded drapes and sheets tied to the surrounding trees with twine.

"Come on in," Tim says, opening the gap wider to reveal a small, thin rug spread out on the ground. There are old pop cans strewn about and a pile of magazines. Cate looks down and sees a photo of a naked woman on the magazine on top.

"That's gross," Cate says, stifling a gasp. She feels uneasy. "Maybe this is a bad idea. Let's go, Kimi."

"Not so fast," Tim says, turning the magazine over. He smiles, his silver braces like train tracks across his teeth. "You've come all this way, and all we want to do is hang out, that's all."

Cate isn't sure, and Kimi looks reluctant.

"C'mon, Kimi," Derek says, patting the ground beside him, his long, lanky legs crossed awkwardly, his knees high in the air. "I don't bite."

Kimi looks at Cate and shrugs her shoulders. The girls sit down beside one another. Tim offers them both a can of Pepsi, and Derek produces a deck of cards. They play a few hands of rummy. Cate is beginning to relax a bit. She's having fun.

"Let's play a different game," Tim says, gathering up the cards. "How about Truth or Dare?"

"I don't like that game," Kimi says. "And besides, I think it's time for us to go."

"Aw, c'mon, don't be such a spoilsport," Derek says.

Cate has played this game with her cousins before. She knows the drill. She feels a strange mix of excitement and fear.

"Maybe we can play, just for a little while?" Cate says. She looks Kimi in the eye.

"You stay if you want," Kimi says, "but I'm going."

"I dare you to kiss me," Tim says, before Cate can switch gears. He grabs her by the shoulders and pulls her to him. He kisses her hard, on the mouth. Cate struggles to push him away, but Kimi clocks him in the side of the head with her closed fist.

"Ouch!" Tim cries out, in shock. He rubs his head and scowls.

"She doesn't want to," Kimi says. "C'mon, Cate, let's get out of here. These two aren't worth our time."

Cate pushes herself up and wipes her sleeve across her mouth, a tear in her eye.

"Go ahead, leave, you frigid bitches," Tim says with a sneer.

Cate and Kimi run through the gully and back to their bikes.

"I think that hawk was warning us," Cate says. "Next time I will listen to you. I'm sorry I got us into this."

"It's okay," Kimi says. "It could have been worse, especially if you'd gone by yourself. I'm glad I was there."

"Me too."

When Cate gets home, she is relieved to discover no one is there. She goes into the bathroom and scrubs her lips with a face cloth. She looks in the mirror and sees a brief flash of a wolf. She shudders, goosebumps rising on her skin, and goes to her room. She rummages in her drawer for her diary and plops down on her bed to write.

September 18, 1976
Dear Diary,

    I'm so upset and confused. Why do some boys have to be so gross and disgusting? I've been getting these urges I never had before, like I want to kiss a boy, but I want to do it properly. I don't even know what that means, except maybe softly? With my permission? It would be nice to be asked, not forced. I didn't know there were so many mean boys. My dad and my brother are so kind. I wish I could meet a boy like

*them. When Tim grabbed me, I had a flashback to the
Magician. I'd forgotten all about him for a while there.
I wonder if I'll ever be able to forget those horrible
memories? Maybe I'll just have to give up on love
altogether and become a nun when I grow up. But then
I feel these tingles. I'm so upset and confused. I wish I
could talk to someone, but I don't know who. I can't
imagine sharing these feelings with anyone, not even
Kimi or Cindy.*

The next day at school, Cate is reading at her desk when she
feels a chill run down her spine. She looks behind her to see
Tim, crouching and leaning his head towards her, his
jet-black hair like an ominous cloud getting closer, brushes
her cheek.

"Ew, what's that smell?" Tim says, making an
exaggerated sniff. "Kimi, you should tell your friend about
deodorant."

Cate is mortified. She tries to sniff inconspicuously
at her armpits, but everyone in the class is looking at her,
smirking and giggling.

"What's going on?" Mrs. Wright asks, looking up
from her desk.

"Nothing," says Cate, looking down.

Tim high-fives Derek and walks back to his desk,
snickering, while Mrs. Wright continues marking
assignments.

At the end of grade five, Cate has earned straight A's on her
report card. Donna thinks Cate needs a bigger challenge.

Before the teachers leave for summer vacation, Donna sets up an appointment with the principal to advocate accelerating Cate up a grade. He agrees that Cate would likely fit in better socially as well, and the decision is made to skip her to grade seven in the fall.

All summer Cate worries and stresses that it will be too hard, that she won't be able to keep up with the curriculum, but she's confident that she will remain the best of friends with Kimi and Cindy, no matter if they're in the same class or not, and she's happy she won't be in the same classroom as Tim. The nightmares return to haunt her. In her dreams Tim leans in to kiss her, then transforms into a wolf. He sets his sharp teeth into her skin and bites down, hard. The blood pours out of the wounds in her neck, forming a dark crimson stain on the neckline of her shirt. The wolf howls as an eagle screeches in the sky overhead.

Chapter 7

*I*N THE SPRING OF 1980, just after she turns fourteen, Cate is at her locker when she hears her and Michael's names called out over the school intercom.

"Would Michael and Cate Henderson please come down to the office, immediately."

Cate has a sick feeling in the pit of her stomach as she pushes her locker closed and snaps the lock in place. As she walks in the direction of the school office, her mind buzzes with possibilities.

When she enters the office, Michael is standing at the school secretary's desk, waiting for her.

"Oh, good, you're both here now," the secretary says, a look in her eye that Cate recognizes as pity. Cate goes over to stand beside her brother and he takes her hand in his.

"I just received a call from your mother, and I'm afraid I have some difficult news."

"What is it?" Michael asks.

"Your dog's been hit by a truck and killed," the secretary says. "I'm so sorry for your loss. Your mother asked that you be dismissed early, so that you can say goodbye to your dog before the burial."

Cate feels like she is going to faint. The room swims. Michael steadies her, putting his hands on her shoulders.

"It's okay, Sis. You're going to be alright."

"Trixie's so street-smart. It's just so hard to believe she could have been hit by a car," Cate says.

On the walk home, Cate confides to Michael.

"I'm kinda freaking out, to be honest," she begins. "I had a dream about a week ago. I didn't realize then it was a premonition. I dreamt I was at school camp, on my own in the woods, when I spotted a group of classmates out on the dock, pulling an animal out of the water. I couldn't recognize what it was, but it was black, Trixie's size. They left it there on the dock. I knew it needed to be in the water to breathe, and it was trying, without success, to drag itself to the end of the dock and back into the water, but I just watched, frozen, and didn't do a thing to help the poor creature."

Maybe I'm the one who is a Seer, Cate thinks to herself, remembering her conversations with Kimi. Her heart constricts, thinking of how close they used to be.

"That is kinda freaky," Michael agrees.

When they get home, their mom and Grandma Henderson are sitting at the kitchen table, both in tears.

"Oh, thank goodness," Donna says when she sees them. She gets up from the table and rushes over to put her arms around her children.

"I can hardly believe it's true," Cate says.

"I know, it's a shock for all of us," Donna says. "We wanted you to be able to say goodbye to Trixie before we bury her out in the yard. Neither your dad nor I feel comfortable leaving her exposed, outside in this heat. He's on his way home from work now."

"Trixie's too smart to get hit by a car," Cate insists.

"Well, I don't think it was an accident at all," Grandma Henderson says. "Trixie was out exploring as is, was, her way. I was washing dishes at the kitchen sink when I happened to look out. There was a monster black truck, one of those godawful jacked-up-on-huge-wheels things, going way over the speed limit. I saw Trixie try to cross to our side of the road, and the truck swerved to hit her. I could see the maniacal look on the driver's face, he looked like a psychopath if you ask me. I ran outside but he took off with a squeal of his tires, leaving burnt rubber on the road. Trixie tried to drag herself home, but her back legs were broken." Elizabeth pauses to compose herself. "The poor thing, it was a blessing she passed soon after, as she was clearly in a great deal of pain. I'm just glad your mother and I were there to comfort her as she left this world."

"That makes my dream even more of a premonition," Cate says with a gasp.

"What dream?" Donna asks.

"I was telling Michael, on the way home," Cate says. "An animal in my dream was hurt and dragging its back legs, trying to get back into the lake."

"That was just a dream," Elizabeth says. "Now, do you want to go and say your goodbyes to Trixie by yourselves, or do you want one of us to come with you? Your father should be home any minute, and he'll want to start digging her grave right away."

"I don't want to see her dead," Michael says. "I'll say goodbye once she's buried. Are we going to mark her grave with a cross?"

"One thing at a time," Donna says. "But, yes, I think that is a nice idea. What about you, Cate?"

"I would like some time, just me, alone with her," Cate says. She gets up from the table and slips out the back door.

There is an old blanket covering Trixie on the ground near the back step. Cate kneels down beside her and pulls the blanket back, just to Trixie's neck. Her eyelids are closed shut and she looks so peaceful, like she could just be sleeping. A tear escapes onto Cate's cheek, soon followed by a flood as a wave of grief and loss sweeps over her.

"Goodbye, my dear, loyal friend," Cate says as she buries her tear-streaked face into her dog's fur and sobs. "You were the best dog, ever."

After a month of grieving, Donna comes home from work one day with a new little puppy, another Heinz 57, like Trixie. She's only eight weeks old, all black, with paws that look like she'll grow to a good size. They name her Abby. Everyone falls in love with her right away.

Caring for a new puppy helps to ease the pain of losing Trixie a little, but Cate still stops in at Trixie's grave every day to say a prayer.

Around the same time, William begins to feel fatigued. He isn't able to get a good night's sleep because he wakes up often, in pain. He detests going to the doctor, but when his symptoms continue through all of May, he makes an appointment for a complete physical exam, including blood work, urine analysis, and stool samples.

"The doctor's office called me at work today with the test results," William tells Donna. They are alone in their room, Donna folding towels while William changes out of his work clothes.

"Well? Don't keep me in suspense. What's the diagnosis?" Donna has been in a constant state of worry, anticipating the worst.

"Apparently everything's normal, other than my iron is a bit low."

"What? That doesn't add up." Donna sets the laundry basket down on the bed. "I suppose low iron might explain why you're tired all the time, but it doesn't explain the pain you're in. There's got to be something more."

"I agree. But Dr. Morrison insists there's nothing else unusual. He even suggested it's all in my head. Maybe your old man is going wacko."

"Now that's about the craziest idea I've heard. You're the most level-headed, down-to-earth person I know. They just haven't done the right tests."

"You really think so?" William asks.

"I know so. If you want, I'll call tomorrow to book a follow-up appointment myself."

William sits down beside his wife on the edge of the bed, leans over, and kisses her cheek.

"Thank you, but I'll call," he says. "This is my responsibility. I'm not another one of your kids, even if you like to tease me that I act like one. Besides—"

He's interrupted by a knock at the door.

"Speaking of kids," Donna says, a bit exasperated. "Come on in, it's open!"

Cate and Michael look embarrassed to find their parents in an intimate moment, cuddled up close together on their bed.

"Sorry to interrupt, but we really need to talk," Cate says.

"No problem, your father and I were just chatting while I was doing up the laundry. What's on your minds?"

"Well, it's just that, we've both, I mean, Michael and I, we've noticed some weird things about Dad and we're kinda wondering—"

William stands and swipes at his cowlick. "What do you mean by weird?"

"I don't know, exactly, just weird, not yourself," Cate says. "I've noticed you napping a lot. You never nap. And you haven't played one round of golf yet this spring. I know your baseball team has started practices, but you haven't gone to one. And we've both seen you limping and struggling to open jars."

"You're right, Caty-bug," William says, surprised that his children have paid so much attention. "I haven't been feeling well, not at all. But I haven't said anything because there's nothing to tell. I've been to the doctor and he can't find anything wrong with me, all my tests came back normal. I don't know what else to tell you."

"I'm so relieved!" Cate says, letting the tears she'd been holding back roll down her cheeks. "I thought maybe you and Mom might be getting a divorce or something. Cindy's parents are in the process of getting divorced, and it's all I can think about."

"I thought you might have cancer or something scary like that," Michael says.

"I'm sorry," William says. "I didn't mean to worry you guys. I guess I should have said something earlier, but like I said, there's nothing really to tell."

"No news is good news, I hope," Cate says, "but if you do find out something, whatever it is, please promise to tell me and Michael. Okay, Daddy, will you promise?"

"I promise," William says, and gives Cate and Michael big hugs.

A week later, William goes to a follow-up appointment with Dr. Morrison.

"The doctor will be with you shortly," the nurse says, after leading him to an examination room.

William sits down in the uncomfortable chair in the corner of the room. He drums his knuckles nervously on the armrest while he waits. The wait seems to drag on forever.

"Hello, William." Dr. Morrison extends his hand, and William shakes it.

Dr. Morrison seats himself on a stool. "So, what brings you back in? I thought I asked the nurse to call you with the test results. Have you filled the prescription for iron pills that I called into your pharmacy?"

"Yes, I did," William replies.

"Good, good. Those iron pills should help you with your low energy in a couple of weeks," Dr. Morrison says.

"Yes, I'm aware of all that. The problem is, I'm still suffering from the same things we discussed before. I'm in pain, all the time. My joints feel hot and stiff. It's not only fatigue."

"Well, I really don't know what to say, William. The blood tests ruled out everything I could think of to test for. I checked for hepatitis, rheumatoid arthritis, lupus, and multiple sclerosis. Have you been having any emotional difficulties? You know, trouble with those teenagers of yours, or the wife?"

"Look here, Dr. Morrison, my personal life is my business. And these symptoms I've been having aren't caused by emotions or stress. They came on suddenly, out of the blue." William stops to roll up his left pant leg. "Just look at the swelling in my knee. It's got to be almost twice its normal size. Don't try and tell me I'm imagining that."

"Well, I don't know what to say," Dr. Morrison says, looking uncomfortable. "But sometimes psychological disorders can manifest in physiological ways. I've seen many people whose pain is relieved with a simple prescription for medication that is truly nothing more than a placebo. I just thought—"

"Well, you best think again," William says as he rolls down his trouser leg and stands up. "Our discussion is over. As is my need for your services. I'll be looking for a new GP, thank you very much."

William storms out of the examination room, outraged with the arrogant Dr. Morrison. He can hardly believe the doctor is still suggesting he has a psychological condition. He stomps out of the doctor's office, his knee throbbing painfully with each step.

William tries another physician, who has more empathy but no answers. He begins to sink into a deep depression. He becomes despondent as golf season kicks off and he can't walk the course, let alone swing a club. He tries baseball practice, but even the swinging of the bat causes him pain, and he can't run around the bases without his knees throbbing.

"William, I really think this has gone on long enough," Donna says one evening in June, not long before the school summer break. She is drying the last of the dishes and putting them away in the cupboards.

"What do you mean by 'this'?" William asks, looking up from his newspaper.

"You know exactly what I mean. It's time you went to see a different doctor, a specialist, in a bigger centre, like Calgary or even Edmonton. You can't just give up because the two doctors you've seen here haven't been able to provide a diagnosis. Something is wrong, that much I know is true."

"We can't just up and go to Calgary or Edmonton," William says. "What about work? And the kids? Not to mention the expense."

"We can figure all that out," Donna insists, wiping her hands on the front of her apron and then taking it off to join her husband on the sofa. "You need a diagnosis so you can get the proper treatment and get better. I'm sure there are plenty of competent doctors to choose from in a big city. Please, William, let me get out the phone directory for Calgary right now. You can pick out one or two names from the list and I'll call to set up appointments for next week."

"It sounds crazy to me," William grunts, "but it seems like you've made up your mind."

"Yes, I have."

The next week Donna and William leave Cate and Michael with their grandmother, make the drive to Calgary, and book into a cheap hotel on the Trans-Canada Highway. The doctor believes William is suffering from some kind of autoimmune disease and sends him to the Foothills Hospital for a thorough work up. They run an arsenal of tests, including a complete blood count, an ESR to measure inflammation, a CRP protein test, an ANA antinuclear antibody test, plus numerous X-rays and radiographs to determine the condition of William's joints, eyes, lungs, and other organs.

Despite the fact William's rheumatoid factor shows negative, X-rays show an arthritic nodule on William's right elbow, in his fingers in both his hands, and inflammation in both knee joints. William is diagnosed with rheumatoid arthritis.

William begins his first round of gold injections and starts an aggressive combination of ibuprofen, folic acid, and cortisone over two weeks as part of an in-hospital short-term stay. He's seen by a stream of professionals—physiotherapists, occupational therapists, orthopedic surgeons, and rheumatologists. Registered dieticians meet with him to give him nutritional advice, which he takes with a grain of salt. He is offered the opportunity to attend group counselling sessions, but William declines, adamant that therapy is all a bunch of hogwash.

With a proper diagnosis and support, William feels hopeful for the first time in months. His biggest concern is how to break the news, that he has a chronic, long-term, incurable disease, to his kids. But he promised Cate he would be forthright, and William doesn't break his promises.

Grandma Henderson is busy looking after Michael and Cate and baking bread, cinnamon rolls, and her famous rhubarb custard pie. Preparing food is her way of showing love, and she's stocked up the freezer in the basement, ready for William's return.

"Yum, it smells so good in here," Cate says after a long day at school. "What did you bake, Grandma?"

Abby comes running over to greet Cate and gives her hand a good lick.

"How on earth can you stand letting that dog lick your hand?" Elizabeth says before answering. "I can only imagine how many germs are on her tongue. To answer your question, I made date-oatmeal cookies today, one of your dad's favourites. If you want one for your after-school snack you best go and give your hands a good washing."

Cate laughs and gives Abby another scratch under her chin, then disappears to her room to unpack her backpack.

She retrieves the permission form for the end-of-year dance then goes to wash her hands.

Before diving into her snack, Cate passes the form to her grandma.

"Can you sign this form for me?" Cate asks. "The dance is tomorrow night, and I need to return it tomorrow. Sorry I left it so late, but I wasn't sure if I wanted to go, and then I just kept forgetting."

"Well, you've had a lot on your mind, what with your mom and dad away and your dear father sick with who knows what," Elizabeth says. "Just leave it on the table and I'll be sure to sign it once I finish up here."

Cate goes back into her room. She has a research project on Greece to complete, her final assignment in social studies for the year, but she decides to write in her diary first.

June 21, 1980
Dear Diary,

I'm so worried about my dad. I've barely been able to concentrate at school. I've handed in two assignments late. It didn't feel good at all. I don't like to be late. Daddy has drilled it into me that tardiness is a bad habit, along with overeating and laziness. He can be such a stickler. Yet somehow, no matter how strict he is, I always feel so loved. I really miss seeing him every day, the little things like hanging out watching television or just feeling his presence nearby, when I'm reading on the couch and he's taking a nap. He's been napping so much. I hope the doctors in Calgary have figured out how to help him. I hope he comes home with good news, that he gets better and back to his old self, soon.

Cate and Cindy are on the way home from school the
next day, when Cindy informs Cate of her latest big idea.

"I'm stealing some alcohol from my parents' liquor
cabinet," Cindy says. "It's our last dance of the year, and
I think we should both get a little tipsy."

"You can't be serious." Cate says. "That's illegal."

"That's the whole point," Cindy says with a giggle.
"C'mon and live a little for a change. With your parents out
of town, it should be easy-breezy for you to get some booze."

"I don't know," Cate says. "My parents hardly ever drink.
I don't even know if they have anything, or where they keep
it. And you know what a busybody my grandma is."

Cate hopes her list of excuses will get her off the hook.
She lost her friendship with Kimi at the end of grade eight
because of Cindy's constant sneaky tricks and lies, and now
Cindy is her only friend, other than Michael. She wants to
be cool, like Cindy, but often the things Cindy wants her to
do don't feel right.

"I'm sure you can find some alcohol if you put your
mind to it," Cindy says. "And I'll bring some cigarettes too.
We'll be total bad girls."

Cate has tried smoking before. She didn't like the taste
or the smell, but she did feel grown-up and kinda cool,
holding a cigarette in her fingers and blowing smoke,
like her mom.

"Okay," Cate agrees. "I'll try."

When her grandma is busy washing up dishes after dinner,
Cate goes into the living room to search for her parents'
stash. She looks in the china cabinet, but only finds the
china set they never use, covered in a film of dust.

When Elizabeth finishes the dishes and goes downstairs to do laundry, Cate pulls a chair from the table and climbs up to look in the cupboard above the fridge. She spies a few bottles of amber and clear liquid and pours a few splashes from each bottle into an empty margarine container. Her heart pounds in her chest as she replaces the chair and hurries back to her room to hide the container at the bottom of her backpack, covering it with an old jean jacket.

Cate sneaks into her parents' bathroom and goes into the medicine cabinet where Donna keeps her limited selection of makeup. She plucks her eyebrows then applies bright blue eye shadow and mascara and a coral-coloured lipstick. She doesn't quite recognize the girl in mirror but decides her reflection looks older and more sophisticated than fourteen. The doorbell rings.

"I'll get it," Cate yells. "It's Cindy, here to walk with me to the dance."

"Alright, then," Grandma calls out from the living room, where she is watching television with Michael. "Make sure you are home in time for your ten o'clock curfew, and have a good time."

"I will, goodbye!" Cate yells back. She closes the door quietly and turns to greet Cindy.

"Wow, you look like a knockout!" Cindy says. "Did you get some booze?"

"Yeah, I did, but only a little." Cate doesn't know that almost half a cup of straight up hard alcohol is a lot for a young girl who has never had even a sip of wine or beer before.

Cindy and Cate walk hand in hand to the school, stopping at the playground to glug back their stolen liquor and share a cigarette. Cindy passes Cate a stick of gum and produces a can of hairspray to mask the smell.

At the door, the principal is sitting at a table with a list on a clipboard of everyone who has permission. She scans the sheet to find Cindy and Cate's names, and checks them off with her pen.

"Have a good time," the principal says.

Cate stores her backpack in her locker and walks with Cindy to the gym. Her legs start to feel like rubber and the room spins a little. She stumbles in her platform heels.

"I feel dizzy," Cate whispers to Cindy.

"I know, me too. It's from the booze, it's all normal."

Cate wonders how many times Cindy has drunk alcohol before. She wonders if she really knows her friend at all. She feels carefree and silly, in a way she's never experienced before. She doesn't like it, but it's too late.

Inside the gymnasium the band is set up on the stage and already playing their first set. There are fold-out tables covered with plastic tablecloths laden with large bowls of fruit punch and disposable paper cups. Cindy pours them both a glass. Cate spills a few drops on the floor as she makes her way to the bleachers.

"Do you want to dance?"

Cate has seen Brad around but doesn't really know him. He's tall and well-built, on the school football team, and very popular.

"Sure, but can my friend join us?" Cate asks, a little surprised by his attention.

"Yeah, sure, why not?"

Cate and Cindy follow Brad to the dance floor. The band is playing "Heart of Glass" by Blondie. Cate knows all the words, and she has a good sense of rhythm. Her body moves naturally to the beat. With the alcohol emboldening her, Cate loses all inhibitions and undulates her hips and can tell it's having the desired effect on Brad. The next song is slow and Brad pulls Cate in close. Cate doesn't even notice Cindy slink away, she's so overwhelmed with the tingling sensation she feels.

"Let's go make out somewhere more private," Brad says. He takes Cate by the hand and leads her to the bleachers. They climb to the top and find a spot in a dark corner. Brad kisses her on the mouth. He pushes open her lips with his tongue. Cate feels flushed. Brad moves his lips to her neck. He starts sucking on her skin while caressing her breast through her shirt.

"Stop, please," Cate says, her voice raspy.

"I'm just getting started," Brad says. "And don't lie, I can tell you like it." He pinches her erect nipple, to make his point.

"I said, stop." The room is spinning heavily now. "I think I'm going to be sick."

Before she can pull away and get to a washroom, Cate vomits all over the bleachers.

"Oh my God, gross!" Brad pushes her away, runs down the bleachers, and disappears into the crowd on the dance floor.

Cindy comes to the rescue. She runs to the girls' washroom and returns with a handful of paper towels. She cleans up the mess and steadies Cate on her arm.

"I'm sorry," Cate says. "I'm so embarrassed."

"It's okay," Cindy says. "You're clearly a lightweight. But don't worry, I'll take care of you."

"I just want to go home," Cate moans.

"Not a good idea. Let's sneak out one of the side doors and go to my place. You can call your grandma from there and ask if you can sleep over."

Cate wobbles her way to Cindy's on rubber legs. She throws up again in Cindy's bathroom. Cindy gets her a

warm facecloth and finds some Tylenol under the vanity.
She pours Cate a glass of water from the tap to swallow
it down, but the water makes Cate's stomach heave again.
She's in no state to call her grandma. Cindy tells her mom,
who agrees to be a part of the cover-up, and she calls to let
Elizabeth know the change of plans.

The next day, Cate wakes up disoriented. Her head feels like
a bowling ball and her mouth feels like sandpaper. She rolls
over and sees Cindy's back. She hardly remembers what
happened, her brain is so foggy. She gets up to use the
washroom, noticing she has on one of Cindy's nighties.
She doesn't remember changing.

Washing her hands at the sink, Cate looks in the mirror
and sees a huge red and blue bruise on her neck. A flash of
memory burns into her awareness.

After a shower Cate gets dressed in the clothing she
wore the night before, which reeks like cigarette smoke. Cate
finds a vial of perfume on the vanity counter and sprays
herself liberally. She squirts toothpaste onto her finger and
rubs it vigorously over her teeth and gums, even her tongue.

"Thanks for taking care of me," Cate says to Cindy
before she leaves. She's put on her jean jacket and pulls the
collar up to try and hide her hickey, even though the sun is
already high in the sky, with promises of a hot early summer
day. "I don't know what I would have done without you."

"Yeah, well, it's the least I could do," Cindy says. "After
all, it was my fault, really. I pushed you into it, and you were
way out of your league."

"I'm never doing that again, that's for sure."

Cate walks in the front door, which they never lock, and
tries to tiptoe to her room to change before anyone sees
her, but Abby comes running over barking, wagging her tail
with excitement.

"Shh, quiet, girl," Cate says.

"Is that you, Cate?" Elizabeth calls out. She's in the
kitchen, scouring the floors on her hands and knees.

"Yeah, I'm home," Cate says.

"I didn't appreciate getting a call from Cindy's mom at
ten, with your last-minute change of plans," Elizabeth says
as she gets up. She wipes her hands on a tea towel. She
makes a point of taking a loud sniff. "You smell like a
smoke factory."

"I know, I'm sorry. There was a crowd of kids smoking
outside the gym, but I was just hanging out with them, I
didn't take a puff."

"Well, go on now and put your things in the laundry and
change into something fresh," Elizabeth says. The look on
her face says she knows Cate isn't being truthful. "Your mom
and dad get back tomorrow, and I don't want them to come
home to find their daughter has been misbehaving on my
watch. I want you to promise me, right here and now, that
you won't do whatever trouble you got up to last night, ever
again. Then I won't ever bring it up, if you promise."

"I promise," Cate says. "Thank you, Grandma."

Cate skulks to her room and removes her dirty clothes.
She bundles them into a ball and stuffs them in the laundry
basket. She puts on a turtleneck, totally inappropriate for
summer, then takes her laundry down to put it in the
washer herself.

Her head feels like a lead weight all day and her tummy
rumbles too. After a good night's sleep, she wakes up feeling
like her old self again. She's just finished making her bed and
tidying her room when she hears the front door open.

"We're home," William says as soon as he walks in, carrying in the luggage and holding the screen door open with his foot.

"Daddy!" Cate runs down the hall to greet him. "I missed you so much!" She throws herself against him, almost knocking him over, before he's fully in the door.

"Be careful, young lady," Donna says as she comes through the doorway to join them. "Your father has been through enough already."

"Sorry. I didn't mean to, I—"

"It's okay, Caty-bug," William says with a smile. "I missed my little girl too."

"She's not so little anymore," Donna says with a slight scowl.

"Hi, Mom, hi, Dad," Michael says as he comes out from his room to join them. "How was your trip?"

"Yes, how was it?" Elizabeth asks, amidst the commotion.

"Let us at least get in the door before you pepper us with questions," Donna says.

Everyone talks over one another as they all take a seat at the kitchen table, anxious to hear all the details. They finally quiet down and William fills them in on the diagnosis and treatment plan.

"You should have seen the look on the physiotherapist's face when your father finished his first round of exercises in record speed," Donna says with pride. "It was absolutely priceless." She laughs.

"Aw, now, dear, it wasn't that much of a record," William says. "But I admit she was surprised. I'm stronger and faster than I look, always have been."

"I've never heard of rheumatoid arthritis before," says Cate. "What does that mean?"

"It's different for everyone," William says. "We'll just have to wait and see. But don't worry, Caty-bug, I already feel better, after only two weeks."

"That's the best news, ever," Cate says. She makes a mental note to look up rheumatoid arthritis in the encyclopedia later.

After a while, William tires of all the chit-chat.

"Well, we best get unpacked," William says. He gets up from his chair slowly and winces.

On the last day of grade nine, Cate leaves school with a heavy heart. She's been teased the last two weeks by all the cool kids, who called her a slut. Her hand grazes over the bruise, which has faded to almost nothing. Then, from out of nowhere, Cate feels a thud of something hitting her in the back. She turns around to see the boys who have been bullying her huddled by the bus stop. Brad is the ringleader, holding a carton of eggs.

"You got a problem, Slut?" Brad calls out in a taunting voice.

Cate ignores him. She twists her arm to slosh away the eggshells and yolk that are dripping down her back.

"Hey, I'm talking to you, Slut," Brad calls out again. He throws another egg and it hits her in the shin.

"Yeah, well I'm talking to you."

Cate recognizes her brother's voice. She turns around to see Michael beating the snot out of her assailant. He's not a fighter, but he's tall for his age and two years older than the boys at the bus stop. Even though Michael's outnumbered, Brad's friends scatter. Michael is about to hit him again in his already bloodied face when Cate runs over.

"Michael, stop, it's okay," Cate says.

Michael looks up, as if in a daze, his arm poised mid-air.

"If I ever see you near my sister again, or talking shit like that again, I won't stop until you can't see straight," Michael says. He gets up and kicks Brad in the ribs, then turns to Cate.

"What was that all about?" Michael asks.

"It's my fault," Cate says with a whimper. "I made a big mistake at the dance and made out with that boy you just clobbered. Him and his friends have been calling me names ever since."

"Making out doesn't make you a slut," Michael says. "It's normal at your age. C'mon, let's go home."

He wipes at Cate's egg-smeared shirt the best he can, then wraps his arm around her shoulders. "Don't put up with people talking shit about you like that, Cate. You're a good person, with the biggest heart I know."

Cate wastes no time looking for a summer job. She combs through the help-wanted ads in the newspaper and circles a few that look hopeful, then heads out on her bicycle.

When she walks into the Boston Pizza that just opened up on the main strip along the highway, there are only a few tables with customers. She approaches the hostess station.

"Excuse me, I'm here about the waitress position advertised in the newspaper," Cate says to the sparkly-eyed girl who greets her.

"Okay, I'll go get our manager," she says.

Cate waits at the door, butterflies fluttering in her stomach.

"What can I do for you?" asks a burly, plain-faced woman. Her name tag says *Marita Glocking, Manager.*

"Good morning, Ms. Glocking. I'm interested in applying for the waitress position."

"How old are you?" Marita asks.

"I'm fourteen. But I'm very mature for my age and a hard worker."

"Well, I could really use the help," says Marita with a laugh. "I'll get you an application form."

Cate sits down at an empty table and fills in the form. She writes in her newly issued social insurance number, her address and contact information. She lists her last two babysitting jobs as references, signs her name at the bottom, then hands it back to Marita.

"This all looks great. Can you start tomorrow?"

Cate can hardly wait to share the exciting news, but she keeps it to herself until she's sitting at the kitchen table over dinner that evening.

"I applied for a waitressing job at the new Boston Pizza today, and they hired me right on the spot," Cate says, beaming with pride.

"Wow, that's great news," Michael says. "Congratulations."

"Waitressing, eh?" says William. "That sounds like something you'd be great at, with your outgoing personality. Being so pretty, I bet you'll score some big tips. How much do they pay?"

"Only three fifty an hour," says Cate, setting down her fork. "But Marita—she's my manager—says with tips it's way more. I'm going to save up to buy myself a real leather journal and a fancy ballpoint pen."

"That's all well and good," says Donna. "But does your manager know you're only fourteen? It seems awfully young for so much responsibility. And don't they stay open late?"

"Of course, I told them. It asks right on the application. I didn't ask about the hours, but Marita said if she needs me for the late shift, she'll drive me home after."

"Hmm, I'm not sure how I feel about it," says Donna. "But I guess since you already accepted the position, I'm willing to let you give it a trial."

Cate loves her work at the restaurant. She takes to it naturally, talking easily with the customers and memorizing the menu. And then there's Danny. He's eighteen and works in the kitchen, and Cate thinks she's in love. She daydreams about his big, brown puppy-dog eyes and imagines his full lips kissing her. Softly, gently. Not like Brad.

A few weeks into July, Cate is flying high. She's deposited her first paycheque, and she and Danny have gone on a few dates. He's taken her to A&W for root beer and fries and to the cinemas to see the epic release of *The Empire Strikes Back*. Science fiction isn't her thing, but the movie impresses Cate with its visual effects. They hold hands and kiss, but Danny is a gentleman and never pushes her to do more, never gropes her or makes her feel uncomfortable. She's stopped hanging out with Cindy ever since the dance, making excuses whenever she calls, but with Danny as her new best friend and working eight-hour shifts five days a week, she doesn't have time for much more.

Donna has come around to Cate's new independence, but she insists that Sunday is a day for family and worship and forbids Cate to take shifts on that day. "Even God took a day off to rest," she says.

It's a Sunday evening and the family is gathered around the television. Archie Bunker is complaining to Edith on *All in the Family*. Cate is rubbing the bottom of her feet, aching from wearing her four-inch platform heels to work the night before. When it goes to a commercial, William clears his throat as Donna taps the ashes off the end of her cigarette into the ashtray.

"I have some news to share," William says.

Cate stops rubbing her feet.

"Well, go on now, just tell them," Donna says. She stubs out her cigarette.

"Tell us what?" Michael asks, his eyes still drawn to the images on the screen, an advertisement for Coca-Cola with a catchy tune, *It's the real thing*.

"Well," William begins. "I can't get the kind of treatment I need here in Lethbridge. They just don't have the resources they have in Calgary."

Cate blanches. Her stomach lurches. She knows without question what her father's news is going to be.

"So anyway, I looked into job opportunities in Calgary and there is a position for an accountant that I've accepted," William says. "It's a bit of a pay cut, and God knows everything costs more in the city, but I've made up my mind. We'll be moving to Calgary as soon as possible, before you go back to school in the fall."

"But Daddy," Cate wails. "I just got this great job. And then there's Danny…"

"Look, Cate, I know it isn't great timing, but that's just how it's got to be," William says. "Besides, Danny is your first boyfriend, it's only puppy love. There'll be others lining up in Calgary, I'm sure." William winks at Cate.

"It's not puppy love, Daddy. I love him for real. I don't want to move." Cate starts to cry.

"I know, Caty-bug, and I'm sorry. But sometimes life just isn't fair."

Cate leaps up and storms out of the room. She throws herself on her bed and cries into her pillow. When her tears dry up, she sits up and retrieves her diary from her nightstand drawer.

July 20, 1980
Dear Diary,

   I'm devastated. Dad just announced that we have to move to Calgary in a few weeks. I didn't see it coming. Just when my life is changing for the better. Just when I found someone sweet, good, and kind, like Danny. Why God, does life have to be so unfair? Even as I pout and feel sorry for myself, I know deep inside it's the right thing to do. I know how much my dad is suffering, even though he's always careful to put on a strong face. I catch him wincing. I see him hobbling. Rheumatoid arthritis sucks. Why did my dad have to be the one to get it? I looked it up, and it doesn't sound good at all. I'm so angry. And I'm afraid to move to a big city. Afraid to start over at a new school and to make new friends. Even though we haven't spoken in a while, I'll miss Cindy so much. She seems to always get me into trouble, but she's been my friend through thick and thin since I was six. It's hard to believe it was that long ago. I guess there's no use crying about it. It's going to happen, so I might as well just try and make the best of it. I don't know how I'm going to say goodbye to this place, to everything and everyone I know. At least I'll always have Michael, my forever best friend. I suppose I just have to buckle up, as Daddy would say. Only time will tell what changes lie ahead.

Chapter 8

*W*ILLIAM AND DONNA PURCHASE a small
three-bedroom bungalow in a northwest
community of Calgary that is close to William's work,
a high school with a reputation for academics, and the
public transportation route.

Not long after the move, mid-August, William's new
doctor begins a treatment regimen that includes weekly gold
injections at the Foothills Hospital combined with daily high
doses of aspirin and steroids. There is a string of side effects,
but Dr. Adams hopes it will slow the onset and reduce
the pain. The prognosis and long-term outlook are grim.
Dr. Adams tells William that he will likely continue to
degenerate and will possibly need joint fusion surgery down
the road.

Just before school is set to resume, the Alberta Teachers'
Association announces they are going on strike over wages
and class sizes. Without school as a place to meet new

friends, Cate finds comfort in the company of her brother. Together, they explore the city with the freedom of newly purchased bus passes.

On one of their daily excursions, Cate and Michael catch the number ten bus to their new school, Sir Winston Churchill. They walk around the eight-acre campus that surrounds a huge brick building. Multiple archways line the main entrance that faces a shopping mall to the west.

"Wow, Churchill is like, humongous," Cate says after they complete a walking tour of the perimeter.

"I know, right?" Michael tries to peer in through a window, but the blinds are closed.

"I wonder how many students go here?" Cate says. "And how many classrooms, do you think?"

"Probably hundreds. You're bound to get lost," Michael teases. "But don't worry, I'll be your navigator and protector, always."

"Thank you. I don't know what I'd do without you."

They sit down in the tall grass for a rest. Cate smiles and reaches over to squeeze Michael's hand.

"I'm so nervous," Cate says. "When I looked through the welcome booklet that came in the mail, there were so many choices, it made my head spin. You probably never noticed, but they offer Beauty Culture, if you can believe it. How cool to get credit for cutting hair? I'm definitely going to sign up for that one."

"I didn't know that," Michael says. "But I agree, it's all a bit overwhelming. I think I'll stick to the basic core courses to earn a matriculation, but I can't decide which clubs to join. I'm thinking maybe drama and chess."

"You'll make a great actor. And with your smarts, chess will be a breeze. I think I'll wait and see what the homework in high school is like before I join any clubs. I'd like to get a part-time job. And who knows, maybe I'll meet a handsome boy who will sweep me off my feet and totally distract me."

"You're such a romantic," Michael says. He gets up and dusts off his pants, then points at the convenience store across the street. "I'm dying of thirst. Let's go get a frosty, my treat."

The teachers accept a new contract, and school starts up at the beginning of October. Cate is a ball of nerves in anticipation of her first day. The household clothing budget has been reduced to include only the essentials, and Cate wants the latest fashions, so she's dipped into the savings she stockpiled from her summer job to purchase a new outfit, which is laid out on her bedspread. She cuts off the tags and puts on the skin-tight blue jeans, a low-cut, tight white T-shirt, and a long, shin-length denim jacket that is all the rage. She slips into high-heeled clogs, grabs her backpack, and heads to the kitchen for breakfast.

"Whoa, what's this?" William says when Cate strolls over and pours herself a tall glass of orange juice. "You're not going to school dressed like that. And what's with all the makeup?"

"Oh, Dad. Don't be so old-fashioned. This is how everyone dresses in high school."

"I don't care if the whole planet dresses that way. No daughter of mine is going to go traipsing around in a get-up like that. Go on now and change into a more appropriate shirt with a higher neckline, and take off that lipstick. And those shoes are ridiculous for a girl your age. You need to wear the running shoes Mom bought you for school."

"Fine," Cate says with a sigh. She disappears into her room. She puts her T-shirt and clogs in her backpack to change into later at school, then slips on a grey, cowl-neck top. She grabs a tissue from the box by her bedside and wipes at her lips, then tosses the tube of lipstick into her backpack too. She hates her running shoes, had thought she'd only endure them for gym class next semester, but puts them on as her father has requested.

"Are you happy now?" Cate asks when she returns.

"Yes, that's much better," William answers. "And you can lose the attitude, thank you."

Cate rolls her eyes and looks over at Michael, who is almost finished his breakfast.

"You better hurry up if you're going to be ready in time," Michael says, looking up at the wall clock over the table. "The bus comes to our stop at seven forty-five."

"Ooh, you're right," Cate says. "I'll just grab an apple to eat on the way."

When they arrive at the school, the main foyer is a buzz of students. Michael guides Cate through the chaotic throng to the main office where they pick up their class schedules.

"Can you help me find my home room on this map before you go?" Cate asks, folding the school information booklet open along the crease.

Michael takes a pen from his backpack and circle's Cate's class, then draws a line through the maze of hallways from the office to the circle.

"Just follow this line," Michael says. He gives his sister a high-five. "I'll meet you at the cafeteria for lunch."

Cate finds her homeroom without too much trouble. Mr. Kempler is her homeroom and English 10 teacher. He is standing at the front of the room near his desk, the chalkboard behind him and a clipboard in hand. He has thick brown hair and a beard and is wearing a beige tweed blazer with patches on the elbows. Cate thinks he looks stern and unfriendly. She looks around at the sea of unfamiliar faces. Groups of girls and boys are huddled in animated discussion. Everyone else seems to know someone, probably from junior high.

Minutes later the bell rings and everyone takes their seats. Cate finds a desk near the back of the room close to a window. There is a girl in front of her with shiny black hair. She turns around and smiles, showing straight, white teeth.

"Hi, my name's Tripti," she says.

Before Cate can say anything, Mr. Kempler clears his throat and Tripti turns around at attention.

"Good morning, and welcome to grade ten," Mr. Kempler says. His voice is steady, monotone. "Today is all about orientation. There will be an assembly in the gymnasium very shortly, after the morning announcement."

Just as Mr. Kempler finishes his statement the intercom comes on. The principal makes a speech, the static muffling his words now and again. Cate's stomach feels about to reject the half-eaten apple she had for breakfast.

After the assembly, Tripti sidles up beside Cate as they are returning to class.

"I didn't catch your name. Did you go to F. E. Osbourne last year?"

"I'm Cate, I just moved here from Lethbridge."

"That's cool," Tripti says. "None of my friends from last year are in our homeroom. Maybe we can hang out?"

"Yeah, sure, I'd like that," Cate says. Her stomach settles, if only a little.

Within a few weeks Cate starts to adjust to her new life at school. She loves Beauty Culture and thinks biology is interesting. Math is hard, but she has a good teacher. Unlike Mr. Kempler.

For their first writing assignment, Mr. Kempler assigns a short essay response to the novel *Lord of the Flies,* by William Golding. Cate finds the story terrifying. She chooses to write about the factors that contributed to turning the boys into predators, turning against each other. She is proud of what she submits, thinking she demonstrates wise insights, but when Mr. Kempler gives their assignments back the following week, Cate is horrified and stunned. Her paper is a sea of red marks and at the top, circled for emphasis, is her mark of 45 percent beside a huge letter F. Cate flips to the back, where in the comments he has written that Cate's grammar is horrendous, as is her attention to detail. He doesn't say anything about the content, about her creativity. She looks back through the pages of handwritten work. He has taken a mark off every time she missed dotting an i, crossing a t, and including a page number, not to mention all her spelling errors and incorrect tenses. It's all she can do not to cry. She crumples her paper and throws it in the trash, along with her hopes of becoming a writer someday.

When William asks her how she did, she lies, saying she earned a B. Then, when he asks if he can read it, she lies again, saying she spilled chocolate milk on it and had to throw it out. It shocks her, how adept she's become at lying. She wonders if her father suspects anything.

Michael makes friends with John, the boy next door who's in the same grade as him. Cate hangs out with Tripti, who lives in Varsity, a community not too far from Cate's house, close to Market Mall where Tripti works at the cinemas.

"You should apply," Tripti says. They are sitting at her kitchen table, doing their homework. "It's easy work for the money, and the hours work well with school."

When Cate gets home later that day, she brings up the subject of work at the dinner table.

"I'd like to apply for a job at the cinemas at Market Mall," Cate says.

"I don't love the idea of you working while going to school," Donna says. "It's one thing to work over the summer holidays, but school needs to be your priority."

"It would only be one night a week and two shifts on the weekend," Cate says. "My new friend Tripti works there and her parents approve."

"I think it's a great idea," William says. "It shows initiative, and Cate is smart enough to manage working part-time while keeping her grades up."

"Thanks, Dad," Cate says.

"What about getting to work and back?" Donna asks. "We only have one car and it might not always be feasible to drive you."

"That's no problem," Cate says. "I can take the bus easy enough."

"Well, I suppose since your father is keen, you can give it a trial," says her mother. "But if your grades slip, you'll have to quit."

Cate's application is accepted the following week. She starts to work that Saturday, on the matinee shift with Tripti, behind the candy counter. She slings popcorn and pours plastic cups of soda pop. She totals up customer orders in her head, then mops the sticky, greasy floors. When she gets home, she feels a crazy mix of excitement and exhaustion. She decides to write about it in her journal and heads to the privacy of her room.

October 25, 1980

I started working at the cinemas with Tripti. My first shift was today, the Saturday matinee. My boss wanted me to work Saturday and Sunday, plus two weekday nights, but I told her about Mom's old-fashioned "no work on Sunday" rule and she said that was fine, I can work Friday night instead. It's the busiest night of the week, and I'm a bit nervous. It was hard enough working the matinee. I was shocked when Tripti gave me the drill and I found out they don't use cash registers, you have to add up everything in your head. Mental math isn't my strong suit, but I managed, even though it was totally chaotic during the pre-show rush. I'm excited to be making my own money again, especially now that Mom and Dad are tight on cash. I want to save up enough money to buy everyone in my family something super special for Christmas.

Then there's Joe. He's one of the doormen. His big brown eyes remind me of Danny, but that's where the similarity ends. Instead of tall and blonde, he's short and dark. But he's cute, kind of shy, but funny.

I still miss my old friends in Lethbridge, but Tripti is so nice. I met her parents the other day. Her mom is from India and her dad is Canadian. Tripti said he grew up in BC. She has two older sisters and they are both as gorgeous as she is—tall, with beautiful black hair that is thick and shiny. It was a full house, a bit chaotic for my liking. Whatever her mom was cooking smelled exotic and delicious. I hope she invites me to stay for dinner someday. I've never tried Indian food before. Dad says it's too spicy, that it blow-torches his taste buds right off.

When the temperature drops below zero at the end of the month, just before Halloween, William suffers from more stiffness, especially in his hands and knees.

"Damn stupid hanger," he curses as he drops his coat for the second time.

"Let me get that for you," Donna says, bustling in from the kitchen after hearing the garage door close.

"I can get it, it just slipped, that's all," William says through gritted teeth.

"I know you can. But it's hard on your knees and hips to bend over, and I'm here so why don't you just let me help once in a while?"

Donna picks up the coat and hangs it neatly on the hanger, then closes the closet door.

"It's Cate's turn to make dinner, but she has to work tonight and cancelled on me last minute," Donna says. "Dinner will be a while yet. Would you like a hot tea while you watch some television?"

"Sure, that sounds nice, maybe with a touch of honey?" William ambles slowly into the living room and plunks himself down on the rust-coloured velvet La-Z-Boy chair, then flicks on the television to the sports channel.

By late November, William finds a full day of work too exhausting. It's a huge blow to his self-esteem to switch to part-time, not to mention the decrease in pay. Donna decides to give real estate a try and enrols for six weeks of pre-licensing classes. Michael loves school. He ends up in drama club, with a small role in the school play, the musical *Jesus Christ, Superstar*, that's set for a performance in the spring. He manages to find time for chess club, and he and

John take up downhill skiing at Paskapoo, the ski hill on the west side of the city limits.

Cate and Tripti become the best of friends, but Tripti's old friend from junior high, Carly, is jealous. She makes it clear she doesn't appreciate Cate encroaching. She shoots Cate nasty looks when Tripti isn't watching. Cate recognizes the uneasiness that whispers in the back of her mind, but she chooses to ignore it.

In the new year, everyone in the Henderson family is adjusting to their new life in the city. Cate has started a new semester at school, is dating Joe, and enjoying her friendship with Tripti.

> *February 14, 1981*
>
> *The big day of Michael's play is coming up and I'm so excited for him. I hardly ever see him anymore, he's so busy with rehearsals. I miss hanging out with him like crazy, but I'm really excited to watch his performance.*
>
> *School just feels like something to get through these days. I hate P.E. I'm such a klutz, no one ever wants me on their team. At least English is finished. Mom kinda flipped out when she saw a C+ on my report card and threatened that I needed to quit work, but I told her I was trying my best, that Mr. Kempler had it in for me. Dad pointed out that a C+ was still a pass, and with my B+ in math and A's in biology and Beauty Culture, I had a decent average. That's my dad, always rooting for me. Mom called me Hyperbole Henrietta, then offered to help me improve my grammar over the summer for next year. That doesn't*

*sound like a fun way to spend my summer vacation
at all, but I kept that to myself.*

*I think I'm going to break up with Joe, but not
today, on Valentine's Day. Soon, though. He's sweet,
so it doesn't really make sense, but I just don't feel that
attracted to him. I'll never meet the right guy if I stay
with him. Tripti says I'm too young to want to meet the
right guy, but I'm not interested in school girl crushes.
I want a grown-up relationship, with a mature boy,
but there seems to be slim pickings, at least in my little
circle of friends.*

Near the end of the school year, Carly appears to have a
change of heart. She invites Cate to watch her boyfriend,
Luke, play football at his school, the Catholic high school
a few miles from Churchill.

"Do you want to come to a party this weekend at my
family's farm?" Carly asks.

They are sitting in Luke's truck after the game, in the
parking lot outside his school.

"Uh, sure," Cate says. "But I'll have to ask my
parents first."

"Maybe we can double date?" Carly says. She places her
hand on her Luke's thigh while looking at Cate.

"Oh, Joe and I broke up. Sorry."

"Oh, right," Carly says. "I remember." Then she points
to a group of boys standing in the parking lot a few vehicles
down, smoking. "We could set you up with our friend Peter.
His girlfriend ditched him a few weeks ago."

"Which one is Peter?" Cate looks over in the direction
Carly is pointing.

"He's the tall one, with the mocha skin and outrageous afro."

"Oh. Thanks, but no thanks, he's not my type." Cate has no way to explain the sudden shiver that crawls up her spine. Peter's profile has an uncanny resemblance to the Magician. He tilts his head back and laughs, then looks over their way. He catches her looking at him and winks. Cate thinks his smile looks sinister and looks away, a lump in her throat.

"What, are you prejudiced?" Carly says. "I never took you to be like that."

"No, God, no, it's nothing like that. I, well, it's just that…." Cate's heart races as she experiences a mini panic attack.

"Never mind," Carly says with a slight snarl. "You can still come, solo." Her voice is all sugary sweet again. Cate wonders if she only imagined it.

"Isn't Tripti coming?" Her heart rate has begun to slow down already. "She doesn't have a boyfriend either. She can be my date."

Carly laughs. It sounds hollow. Cate pushes away the uneasiness she feels and tells herself not to let her imagination get carried away.

The night of the party, Cate stresses over what to wear. She wants to look her best, but it's at a farm and her high heels won't suit. She looks at her runners, the only flat, appropriate shoes she has. Then she remembers the cowboy boots in her closet, still in the store cardboard box, that she bought for the Calgary Stampede. She chooses her favourite pair of tight Jordache jeans and the snug white T-shirt her father had forbidden her to wear the first day of school. The boots are brand-new stiff, but she slides them on over her slim calves and pulls her flare-legged jeans down over them. She zippers up her hoody. She glances in the hall mirror on her way out the door and approves of her charcoal-rimmed eyes, eyelashes triple coated with Maybelline blackest black mascara.

"I'm heading out now," Cate calls out from the front landing. She crosses her fingers and hopes her parents don't disrupt their bridge game with the neighbours to come say goodbye.

"Have a great sleep-over at Tripti's," her mother calls out.

"Yeah, have fun, Caty-bug," her dad adds. "See you tomorrow morning."

On the bus ride to Tripti's, Cate applies another coat of mascara and adds some pink lip gloss. It's a short five-minute walk from the bus stop to Tripti's house. It's a beautiful early summer evening with a cloudless sky, streaked pink and purple as the sun begins to set. Cate goes around the back and knocks.

"Hey, Cate, come on in," Tripti says. "I'm so excited. Carly just called. She said they'll be here in ten minutes to pick us up."

"Guess I made it just in time," Cate says.

"You can put your stuff in my room. Then we'll wait outside."

Cate stows her backpack and walks to the bus stop with Tripti where Carly and Luke have agreed to pick them up. Cate gets out a pack of Du Mauriers from her purse.

"Want one?" Cate asks, holding open the flap of her pack of smokes.

"Sure, thanks."

Cate gets out her lighter and lights both their cigarettes. The air fills with smoke.

"Have you ever been to Carly's farm before?" Cate asks. She attempts to blow smoke rings, but they look more like deflated balloons.

"No," Tripti says. "Her parents just bought the land. I don't think there's much there yet, just big open fields."

"I'm just glad Carly has come around to us being friends," Cate says.

"Yeah, me too."

It's a tight fit with Luke, Carly, Tripti, and Cate all crammed into the cab of Luke's truck, but no one complains. Luke has the stereo on high, and the girls have to yell over top one another. The three girls sing along to Blue Rodeo while Luke drums with his thumbs on the steering wheel, keeping rhythm. After ten minutes or so, Luke turns off the highway onto a gravel road that leads to the farm.

"Turn here," Carly says, pointing at a worn-down sign. "You can park anywhere you like."

Cate looks around. Tripti was right. There isn't much in the way of development, just an old, crumbling shed. A few of Luke's friends have arrived ahead of them and started a fire in the middle of a field. There is a card table set up with coolers stored underneath and bottles of booze on top.

"I know, it's not much to look at," Carly says, as if reading Cate's mind. "But there's no adults around for miles to keep track of us." She laughs. "Go on then, open the door and hop out, Cate."

"Is there a bathroom somewhere?" Cate asks once they've all piled out of the truck.

"Nope, just a roll of toilet paper over by those bushes," Carly says, pointing off in the distance. Cate hopes she can hold it until they get back to Tripti's.

Over by the fire there is a group gathered, drinking beer. Luke turns up the music on his truck stereo even louder and leaves the door open.

"Can I get you a cold one?" Luke asks.

"Sure, thanks." Cate's never had a beer before, but she tries to act casual. She remembers the fiasco from the school dance and hopes the beer won't make her sick. She notices Luke's friend Peter from the other day, over at the fold-out table. He is pouring hard booze into plastic cups.

"Let's go try a shot at the tequila station," Carly says, as Cate drains the last drop of beer from her bottle.

"Where did Tripti go?" Cate asks.

"I heard she's making out with some hot guy in his car," Carly says with a sly smile. She nods her head in the direction of several newly arrived cars. "C'mon."

Cate and Carly walk over to the tequila station where Peter is pouring shots. There are cut-up lemon slices and a shaker of salt on a paper towel.

"Pour a special one for my friend here," Carly says with a wink at Peter.

Peter turns his back to the girls and then turns around with a glass for each of them. He and Carly demonstrate how to lick salt sprinkled on their hands, shoot the tequila, and then suck on a slice of lemon.

"I'm not sure about this," Cate says. "Maybe I'll just stick to beer."

"C'mon, don't be a wuss." Carly takes the salt shaker and pours salt on Cate's hand. "It's fun."

Cate downs the tequila. It burns in her throat and tastes horrible. The lemon does little to improve the situation. She turns and heads back to the fire, looking for Tripti. She's barely made a few steps when her vision starts to blur. She wobbles. She feels someone grabbing her arm, just as she topples, almost right into the fire. She feels like she is going to faint. Then everything goes black and she pitches to the ground.

Cate regains awareness when she feels something hard pressing into her back. She peers into the darkness, her vision like broken glass. Someone is pulling her by the feet through the gravel. It looks like Carly, but she isn't sure. She tries to speak, but her mouth feels like it is full of marbles. She closes her eyes. She's so tired. Then the movement stops. She's no longer on gravel, but a cold, earth floor. Her brain is foggy. She hears voices close by. She can't make out what they're saying, her ears feel full of cotton balls. She closes her eyes again and drifts off.

Cate wakes up to a searing pain in her vagina. She opens her eyes, mere slits. Someone is on top of her, the weight heavy. She knows what is happening. She recognizes Peter as he shoves and grunts inside her.

"Stop, please," Cate says. "Please, Peter don't do this…" She tries to push him off her, but her arms feel like dead weights; she can't even lift them off the ground. Tears pour down her cheeks. Peter shoves in deep a few more times, then lets out a moan before falling on top of her, his breath hot and laced with alcohol beside her cheek.

"Looks like I'm your type after all," Peter says with a sneer. He pushes himself up on his elbows, then lifts himself off her. She can feel the warm stickiness between her legs. He pulls up his jeans that are bunched around his ankles. Cate's tears streak down her face. She's peed herself; she can smell it and feel the pool of warmth beneath her bum, but Peter doesn't seem to care. She hears him talking to someone. "C'mon, help me get her dressed."

"Serves you right, you uptight bitch," Carly says.

Cate can't believe what just happened. That Carly was in on it. She sobs.

"Shut the fuck up," Peter says.

Carly and Peter struggle to get Cate's jeans back on, then drag her back through the gravel again. They heave her into the bed of Luke's truck. Cate stares up at the star-studded sky, then blacks out again.

"What are we gonna do now?" Cate hears as she regains consciousness.

"I don't know, but this is her house," Carly says. "Let's just leave her on the front step. She can figure it out."

Cate feels herself being pulled and lifted from the truck. Luke tries to steady her on her feet.

"Do you have a key?" Luke asks.

Cate looks around. She's at her house. The lights are all out. She has no idea what time it is or where her key is.

"Huh?" Cate slurs.

Carly takes out a credit card and easily unlocks the door. She pushes Cate inside.

"Good luck, you fucking slut," Carly says.

Cate crumples to the floor and groans. She manages, somehow, to crawl to her room and into her bed.

It is late morning, approaching noon, when Cate wakes up. She feels the worst she's ever felt in her life. Her memory is fuzzy, but not so fuzzy that she doesn't remember what happened. She recognizes that she is in her bed but doesn't remember coming home. She was supposed to sleep over at Tripti's. *How am I going to explain this to my parents?* Cate wonders. She pulls herself into a ball and cries. She doesn't want to get out of bed and face the world. She falls back asleep.

It's two in the afternoon and Donna is worried. She hasn't heard from Cate. Donna finds Tripti's number and calls.

"Hello?"

"Hello, this is Donna, Cate's mom. May I speak to her, please?"

"Oh, hi Donna, I'm Tripti's mom, Anushka. I'm sorry, but Cate's not here."

"What? I thought she slept over last night."

"Yes, well, she and Tripti went to Carly's house for a few hours," Anushka says. "But Tripti got in around eleven and Cate wasn't with her. I assumed she changed her mind and went home or stayed at Carly's."

"Oh, well, her door is closed, I never thought to look. Sorry to have bothered you."

There's no answer when Donna knocks on Cate's door, so she opens it and looks in. Cate is curled up in a ball. She looks terrible, with mascara-smudged eyes and her long ash-blonde hair tousled and tangled. As Donna approaches the bed, she can smell cigarette smoke and the acrid stench of vomit. She puts her hand over her nose and shakes her daughter.

"Cate, wake up."

Cate looks up at her mother, disoriented. She moans and pulls the covers over her head.

"Cate, c'mon, I said wake up. It's two in the afternoon, for goodness sake, and you look and smell absolutely horrible. You were supposed to sleep over at Tripti's. You've got to tell me what's going on."

Cate pulls the covers back down and sighs.

"I, well, I don't know where to start or what to say," she says. She sniffles, then reaches for a tissue from the box on her nightstand. She blows her nose and wipes at her eyes. Donna has never seen her daughter look like this before and she is alarmed, but she does her best to keep her composure.

"Why don't you just start at the beginning," Donna says.

William peeks his nose in the door.

"It smells like a brewery in here," he says. He walks into the room, his arms crossed over his chest. "What the hell is going on?"

With her mother sitting on her bed and her father standing over her, Cate feels heavy with guilt and shame. She's never wanted to turn back the hands of time more in her life.

"Well, first of all, I lied about going to Tripti's," Cate begins with a sob. "Well, it wasn't a total lie. I did go to Tripti's. But then we told her mom we were going over to Carly's house."

"Who the hell is Carly?" William interrupts.

"She's Tripti's best friend," Cate says. "Anyhow, we didn't go to Carly's house either, at least not exactly. Carly's parents just bought some land not far out of town, on the way to Cochrane, and Carly was throwing a party." Cate stops to catch her breath for a minute. "I had a beer, and then a shot of tequila, and then everything goes hazy," Cate says.

"Tequila?" William says. "How the hell did you come across beer and tequila at your age?"

"William, that's not the point," Donna says. She turns back to Cate. "Go ahead, go on, darling."

"I, I think I was raped," Cate says.

Donna gasps and puts her hand to her throat. William's eyes cloud over and he stares down at his shoes. He thrusts his hands deep in his trouser pockets. There is a long, awkward, drawn-out silence.

"You said *think*," William says. "It sounds like you're not sure…"

"I was so wasted," Cate admits. "I never knew alcohol could affect you like that. It might have been a hallucination, everything feels so muddled."

Inside, Cate knows it would be impossible to imagine or hallucinate something so traumatic. And she can't pretend she doesn't feel it. Her vagina is still sore. But she decides in that moment, seeing the distraught look on her father's face, that she'd rather he believed it never happened.

"It sounds like more than alcohol was involved," Donna says. "Did you take any drugs?"

"No, Mom, honest, I didn't," Cate says. Fresh tears burst forth.

"Well, I think it's possible you were drugged," Donna says. "Did you pour your own drinks?"

"Actually, no…" Cate says. Suddenly she feels certain that Peter drugged her.

"You've got to report this to the police," Donna says.

"No, Mom, I can't, I'm so ashamed, please…"

"She has a point," William says. "If she reports it, the police will have to investigate. I know the drill. They'll interrogate her. And God knows what the boy and his lawyer will do to defend him. I've heard of cases where the prosecution paints a sordid picture of the girl, questioning her morality. I don't want that for my girl."

William's knees buckle and he lets out a strangled sob like nothing Cate has ever heard before. He gathers his strength and walks over to Cate's bed and sits down on the other side of Donna. He takes Cate's hands and puts them in his.

"I hope to hell it didn't happen," her father says, tears welling up in the corners of his eyes. "But if it did, it can't be undone. What happens next needs to be up to you. Your mom and I will support whatever course of action you choose."

"Yes, darling," her mother says. "Although I still feel you should report this to the police, for justice to be served, but it's your decision."

"I just want to forget all about it," Cate says. "I'm never going to drink again, or go to a party. I'm not going to trust anyone. Except you guys, and Michael," Cate says. "I'm so sorry." She sobs. "I never meant, I never thought, I was just trying to…"

"Hush, now, it's okay," William says. He folds his daughter in close to his chest and holds her to him. Donna cries too, her hand on Cate's leg over the covers.

In the end, nothing happens, legal or otherwise. No charges are laid. There seems a silent agreement between Cate and her parents not to ever mention the incident again. And while Cate does her best to try and forget, the memories haunt her, nightly. In her dreams, Peter transforms into a cartoon magician and pulls a quarter from between her legs. He opens his magician's cape to expose his hard-on and laughs. His laugh turns into a howl as he changes again, into a wolf. He snarls, revealing his sharp, white teeth. Cate thinks of Red Riding Hood and remembers the story she wrote, back in grade three, about the princess and the hunter who could transform into a wolf. She wonders, not for the first time, if she isn't a Seer after all.

Chapter 9

SOMETHING CHANGES INSIDE CATE after the rape. Something she doesn't understand and avoids thinking about. The bright light inside her that is a beacon of joy is still visible to everyone around her, but she feels numb, angry, and ashamed. She starts to restrict her food. She wants to have sex with someone she chooses, on her terms.

When school gets out for the summer, Cate finds work again as a waitress, at the Boston Pizza on 16th Avenue. It is quite a trek to get there and back, a forty-minute commute with two bus transfers, but Cate takes comfort in the familiar routine. She's still a voracious reader, and passes the time in transit reading romances by Danielle Steel and thrillers like *Bloodline* by Sidney Sheldon.

On a Saturday night, when she is scheduled to work until two a.m., a good-looking man comes into the restaurant, not long before closing. Two tables are occupied, one with the manager and his regular buddy, the other with two middle-aged men who look like they might be truckers. With an air of confidence in his stride, he brushes past Cate as she is clearing some dirty dishes away, and takes a seat in a booth near the back.

"Hello, welcome to Boston Pizza, may I take your order?" Cate asks with her customary cheery welcome. She takes her order pad from her apron and has her pen poised and ready.

"That depends," he says. "I don't see what I'm looking for on the menu."

"If it's pizza you want, you can choose your own toppings," Cate says. She leans in and points to the large pizza section. "Or if you just want a late-night snack, we have a decent selection of appetizers. I like the buffalo wings myself."

He looks up from the menu, his face only a foot from Cate's waist. He glances at her name tag.

"Hi, Cate, I'm Leo. I was hoping I could place an order for Cate Henderson."

Cate's hand flutters to her name tag and she blushes. She is too shocked to come up with an appropriate response, but Leo is quick to close the awkward gap of silence.

"What time do you get off work, Cate?"

"Um, not for another hour," Cate stammers, looking at her watch. "And there's cleanup."

"I don't mind waiting," Leo says. "If you'd like me to."

Cate hesitates. She looks into his steel-grey eyes. She notices his tanned skin and full mouth. She admires his fit body. She's feeling reckless and decides it is the opportunity she's been waiting for. Her mom and dad are already unhappy that she is working such late shifts, and Cate doesn't know how she'll handle the situation, but she decides she can deal with that later.

"I would like that. Can I bring you something while you wait?"

"I'll have a Canadian," he says, closing the menu and handing it to Cate, brushing her fingers with his. "And an order of the buffalo wings you suggested."

When it's time to close the restaurant, Leo tells her he'll be in his car, the black Toyota Celica in the parking lot out back. Cate finishes her close-up checklist in record time and says good night to the manager, and that she has arranged her own ride home.

Cate feels her heart race as she walks toward Leo's car. She knocks on the passenger window and Leo leans over to open the door. As soon as Cate sits down, Leo reaches across the console and tucks her hair behind her ear, then lifts his hand to graze her cheek before pulling her to him. His kiss is practiced, perfect, like nothing she's experienced before. It's several minutes before they stop. Cate's heart races faster. The tingling sensations are intense.

"Can I take you to my place?" Leo asks.

"Yes, please," Cate says.

Cate makes love with Leo over the course of several hours. They have a bath together and start again. He goes down on her and she does the same to him. With each touch and caress, Cate feels as if Leo is erasing the memories of the night Peter raped her.

When they're both satiated, Cate snuggles up beside him and traces her hand across the hairs on his chest.

"Was this your first time?" Leo asks.

"No, but sort of." Cate notices the alarm clock on his bedside table. "Wow, it's four thirty. I'm going to be in so much shit with my parents when I get home."

"Parents?" Leo says, lifting up onto one elbow. "How old are you anyway?"

"Fifteen."

"Holy shit!" Leo jumps out of bed and starts pulling on his jeans. "I thought you were twenty. Or at least legal age. I could get into fucking big trouble for having sex with a minor."

"It's okay, calm down. It's not like I'm going to report you. And I won't tell my parents. I'll make up something convincing."

"Yeah, well, thanks, but I think I best get you home. C'mon, grab your things."

Leo drops off Cate a few blocks down from her house. When she asks when she'll see him next, he tells her he'll drop by the restaurant, but Cate never sees him again.

At the end of August, Cate quits her waitressing job and reapplies to the cinemas. She goes on a ten-day fast and drinks nothing but a concoction of water, maple syrup, and cayenne. She weighs herself every day. She passes out shopping for back-to-school clothes at the mall. When school starts up after the September long weekend, she's dropped from 120 to 105 pounds. Her high cheekbones look even more prominent, and her stomach, which used to be slightly rounded, is flat as a board.

Mr. Scheer, Cate's English 20 teacher, is young and attractive. He has a full moustache and thicky, wavy hair, with deep blue-green eyes, the colour of the sea. His eyes often drift to her breasts, solid C-cups, and linger longer than appropriate, but Cate takes the attention as a compliment, as a sign of her maturity.

A few weeks after school starts, Mr. Scheer distributes an outline for a creative writing assignment. Cate's stomach curdles. She remembers the criticism she received from Mr. Kempler. But the writer inside her, who has lain dormant for over a year, is excited. She works on her story in every free moment, making revisions right up until the night before it's due.

"Cate, can you stay after school to go over your story?" Mr. Scheer asks when the bell rings.

"Sure." Cate's heart constricts and her stomach does somersaults.

The students in her class file out of the room. Cate collects her purse and her binder, her heart beating so loud, she's sure Mr. Scheer must be able to hear it. She approaches him at his desk. He flips through the stack of papers and produces Cate's short story, "The Girl Who Could See Into the Future." There is an *A* in red ink beside her name.

"What did you want to talk to me about?" Cate asks, a gleam in her eye. She can hardly believe how the tables have turned in one year. And she didn't even take her mom up on her offer for grammar lessons over the summer.

"This is really, really good," Mr. Scheer says, tapping his fingertips on the front page. "Your writing is incredibly mature for someone your age. You've created such vivid scenes. I could completely imagine it. In fact, I almost felt like I was there. When did you start writing like this?"

"Well, I've loved writing since I was a little girl," Cate says with a blush. "I wrote my first chapter book in grade three. But then last year, Mr. Kempler hated everything I wrote for him. I could never seem to do anything right in his eyes."

"Well, I happen to know Mr. Kempler is a stickler for precise grammar and spelling, and it's true, you do have some work to do in those areas. But anyone can figure that stuff out. Not everyone can write like this."

"Thank you," Cate says. "That means a lot."

"I'd like you to submit it for publication," Mr. Scheer says. "But first you'll need to get a better understanding of the grammar side of things. Would you be interested in staying after school for some tutorials?"

"Yeah, sure. I have work today, but I could start next Monday."

"That's great," Mr. Scheer says. His hand grazes over hers as she reaches for the paper. A small shock goes up her arm.

The next Monday, Cate stays after the bell. She pulls up a chair beside Mr. Scheer's desk and sits down next to him.

"Let's get started with this," Mr. Scheer says. He picks up a copy of *The Elements of Style* and flips through to the section on adverbs. He reads from a page and then passes Cate her story.

"See if you can apply this rule about avoiding passive voice to your sentence, 'Her first kiss would always be recalled to her as an example of male entitlement.'"

"I could change it to, 'She recalled her first kiss as a feeling of male entitlement,' Cate says out loud as she writes in the minor change.

"Doesn't that read more concisely?" Mr. Scheer asks.

"Yes, it does sound better."

"I'm curious, though," Mr. Scheer says. "Is this completely fictional, or is that what your first kiss was like for you?"

Without waiting for an answer, Mr. Scheer moves his head in closer, his lips so close to Cate's they brush against hers, ever so slightly. He pauses for what feels to Cate like an eternity.

"Well, are you going to invite me to kiss you?" Mr. Scheer's breath is peppermint-chewing-gum sweet. "I wouldn't want to appear entitled. But you must know when you strut around wearing tight, low-cut T-shirts, you're sending a message, an invitation of sorts."

Cate pulls her head back and stands up.

"No, I didn't know that." Cate picks up her story. "In fact, I think how I dress is my business, and it is nothing to do with you or any other man."

Mr. Scheer stands up, revealing an erection straining against the fabric of his trousers. Cate wrinkles her nose in disgust, turns on her high heels, and leaves.

Cate rekindles her friendship with Tripti when she returns to work at the cinemas, but they both find conversation awkward ever since the night at the farm. They've never spoken about it, and Cate isn't sure if Carly filled Tripti in on the details, but it's not the same as it was before. Cate makes a new friend in her Beauty Culture class, the shy and soft-spoken Rose.

Rose's blonde hair falls down to her waist in thick waves. Her small, pale blue eyes shine with intelligence, but Rose is a huge introvert and doesn't let many people into her inner world. She lives only a few blocks away from Cate and they often get together at one another's house after school and experiment with makeup and new hairstyles. Cate purchases a home highlighting kit, and Rose threads Cate's ash-blonde hair through the holes in the cap, then lathers on the cream that will transform the strands to platinum. They make faces at themselves in the mirror, posing like models and giggling at their reflections. Rose opens up with Cate, often sharing her opinions on politics and philosophy. Both girls feel like fish out of water with their peers, who seem to be only interested in playing social games and who is wearing what.

"My brother says the new pub a few blocks away doesn't ask for ID," Rose says one afternoon in Cate's room. "With your new hair and makeup, I bet you could pass for eighteen. Do you want to try and get served? We could go right now."

Cate thinks about her two past experiences with alcohol. They were both a disaster. She decides that perhaps it's time to transform those experiences too, like she did with sex, with Leo.

"Yeah, sure, why not?" Cate says. "That sounds like fun."

Cate and Rose add some black eyeliner. Cate puts in her contacts.

"Rose and I are just going out for a stroll," Cate calls out when they're ready to leave.

"Okay, just be back in time for dinner," Donna yells back from the kitchen where she is chopping onions for spaghetti sauce.

Inside the pub it is dim after the bright afternoon sun, the window shades drawn and the lighting low. Rose and Cate take seats in a booth and nervously look over the beverage menu.

"I have no idea what any of these drinks are," Cate says. "Except the Molson Canadian, and I can't stand the taste of beer."

"Me neither," admits Rose. "But they sound exotic. I can't decide if I want to try a Blue Monday or a Long Island Iced Tea."

"I know, right? I think I'm going to try a Singapore Sling, it sounds delicious."

The server takes their orders without requesting identification, as Rose had predicted.

"I feel so badass," Cate whispers. "We obviously look way older than we are."

"Yeah," Rose agrees. "And do you see those two guys across from us at the bar? They've been giving us the eye."

Cate turns her head to look over.

"Don't be so obvious," Rose says, kicking Cate's shin under the table.

But it's too late. The guy with the dark, curly hair that falls to his shoulders and big brown eyes makes eye contact with Cate. He smiles and Cate swoons. He gets up from his bar stool and approaches their table.

"Hi there," he says. "I've never seen you two gorgeous ladies in here before."

"Hi," both girls answer in unison.

"This is our first time," Cate says, blushing.

"In this pub," Rose adds, not wanting them to appear as novices.

"I'm Billy, nice to meet you." He shakes each girl's hand.

Cate feels the scrape of a callous but likes the feel of his strong grip.

"Would you like some company?"

"Sure," Cate says. She withdraws her hand from his, still tingling from his touch, and slides over to make room. Billy hasn't taken his eyes off her since he came over, but he turns away to call over his friend, then slides in beside Cate in the booth.

"This is my friend Ken," Billy says as Ken approaches. Ken has ginger hair, cut short, bright green eyes, and a spattering of freckles across his pale cheeks. He takes a seat beside Rose, who introduces herself. They all start talking about the beautiful extended summer they've been having. The waitress brings the drinks Cate and Rose ordered, along with two large mugs of beer for the boys. Cate takes a sip.

"This is so delicious, I can hardly believe it has any alcohol in it," Cate says. She draws on the straw again.

"You have to be careful with those sugary drinks," Billy warns. "They can sneak up on you."

"Don't worry," Cate says. "Rose and I can hold our alcohol."

After three rounds of drinks, both girls are more than a little tipsy, but Cate feels nothing like she did when she drank straight alcohol before. She feels flirty, confident, and sexy.

"Let me get this," Billy offers, when the waitress brings two separate bills.

"That's so sweet of you, thank you," Rose says.

"Yeah, thanks," Cate agrees with a smile that she hopes will encourage him.

"Do you have plans?" Billy asks.

"I don't have to be home for another hour," Cate says, glancing down at her watch. "What about you, Rose?"

"It depends, what are you thinking?" Rose asks. The four of them have vacated the booth and are walking toward the door.

"I was wondering if you'd like to take a spin in my new car," Billy says, pointing to the white Camaro Z28 in the parking lot that gleams in the late afternoon sun.

"Wow," Cate says. "What a cool car. I'd love to!"

Cate hops in the front with Billy after Ken and Rose climb into the back seat. The red fabric interior is pristine and the black console gleams like it's been newly polished. Billy presses a button on the dash and the windows of the T-roof slide open. He turns up the stereo, then pulls out with a screech of his tires.

Billy drives down Crowchild Trail toward the city limits, then takes up the speed to 130 once he's on the highway.

He turns into a roadside pull-off with a view and lowers the volume on the music.

Cate discovers over the course of their conversation that he is twenty, working in construction. He shares the rent of a duplex in the northeast with two of his friends from work. By the time Billy drops Cate and Rose off at Cate's house, it is clear that they are both interested in one another.

"Do you want to do this again?" Billy asks.

"Yes, I do," Cate says. "Why don't you pick me up from work on Friday?"

"Okay," Billy says. "It's a date. I'll be waiting outside the mall doors, in the parking lot. What time do you get off?"

"Around ten." Cate leans across the stick shift and kisses Billy on the lips, then gets out of the car.

A week later, Cate is sitting on the front steps of her school, waiting for Billy to pick her up. She's decided to skip her last class, which is English with the perverted Mr. Scheer.

The sun is warm on her back and she takes off her sweater and ties it around her waist. The leaves have turned their glorious fall spectrum of autumn colours and a few have begun to fall, blowing in the light breeze. Cate is watching the leaves dance, off in her own world, when she hears the roar of Billy's new Harley. She looks down the street and sees him speeding over the school zone limit before sidling up to the curb, the engine idling.

Billy grins. "Hop on." He passes Cate a helmet.

"Have fun!" Cate hears someone call out from behind her. She turns around to discover a boy from her English class, then sees the whole class, including Mr. Scheer, sitting on the grass of the school's front lawn with their novels for silent reading. She is totally mortified.

"You know that scrawny bastard?" Billy asks, a jealous tone to his voice.

"He's just someone in my class, that's all," Cate says. She throws her leg over the seat of the motorcycle, then slides her body up close against Billy.

"Where are we going?" Cate asks. But the noise of the engine drowns out any chance of conversation.

Billy parks in the lot outside Nick's Pizza, where he's taken Cate before. It is dark inside the seventies-style restaurant.

"A table for two?" the waitress asks.

"Yes, please," Billy says. "My woman prefers a booth."

Cate blushes as the waitress leads them to a booth with orange leather seats on either side of a deep mahogany table in a cozy corner. She doesn't like Billy calling her his woman, but she doesn't say anything. She slides in next to the wall and then, instead of sitting across from her, Billy takes a seat beside her. He kisses her, long and deep.

"I've missed you," Billy says.

"Me too," Cate says, but changes the subject as she scoots over a little. "That was so embarrassing, my English class seeing me as I climbed onto your bike. I'm going to be in shit for skipping class, but I hate that class so much."

"I thought you're planning on going into journalism? That seems weird that you don't like English."

"I love reading and writing. But my teacher is a pervert."

"What?" Billy says. "That son of a bitch better not have touched you or I'll beat his face in, teacher or not."

"It's okay, babe," Cate says in a soothing voice. "He hasn't done anything except leer at me." She puts her hand on Billy's thigh.

The waitress returns. "You two lovebirds ready to order?"

"Yeah, two rum and Cokes to start," Billy says. "Are you hungry, Cate?"

"Yeah, I skipped lunch." Cate is still obsessed with counting calories. "I could have a piece of pizza."

"Okay, we'll share a medium Bulldogs special," Billy says, handing the waitress the menus.

He turns back to Cate, runs his hand up and down the inseam of her jeans, and leans in to kiss her.

"Want to come over to my place after?" he asks.

"Yes, please," Cate says, thrilled by his touch.

A month goes by and Cate and Billy see each other every chance they get, but Cate keeps the information close to her chest, telling nobody except Rose about her burgeoning feelings. One Sunday night at the beginning of November, just after the first snowstorm, Cate returns home from a secretive afternoon date with Billy, having told her parents she was meeting Rose at the mall. She pops into the kitchen where Donna is busy preparing dinner.

"When will dinner be ready?" Cate asks.

Donna turns from her task and looks at Cate with a critical eye.

"You'd best get yourself more presentable before your father sees you," Donna says.

"What are you talking about?" Cate says. She disappears into her room to look at herself in the dresser mirror. Her hair is a bit wild and her cheeks are flushed, but other than that, she can't discern what her mother feels is unpresentable. She gives her hair a quick brush and returns to the kitchen, lifting the lid off the pot of boiling potatoes.

"What are you making for dinner?" Cate asks.

"A pork roast with apple sauce, mashed potatoes, and green beans. And my famous Queen Elizabeth cake with ice cream for dessert."

"Yum! One of my favourite dinners. I'll set the table."

"That's thoughtful of you," Donna says as she slices apples into a pot.

"Do you know where Dad and Michael are?" Cate says once she's finished placing the last set of cutlery.

"Your father is outside I think, shovelling off the driveway," Donna says. "Michael is next door."

"Okay, I'm going to hang out with Dad until dinner."

Cate finds William cursing as the shovel slips from his gloved hands and falls to the ground. She tramps across the snow-covered grass, leaving deep dents in the icy-crisp snow.

"Sorry for swearing," William says.

"Why are you even bothering with that stupid old shovel?" Cate asks. She grabs the shovel by the worn and peeling handle. "You ought to buckle up and buy a new one."

"Buckle up, eh? That's a new one." William chuckles. "And can you point me in the direction of the money tree?"

"Oh, didn't I show you?" Cate giggles, relieved to hear her father laugh. "It's just over here." Cate sets the shovel against the wall and scampers across the yard to the planter that runs along the length of the fence, filled with evergreen cedars. Nestled among them is an ornamental cherry tree, only eight or nine inches tall, frozen and asleep for the winter.

"Well, I don't see that runt producing much cash, other than some dimes and nickels maybe. Not enough for a new shovel," William says.

"You just wait. By the time you're a grandpa, this magical tree will be growing hundred-dollar bills by the pile.

You'll need a new rake, as well as a shovel, to gather them all up."

"Twenty years is a long time to wait for a new shovel," William teases. "I hope you have a backup plan."

"I'll be thirty-five in twenty years," Cate says. "I'm not waiting that long to have kids."

"Okay, maybe twenty years is pushing it," William admits. "But I still say this tree has got lots of time to grow before I have any grandchildren to run around it. If you're going to follow through with your dream of becoming a journalist when you finish high school, you won't want to get married and have kids right away. You'll want to enjoy your career."

"That's true." Cate's stomach growls. "What time is it anyway?"

"Just past six thirty," William says, looking at his watch.

"Let's go in for dinner then." Cate jumps down from the garden border and sidles up beside her father, then slips her hand comfortably into the crook of William's arm.

Everyone is enjoying another one of Donna's home-cooked Sunday dinners when Michael clears his throat.

"So, Cate, who was the guy you were making out with in the car parked up the street this afternoon?"

"I don't know what you're talking about," Cate stammers, almost choking on a mouthful of beans.

"What the hell?" William asks. "I thought you were through with boys, Cate."

"Well, I was, but Billy isn't a boy. He's a man."

"A man?" Donna says. "What on earth? How in the heck would a young girl in high school meet a man?"

"I met him at work," Cate lies. "He's really nice, and so good to me. I'm sure you'll like him."

"How old is this man?" Donna asks.

"He's twenty. But—"

"Twenty!" William's voice is raised. "What the hell is a twenty-year-old man thinking, dating a fifteen-year-old girl? It's not right, Cate."

"Well, he didn't know how old I was when we met. It never came up until later, when we'd already—"

"I don't care how nice he is," Donna interrupts. "You'll just get into trouble hanging out with someone so much older. He has a different life. He's of legal age and can drive and drink, all kinds of things you can't do yet. I don't think it's a good idea at all."

"I agree," William says. "You need to break up with him, the next time you see him."

"I wasn't asking for your permission," Cate says. "It's none of your business who I date."

"As long as you live under our roof, it sure as hell is our business," William says.

"And you know, it's against the law," Donna says. She sets down her fork and wipes at her lip with her linen napkin. "You shouldn't be dating a man five years older than you."

"What?" Cate says. "You can't be serious."

"I'm totally serious," Donna says. "If he ever steps his foot in this door, I will call the police and have him arrested for taking advantage of a minor. You're so headstrong, there's no telling what trouble you'll get yourself into."

"You can't do that! Mom, please, I love him!" Cate turns to Michael. "Thanks a bunch, for starting all of this."

"I'm sorry, Cate," Michael says. "I didn't know he was old. I was just teasing."

Everyone stares at their plates for a few strained moments.

"You know what? You can just screw off, all of you!" Cate yells. She gets up from the table in a flurry, bumps her knee on the table leg, then runs from the kitchen into her room and slams the door. She throws herself onto her bed and bursts into tears. Footsteps come thundering down the hallway, and the next minute her father explodes into her room.

"Young lady! Did I just hear you tell me to *screw off*?" William yells.

"Now William, calm down," Donna says, coming into the room after him.

"Calm down? After our daughter just told us to screw off? I bloody well don't think so!" William fumes, hardly able to contain himself. He pushes past Donna and pulls Cate off her bed, yanking on her arm, hard.

"I'm sorry!" Cate cries out, in shock. "I'm sorry I said that, Dad." She pulls her arm away. William looks at his hand, as if it doesn't belong to him. His arm drops to his side and his eyes soften.

"I'm sorry," William says, his voice lowered, back to its usual calm tone. "I totally lost my temper, but it's no excuse. It's just that I worry about you, so much. I really don't think it's a good idea for you to date someone who is twenty. Will you at least consider our advice?"

"No, I won't. I love Billy and he loves me. Would both of you just leave me alone, please?"

"Okay, we'll back off a bit for now." William shakes his head. "But this isn't over." He and Donna leave, closing the door behind them.

Cate sits stunned. She buries her face into her feather pillow and cries until she feels as though she's cried herself dry. She opens her nightstand drawer and retrieves her journal and pen.

My dad just yanked on my arm so hard, it felt like he was going to pull it right out of my shoulder socket. It hurt, like hell, but the pain in my heart, that my dad could lose his temper like that, with me, has my head spinning. And what was with Mom threatening to call the police? Talk about drama.

I know I haven't been the same since the farm. I've felt so much shame. But since I started dating Billy, I feel different. I love him and I'm pretty sure he loves me too. I know I've only been dating him a short time, but I think about him every minute of every day. My parents can't make me stop seeing him. In fact, I'm going to see Dr. Adams, in confidence, and ask for a prescription to go on the pill. Billy doesn't like using condoms, and I'm not fond of how they smell. I just hope Dr. Adams agrees, that he doesn't make me inform my parents. I'd rather die than admit to my dad that I'm having sex. They'd likely go through the roof if they knew.

Cate dates Billy for all of grade eleven, over the summer, and through to grade twelve. Her parents never really come around, but they accept that Cate is a stubborn teenager with her own mind.

Over the Christmas break of 1982, Billy and Cate go with his parents to Black Diamond, a dinky little town southwest of the city, to visit with his relatives. They stay overnight at his grandpa's house, in separate bedrooms. Cate has gone off the pill. Her new female doctor says it is risky at her age, especially since she's a smoker, and has prescribed her a diaphragm. But when Billy appears in Cate's bedroom at three in the morning and tells her about a bad dream he had, where she was walking around at a party in a bikini, flirting with all of the guys, he wants her to console him, with sex. In her groggy state, Cate forgets all about the diaphragm, stowed in a plastic container in her overnight bag.

Afterwards, Billy rolls over and falls right back to sleep, squished in beside Cate in her single bed. She can't sleep. She creeps quietly out of bed and gets out her journal and pen. She sits in a chair in the corner to write by the light of the full moon shining through the sheer drapes of the floor-to-ceiling window.

I can hardly believe what I just did. I made love with Billy and forgot to put in my diaphragm. Shit. What if I just got myself pregnant?

Cate stops to look down at her flat abdomen. She lifts her nightie and places her hand just below her belly button.

That would suck, big time. But I did just finish my period a few days ago. I shouldn't be ovulating for another week. And it was only this one time. I'm sure I'm fine.

Cate crosses her fingers and prays, something she rarely does anymore.

God, if you're there, please, please, please don't let me be pregnant. I'm not ready. I know Billy's not ready. I've got dreams of enrolling in a journalism program when I finish high school next year. I want to get married and be a mom, so much. But not now. Not yet.

Two missed periods later, Cate goes to the doctor. She provides a urine sample for a pregnancy test. A few days later, she makes the call to the doctor's office from a pay phone at the cinemas.

"Hi, this is Cate Henderson. I'm calling for my test results."

"Just one moment please," the nurse says.

Cate waits. Her stomach lurches. She rolls the silver, coiled phone cord nervously between her fingers and stares down at the floor.

"Hello?" the nurse says. "I have your results. They're positive."

"Positive?" Cate mumbles. "What does that mean?"

"You're going to have a baby. Shall I make a follow-up appointment for next week?"

"Um, well, actually, I'll call back later, thank you." Her head is spinning and she feels about to keel over. She hangs up the phone and stares at it, then walks, as though in a trance, back to the candy counter where Tripti is restocking chocolate bars.

"So, what did they say?"

"It's confirmed, I'm pregnant."

Both girls stare at Cate's flat stomach in disbelief.

"Ooh, I can hardly believe it," Tripti says. She places her hand on Cate's tummy and then pulls it quickly away, like she's just touched a hot stove. "What are you going to do?"

"God, I don't know. Can you cover for me while I go and call Billy?"

"Yeah, sure, here's a quarter for the phone," Tripti says.

Billy's phone rings several times before he answers. Cate's stomach is in knots and her heart thumps in her chest.

"Hello?" Billy answers.

"Hi, it's me. I just got off the phone with the doctor's office. I'm pregnant."

There is a long pause.

"What? Pregnant, with a baby? I, I'm not ready to be a dad. I hope you're planning on having an abortion."

"We can talk about it later. Come and pick me up after my shift at work."

Cate hangs up and lets out a huge sigh. She's not ethically opposed to abortion. She believes that every woman should have a choice. But it doesn't feel like something she's prepared to do.

The rest of her shift goes by in a haze. When Billy picks her up, they get into a fight, neither one of them willing to budge on their opinion of what to do.

The next day Michael is out with friends from university and Cate decides she might as well break the news to her parents. They are watching curling on TV when she comes into the room and turns the television off. She plops down beside her mother on the couch, her dad in his customary spot in his recliner.

"I've missed two periods," Cate begins without preamble. "And my test results confirm, I'm pregnant."

"Pregnant?" William repeats, as if she's just said she's returned from a visit to Mars. "How can that be?"

"Honestly, William. You know perfectly well Cate and Billy are sexually active." Donna turns her attention to Cate. "How far along are you?"

"It happened when we were in Black Diamond. I haven't scheduled a follow-up appointment yet. I guess around three months. Why?"

"Well, it's very important," Donna says. "It's dangerous and cruel to have an abortion when you're too far along."

"I'm not getting an abortion."

"Before you make any hasty decisions, you should consider carefully all of your options," Donna says. She takes Cate's hand in hers and gives it a squeeze. "If you don't get an abortion, you'll have to give it up for adoption. At least I can't imagine you're considering keeping the baby, are you?"

"I haven't thought that far. Billy wants me to get an abortion too."

"I didn't say I want you to," Donna says, "but it's the best option for you, I think.

"Aw hell, Cate, I wish you'd been more careful," William says. He lets out a deep sigh and leans forward in his chair. "Is there any possibility the two of you will get married? That would be the right thing, if you ask me."

"You can't be serious," Donna says. "She's just turned seventeen, she's too young to get married and have a baby!"

"Look, I really appreciate you guys looking out for me. You're handling this way better than I imagined. But I've already made up my mind not to have an abortion. I should have been more careful. This is my responsibility. I'm obviously not in a financial situation to raise a baby, so unless Billy changes his mind, I guess I'll have to give it up for adoption." Cate drops her mother's hand and moves hers to her belly, stroking it absently.

Donna notices for the first time that her daughter's waist has widened a little, that her breasts are fuller.

"Well, that is likely the best choice if you're determined to carry this baby to term," Donna says. "Your dad and I are in no position, what with his illness, to have a newborn in the house."

"You don't need to decide what you're going to do just yet," William says, getting up and coming over to sit next to Cate. He puts his arms around her and pulls her close. "You've got six months to figure that out. And who knows, Billy just might come around."

"Thank you, for being so supportive, for not getting mad at me," Cate says. She hugs her father back and pushes her painful feelings away.

Deep down she thinks she'd make an excellent mother. She's already feeling maternal and has even caught herself singing lullabies to her baby. But still, she's scared as hell of what the future will hold for her and her baby. Cate says a little prayer under her breath and hopes for the best.

Chapter 10

WHEN CATE STARTS TO show, the school principal calls up William and Donna to request a meeting. He strongly suggests that Sir Winston Churchill isn't the appropriate place for an expecting mother and gives Cate a registration form for the school for pregnant girls.

Louise Dean School is downtown in the quaint, older area of Mount Royal. Cate has to catch two buses to get there. It is a beautiful brick building, surrounded by lush gardens and huge oak trees, but the interior needs some repairs. There are two classrooms, a kitchen, a meeting room, and a lounge where the girls can go to rest between classes. In Modern Living 30, which is really a prenatal class the girls get credit for, Cate embraces the activities with enthusiasm and earns an A grade.

"I don't think I need to tell you how much I enjoyed having you in my group," Mrs. Crowther writes in the comment section of her report card. "Your perceptiveness, sensitivity, ability to communicate your ideas and feelings, as well as to listen to others, were unmatched by anyone."

In English 30, Cate writes a poem that she hopes will give clarity into the difficult and complex feelings she is trying to process. She earns an A for it too.

> **Teenage Pregnancy**
> *The sadness is the hardest part to bear.*
> *It hurts to hear,*
> *"We don't want her at our school."*
> *On the bus to my new school, the one for*
> *"girls like me,"*
> *Old ladies across the aisle whisper and stare*
> *disapprovingly.*
> *I tuck my naked fingers under my thighs,*
> *Feeling the heaviness of their condemning sighs.*
> *I cast my gaze downward.*
> *No announcements slipped into mailboxes.*
> *No congratulations.*
> *I stay quiet, I hide,*
> *when all I desire is to shout from the rooftops:*
> *"There is a little miracle growing inside!"*
> *I save my joy for private moments, alone*
> *in my room.*
> *Where I whisper to my baby,*
> *"You are so loved; you are so wanted."*

Cate's parents watch in wonder as their daughter transforms from a rebellious teenager to a mature young woman in a matter of months.

"I'm so proud of you," Donna says one early summer morning. Cate is in the kitchen, preparing a healthy morning snack of sliced apples with peanut butter, her eating disorder now a thing of the past.

"Thanks, Mom. What for?" Cate dips the knife into the jar and spreads more peanut butter onto her plate.

"I don't know where to start," Donna says. "You finished grade twelve with honours, and you've embraced your pregnancy with such responsibility. You quit smoking and you put so much time and effort into creating a healthy eating plan with the dietician at your school, to make sure your baby is getting all the nutrients it needs."

"I couldn't agree more," William says as he walks into the kitchen. "It seems a shame for you to give up that baby, just because of money." William runs his hand along the curve of Cate's belly.

"Yeah, well, that's my situation." Cate puts her hand on top of her father's and pats it. "I'm sad that I have to give my precious little one up for adoption, but I know I'll be making some couple who wants a baby so happy. And let's face it, Billy hasn't come around to the idea of being a father."

"That's true," William says. "I'm not impressed with him. He's the older one, the man. He should be ashamed of himself. But I suppose it's a different time to when your mom and I were young. You know Mom was already pregnant with Michael when we got married?"

"Yeah, I did the math," Cate says. "It was different back then."

"Well," Donna says, "your father and I have been talking, and we've decided we wouldn't be able to live with ourselves if the only reason you give your baby up is because of the financial side of things."

"What? Are you serious?" The peanut butter knife slips from Cate's hand and lands on the counter. She does a little dance and rubs her tummy. "Did you hear that, little one?"

"Yes, we're completely serious," William says with a smile that lights up his face. "You can stay at home as long as you need to get on your feet."

Cate practically glides across the kitchen linoleum. She gives both her parents huge bear hugs, grinning ear to ear. "Thank you, thank you, thank you! You won't regret it, I promise."

That night, before Cate turns out her light, she gets out her journal.

> *I can hardly believe this fantastic shift of fate! Mom and Dad said I can live at home with my baby, if that's what I want to do, for as long as I need! I've never wanted anything more in my life. Even though Billy has become more distant, I don't care. I just I know I can do this, with or without him. True, I'll have to put my dreams of being a journalist on hold, but I can figure out a career that will suit being a mom that is satisfying too. Maybe nursing or teaching? But that decision is so far down the road, first things first. I'm going to be a mom!!!*
>
> *Rose had the nerve to suggest Billy is cheating on me. She said she saw him at a hockey game with a gorgeous redhead. But when I confronted him, he promised me she was just a friend from work. And he made a good point, that he never thought of asking me, since I'm clearly not interested in sports.*
>
> *He still hasn't come around to being a dad, but I'm so proud of him for making the decision to go to university as a mature student. He's enrolled in general studies starting in September and has plans to apply to*

business education. Maybe everything is going to be all
right after all.

A few weeks later, Billy surprises Cate when he calls her
and tells her to dress up, he's taking her out for dinner.
He hasn't taken her out in months and Cate is excited, but
self-conscious about what to wear. On her limited budget,
she doesn't have much in the way of fashionable maternity
clothes. She chooses the grey dress she wore to her
graduation ceremony at Louise Dean and white sandals, the
only footwear she can manage to squeeze her swollen feet
into. She's just putting on some pink lip gloss when she hears
the honk of his horn.

"That's Billy," Cate calls out to her dad. Her mother is
out showing a new listing to prospective buyers. "I'll see
you later."

"That's so rude of him not to come in," her father says
as he hobbles over and gives Cate a kiss on the cheek.

"I don't think he's being rude," Cate defends. "He's just
uncomfortable around you and Mom. He knows you don't
approve of him."

"Well, that's no excuse not to be a gentleman. But I'm
glad he's taking you out for once and I don't want to wreck
it. Have a good time, Caty-bug."

"Dad, I'm far too old to be your Caty-bug anymore,"
Cate says with a smile. "But thank you for always looking
out for me. I love you."

Cate lowers herself with some effort into Billy's car.
"Where are we going?"

"To a new restaurant that just opened on Centre Street
that's getting great reviews. I remember you loving the
souvlaki and tzatziki dip the last time we had Greek food."

"That's so thoughtful of you," Cate says.

He parks across from the restaurant and comes around to Cate's side to help her out of the car. The table he reserved is in a quiet, dark corner. He orders a beer for himself and a sparkling water for Cate.

Billy seems distracted, with little to say in the way of conversation, the silence uncomfortable as they look over the dinner menus.

"Is there something on your mind?" Cate asks.

"No," Billy says.

The awkwardness continues throughout the meal. Neither one of them has much to say to the other. Cate chews nervously on her cuticles. She picks at her food, her stomach doing somersaults. She smoothes the starched white tablecloth and then drums her fingers on the table. The waiter clears away their dishes.

"Well, that was nice," Cate says, patting at her mouth with the napkin and setting it on the table. "Shall we ask for the bill and get going?"

"No, not yet," Billy says.

"Oh? Do you want to order dessert? You don't usually have any."

"No, that's not it." Billy gets up from his chair and walks over to where Cate is sitting, then drops to his knee. "Cate Henderson, will you marry me?"

"What?" Cate says with a gasp. She looks around the room, embarrassed and thrilled at the same time. "I wasn't, I didn't…"

Billy laughs. "Seems I've succeeded in surprising you." He pulls out a velvet ring box and opens it to reveal a diamond engagement ring.

"Are you serious?" Cate drops one hand to her belly, the other lifts to her heart. "You really mean it?"

"Yes, I really mean it. I want us to be married. It's obvious to anyone with eyes how much you love this little one. And I want him to have a mom and a dad. So, I'll ask you again, will you marry me?" He's already sliding the ring onto Cate's finger.

"Yes, Billy, a thousand times, yes."

Two months later Cate and Billy still haven't made any concrete wedding plans. Cate's due date comes and goes. She has Braxton Hicks contractions that have her parents taking her to the hospital twice, only to be turned away when her labour pains stop. It is an early October morning when Cate first knows something is wrong.

"Mom! Come here, quick!" She falls to her knees in the hallway. Her hands cradle her massive abdomen. She winces. Abby comes over and licks at her hand.

"What's the matter?" Her mother's voice rises at the sight of her daughter. She shoos Abby away. "Are you in labour?"

"I, I don't know. I think so. I was walking off what I thought to be mild contractions." Cate gasps as another sharp pain grips her. "And then suddenly I felt this tearing sensation. I can't quite describe it, Mom, but it feels like something is wrong."

Her father is at work and Michael is at the university. It's just the two of them.

"Okay, try not worry, darling," Donna says, trying to convince herself as much as Cate. "Let me help you up."

Donna supports Cate to stand and leads her to the garage. She forgets all about the overnight bag in Cate's room that's been packed and ready for weeks. Cate hunches over as she walks, each step a giant effort. Her breathing is fast.

"Try to calm down, take some deep breaths," Donna says as she helps her daughter into the car. "Everything's going to be okay."

At the hospital Cate leans on her mother as they come through the automatic doors of Emergency.

"We need some help here," Donna yells. "Please, someone, hurry up!"

The few people in the waiting room look up to watch the drama while one of the hospital staff pushes a wheelchair over for Cate.

"Thank you," Donna says. "I can wheel her into an examining room."

"Not so fast," he says. "You need to fill in the proper paperwork."

"You can't be serious. My daughter's baby is in distress, could possibly be dead already—" Donna puts her hand to her mouth. "Oh, I'm sorry, darling, I don't mean to cause you any more anxiety."

Cate is bent over in pain, moaning and unable to respond.

"All right then, follow me," the young man says, with clear reluctance. He grabs the handles of the wheelchair and begins to walk toward the elevator. "You can fill in the paperwork for your daughter while she is examined. Do you have her Alberta health card?" He pushes the button for the fifth floor.

"Oh, no…" Donna says, flustered. "I forgot Cate's things at home. But I have mine, in my purse."

When they step off the elevator, the attendant leads them to the nursing station.

"We'll take over now," the nurse behind the counter says to Donna. She hands her a clipboard and a pen. "Please, take a seat and fill in the forms."

Another nurse leads Cate to an examining room. She asks her questions along the way. The contractions are getting heavier, and Cate is having difficulty concentrating. She hears the nurse say to her colleague, who has just joined them, "She's likely only having a panic attack at the idea of delivering a baby, now that the time has come. By the look of her, she can't be more than eighteen." Cate doesn't have the energy to be insulted or angry. The two nurses lift her onto an examining table. One of them does an internal exam while the other starts to hook Cate up to a fetal monitoring machine.

"You're only three centimetres dilated. You've still got a long way to go and it's only going to get worse. I'll see if the doctor on call can order some pain medication."

Donna comes into the room. "Why on earth is the doctor not here yet?"

"There's no need," the nurse says. "Your daughter is barely into labour. We'll contact her doctor when she's closer to delivering."

The other nurse is strapping a pair of belts to Cate's abdomen, a Doppler to measure the fetal heart rate and the other to measure uterine contractions.

"Hmph, something must be wrong with this machine," the nurse says. "There's no reading of the baby's heartbeat. I'll go exchange it for another."

Cate turns to her mother. "Is my baby okay?"

"Yes, darling, I'm sure everything is fine," Donna says, but her face conveys as much uncertainty as Cate is feeling.

The nurse returns with a new monitor and hooks it up. Still, there is no heartbeat. The energy in the room changes swiftly, as the nurses recognize that perhaps something is wrong with the baby after all. In an instant a new nurse shows up with an internal fetal heart monitor that she inserts into Cate's vagina and places on the fetus's scalp.

"Rapid response! The baby's heart rate is only fifty-six beats per minute," the nurse snaps.

Suddenly there is a flurry of activity as doctors and specialists pour into Cate's room.

"Fifty-six?" Cate mumbles. "What's it supposed to be?"

"The normal range is 120 to 160. I'm sorry to say you were right to be concerned. There must be something wrong."

"That's what I've been trying to tell you," Donna says, her top lip trembling. She strokes Cate's arm and murmurs reassurances.

A group of medical students gathers at the doorway to observe and take notes as intravenous lines are inserted into Cate's arm. A catheter is inserted into her bladder and a blood sample is taken from the baby's head. The stress and the pain have Cate in convulsions. Her body lifts off the table like a scene from The Exorcist. She has three contractions before the anesthetist enters the room. As he is about to give Cate a general anesthetic, a hospital administrator comes into the room with a permission form for an emergency Caesarean.

"I can sign that," Donna says, reaching for the form. "She's not yet eighteen."

"Please, God, let my baby be all right," Cate whispers, her last words before the anesthetic takes hold.

When she regains consciousness several hours later, Billy's voice is the first thing she hears.

"Congratulations, little momma," Billy says. "We have a baby girl."

"What?" Cate says. Everything is a blur, but then images return of the moments before she went under. "A baby girl? It's, she's, all right?"

"She's more than all right, she's gorgeous. Now that you're awake, why don't I wheel you down to the nursery to meet her?" Billy leans down and kisses Cate on the top of her head.

"Oh my God, yes please! I can't believe we have a girl, that she's okay." She sits up, then winces from the pain of her incision and lies back down.

As Billy pushes Cate's bed down the hall toward the nursery, Cate spots her mother, father, and Michael huddled together in a semicircle. When they see her, they rush over, talking over one another.

"Dad, Michael, when did you get here? How long have I been out?"

"That's a long story," Michael says.

"It's half past three," William says.

"You've been out almost two hours," Donna adds.

"I'll tell the nurse you're awake and ready to meet our baby girl," Billy says.

William kisses Cate on the top of her head and Donna squeezes her hand while Michael beams.

"I never thought it would feel so amazing to be an uncle," Michael says. "Oh, here she comes."

Billy walks over with the nurse, who is holding a pink bundle. She places the baby in Cate's outstretched arms. Tears pour down Cate's face as she gazes at her daughter for the first time.

"It's so wonderful to meet you." Cate's voice catches as she pulls open the blanket to count her fingers and toes. "One, two, three...all ten accounted for. She's so pink and perfect." She kisses her daughter. Her skin is soft and delicate. "I could gobble you up, you smell so amazing." She nuzzles her face into her daughter as she pulls her close, next to her breast. "She looks just like you, Billy."

"Speaking of your little one," says William. "Have you two decided on a name?"

"No, actually," Cate says. "I was so certain she was a boy. I've been calling her Christian for the last few months." She laughs, then flinches at the painful pulse in her incision. "I told Billy if it was a girl he could name her, thinking I was being clever when we couldn't agree, but I guess he gets the last laugh." She turns to Billy. "Do you have a name picked out?"

"I do, but only if you approve. What do you think about Celeste? It's a Latin word meaning *heavenly*."

"I think it's perfect, don't you, my little angel?" Cate coos.

"It's lovely to see you bonding with your baby," says the nurse. "But you have some recovering to do and need your rest. A Caesarean is a major operation, you know." She reaches to retrieve Celeste.

"But, can't she stay with me? I want to start breastfeeding her right away. I was so hoping she could stay in my room."

"That can be arranged later," the nurse concedes. "For now, you need to rest. Don't worry, your baby is in good hands. We'll bring her back to you when she's ready for her first feeding."

Cate doesn't want to let go of Celeste, but already her eyes feel heavy.

"I guess I am a little tired," she says with a yawn. She's sound asleep before Billy has her back in her semi-private room on the ward.

The first twenty-four hours after Celeste's birth pass in a blur. Cate is injected with morphine every four hours to manage her pain. In her lucid moments, she finds out that the reason for the emergency Caesarean was a placental abruption, not uncommon in post-term babies. She learns that Donna called William at work and somehow managed to get hold of Billy, who was in class at the university and got quite a shock when his professor called him to his desk to give him the news. By some crazy twist of fate, Billy ran into Michael in the campus parking lot and gave him a lift to the hospital. Celeste was brought into the world less than ten minutes after Cate went under.

Two days later, Cate is recovered enough to have Celeste's crib moved into her room. A pink index card labelled *Baby Girl Henderson, Room 62B; weight 8 ½ lbs, height 21"* is taped to the side. When Celeste is asleep, all bundled in her receiving blanket, a skiff of dark hair and long lashes on pink cheeks, Cate gets out her journal from her overnight bag.

> *It almost feels like a dream, but it's true. I'm the mother of a beautiful, perfect baby girl. I'll admit, I did feel a bit disappointed at first, that Billy, Mom, Dad, and Michael all got to meet my little angel before me, but then I reminded myself the important thing is that she's healthy. That she's alive. My last thought before I went under was that I was going to lose her.*
>
> *Mom didn't spare me any of the details. She told me my uterus was green, that Celeste had pooed from distress, although apparently the medical term for pre-birth poo is meconium. When Mom told me that the doctor put my liver on a tray, that kind of grossed me out. I imagine now I have dust on it. I know that's silly, but that's how my brain works.*

The doctor told me that Celeste swallowed some of the meconium and they had to put a scope down her throat to vacuum it out. I gasped, but he said not to worry, she might just have a bit of hoarse cry, and maybe a scratchy voice when she starts talking. It's hard to imagine her talking. She barely cries, she's such a contented little thing. And she latched onto my nipple like an old pro. The head nurse came into our room this morning and asked me if I'd be willing to demonstrate how to bathe a baby to the other mothers next week, since Celeste has such an easygoing disposition, and I said sure. The doctor says I have to be in here for ten days. That feels like an awful long time to be cooped up in here, with the dreadful hospital food. I would like to go home already, but I suppose the medical professionals know best. It is kind of fun to pick out my meals on the selection card. And all the flowers I've received look so gorgeous, lining the border along the windowsill. Pinch me, I'm dreaming, the best dream I've ever had in my life.

Cate is discharged after a week as her young body recovers quickly. Celeste has won the hearts of all the staff with her charming personality, and they all come in to wish Cate well on the morning of her release. Cate is busy packing up their things, Celeste sleeping contentedly in her crib, when Billy arrives.

"Looks like you're all ready to go. Has the doctor signed off yet?"

"Yes, I was just waiting for you to come." Cate turns around to give him a kiss. She holds her body back a few inches, self-conscious of her extra weight, her tummy now a floppy, distended thing that looks more like bread dough with stretch marks streaked across it.

"Perfect, let's get a move on then. I'll take your things, you can carry Celeste."

The nursing staff all shout goodbye and wave as they head down the hall to the elevator.

Out in the parking lot, there is a light breeze in the air. Cate pulls Celeste's blanket over to protect her face.

"Mom bought us a travel bed for the car," Billy says, pointing to the back seat.

"Oh, I'll just hold her on my lap." Cate doesn't want to let go for even one minute.

"It feels strange, taking you home to your parents," Billy says as he navigates the car down Crowchild Trail. "I feel like I should be taking you home, with me. But there's my roommates, and—"

"Don't worry," Cate says, interrupting. "I understand. I never expected anything else, what with us still not married. You know that I converted my room to a nursery, to be ready for her, months ago." She strokes Celeste's cheek.

"I know, it's just that, now that's she here…"

"We can sort that out later." Inside, Cate's grateful that she's going home to her parents' house, where she knows she'll get the support she wants and needs. She can't imagine Billy being much help. He seems nervous just to hold Celeste.

"Yeah, you're right," Billy says. "Maybe after Christmas we can talk about setting a wedding date and getting a place together."

Christmas comes and goes, but there's no talk of weddings or new living arrangements. Cate and Celeste fall into an easy flow, but even though Celeste is a content baby, getting up in the night several times to feed her has Cate exhausted. She's grateful that, despite her father's illness and her mother's worry, they both dote on her and Celeste.

"Since it's Saturday, why don't we take turns grabbing a nap?" William says. "You go on now, Cate, I'll look after Celeste."

"Thanks, Dad, I could use some sleep," Cate says with a yawn.

Two hours later Cate enters the living room on stealthy feet to discover her father rocking Celeste over his shoulder and singing the mockingbird song, just like he used to do with her.

"Looks like she's in good hands," Cate says as she walks into the room. "I'll take her now, Dad, she's probably ready for some milk."

William passes over Celeste and Cate takes her to the couch. She releases her left breast from her nursing bra, engorged and ready. Cate strokes Celeste's cheek and she nuzzles in.

"I never saw your mom breastfeed," William says, his face an expression of awe. "Back in those days, women covered up. In fact, your mom used to take Michael into his nursery to feed him."

"I'm glad times have changed. It would practically kill me to have to miss out on social interaction to hide out in our room. Babies eat so often when they're newborns."

"Yes, you've always been a little social butterfly. And I have a feeling this little one is going to be much the same." William reaches down and runs his gnarled, arthritic finger across Celeste's cheek. "Well, I think it's my turn for a nap, see you in a bit, Caty-bug."

Cate smiles to herself. She knows she's too old for such things, but she still loves it when her dad calls her Caty-bug.

Before Cate turns eighteen in March, she applies for university and student loans for the fall semester. She meets with a social worker to arrange for social assistance until her student loans are approved. With the social worker's help, Cate finds an apartment on the allotted budget.

Cate and Celeste will move into their first home together on April first, a modest two-bedroom unit in Brentwood with a balcony, conveniently located near the university, a playground, and a shopping centre.

"Are you sure you're ready for this big transition?" Donna is helping Cate load up boxes of clothes and the mountain of Celeste's toys and baby gear.

"I'm absolutely sure," Cate says. "These first six months at home were such a blessing. I discovered how capable I am inside the safety net of your and dad's support. I'll be forever grateful."

"It's been our pleasure and joy," Donna says, wiping a tear from her eye. She picks up a pastel pink velour sleeper with little ears on the hood. "Where did you get this adorable outfit? It should fit her soon." She folds it neatly and places it in a cardboard box.

"Oh, that one is a gift from John. I must say, I was surprised when he showed up bearing gifts for Celeste."

"Yes, I do remember now," Donna says with a sigh. "I think he's had his eye on you since he and Michael became friends. I've seen him cast furtive looks in your direction, even after it was clear your heart belongs to Billy."

"Yes, well, that hasn't amounted to much, has it? Billy gave me this ring, but there's been zero follow-through." She turns the ring around her finger several times. "Every time I try to bring up wedding plans, he manages to change the subject. I thought for sure, when I told him I was ready to move out on my own, that he would suggest we move in together, but it never happened."

"It is a shame," Donna agrees. "He's clearly batty about Celeste, but it would seem he isn't up for the responsibility of helping to raise her."

"Yes, well, at least he was honest from the beginning. I never expected anything, so I'm not disappointed. Although I must admit, when he proposed it did get my hopes up." Cate gets up and goes over to the crib where Celeste is sleeping and runs her fingers along her forehead, down her cheek. "You and me against the world, sometimes it feels like you and me against the world," she sings to Celeste in her off-tune country twang, the words from Linda Ronstadt's hit.

"Don't give up just yet," Donna advises as she places the last item on top and closes the box. "Who knows what the future has in store?"

Finding a good daycare turns out to be more challenging than Cate had anticipated. She makes a list of all the daycares in the northwest of the city and drops by unannounced, with either her mother, father, or both in tow. Cate thinks several of the ones they visit ought to be condemned, the standards of cleanliness almost non-existent. Others are low on staff, and the resulting staff-to-child ratios create an atmosphere of utter chaos. Cate has crossed seventeen of the twenty candidates off her list when William shows up to accompany her to Little Stars in Silver Springs.

"Are you sure you want to check this one out?" William says, looking at the address Cate has circled on the map.

"It's one heck of a drive to make every day and then backtrack to the university."

"I know, it is a bit of a hike," Cate concedes. She balances Celeste on her hip as they make their way to William's car. Cate's new-to-her used car is at the mechanic's for service again. "But if it is clean and well staffed, it will be well worth it."

"That's true enough," William agrees. "We've seen our share of duds."

William parks a few blocks down the street from the daycare. Cate unfolds Celeste's stroller and buckles her in.

"This grassy area right across the street is a perk," Cate says, pointing to the open field to their left.

"Yes, this neighbourhood does feel quiet and safe. Do you have your checklist with you?"

Cate chuckles. "One step ahead of you, Dad. It's in the pocket of Celeste's diaper bag." Celeste coos and jabbers in a delightful sing-song voice, her face lit up like the sun. At nine months old, she is just beginning to say a few words like *mama* and *up*.

"After you," William says, holding open the door.

As they cross the threshold, Cate's eye is drawn to the tidy cork bulletin board in the entrance that resembles something you'd find in a school classroom. She takes in the fresh scent of lemon cleaner and makes two checks on her list.

"Hello, can I help you?" a young woman asks. She looks not much older than Cate, with a very positive vibe.

"Yes, I hope you can," Cate says. "I'm looking for a placement for my daughter for when I start classes at university in September."

"My name is Suzanne, and who's this little cutie-pie?" Suzanne asks. She reaches her arms out to Celeste.

"Her name is Celeste," Cate says. "Do you know if you have any openings?"

"I'm not sure, you'll have to talk with our director," Suzanne says with a smile. "But I can take you for a tour if you like, I'm on my break."

"That would be wonderful," Cate says.

"Do you want out of there?" Suzanne asks, already undoing the safety strap to lift Celeste from her stroller. "I can hold her."

Cate and William follow Suzanne, Celeste perched on her hip, for a tour of the daycare. It is divided into four sections: a nursery for babies under eighteen months, a toddler room, a preschool class, and a before- and after-school room for older kids. There is a bright, clean kitchen where a staff member is peeling carrots and a pot of rice is boiling on the stove. When the tour is complete, Cate knows for certain she's found the right place for her daughter and makes an appointment with the director to complete the paperwork.

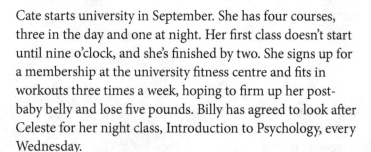

Cate starts university in September. She has four courses, three in the day and one at night. Her first class doesn't start until nine o'clock, and she's finished by two. She signs up for a membership at the university fitness centre and fits in workouts three times a week, hoping to firm up her post-baby belly and lose five pounds. Billy has agreed to look after Celeste for her night class, Introduction to Psychology, every Wednesday.

The first Wednesday, Billy calls last minute to say he's been called in to work at the pizza joint where he does delivery service part-time. Cate has to scramble to arrange with her mom and dad to take over babysitting duty. The

next Wednesday, Billy drops the ball again, calling from
a bar during happy hour to say he forgot what day it was.
Cate is furious, but she bites her tongue. She asks her parents
if they will take on the weekly responsibility for the entire
semester, and they agree.

"It's no trouble at all," William insists.

"You're doing us a favour, really," Donna says. "We miss
having her around so much."

By the end of the year, Billy rarely comes around to see
Cate and Celeste anymore. Then, with just a few days' notice,
he invites Cate to a New Year's Eve party at a club with some
of his friends. William and Donna agree to take Celeste for
the night. Having just turned one, it's her first sleepover
without Cate.

On the night of the party, Cate is excited and nervous.
She hums and haws over what to wear, then chooses a pair
of black jeans she can finally fit into again with a cherry-red
blouse and heels. Her hand trembles as she applies mascara.

She's dressed and ready, on time, but there's no sign of
Billy. Cate waits and waits. An hour after he was supposed
to pick her up, Billy calls with another excuse. He says he has
to work last minute, that they're short-staffed. Cate can't
believe she fell for his bullshit again, but instead of sulking,
like usual, she decides to go the party anyway and
catches a taxi.

"Another round of Sex on the Beach shooters, and a
round of champagne too," Ken says to the server a few
minutes before midnight.

Cate laughs, already quite tipsy. "I can't possibly have
another drink and walk out of here. But I will have one sip
of champagne to toast the new year."

"Do you have any resolutions?" Ken asks.

"I'm going to try and quit smoking," says Cate. When Celeste stopped nursing, Cate started smoking again with the stress of exams. "How about you?"

"I'm thinking of going back to school as a mature student, like Billy did," Ken says. "But I wish I had a girlfriend like you. I can't believe he doesn't see what he has, right in front of him, that he cheats on you and you just put up with it." Ken is slurring his words a bit, but continues. "I have to admit, I never pegged you to be one to put up with that."

"What are you talking about?" Cate asks, suddenly feeling sober. "Billy has never cheated on me."

"You're kidding, right?" Ken laughs out loud. "You can't possibly be that naive."

"I'm not kidding, I—" Cate is about to defend Billy when Ken turns to the crowd.

"Hey, everybody, Cate here says Billy has never cheated on her." Ken keels over, laughing as if it is the funniest thing he's ever heard. "Can you believe it?"

There is an awkward silence as everyone at the table looks at Cate. It's clear they all know.

"We all assumed you knew," Ken says. "Billy has been with at least five different girls since you started dating. He was with other women throughout your pregnancy. In fact, he's at his latest girlfriend's house tonight, at her New Year's party, instead of being here with you."

"I, uh, I..." Cate says. "While I was pregnant with Celeste?" She can hardly believe the words that are dripping off Ken's tongue like venom.

"Yeah, honestly, Cate," Ken says. "He's been seeing other women right from the start, maybe six months after you started dating. I can't believe you didn't know. I'm sorry to be the one to break your bubble."

"No, Ken, it's better that I know." Tears form in her eyes and she wipes at them with the back of her hand. "I guess now I have another resolution. Here's to giving Billy the boot!" Cate takes one of the shot glasses from a tray on the table and lifts it to clink glasses with Ken. She spills a few drops before throwing it back in one gulp.

Cate wakes to a serious hangover. The first thing she does after glugging back some water and a couple of aspirin is call Billy. His phone rings and rings, no answer. She leaves a message.

"Goodbye, Billy. I just wanted that to be the first thing you heard from me this year. I went out with Ken and some of your other friends last night, to the club you were supposed to take me to. They told me that you're cheating on me, that you have been all along. That you're dating someone else. I imagine you're with her, even as I speak. It all makes sense now. The lack of commitment, of wedding plans, of moving in together. I can't live like this. So yeah, goodbye, Billy. It's been fun. I loved you. I still do. But it isn't enough."

Chapter 11

AFTER A FEW MONTHS, Cate begins to recover from her breakup with Billy. She is too immersed in her school work and running a home as a single mother to give romance much thought. When she receives her marks in the mail at the beginning of May, she is thrilled to discover she earned a high grade point average and is on the dean's honour roll.

"I've decided to enrol in the bachelor of education program this fall," Cate says to Michael. They are at Bowness Park with Celeste, enjoying the first of the warm weather. The grass has transformed from dry and brown to patchy, pale green, and their favourite spot near the playground across from the Bow River is packed with Calgarians jazzed to be outside after being cooped up through the long, cold winter.

"You're sure you want to give up your dream of being of a writer to teach?" Michael asks. "It seems like you've wanted to be a writer for as long as I can remember."

"Yeah, well, life surprises you sometimes, things change." Cate looks over at Celeste, sitting on the blanket beside her, building a tower with her blocks. At just over nineteen months, Celeste has a halo of soft curls, so like Cate's at her age, but dark brown, like Billy's. Her coffee-coloured eyes, framed with thick eyelashes, are so bright and joyful, almost everyone who passes by stops to look at her.

"Without Billy in the picture, I can't imagine how I would manage the unpredictable hours and late nights as a journalist," Cate continues. "And the income from writing would be unsteady too. As a teacher, I'd have stable hours and a salary, not to mention summers off. I'm still going to major in English, and can pass on my love of reading and writing to my students."

"Sounds like you've put a lot of thought into it," Michael says. "And you know I just love hanging out with this little one, if you need more help with child care." He leans over and tickles Celeste on her bare toes, and she giggles, an infectious, joyful sound that has both Cate and Michael smiling so hard their cheeks hurt despite the seriousness of their conversation.

"Thank you, I appreciate you so much," Cate says. "But I'm sure a handsome, eligible bachelor such as yourself must have better things to do than look after his niece."

"Oh, you know me," Michael says. "I'm so shy and awkward with girls, not like you at all." He pushes his hair back out of his eye and peers over at Cate. "You seem to attract the attention of men so easily, you're like a love-magnet. You know John is still absolutely smitten with you."

"Yeah, I know, but that's all too weird, him being your best friend. He feels more like a brother, really."

"I suppose you're right, but he is a good guy. He'd never cheat on you, like Billy did. I still get furious when I think about it."

"You don't need to protect me anymore," Cate says. She takes her brother's hand in hers and squeezes it. "Besides, dating is the last thing on my mind right now. I want to give all my love and energy to Celeste."

"That's all good," Michael says. "But don't you think she deserves to have a dad who is in the picture, too?"

"Celeste deserves to have everything amazing that the world has to offer," Cate says. "But at least she has you, and Dad. You two are the real deal, the best male role models I could ask for." Tears form in the corners of her eyes, and she needs to take a moment to compose herself.

Celeste has stood up and ventured off the blanket, heading toward the swing set.

"Untle Mitel, pus' me?" Celeste says as she toddles her way across the grass.

"Right behind you," Michael says. He pushes himself up and chases after his niece, then scoops her into his arms and carries her over to the baby swing. Cate watches from behind her sunglasses, her eyes wet with tears, her heart heavy.

Diane, a tall brunette, is in Cate's Canadian literature class. The September term has just started when she catches up with Cate after class.

"Uh, excuse me, Cate, isn't it?" Diane says, her pale cheeks blushing pink under a smattering of freckles. "I couldn't help but notice how passionate you are about our assignment, to develop the theme of alienation of women. I was wondering if you'd consider helping me? I hate to admit it, but I didn't get the symbolism at all. *Surfacing* was a drudgery for me to get through, let alone comprehend."

"Drudgery?" Cate says with a dramatized look of horror on her face as she turns to acknowledge Diane with a quick handshake. "Yes, I'm Cate, and Margaret Atwood is a master, my idol and inspiration. I'd be happy to bring you over from the dark side."

"That's awesome, thank you," Diane says with a shy laugh. "Should we start now, or do you have other plans?"

"I have a few hours before I pick up my daughter from daycare," Cate says.

"Your daughter?" Diane says. Her eyes, almost as bright emerald as Cate's, light up. "That's trippy."

"Hmm, I can think of more appropriate adjectives." It's Cate's turn to laugh, hers a guffaw loud enough to attract the attention of passersby. "Although now that you say it, I suppose it is kinda trippy, being Celeste's mother. She means everything to me. But I won't bore you with my litany of Celeste stories. Let's go grab coffees and get started."

Cate and Diane become friends over that first study session. Soon they are hanging out on the weekends, berating men and sharing their woes over bottles of cheap red wine at Cate's apartment after Celeste is tucked in, asleep in her crib, and they've finished their assignments.

"You've left a graveyard of shit relationships with men in your wake," Diane says, well into her second glass. She's seated on one of the second-hand, psychedelic-coloured fabric chairs Cate picked up for next to nothing from an ad in the paper. "I can't decide which dud I hate the most."

"Yeah, well, get in line. I seem to attract the duds, what can I say?"

"Not only duds," Diane says. "You attract the good guys too. You've got a light about you that is compelling, that lights up a room and makes everyone in it want to be with you, girls included."

"That's so kind of you to say," Cate says. "But I think you're a bit partial. Best friends aren't exactly objective."

"Say what you want, but I think it's true. You just haven't picked the right guy out of the lineup yet. I think you feel sorry for the screw-ups, that you think you can change them by showering them with love. That's never a good place to start."

"Since when are you the love guru?" Cate teases. She sets her wine glass on a coaster on the glass coffee table. "Although, if you've got some good advice to offer, I'm all ears."

"Well, if you want my humble opinion," Diane says, then takes another sip of wine, "I think you let your emotions drag you around and they get you into trouble. And as you've discovered, being attracted isn't enough. There needs to be compatibility. You don't know what you want or what you're looking for. Hell, Mr. Perfect is likely right in front of you, but you're too unaware to see it."

"You really think so? That's what Michael said too."

"What you need to do is get clear on what you want in a relationship. I think you should make a list of all the qualities you value in a man."

"That's a good idea. Worth a try at least. What harm can it do? And I already know the first item on my list will be that he is faithful."

After Diane has left and Cate has tidied up, she pulls out a stack of foolscap and sits down at the kitchen table that she also uses as a desk. She fills two pages, both sides, of every detail, big or small, that she thinks she wants in a man. When she is finished, she sets down her pen and closes her eyes. In her mind, she sees words forming in golden handwriting. *Johnathon Jeffrey Downing*, the full name of Michael's friend, John. Cate smiles and folds the paper neatly, then slips it into an envelope and tucks it into her nightstand drawer.

Michael calls the next day and invites Cate to a live music event at the MacEwan Student Centre the following weekend. Cate asks her parents to babysit, and Donna invites Cate and Celeste to sleep over.

Cate picks Celeste up early from daycare on Friday. After one of Donna's home-cooked meals, Cate gives Celeste a bath.

"Alright, angel, what story would you like me to read to you tonight?" Cate asks.

"Tan Drampa read to me?"

"I'm sure he'd be delighted, let's go find him."

They find William sitting in his chair, watching television. Celeste runs over as fast as her little legs can carry her and throws herself against his legs.

"Read to me Drampa?"

"I would love to, climb on up," William says, turning off the TV.

Celeste tucks her head into William's chest for a snuggle. Cate is touched to see how deeply the two of them have bonded. She goes into her old room to fetch one of Celeste's favourite books and passes it over to her father. William sings the words of the story and Celeste joins along, clapping her hands, having memorized most of the words. When William closes the cover, Celeste buries her face into her grandpa's chest and he holds her close.

"Come on then," Cate says. "Mommy and Uncle Michael are going out, and we need to get going. Into bed for your good night song before I go."

Cate sings their "Me and You Against the World" song. She runs her fingers along Celeste's forehead and down her cheek, then gets up and turns out the light. From the doorway she whispers, "I love you so much, my little angel."

"I wuv you too," Celeste says with a yawn.

The hall is already packed when Michael and Cate arrive. They can hear the dull roar of people talking, and the music blares. Michael purchases a roll of drink tickets.

"C'mon, Sis," Michael says, taking Cate by the arm. He leads her through the throng. They see John sitting at a table. He's grown a thick beard since Cate saw him last and changed from glasses to contacts that highlight his steel-grey eyes. He waves them over.

"Hey, buddy, thanks for saving us a seat," Michael says, pulling out a stool for Cate.

"Hi, John," Cate says, a little unnerved. "Michael forgot to mention you were going to be here."

"Did he now?" John says with a wink at Michael. "Well, I hope it's a good surprise." He looks Cate up and down and lets out a whistle. "You look gorgeous. You'd never guess you had a baby with that body."

"Uh, thank you," Cate says with a blush.

"Oh, please, spare us your lines," Michael says, rolling his eyes. "Cate is a knockout, I'm sure we can all agree. I think she's more fit now than before she had Celeste. But enough of the compliments, we don't want to bloat Cate's ego."

"I've worked hard to get in shape, and it does feel good," Cate says. "But don't worry, Michael, I won't let it go to my head."

"I'm going to grab Cate and me a drink," Michael says. "Can I get you anything, John?"

"Sure, thanks, buddy. I'll have a beer."

Over the course of several hours, the threesome enjoys listening to the band. They all take to the floor for a dance, then chat at their table between sets.

"So, how is Celeste doing?" John asks. "I haven't seen her in a while now. I can hardly believe she's going to turn two next week. Is she as precocious as ever?"

"Yes, she is," Cate says. She is a little taken aback that John remembers Celeste's birthday. "She has quite an advanced vocabulary for her age, but she still struggles with her *g* and *k* sounds. Her pediatrician says she'll grow out of it soon enough. Many children aren't even speaking at her age, let alone in full sentences."

"Yeah, it's so cute, though," Michael says. "When I copied her way of saying Grandpa, she insisted, 'not Drampa, Drampa!'" Michael laughs, his rat-a-tat-ho-ho chuckle that has Cate and John joining in.

"You should invite me over to see her, the next time you're visiting your parents," John says.

"Okay, I will."

By the end of the evening, they've all had too much to drink to drive safely. They leave Cate's car in the parking lot and the three of them catch a taxi home.

"I can drive you back in the morning to pick up your car," John offers. "Just come over whenever you're ready."

"Thanks, John, I appreciate that."

John bends down and kisses her on the lips. It's tentative and brief, and almost as soon as he's begun, he is backing away, waving good night.

The next day, Cate and Celeste share a lazy morning watching cartoons and reading books. When Donna gets up, she makes Celeste her favourite pancakes, with chocolate chips to make a smiley face.

"I noticed your car isn't in the driveway," William says, looking up from his newspaper. "That was a good choice, if you were drinking. Do you need a ride to pick it up?"

"No, thanks, John offered," Cate says.

"John the lovebird?" Michaels teases, coming into the room, still in his pajamas with a head full of rooster tails. "He kissed Cate last night," Michael informs their parents.

"It was nothing," Cate says with a blush. "I think Michael has his eye on the Cupid role that wasn't advertised."

"Cupid, eh?" William says with a chuckle. "Well, that would certainly be a sight, Michael with a bow and arrow, stark naked."

"What's a tupid?" Celeste asks. "And what's start nated?"

"Never mind, sweetheart," Cate says. "Your grandpa is only teasing."

John picks Cate up to go to collect her car while Celeste stays with her grandparents. It's a bit strained for the first few minutes, but soon John is telling Cate about the structural engineering contest he's entered, along with some funny stories about the last scavenger hunt pub crawl he was at, and they fall into an easy conversation. He kisses her again when they get back and asks her if he can call her, and Cate says yes.

Cate is eager to get back home, so she packs up Celeste's toys and books and takes her back home to their apartment. After lunch, Cate tucks Celeste in for her afternoon nap and gets out her journal.

Wow, I can hardly believe the series of events that have unfolded. First Michael reminded me John is still interested in me and told me I should be thinking about dating again. Then Diane said I should consider what I want in a man and write out a list. I imagined John's name in golden handwriting. And then last night. The way John looked at me when I walked into the music hall, there was no denying he's still interested. When he kissed me good night, it was short, but intense. When he kissed me this morning, it was long and luscious. Who would have thought?

It feels so strange. He's always had a crush on me, but I thought it was just that, a crush. He's been the neighbour. Michael's friend. The chess geek. The engineering nerd. But then, as Diane pointed out, maybe it's time to give up going for the bad boys who need fixing. When I think of some of the things I wrote on my list, he certainly fits the bill. He's responsible and smart. When he graduates from engineering, he'll likely score a good job easy enough. And he's from a good family. Maybe something is unfolding. I hope Billy will be okay with it. Even though we've been broken up for almost a year now and he's moved in with his latest girlfriend, he can still be so possessive of me. And he'll always be Celeste's father. But I'm getting way, way ahead of myself.

By the beginning of October, John and Cate have officially started dating. Everyone seems to approve, even Billy.

Cate wants to take it slow. She is focused on her education and doesn't want to send conflicting messages to Celeste. She only invites John over when Celeste is asleep or having a sleepover at Cate's parents'. But John is adamant he wants to be a part of Celeste's life too. They've only been dating a month when they have their first big fight.

"I don't know why you have to be so intense," John says, his voice rising, his cheeks flushed red. "I don't see what harm there is in including Celeste once in a while. If I'm going to be her dad—"

"Hold the phone and whoa a minute," Cate says, holding her hand up like a crossing guard. "I've already told you a million times. We've just started dating. It's way too early to be talking about being her dad. She already has a dad."

"That fuck-up? What kind of dad has he been? He's never around. I bet he doesn't even help you out financially. And we may not have been dating long, but I've known you forever."

"What Billy does or doesn't do is none of your business," Cate says. "If you can't accept my rules, perhaps we should just break up."

"Break up?" John is yelling now. "Where the fuck did that come from?"

"Lower your voice." Cate turns her back to him and starts folding the basket of clean clothes on the counter, trying her best to stay calm.

John grabs her by the arm, hard, and yanks her back to face him. He towers over her, a full foot taller. "Are you listening to me?"

"No, I'm not, because you're yelling," Cate says. "Let go of my arm. I think it's time for you to go."

"Hey, c'mon, it's okay, I'm sorry." John shakes his head and his voice mellows to silky soft. "I didn't mean to let my temper get the best of me. I just want so much to make you happy, to be a family." He takes Cate's hand and lifts it to his mouth for a soft kiss. "Forgive me? We don't have to do anything until you're ready, I promise."

Cate can't switch gears so easily. "If you're going to criticize Billy and be so damn pushy, it's never going to work," she says. She is too worked up to forgive John in the moment. "I need some time to cool down. Please, John, just leave." She points at the door.

"You're way overreacting," John says. He tries to regain his composure as he fumbles for his shoes. "I'll go, but I'm not giving up that easily."

John leaves a litany of long voice messages on Cate's machine all the next week. He pops by the cubicle where he knows Cate likes to study and drops off love notes. When Cate is having coffee with Diane at the cafeteria, he shows up with flowers. By the end of the week, she has all but forgotten the reasons for their disagreement and is ready to make up.

When John calls the next time, Cate invites him to come over after Celeste's bath to be a part of storytime. He looks smitten as he turns the pages and reads the story with enthusiasm, giving different voices to the various characters.

After Cate tucks Celeste into bed, they go into the living room. Cate opens a bottle of wine and pours them each a glass. John has a few sips, then moves from his spot on the chair opposite Cate to the empty space beside her on the loveseat. He leans in and kisses her while his hand reaches for her breast.

"I want you," John says, his words husky. "Can we move this into your room?"

"Okay, but we need to be quiet," Cate says. "I don't want to wake Celeste."

John puts his finger to his lips and makes a point of exaggerating his tiptoe steps. He closes Cate's door and wastes no time in removing her clothes, then his. He takes her hand and leads it to his hard penis.

"Will you go down on me?" John asks. "I want to watch you do it, in the mirror."

"Okay," Cate says. She grabs a pillow off her bed to rest her knees on. John is well-endowed, and she can't take in all of him. When she pulls away a little, he grabs her by her hair and presses her face into him. Cate starts to choke, but he doesn't release his hold. Cate pushes away from him with her full force, then stands up.

"What the hell is your problem?" Cate says, a little louder than she intended. "You were gagging me."

"I, uh, I'm sorry." John looks as though he is waking from a dream. He shakes his head. "I guess I got a little carried away, it, you, felt so good."

"Yeah, well, you didn't feel good at all," Cate says. "I think you should go now."

John leaves, but not until after they've had another big fight. Cate crawls into bed, shaken and confused. As she drifts off, in her half-asleep state, she sees a wolf at her window. His green eyes stare with a sinister expression and then he opens his mouth in a slobbery grin, revealing sharp, white teeth. Cate startles, terrified. She hasn't thought of the wolf in years. She shivers as an uneasy feeling travels up her spine. A feeling of urgency comes over that she can't explain. She pushes into her slippers and goes to Celeste's room. She is sound asleep and looks so peaceful. Cate breathes a sigh of relief. She kisses her daughter lightly on her forehead and goes back to her room but sleeps fitfully for the rest of the night.

Cate wakes up super early, before Celeste, a feeling of unease still with her. She decides she needs to process her feelings, and gets out her journal.

> *I'm so confused. John can be so polar. One minute he's kind and loving, the next self-centred and demanding. I never know what to expect. It doesn't make any sense. After all, I saw his name, clearly. In golden handwriting. Maybe it's his inexperience with sex that's the problem? He told me he's a virgin. Maybe I just need to teach him how to be more present and engaged with me? Maybe I need to show him? But then again, perhaps he's into that aggressive bullshit. I've heard about S&M. If that's true, I'll have to break up with him, for good. There's no place for stuff like that with me. So many questions.*
>
> *And then there's the appearance of the wolf at my window. That's what has me the most rattled. I don't know what it means. Does it mean John is a transformer? It seems unlikely. Michael knows him so well. Maybe his behaviour triggered something old that's been dormant inside of me? Maybe I'm the one who's fucked up? But then, I never felt anything like this when I was with Billy. I pray that I will find the answers, that I will know what to do.*

Cate is so busy with end-of-term exams and final essays, she forgets all about John and her vision of the wolf. When the Christmas break starts, Donna invites Cate and Celeste over to bake sugar cookies, decorate the tree, and have a sleepover.

"I've invited John and his parents over for a small Christmas Eve gathering after church," Donna says as she scrapes down the sides of the icing bowl. "Would you like to invite Diane? Or perhaps Rose or Tripti?"

"John?" Cate drops the rolling pin on her finger. "Ouch, there I go again, clumsy ol' Cate."

"Yes, John. You're back together again, aren't you?" Donna pauses from her task to look Cate in the eye.

"I guess so," Cate says with a sigh. "I have to admit, it can be such a rollercoaster with him. You and Dad are always so steady."

"All couples have arguments and things they disagree on, including your father and I. But we choose to keep those discussions private."

"Yes, well, in that light, let's change the subject," Cate says with a nod of her head in Celeste's direction. "What can I bring to the party?"

On Christmas Eve, Cate packs up overnight bags for her and Celeste. Celeste dances around the tiny kitchen of their apartment in her new black patent shoes, dazzled by the bows and ribbons on her new dress, an early present from Billy.

"I so esited for the party," Celeste says. "Did you see all the pwesents under Dramma and Drampa's twee?"

"Yes, I did," Cate says. "But you know Christmas is about a lot more than presents."

"Uh huh," Celeste says. "It's Jesus was born and tooties and singing. I so esited."

"I am too, angel. Go and grab your toothbrush from the bathroom, and don't forget to pack your favourite stuffy and then we'll be ready to go."

After the church service, Cate and Celeste walk up the sidewalk to Cate's childhood home, leaving footprints in the newly fallen snow. Her dad has already turned on the outdoor lights, and the decorated artificial tree in the bay window twinkles.

Cate has just stowed away their overnight bags when the doorbell rings. She overhears John announcing his entrance with a "merry Christmas."

She walks into the front entrance to see John with a stack of gifts a mile high. She takes them and sets them under the tree. John's parents arrive right after, followed soon by Diane. Michael leads the assembly in singing Christmas carols, accompanied by their mother on the piano. The drinks are flowing and Cate is feeling happy. John is being nothing short of a gentleman, helping William to pour drinks and playing with Celeste. Before Cate takes Celeste off to bed, John helps her set out cookies and milk for Santa, along with the customary carrots for the reindeer.

"I hope Santa brings you everything you asked for," John says to Celeste.

"It's time for a certain little girl to head to bed," Cate says. "C'mon then."

"But Mommy, I too esited to sleep," Celeste says with a yawn, her eyelids drooping.

"It will be morning before you know it," Cate says.

The party carries on for a few more hours, with games of charades that have everyone in stitches.

"Well, I hate to be the first one to throw in the towel," Cate says as she gathers up her empty eggnog glass and plate of half-eaten goodies. "But that little one of mine is an early bird."

She's in the kitchen, scraping her plate into the trash can, when John sidles up behind her and presses close.

"I hope we can start fresh," John says. "And I don't want to wait for the New Year. I know I've been a complete dolt, but I love you, Cate. I want to learn how to be the man you need me to be, and I think I can, if you're willing to teach me."

Cate turns around to face him, tears welling.

"Okay. I'm willing to give us another try." She blinks the tears back.

"That's the best Christmas gift I could have asked for." John leans in and kisses her, softly. "I know you guys have your family Christmas traditions tomorrow, but can I take you to a holiday movie on Boxing Day?"

"Yeah, that sounds like fun. I'll see if Mom and Dad can look after Celeste."

"I was thinking a family movie, that all three of us could go to," John says, a hurt look on face.

"John, please don't start up already," Cate says. "And besides, Celeste is far too young to go to the movies. You've seen for yourself, she can't sit still for more than ten minutes. Let's go see something romantic, just the two of us."

"Okay," John says. "Good night and merry Christmas."

The rollercoaster that is her relationship with John continues in the new year, despite John's promises. He's loving and attentive one minute, controlling and dismissive the next. Cate isn't sure how or when it happens, but somewhere along the way she convinces herself that she's happy.

John graduates in the spring and accepts a job working in the oil sands in Northern Alberta. He knows full well that Cate still has a year before she's done school and accepting the job will mean living in separate cities, an eight-hour drive between them.

"There's so much to celebrate," John says, in one of his expansive moods. He's stretched out on Cate's sofa. "I'm going to make so much money at this new job, I want to take you away for a tropical vacation somewhere. What do you think?"

"That's very generous of you," Cate says. "I can't contribute much at all. And then there would be the issue of child care for Celeste. How long were you thinking?"

"I don't know, maybe a week or two," John says, sitting up. "Does this mean you're interested? That you'll consider it?"

"Yeah, it sounds amazing. I've never gone anywhere before, except camping trips or to Peachland and Winnipeg to visit family. I haven't been in a plane since Mom and Dad splurged on our trip to Disneyland. That was forever ago."

"And you're cool with leaving Celeste?" John jumps up off the couch. "I can hardly believe my ears. I was sure you'd say no."

"Don't get too excited yet," Cate says. But his enthusiasm is contagious. "I still have to ask my parents and—"

"I'm going to call the travel agent right away." John is already making his way to the phone.

John books them an all-inclusive, ten-day holiday at a resort in Playa Cozumel, Mexico. Cate's parents agree to take care of Celeste, with support from the daycare and Michael. Even Billy agrees to lend a hand.

On the day of the departure, Celeste cries at the airport. Cate feels like her heart is going to break in half. She's never left Celeste for more than a night before.

"My angel, don't cry." Cate crouches down to look Celeste in the eye. She strokes her cheek. "Mommy will be back in ten sleeps, and you're going to have so much fun at Grandma and Grandpa's."

"Don't doe, Mommy." Celeste cries even harder.

"Go on, now," William says, taking Celeste by the hand. "You know she'll be fine as soon as you leave. She's in good hands."

"I know, I know," Cate says.

"Yes, it's time," John says. He takes Cate by the arm and grabs her suitcase, then leads her through the entrance for departures. Cate turns and waves to Celeste and her mom and dad, feeling as though a part of her body has been severed.

Once they land in Mexico and get settled into their suite, Cate embraces the fun energy of the tropics. John takes her on several excursions. She tries snorkelling for the first time in her life, in a bay where the water is so clear she can see schools of brightly coloured fish all around her. They ride a hot, stuffy, over-crowded bus to the Mayan ruins and climb the ancient crumbling stone stairs. But what Cate loves most is relaxing on the beach caressed by the hot, humid air. The time seems to fly by and soon it is the last night of their holiday.

"I've planned a romantic candle-lit picnic on the beach tonight, if that suits you," John says.

Cate is lying on her navy and white striped towel, clad in a polka-dot bikini, her skin bronzed and glowing with tanning oil. She puts down her book, *Kane and Abel*, by Jeffrey Archer. "That sounds lovely. What time?"

"I was thinking around five thirty, before the sun sets. I want you to leave everything to me. All you have to do is show up. You should wear that sexy black sundress with the low neckline, with nothing on underneath."

"Sounds like you've got it all planned out," Cate says with a smile.

At five Cate trudges up the stone steps that lead from the beach, through the common area of the resort, then up to their room. John is rustling about in the tiny kitchenette.

"I'm going in for a shower," Cate calls out. She heads into the bathroom without waiting for a reply and turns on the taps. It takes a few minutes for the heat to come on. Once the water is tepid, she steps inside the cramped enclosure and lathers soap across her breasts, thinking about John's request for her to wear nothing under her dress. Her nipples are hard and she feels moist between her legs. The glass panels of the shower are steamy and Cate feels in a dream as she moves her hand down.

When she steps out onto the bath mat, the mirror is so fogged up she can't see a thing. She swipes a spot clear so she can put in her contacts. She blow-dries her hair, applies some mascara and lip gloss, then goes into the bedroom to slip into her sundress. It feels very naughty to be wearing nothing underneath, and she's aroused again.

John has put a great effort into creating an inviting space. He has spread out the colourful handwoven blanket he purchased at one of the markets. Hundreds of tea lights surround the space like a shrine. A bottle of champagne sits on a bed of ice in a silver bucket in the centre, and a wicker picnic basket is off to the side in the sand. Cate sits down where a folded linen napkin marks her place and sighs with contentment.

"This is absolutely beautiful," Cate says. "Thank you so much. These ten days have felt like paradise, and I'm so grateful."

"I think that statement deserves a toast." John pops the cork and pours them both a glass of champagne. "To the first of many exotic adventures."

"The first of many?" Cate says, clinking her glass with John's. "Sounds like you're thinking well into the future."

"You must be reading my mind." John can barely suppress his excited energy. "Why don't you spread out your napkin and I'll serve you some fresh lobster for the first course?"

Cate picks up her napkin. There is a ring box hidden underneath.

"What's this?" Her hand goes to her throat as the words seem to catch.

"I'm sure you know," John says with a grin. "Go ahead, open it."

Cate opens the box to find an engagement ring nestled inside the velvet enclosure. It sparkles in the light of the candles.

"Well, what do you say, Cate Henderson? Will you marry me?"

Cate wants to say yes, and yet she hesitates.

"Cate? You will marry me, won't you? I love you and I love Celeste and I want to spend the rest of my life with both of you, as a family."

"Yes, John," Cate says after a moment. "I will."

The gorgeous meal that John has put together stays mostly untouched. John moves in closer to Cate and slides his hand up her dress. He opens her legs wider and rubs her sweet spot. Cate moans and John lowers his head. They make love on the sand under a moonlit sky.

Back in their room, John conks off to sleep as soon as his head hits the pillow, his body still encrusted with pebbles of sand. Cate is wide awake, her mind spinning. She gets out her journal and tiptoes over to the chair by the window to write.

> *Well, I've done it. For the second time in my life, I've accepted a marriage proposal. I wonder, will this one end differently? Will there be a wedding? Or will John end up abandoning me and Celeste too? It seems unfortunate to be having such thoughts, so soon. But that's how I feel. Scared shitless. What have I just committed to? I can imagine spending my life with the John who has shown up every day since we've been here in Mexico. It's been so magical. But I can't seem to put out of my mind all the fights or the many times he's come to my bed and been aggressive. He's always sorry after and begs my forgiveness. And then it happens again. Usually, he's had too much to drink. I asked him if he would consider giving up alcohol, but he practically lost it, telling me I'm a control freak. Maybe I am. Maybe it wouldn't matter if Prince Charming*

*himself asked me to marry him. I'd still be fucked-up
me, who can't tolerate the slightest rough gesture. John
tells me what he wants is all perfectly normal. That
when it's between two consenting adults, anything goes.
That it turns him on when he pins me down or ties my
wrists to the headboard. I've tried to explain that it
brings up past experiences that were painful for me,
but he doesn't listen.*

*I hate that these are my thoughts, tonight of all
nights. I need to tuck away this negativity and focus on
the positives. He's been generous and giving this whole
holiday. Maybe he is willing to change for me. Maybe
this is the first step on a new journey.*

When they get back from Mexico, John can hardly wait to
show everyone the ring on Cate's finger and share the good
news. Cate is a ball of nerves as they walk together up the
front steps to her parents' house.

"We're home!" Cate calls out from the front entrance.

"Mommy!" Celeste squeals. She runs over and throws
herself against Cate's legs. "I missed you so much!"

"I missed you too, angel," Cate says, as her father shuffles
into the room, followed by her mother and Michael.

"How perfect, everyone is home," John says. "Cate has
something special she brought back with her to show you,
right, Cate?"

"Yes, er, I do." He has caught her a little off guard, not
wasting any time.

"Go ahead, show them," John says. He gives her a
little nudge.

"Show us what?" William asks.

"We got engaged," Cate says as she holds out her left hand, tanned against the sparkle of her diamond ring.

"Wow," Celeste says. She looks at the ring with awe. "What is endajed?"

"It means your mom and I are going to be married." John digs into the side of his carry-on and produces a replica of the box that Cate's ring was in. "And don't worry, I didn't forget about you."

Everyone looks shocked, stunned into silence as John bends down on one knee in front of Celeste and opens the box to reveal a gold ring that is just the right size for a little girl's finger.

"Can I be your daddy too?" John asks.

"Two daddies?" Celeste says. She turns to Cate.

"Yes," Cate says with a weak smile. "If John and I get married, you'll have two daddies."

"If?" John says. "I think you meant to say 'when.'"

Everyone starts talking over one another with excitement as they clamour to hear about Mexico and to plan the wedding. The conversation goes by in a blur for Cate. She looks over at one point and sees Celeste gazing with bright eyes at her ring. *I guess it doesn't matter that John didn't ask me first,* she thinks to herself. *Celeste is clearly thrilled, as is the rest of my family. This is what I said I wanted. Maybe everything is going to be all right.*

Chapter 12

*I*N THE FALL OF 1987, John is still living up north, working at the oil sands project, and Cate is starting her final year of university. John makes the eight-hour drive to Calgary twice a month, having a three-day weekend every second week. Cate is so busy, with a full course load plus her practicum and teaching preparation tasks, she barely has time to miss him in between.

Three weeks before the end of first-term exams, Cate's parents are helping out with child care for Celeste. Donna has insisted that Cate take a break from her studies to join them for dinner, and everyone is gathered in the kitchen.

"It sure will be nice when I use a can opener again," William says through gritted teeth. He's clutching the opener in an awkward grip, the can of brown beans pressed up to his torso for leverage.

"What do you mean, 'when'?" Cate walks over and takes the can and opens it easily.

"I imagine he means when he is fully recovered from his surgery," her mom says.

"Surgery?" Cate drops the opener on the counter and turns around.

"William, have you still not told her?"

"I've meant to. But she's been up to her neck in school work. There just never seemed like a good opportunity."

"It's okay, Dad. I understand. I assume it's for your hand?" Cate picks up her father's gnarled right hand and kisses his knuckle. "I was so hoping the methotrexate you started taking would help, but I guess it's been another fail. When is the surgery scheduled for?"

"Unfortunately, they slated me in just a few days before Christmas, on Tuesday the twenty-second." He rubs his knuckles. "I'll be laid up over the holidays, sorry to say."

"That timing is perfect," Cate says, putting her arm around him. "My last exam is that Monday. Celeste and I can come and stay over for the two weeks of term break and help you and Mom while you recover."

"I would love that," her dad says. "Having you and Celeste here will help lift my spirits, especially now with Michael in Toronto. It's so quiet here, just your mother and I."

"Yes, and I'll appreciate having you to enforce the post-op rules," her mom chimes in. "You know how well your father listens to me."

Cate doesn't waste any time. As soon as the dinner dishes are cleared up, she sits down beside her daughter at the kitchen table and begins to scratch out a post-operation recovery plan for her father.

William's day surgery is at the Foothills Hospital. It is a complicated procedure, with the surgeon performing both a finger fusion and a total knuckle replacement on his right hand.

On the morning of the surgery, William and Donna head out early, with Celeste and Cate waving from the front step. A chinook blew in the day before. Cate notices piles of mud and slush beginning to form. She hopes the warm afternoon sun will have the snow and ice melted, making her task of clearing the driveway easier.

Once they've left, Cate enlists Celeste's help in preparing meals, as well as some of her grandpa's favourite baked goods.

"When Grandpa gets home, he'll have a splint over his hand and wrist, so you'll have to be extra careful."

Celeste is counting chocolate chips and raisins as she places them in a measuring cup. "I will, Mommy. Grandpa and I are going to watch all the holiday specials together."

"That sounds perfect. Grandpa is lucky to have a girl as special as you around. Maybe we can stop in at the video store later and pick out a few movies too."

"Thanks, Mommy," Celeste says with a smile. "I love Grandpa so much. I hope he gets better real soon, and that his hand works better after too."

"It will take quite a while, maybe three months to totally heal. But yes, we're all praying that Grandpa's surgery will be a success."

Abby is the first one to hear the garage door opening and runs to the front entrance, her tail wagging. Celeste follows, with Cate right behind her.

"Welcome home, Grandpa. Mommy and I made homemade chicken soup and Jell-O! And Mommy fixed up a spot for you on the couch, with extra pillows and a blanket!"

"You two are the best." William winces and smiles weakly as he steps into the entrance and wipes his shoes on the mat. "It smells delicious in here. And I noticed the driveway all cleared too." He tries to remove his coat with only his left arm in the sleeve.

"Let me help you with that," Cate says.

"Thank you, Caty-bug." He groans and wiggles his good arm while Cate gives his coat a good tug.

"Does it hurt, Grandpa?" Celeste's brows furrow as she takes in William's splint, which runs from his hand up to his elbow. White cotton bandages are wrapped around it, and some blood has seeped through, from his incisions.

"Only a little," he says. "Watching a good show on TV with my favourite granddaughter will help distract me."

William struggles to get settled on the couch that Cate has made all cozy. He sets his arm carefully on one of the cushions, then notices the glass with a straw on the end table.

"What's this?"

"Mommy bought ginger ale. And she thought it might be easier, since you have to use your left hand, if she bought some straws."

"My mouth does feel dry as a bone," William says. "Do you mind passing it to me? Then you can fetch the TV guide and see if there's anything good on." He pets Abby, who is curled in a ball at the foot of the couch.

"We don't have to check what's on TV. Mommy and I picked out two videos at Blockbuster." Celeste points to the TV stand. "Which one do you want to watch first, *A Muppet Family Christmas* or *It's a Wonderful Life*?"

"Ooh, that's a tough choice." He rubs his chin. "Those Muppet characters tickle my funny bone, but *A Wonderful Life* is a classic. You choose."

"Okay, Grandpa, I choose the Muppets. I want your funny bone to be tickled."

On Christmas Eve, John drives back to Calgary to stay with his parents for his two weeks of Christmas holidays. He calls Cate to see if her dad is up for having a visitor, then, true to form, shows up with a stack of gifts for under the tree. Cate's mom brings out a plate of Christmas baking once John is seated in the living room, and everyone gathers around to share their latest news.

"It was so cold when I left Fort McMurray," John says with an exaggerated shrug of his shoulders. "My car wouldn't even warm up until I got past Edmonton. I had to wear my parka and cover the grill with cardboard. The radio said it was minus fifty-four with the wind chill, if you can believe it."

"Brr, that does sound frigid," William says. "I suppose it's nice to be back home for a bit of a reprieve, especially with this warm chinook weather. How are things at work?"

"It's a great experience from a professional point of view," John says. "Quite challenging. And of course, the pay is phenomenal. But I miss these two like crazy."

"Yes, well, speaking of these two." William nods his head toward Cate and Celeste. "Cate's on the home stretch now, about to graduate herself. What's going to happen then? Are you going to keep living apart? Or do you expect Cate to look for work up there? And when are you two going to set a date for your wedding anyway?"

"Whoa, Dad, enough with the drill sergeant," Cate says. "It's still early to make these decisions. John and I haven't figured any of that out yet."

"Well, I think it's high time you put some thought into it," her father says.

"I couldn't agree more," John says. "I haven't had a chance to talk to Cate about it, but I was hoping to convince her to move in with me after she graduates. With the teacher surplus in Calgary, I bet she'll have a better chance of getting a job up north, where they always need teachers. As to a wedding date, I'd like to save some more money first, so I can buy Cate and Celeste fancy gowns and rent a huge hall and have a grand honeymoon too."

"Sounds like you've got it all planned out," Cate says.

"And that's very responsible of you, John," her father says with a nod of his head. "I'm glad you're considering the financial end of things. My girls deserve to be spoiled."

"What's a fancy gown?" Celeste asks.

"It's just a different name for a dress that's for special occasions," Cate says.

"Yes, and I want yours to be a miniature replica of your mommy's," John says. "Maybe we can go to some bridal shops while I'm in town?"

"That sounds fun!" Celeste says.

"Yes, well, we can talk about that later," Cate says. "It's Christmas Eve and it's getting late. We still need to get Santa's cookies out and write him a note. And I'm sure Grandpa is past ready for bed too. I think it's time to say good night, John."

"It is getting late," John says with a glance at his watch. "Cate, you can walk me out?"

Cate takes John by the arm and leads him to the door.

"I hope you're as excited to start planning our future as I am," John says. He bends down to kiss Cate, not waiting for a response. "Good night, Cate. I'll be by tomorrow afternoon, in plenty of time for Christmas dinner."

Once Celeste is tucked into bed, Cate gets out her journal to write in the dim glow of the night light, feeling a little overwhelmed.

> *My head is spinning. It's exciting to think about wedding plans and moving in together after all this time, but I didn't appreciate John sharing his thoughts with Mom and Dad and Celeste before running it by me first. Sometimes he's so damn impulsive. He doesn't stop to think how it will affect Celeste if he doesn't follow through. Often his big plans fall flat. I really can't fathom the idea of moving to Fort McMurray. From John's own description, it sounds like a frozen ice sculpture for six long months of winter and a massive mosquito and blackfly infestation in summer. I can't imagine moving away from my mom and dad. They support me and Celeste so much. But I suppose, when John and I get married, things will change. He'll become more involved. Still, there's Dad's ongoing struggle with RA. He hasn't had one remission yet. And who knows how effective this surgery will be. The doctor warned us that it has a high complication and failure rate. And his left hand is almost as bad, not to mention his poor feet. I don't know how he walks on those inflamed metatarsals of his. I can't imagine abandoning him. It's a lot to consider. The last thing I need right now are distractions like shopping for dresses.*

It's just like John to drop a bomb like this over a family gathering, just as I'm about to enter my final semester of school. In two weeks, he'll bugger off, and I'll be the one left holding all the pieces. I bet he has no idea how much work it is to pull off a big wedding. And who said I want a big wedding anyhow?

Wow. I'm really on a tangent, going in circles. I should be happy. I am. I guess. But I'm not ready to make all of these big decisions.

I'm not looking forward to discussing this with him tomorrow. I hope he doesn't lose his temper. God, what a mess, I feel so much stress, too much pressure. I feel like I'm drowning and there isn't a lifeboat in sight, no end to my fright, of a fight. Good night, sleep tight, time to turn out the light.

John gets a bit sulky when Cate tells him it's too soon to make plans, that she wants to focus on school, but in the end, he concedes without too much drama. They spend most of the Christmas vacation over at her parents', watching movies and playing board games. A trip to the zoo's Winter Wonderland gets thrown in. When it's time for John to drive back to Fort McMurray and for Cate's classes to resume, her dad has had his stitches removed from his right hand and is adjusting to using it quite well. Cate and Celeste settle back in their apartment and into their routines. The months seem to fly by, and before Cate knows it, she's written her final exam.

"I suppose now that you're finished school we can talk about our plans," John says one night over the phone. "Have you given any more thought to moving up here?"

"I only finished yesterday, for God's sake," Cate says. "But to be honest, I have been thinking about it. It probably would be easier to find a job, but I don't know if I'm prepared to leave Mom and Dad."

"You need to get out from under their shadow one of these days. You still haven't cut your apron strings, and you're twenty-two years old. I don't think you should let that deter you. Even Michael has taken wing and flown the coop."

"Yes, well, Michael doesn't have a child, does he?"

"When we're a real family, I'll take up where they leave off. Maybe moving is just the push you need."

When John arrives for his bimonthly weekend visit the following week, he asks Cate if he can stay with her instead of with his parents, and she agrees. Cate is busy writing a rough draft of her resumé, and Celeste is playing with her Barbies on the living room floor while John watches his favourite television program.

"Speaking of resumés," he says on a commercial. "I've applied to a few architectural and engineering firms in Calgary."

"What?" Cate says. "That's great news!"

"Yes, well, I've only just applied," John says. "I don't have any offers yet. I thought it might be a nice compromise if you apply with both the Calgary and Fort McMurray school boards. Then we can make a decision based on what opportunities come up for both of us."

"That sounds very reasonable," Cate says.

"I don't want to move," Celeste says. "I want to start kindergarten with Gillian."

"We haven't made any decisions yet, angel," Cate says.

"What I want to know is when are you getting married?" Celeste says. She looks at the ring John gave her.

"I'd like to know the answer to that one too," says John. "I think we should pick a date for next summer. We can plan to have the wedding in Calgary, regardless of where we are living. That way it will be easier for all our family and friends to attend."

"What do you think, Celeste?" Cate asks. "Should we pick a date for next summer?"

"Yes, please!" Celeste says.

John and Cate set their wedding date for the second Saturday in August, the following summer. They both get job offers in Calgary, and John moves in with Cate and Celeste in their small apartment. John's work is downtown, Cate's school is in the far northeast, and Celeste's kindergarten is across the street from her daycare. It's a bit of a challenge to get their schedules sorted out, but they manage to develop a routine of sorts. Living under the same roof 24-7, Cate realizes how quickly and frequently John's moods can shift.

"What the hell?" John storms into the living room where Cate and Celeste are snuggled up on the couch reading one of the books Cate wrote for Celeste. "You haven't even started making dinner yet? You two have been home for hours, and I'm starved!"

"Lower your voice, please," Cate says. She strokes Celeste's cheek. "I had an emotionally exhausting day at work. The little girl I told you about who has fetal alcohol syndrome was really struggling, and—"

"I don't give a shit about some girl in your class," John says.

"John, really, mind your language."

"Is 'shit' a bad word?" Celeste asks innocently.

"Now see what you've done?" Cate seethes. She gets up off the couch. "Honestly, John, how on earth did you manage when you lived on your own? It's not my job to wait on you hand and foot. You're perfectly capable of making your own damn supper."

"Now who's using profanity? And it isn't about being capable, it's about you not being thoughtful."

"You can't be serious," Cate says. "That's the kettle calling the other kettle black."

"There you go again, mixing up your metaphors," John says. It's 'the pot calling the kettle black.'"

"Whatever, you know what I mean. If ever there was someone who wasn't thoughtful—"

"I know," says Celeste, her voice rising above the din. "Why don't we go to McDonald's for dinner?"

"That's a great idea, Celeste," John says. "I'll go change out of my work clothes while you and Mommy go pick up some takeout."

"Okay then, let's go," Cate says. She snatches her purse and jams her feet into her shoes, crushing the heels, then lets the door slam with a loud bang.

Cate is uncharacteristically quiet on the drive, but Celeste is too excited about her Happy Meal, a rare treat, to notice. When they get back home with their paper bags of food, John is watching television and appears to have showered off his bad mood, but Cate is short with him for the duration of the evening. She feigns a headache. As soon as she's tucked Celeste into bed she goes into their room and closes the door. She gets out her journal.

> *It's more than anger, deeper than sadness, this feeling I have, of built-up resentment. We're not even*

*married, yet already John seems to take our relationship
for granted. He has unrealistic expectations. But it's
worse than that. He can be such a self-centred
chauvinist pig. I hate feeling like this. Sometimes I just
want to run away and start over. Just me and Celeste.
Then, just when I'm feeling ready to throw in the towel
and jump ship, John will do or say something so
incredibly sweet, all my resolve seems to disappear
in a puff of smoke. The ties just keep getting stronger,
especially now that we're living together. We've put
the deposit down on the hall for the wedding reception.
Celeste and I have picked out our dresses and they're
at the seamstress's for alterations. Last weekend John
announced he wants us to buy a house, and we went
to a few open houses. Celeste has even started calling
him Dad. How on earth do I turn things around now?*

*I was watching Oprah the other day and her guest
was Gary Chapman. He wrote a book called* The Five
Love Languages. *It sounded really interesting. Perhaps
this weekend I'll pick us each up a copy and suggest
we do a book study together. Mom says all relationships
have ups and downs, that all couples have to work at it.*

*I feel better already, just writing my feelings out.
I'm going to bury my resentment hatchet and start
fresh with John, with a new attitude, tomorrow.*

Somehow the year flies by, as time often seems to do when
you're busy, and before Cate knows it, the day of their
wedding arrives. Diane is her maid of honour and Tripti and
Rose are both bridesmaids. Michael has flown in from
Toronto with his girlfriend, Ashley. He is John's best man

and two of John's other friends from university that Cate hardly knows are his groomsmen.

Celeste and Cate sleep over at her parents' the night before so they can surprise John at the church. Michael and the other guys are all staying over at Cate and John's house, a brand new two-storey in a community on the western edge of the city.

"Mommy, how many hours is it until the wedding?" Celeste asks as she glides into the kitchen. She does a pirouette and spins around, her favourite move since she started ballet classes.

"Celeste, that is the zillionth time you've asked me," Cate says, with a roll of her eyes. She looks at her watch. "There's still three more hours, but it is lunch time. What would you like me to make? Grilled cheese sandwiches or Kraft Dinner?"

"My tummy is too rumbly to eat," Celeste says. "Can I watch *The Little Mermaid*?"

"You need to eat something or you'll never make it until dinner. But yes, you can put on *The Little Mermaid*. I'll make you a snack-lunch that you can nibble on while you watch."

Celeste does another spin and goes up on her toes, then does a plié before disappearing into the living room to put the video on. Cate finds her father in the kitchen, shining his black patent shoes to a military sheen.

Cate goes over and gives him a hug. "Need any help with that?"

"I'm almost done. But I could use some help getting my orthotics in place. It's so awkward with my damn ol' bent-out-of-shape hands."

"Okay, no problem. I'm going to put together a few snacks for Celeste and me. Can I make up a plate for you and Mom?"

"That would be great, thank you." William gathers up his polishing kit and washes his hands at the kitchen sink. "I was just thinking about having a bite to eat."

After lunch and the movie Celeste is ready for Cate to do her hair. Cate pulls Celeste's long dark chestnut strands into plaits to create a French braid. She weaves in some baby's breath and clasps on the pearl barrette they bought at Claire's.

"You look absolutely stunning, my angel," Cate says. "Now all that's left to do is get dressed."

Cate and Celeste put on their matching traditional, floor-length lace dresses and then meet up with Cate's parents and the wedding photographer in the front room.

"Wow," William says with a whistle. "Look at our gorgeous girls."

"Do you really think so?" Celeste asks with a twirl and curtsy.

"I know so," he says. "You're picture perfect. Now all you have to do is smile for the camera."

On the way to the church a half-hour later, Celeste can hardly sit still. She squirms on the leather seat of the black town car they've rented. She twirls the ring on her finger and looks out the window, then batters Cate with questions.

"It's all going to be just like we practiced at the rehearsal," Cate says. "Only a few more people. Nothing to be nervous about."

"Daddy said more than three hundred of the guests we invited said yes," Celeste says. "That's way more than a few."

"That's true. But they are mostly family from his side that we don't even know. Try to stay focused. Smile your beautiful smile and enjoy yourself."

"I hope I don't trip or forget my words," Celeste says, twisting the handle on her mini clutch purse.

"You won't. But if you do, it's no big deal. We'll just carry on."

William pipes up from the front. "Grandpa will keep you steady. And before you know it, the formal part will be done."

"Yes, and the photo shoot will be fun, since it's all outdoors, and it's such a gorgeous day," Donna chimes in. "After dinner, it's the dance. You've been excited about that for weeks now."

At the church, Cate's parents escort her and Celeste to the bridal room, and then Donna goes to sit in the front pew. Grandpa holds Celeste's hand until they hear the music to signal that it's time for them to walk down the aisle. Cate takes her place on the other side, and the three of them make their way to the front of the church where John is standing with his groomsmen. Michael winks at Celeste and her smile lights up the room. Cameras flash and the congregation stares. Then they're at the front and William is giving his daughter and granddaughter to John and taking his seat beside his wife.

"We're gathered here today to witness the joining of three people who are coming together as a family," the minister says with a smile in Celeste's direction. "We'll begin with the traditional exchange of vows between man and wife, followed by a not-so-traditional recitation with young Celeste."

After the ceremony, the bridal party is ushered into a backroom to sign the official papers. Cate is keeping Henderson as her surname. She wants to have the same last name as Celeste. Her decision caused some friction with John initially, who wanted them both to take Downing, but after a few heated arguments he let it go.

"Is it almost time for the dance?" Celeste asks on the drive to the park where they're having the formal photos taken. She's squished in the back of the decorated bridal car, sandwiched in between John and Cate.

"Only a few more hours," Cate says.

"Well, how does it feel to be married and now a real family?" John asks.

"No different at all," Celeste and Cate say at the same time. Celeste bursts out laughing.

"We were already a family," Cate says.

"And my real daddy says he'll always be my daddy too," Celeste says. "He says families don't always look the same, but it's what's in your heart that matters. Some kids don't have a mom, some don't have a dad. Some are even orphans, or live with their aunts or grandparents. But lucky me, I have two daddies."

"That's because you're extra special," Cate says, as she puts her arm around her daughter. She can't help but notice the hurt look on John's face. "And I feel lucky too, to have you," she says to him.

John's smile returns and he leans over to kiss Cate, but then he turns his face away to stare out the window in quiet contemplation.

After the photo shoot they climb back into the car and drive to the hall. Their guests have already begun to arrive. John's mother has requested that the bridal party have a traditional receiving line. With three hundred guests, it's a lot of standing around shaking hands with virtual strangers, especially for Celeste.

"There are a few people who want to congratulate this beautiful young lady," Cate's dad whispers to her as he walks over and reaches for Celeste's hand. Then, to Celeste, he adds, "Your great-grandma Henderson has driven out all the way from Winnipeg. She hasn't seen you since just after you were born."

"The procession isn't finished yet," John says, a bit more curtly than necessary.

"That's okay," Cate says. "She's hung in long enough. Off you go with Grandpa, Celeste. Mommy and Daddy will join you soon."

"There you go again." John seethes behind a fake smile. "You're such a softie, you let Celeste get away with way too much. It wouldn't hurt her to learn a bit more patience."

"This isn't the time for a debate on parenting," Cate says, with a similar pasted-on smile.

"Fine, but I expect to address this later." John turns his attention back to the lineup of guests.

Dinner turns out to be a long, drawn-out affair too, with speech after speech from family and friends who seem to keep popping out of the woodwork with stories they wish to share about John and Cate's courtship. Michael's speech is the most touching. Cate gets tears in her eyes when he describes how lucky John is to have someone as special as his sister. Then her parents welcome John into the family.

"I'm so happy my little girl has someone to help her raise her little girl," William says.

"Yes, we're both just delighted to welcome you into our family," Donna adds. She raises her glass. "Here's to John."

Celeste starts to squirm and fidget as more people make their way to the podium to offer their congratulations. Cate wants to excuse her from the table to go stretch her legs, but she worries how John will react. The last thing she wants is to create a scene.

"I'm going to take Celeste with me for a washroom break," Cate whispers in John's ear. She doesn't wait for a response but takes Celeste by the hand.

"Mommy, I think I'm going to go crazy if I have to sit in my chair one minute longer," Celeste says as they are washing up at the sink.

"I know," Cate says. "I'm a grown-up and I'm tired of it. But you know what a stickler Daddy can be about protocol."

"What's 'protocol' mean?"

"It's a certain way of doing things, the social rules so to speak."

"But, aren't you the boss?"

"Yes, well," Cate says with a laugh. "That is perceptive of you. And as the boss, I hereby give you permission to go and mingle with our guests."

"Thank you, Mommy," Celeste says with a huge smile.

Celeste skips over to one of the other tables and Cate returns to her spot.

"Where is Celeste?" John asks.

"She's going around to talk with all of our guests," Cate says. "She needs a stretch. Who knew this would take so long?"

"Yes, well, your family is all so long-winded. But that's no excuse."

"Since I'm the one with the degree in child education, and I'm the one who has parented Celeste for five years on my own, I think you can just keep your opinions to yourself, thank you," Cate says firmly. "I'm not interested in your judgment. Your family is always more concerned with how things look than how they are."

"Is that how it's going to be?" John says. "Well then, you better not look to me for any support either. You can't have it both ways."

"Is it really necessary for us to discuss this, today of all days?" Cate says with a sigh. "Could we please just relax a bit and celebrate?"

"I couldn't agree more." John picks up his rye and Coke and glugs it back in one gulp. "Let the party begin."

John drinks more than anyone should in one evening. He gets carried away and goes a little crazy with his moves on the dance floor. He becomes loud and obnoxious, slurring his words and making crass jokes. Deciding she might as well join him rather than stay sober and feel annoyed, Cate drinks more than her usual.

It's past two in the morning when Cate finally convinces John to call it quits, only a few stragglers left. She falls asleep in the back of the taxi on the way to the hotel.

"Wake up," John says. "We're here." He shakes Cate gently, then more firmly.

"Uh, what?" Cate blinks and looks around. "Wow, I was sound asleep. I can hardly wait to crawl into bed."

Minutes after they've walked through the door of their honeymoon suite, Cate says, "I'm ready to crash."

"What do you mean?" John says with a thick tongue. He throws his jacket onto the floor and slips out of his shoes. "It's our wedding night."

"I know. I guess all the late nights are catching up with me. I'm just so exhausted. We can be together in the morning."

"Are you serious? I've been waiting for this all night."

"It's not like we haven't consummated our love many times already. I'll be much more responsive after a few hours of sleep. But I do need your help to get out of this dress, please."

John comes over to where Cate is standing with her back to him, ready for him to undo the tiny buttons that line the back of her gown. He pushes her onto the bed.

"I want you way too much to wait until the morning." He climbs on top of her, pulling her dress up with one hand, her panties down with the other.

"John, please," Cate cries out. "I said no. I don't want to start our marriage out like this."

"It's too late for that," John says, already forcing his way. "You said your vows." He moans. "From this day forward, in sickness and in health, you're mine."

Cate feels like she is going to suffocate, John is so heavy on top of her. She almost wishes she would. But then she sees Celeste's face in her mind. She grits her teeth. Tears stream down her cheeks into the pillow.

It isn't long before John climaxes. He falls down on top of Cate and passes out, his face buried in her neck. Cate lifts up to roll him off her and gets out of bed. It's near impossible to remove her gown by herself, but she manages somehow. She walks, as if in a trance, to the bathroom. She stares at her tear-streaked, mascara-smeared face in the mirror. She's no longer tired, even though she's exhausted. She runs a tub and crawls in. Fresh tears pour forth, down her breasts and into the bathwater. She soaks herself numb until the water is cold, then climbs out and dries off vigorously. She finds the complimentary hotel robe and puts it on, then takes her journal out from the side pocket of her overnight bag.

I'm reeling. It's my wedding night and I should be deliriously happy, but instead, I feel like I'm drowning in my own tears. I can't stop crying and when I do, it just feels as though they are trickling backward, down my throat, into the pit of my stomach. I've imagined this night so many times, but nothing ever came close to the reality of what just happened. I know John would never behave like that without having drunk so much. I'm more confident now than ever that he has a drinking problem. I suppose the bright side is that there are ways to manage alcoholism, although I have heard that addiction is one of the hardest illnesses to overcome. I'm going to talk to John about us going to an AA meeting together, sooner than later.

Chapter 13

*C*ATE WAKES UP TO the sound of John hurling in the bathroom. He comes back to bed, the acrid smell of vomit laced with mint mouthwash on his breath.

"Good morning, wife." He moves in to spoon up next to her.

"Please, don't." Cate inches away, to the edge of her side of the bed.

"What do you mean, 'don't'?" He pushes up closer. "It's our first day as man and wife, and all I want to do is hold you close to me."

"Yeah, well, after last night, I'm not really feeling the love," Cate says. "Please, just go back to sleep."

"What do you mean, 'after last night'?"

"You don't remember?" She rolls over to look him in the eye.

"Remember what? Everything after we arrived at the hotel is a blur for me, I'm afraid. I guess I passed out. I'm sorry. I shouldn't have had so much to drink, but once I got going—"

"John, you didn't pass out right away," Cate interrupts. She sits up. "You seriously don't remember? You forced yourself on me, when I said no."

"What?" His jaw drops, his eyes widen. "There's no way I would do that." He lowers his gaze and moves back to his side of the bed.

"Well, I didn't bloody well imagine it." The distraught expression on John's face looks sincere, but Cate isn't certain.

"If you say I did, it must be true," John says, so quietly Cate can barely hear him. "But I honestly don't remember. I'm so sorry, Cate. Will you please forgive me?" He keeps his eyes downcast, his shoulders slumped forward, his hands folded in his lap, as if in prayer.

"I believe you." She softens, a little. "But that's almost scarier. To think you could drink so much to not remember. Who knows what other shit could happen, in the future? I really think you need to stop drinking, like I've said before."

"You have every right to be upset," John says, sitting up a little straighter. "And I agree, I need to get a hold of my drinking, but I'm not prepared to stop completely. Drinking helps me to relax and to calm my social anxiety. I will commit to never getting wasted again. I promise to keep my limit to three drinks."

"Three drinks is still quite a bit. But if you can guarantee me that you'll stop at three, I guess I'm willing to give you another chance. I don't want to have this conversation again, ever."

"I agree. Let's try to forget this ever happened. We'll start over, fresh, today."

John falls back to sleep no sooner than he's turned over on his side, but Cate is wound up. She gets out of bed and showers. She turns the TV on low volume and flips through the channels, but there isn't anything much other than news and old reruns. She wishes she hadn't left her book at home. Cate stares at a spot on the floor as her mind plays over what happened again and again like a broken record.

Much later, when John's in the shower, Cate puts on her makeup and straightens her hair with the hot iron, then gets dressed in the new outfit she bought for the gift opening that her parents are hosting.

"Wow, you look amazing," John says. "I don't want to mess with your look, but..."

"Really, John?" Cate says. "I need some space." Then she remembers the resolution she just wrote in her journal in the early hours of the morning, to be more agreeable. "I don't want to ruin my freshly applied makeup, and we're tight on time as it is. Why don't you go back in and take a cold shower?"

John sulks back into the washroom, but when he emerges later, he's all smiles.

"Are you ready?" He grabs his duffel bag and his tuxedo tucked inside the garment bag.

"Yes. Let's go."

When they get to their old neighbourhood, they discover a sea of cars.

"Looks like many of our guests beat us to it," Cate says. "You might have to park a few blocks away."

"Yeah, we're only ten minutes late, but I can't find a spot anywhere," John says. "You'll have to walk a bit, in those sexy high heels, I'm afraid."

John parks in a cul-de-sac a ten-minute walk from the house. As they make their way up the driveway to her parents' home, Cate spots a group of people congregated in the living room around the bay window, holding Styrofoam cups of coffee and paper plates of food. She hopes her mask of wedded bliss is convincing.

"The newlyweds have finally arrived," her father yells out as they walk up.

"Hi, Dad," Cate says with a hug. "Sorry we're late."

"That's okay," he says with a wink at John, who shrugs his shoulders and grins. "It's allowed, the morning after your wedding."

"Where is Celeste?" Cate says, quick to change the subject.

"She's out back, with some of the other children, throwing a ball around for Abby."

"I'm going to go say good morning to her." Cate gives her father a peck on the cheek.

When Celeste sees Cate, she drops Abby's ball and runs over.

"Mommy, you're here!" She throws herself against Cate. "Did you and Daddy have fun in your honeymoon suite?"

"It was fine, angel," Cate says, straining a smile. "What about you? It was a late night. Were you able to sleep in a little?"

"No, I woke up early, like usual. But I let Grandma and Grandpa sleep while I watched *The Land Before Time*. When they got up, Grandma made me pancakes for breakfast."

"That all sounds lovely. You might need a nap this afternoon."

"When are you going to open up your gifts?" Celeste points to the growing pile of presents stacked on the fold-out table covered with a floral tablecloth.

"Soon. I'm going to mingle a bit with the guests. When we're ready I'll come find you so that you can open a few too."

"Thanks, Mommy." Celeste gives Cate a kiss and runs back to join the other children on the lawn.

Cate almost walks right into Michael on her way back into the house.

"Hey, Sis." He gives Cate a big bear hug. "Can I get you a cup of coffee? You and John were well into party mode when Ashley and I left at one."

"Yes, please," Cate says with a blush. "We did get a little carried away with the celebrating. A coffee sounds wonderful. I'm just going to use the facilities. I'll be right back."

Cate goes into the washroom and locks the door. As she washes her hands at the sink, she looks in the mirror and sees a woman in deep pain. *How is it that no one can see?* she wonders. The wolf flashes briefly in her mind, making her shudder. She shakes her head and dries her hands, more determined than ever to overcome her challenges with John.

More people have arrived. Michael brings her a coffee, as promised.

"I just saw Diane walking up the driveway," he says.

"Oh, thanks, I'll go meet her." Cate takes a sip of her coffee and heads out front. Diane is standing next to the ornamental cherry tree talking with one of John's many cousins.

"Hi, gorgeous," Diane says with a grin. John's cousin excuses himself and heads inside.

"Hi, glad you could make it. I hope you're faring better than I am this morning."

"You and John did go a little crazy," Diane says. "I never knew John could throw them back like that. And those dance moves of his. I nearly fell over laughing when he kicked off his shoe and it hit the ceiling while he was doing his rendition of 'Rasputin'..." Diane trails off with a belly laugh.

"Yeah, well." Cate looks off into the distance.

William walks over to join them. "You two coming in so we can get the gift opening under way?"

"Yeah, sure, Dad. Will you go on ahead, Diane, and round everyone up? I just want a moment with my dad."

"Sure thing."

When the door closes behind Diane, Cate turns to her father.

"Do you remember when I said this was a money tree?" She glances at the still fledgling cherry tree.

"I sure do," he says. "It wasn't that long ago, but it seems like a lifetime, so much has happened." He puts his arm around Cate's waist and pulls her close. "My sweet Caty-bug, all grown up and married. To the boy next door, no less."

"Yes, well," Cate says, a tear in her eye.

"Is something wrong?"

"No, Daddy, everything's perfect. I'm just emotional, remembering those days. You know how I can be."

"Yes, I do." Her father gives her a squeeze. "And you're perfect, exactly as you are. As for me, I just feel so relieved, that you and John have finally tied the knot."

"I'm glad you're happy," Cate says. She takes her father's gnarled, arthritic hands in hers.

"I just hope the hardest times are behind you now," William says, a twinkle in his eye. "Let's go on now and join the party."

The next day, John surprises Cate and Celeste with the news that he's made a reservation at a campground near Banff. He borrows his parents' RV and loads up their bicycles for a week of outdoor fun and adventure. Cate is thrown completely out of her comfort zone, with her anxiety around bears and her aversion to dirt and public washrooms, but she encourages herself to embrace nature in all its untidy glory.

When she tucks into bed the first night, not long after Celeste, she feels tired deep into her bones, but she gets out her journal to jot down a few lines.

> When John first told me we were going camping as a family for our honeymoon, I can't deny I was more than a little disappointed. I recalled his toast when we got engaged in Mexico, promising it to be the first of many exotic adventures, and yet there hasn't been a single one since.
>
> I used to love camping when I was kid, but somewhere along the way I've become a little too OCD for my own good. I don't know how it happened. I guess it's like the story of the frog in the pot of boiling water— it sneaks up on you so gradually, you don't even sense it.
>
> I must admit, even with the RV, it's one heck of a lot of work. I have a new appreciation for what Mom and Dad did, while Michael and I were busy playing and exploring. It's so much effort just to prepare a meal, what with the gathering of firewood, making a fire, then washing dishes in the tiny sink. I remember Mom hauling water from the well and boiling it on the Coleman to wash dishes in a rubber basin. At least we have a sink with running hot water and electricity.
>
> Then there's my angel. Celeste is as uncomfortable as I am with uncleanliness. I caught her removing dirt from under her nails after our hike, with a look of disgust on her face. But she seems to love the freedom and the fresh air. She's literally blossoming, like a flower. On our nature walk this afternoon, she was

so curious about everything. She asked questions about the plants, insects, and creatures we happened upon. I think it delighted her to be included on the honeymoon.

The best news of all is that John is behaving like a total gentleman. He only consumed two beers while we sat around the fire tonight. He was patient with Celeste, teaching her how to ride her two-wheeler without training wheels. After I tucked Celeste into bed, he made a move, but when I told him I started my period, he didn't sulk at all, like he often has in the past. He just gave me a big hug and asked if I would like a lower back massage. I'm feeling hopeful, again, and hope, it would seem, makes all the difference.

During summer holidays the following year, Cate has a late period. She dismisses it as part of her recent challenges with irregular cycles. Dr. Cote encouraged her to go off the pill and use condoms to try and sort out her natural hormonal rhythm and warned her things might be erratic for a while.

When another month passes and her period still hasn't come, Cate makes an appointment at the clinic.

"Your urine test confirms your suspicions," Dr. Cote says. "Congratulations, Cate, you're pregnant."

"You're sure?" Cate says. "We've used condoms and spermicide, every time we've had intercourse." In her mind, she recalls the one time when the condom broke.

"Yes, well. Nothing except abstinence is 100 percent. I know you and John have only been married a year, but I hope this is good news."

"Oh, it's wonderful. I'm just surprised."

"Let's schedule a follow-up for two weeks from now, to do some more tests and create a prenatal game plan."

Cate picks up Celeste from daycare on the way home and gets busy preparing one of John's favourite meals, perogies and sausages. She stresses over how to break the news. When the three of them are all seated around the dinner table, she starts to babble nervously.

"I have something to share with both of you," she begins. "I don't know how much you know about these things, Celeste, how babies are made and so forth—"

"Babies?" John interrupts. He drops his fork.

"Yes, babies," Cate says. "I went to see Dr. Cote today. I've just missed my second period, so it's early on, but—"

"Oh my God, you're pregnant?" John says. He quickly goes silent. Cate can't tell if he's speechless with happiness, surprise, dread, or all three.

"You mean I'm going to be a big sister?" Celeste asks, her face an expression of pure joy.

"Yes, Celeste," Cate says with an anxious look at John. "You're going to be a big sister. We're going to have a baby."

"Hooray!" Celeste says. "I can hardly wait! When will it be here? It's in your tummy?" Celeste jumps up from her place at the table and runs over to Cate. She puts her hand on Cate's abdomen and crouches her face close in. "Hello, little sister."

"It might be a brother," Cate says with a nervous laugh. John is still staring into space. He shakes his head and looks over at Cate.

"That's amazing news," John says. He gets up from his spot to join Cate and Celeste in a three-way hug.

At Cate's follow-up appointment, she finds out that she has gestational diabetes. That news, combined with the fact that Celeste was an emergency Caesarean, has Dr. Cote concerned.

"I'm afraid that with two high-risk factors, you'll need to go on maternity leave sooner than you planned," Dr. Cote says. "In fact, in my opinion, you shouldn't bother going back to work in September. I know how much time and effort you put into teaching, and I think you need to concentrate your attention fully on your pregnancy."

"Wow, really? I'm not due until the beginning of March. That's a long time to be off work and stuck at home, especially with Celeste in school all day."

"Trust me, you'll have your hands full soon enough. As I'm sure you recall with Celeste, pregnancy can be exhausting. And with diabetes, you're likely to have lower energy too, especially if we can't get your blood sugars down with the new diet I'm prescribing."

"I suppose you make a good point. The baby's health is the most important thing."

"I'm glad you agree. And even though it's been seven years since you had Celeste, the fact that you needed to have a Caesarean may mean you'll have to have one this time too. We'll want to do regular ultrasounds in the last month to check on the health of your placenta."

"Is it possible I'll be able to deliver this one vaginally?"

"It is possible. But my advice is to not get too attached to any outcomes. Let's just take it one day at a time, beginning with you giving your notice at work and starting the new diet plan."

When John walks in the door after work, Cate is preparing a fresh salad with homemade balsamic dressing, and chicken breasts are baking in an aromatic tomato sauce.

"Mm," John says after a big inhalation. "It smells delicious in here."

"Hi, Daddy," Celeste says. "Mommy is making a new recipe for dinner. Her doctor prescribed it."

"Prescribed? A new recipe?" John hangs up his coat, then he and Celeste join Cate in their open-concept kitchen. "What's that all about?"

"Oh, well, it's nothing really," Cate says, wiping her hands on a tea towel and turning away from the sink to kiss him. "Apparently I have gestational diabetes, but it will go away after the baby is born."

"Gestational diabetes?" John's brows furrow into a scowl. "I've never heard of that. Did you have it when you were pregnant with Celeste?"

"No, I didn't. I'd never heard of it either. Dr. Cote says there are three types of diabetes. Type 1 is the type you get when you're little and need to inject insulin, type 2 develops when you're old and is lifestyle and genetically related, and gestational is brought on by hormone changes in pregnancy. It disappears when the pregnancy is over."

"Hmm," John mutters. "But you say it isn't serious?"

"I don't think so. But Dr. Cote has suggested I start my maternity leave right away, so I can focus my attention on taking care of myself. She's given me a new diet to follow and wants me to test my blood sugar regularly and get plenty of rest. She said later on, when it's closer to my due date, she wants me to fill in daily charts that record the baby's heartbeat and movement."

"That does sound intense," John says. "But if that's what Dr. Cote thinks is the best course of action, I agree. You should give your notice first thing Monday morning."

"Thank you," Cate says. "I really appreciate you being so supportive."

"I want the very best for our little one," John says. He pats Cate's stomach, then pulls her in close in an intimate embrace.

By the end of February, Cate has gained almost forty pounds, double what she gained with Celeste. Despite following the diet plan rigorously, her blood sugars keep soaring and she has to start insulin injections. She finds the days long, the three weeks until her due date stretched out in front of her like a long, dark tunnel, with no light at the end. Before her daily afternoon nap, Cate gets out her journal.

> *This pregnancy has been so different than when I carried Celeste, it's got to be a boy. With Celeste I was round and wide, and with this one, I'm all out front. I can balance a glass on top of my belly, it's like a having my own built-in shelf. I feel like a beached whale, I'm so huge. I just hope I can deliver vaginally this time. Although, thinking back on it, having a Caesarean wasn't that bad. I recovered quickly. It was easy enough losing the first fifteen pounds, but those last five were tough. God knows how long it will take me to lose forty. It seems crazy, when all I seem to eat these days is salad with fish or chicken. I can't tolerate spice, it gives me heartburn. I just eat to live. And still, the pounds keep packing on. I guess the important thing is that the baby is healthy. At the last ultrasound, they estimated it weighs eight pounds already. They asked if I wanted to know whether it's a girl or a boy, but I said no, I want to wait and find out when it's born.*
>
> *John and I haven't been able to decide on a name for a boy, but we both like Dana if it is a girl. He's been*

*amazing this whole pregnancy. We haven't had one
fight. And with me not drinking, he hardly ever has
one anymore either.*

*Celeste is such a sweet little girl. So thoughtful,
almost protective of me. She's always asking if she can
help out with cooking and cleaning. If I need a rest,
she'll lie down beside me and read to me. I've caught
her watching me inject insulin, with a look of concern
on her sweet little face. I'm so lucky to have an
angel like her.*

*I feel so grateful. It looks like my worries are a
thing of the past. Our future as a family looks bright
and promising.*

Cate goes into labour the day before her due date, not long
after lunch. She calls John at work and he comes home right
away. When he walks in, John finds Cate in the living room
clad in nothing but a short nightie, on her hands and knees
and swaying as she moans.

"God, who knew labour could be so sexy," John says.
He kicks off his shoes and joins Cate on the area rug. "Does
it hurt much?"

"It's not too bad," Cate says. "The contractions are still
more than ten minutes apart, and Dr. Cote said I don't need
to go to the hospital until they're five. I just wanted you
here with me."

"I read somewhere that having sex can help speed up
labour," John says. He reaches his hand down and caresses
Cate's bare bottom.

"I'm nervous to have sex now," Cate says. "What if my
water broke?"

"I wouldn't mind," John says, his eyes full of desire.

John and Cate make love, and while it is a pleasant distraction, her water doesn't break. Afterwards, Cate's contractions become inconsistent, one after ten minutes, the next after six, then ten again.

It is after midnight when Cate shakes John's shoulder.

"John, wake up." A contraction grips her and she has to pause to breathe through it. "My contractions have been five minutes apart for the last hour now."

"What?" John says. He jumps out of bed like a man on fire and disappears into the walk-in closet. "Why didn't you wake me up sooner?" He throws on a pair of jeans, grabs a fresh shirt off the hanger, and throws Cate's overnight bag over his shoulder while she changes into a comfortable maternity dress. John calls her parents, as arranged, and Cate brushes her teeth. As soon as William and Donna arrive, John and Cate head to the hospital.

Dr. Cote is already there when they check in at the nursing station on the labour and delivery ward. Once the paperwork is filled in and Cate is settled into the birthing room, the nurse conducts an internal exam.

"You're still only five centimetres dilated," the nurse says.

"What?" Cate says. "I've been in labour since early afternoon. And my contractions are coming so frequently. Are you sure?"

"Trust me, I've been doing this a long time," the nurse says. "One thing I know, every baby comes into this world differently than the next. Try to relax the best you can between contractions, it's likely going to be a while yet until your baby is born."

Cate tries her best to follow the nurse's advice, but she finds herself clenching her jaw with each contraction. She barely catches a wink of sleep and has no appetite, turning down John's offers of packed snacks. Morning turns into afternoon and Cate is still only seven centimetres.

"I think we're going to have to risk breaking your water," Dr. Cote says. "For some women, it doesn't rupture on its own, but labour doesn't progress until it breaks."

"What do you mean, 'risk it'?" John asks.

"Well, if we break the water and the baby doesn't come soon, there is a higher risk of infection. Then we might have to perform a Caesarean."

"I'm good with that," Cate says. "I'm running out of steam here."

"Maybe you want to try an epidural?" Dr. Cote asks. "It would certainly help you to manage your pain."

"Wait a minute," John says. "Isn't an epidural an injection of anesthetic into your spinal cord? That sounds dangerous."

"I know, it sounds scary," Dr. Cote says. "But the risk is extremely minimal. This needs to be Cate's decision though, not yours."

"I trust you," Cate says, just as a contraction takes her breath away. "Hee, hee, hoo, hee, hee, hoo," Cate pants as her eyes roll back into her head.

Dr. Cote breaks Cate's water and the anesthetist sets her up with an epidural. It still takes several hours for Cate to reach ten centimetres, and then the delivery is slow too. Cate doesn't mind because she hardly feels a thing, but when the baby's heart rate starts to drop, Dr. Cote decides the epidural is interfering with Cate's ability to push effectively and has it disconnected. Cate goes from feeling pain-free to feeling like her vagina is a ring of fire in a matter of seconds. She screams and writhes. She vomits green bile into a basin with each contraction, her feet in stirrups, legs splayed. John tries to distract her with jokes and the labour mix playset he recorded on a cassette, but it's no use.

"I can't do this," Cate says, as tears stream down her face, her hair glued to her neck, drenched in sweat. Her eyes are clenched into mere slits as she uses all of her energy to push. "I'm sorry, but I can't."

"You can and you are," Dr. Cote says. "The baby's head is crowning now. My gosh, what a thick head of hair. Okay, you're almost there, just a few more solid pushes."

Cate lets out a huge moan as she pushes once, then twice.

"Here she is! Born at 10:05 p.m. John, would you like to cut the cord?"

"Uh, no thanks," John says, a sickly shade of grey.

"Did you say 'she'? We have a girl? How come I still feel like shit? How come the contractions are still so intense?" Cate says, one thought rushing into the next. "Why don't I feel better, like on the Pampers commercials on TV?"

In the middle of Cate's diatribe, the baby starts to cry, a robust, healthy sound.

"Can I hold her?" Cate asks, her motherly instincts suddenly in overdrive.

"I'm sorry. We need to examine her vitals first." Dr. Cote passes the baby girl to a nurse. "And unfortunately, your placenta hasn't come out all in one piece, like it's supposed to. It's going to take a little more time."

Dr. Cote pushes gently on Cate's abdomen, and her placenta slides out in torn pieces into a silver basin. It looks to Cate like the cow's liver they sell at the grocery store, a deep, dark red, rubbery mass. Cate gags. John turns his gaze away.

"I hope that's all of it," Dr. Cote says with one final massage. "It's so hard to tell."

"What about our baby girl?" John asks. "Is she okay?"

"I'll go check on her now." Dr. Cote removes her medical gloves and discards them in the trash. "Try not to worry."

John holds Cate's hand while she drifts in and out of consciousness. A few minutes later Dr. Cote returns with

Dana, all cleaned up and wrapped in a hospital blanket with a knitted cap on her head.

"Everything checked out perfectly." Dr. Cote is practically beaming herself. "Shall I lay her on your breast, Cate?"

"Yes, please," Cate says. She cries fresh tears as she gazes with love at her baby girl. "Look how precious she is, John. I was so sure she was a boy."

"She looks like a Shar-Pei pup, what with all those chubby wrinkles," John says with a laugh. "I guess she got a bit squished coming into the world, it took so long."

Just then Dana opens her dark eyes and blinks.

"She looks so wise," Cate says. "She must be an old soul. Hello, my darling baby girl. It's so good to finally meet you. You're such a trooper, my little love." Cate pulls Dana to her and offers her breast. Dana snuffles about, her head bobbing into Cate's skin, missing her nipple altogether.

"How cute is that?" John says.

"It usually takes a few tries before they latch on," Dr. Cote says. "And Cate's milk won't be in for a while yet."

"I'm so tired," Cate says with a yawn. "I can barely keep my eyes open."

"You go on now, close your eyes then," John says. "I'll look after Dana while you get some sleep."

When Celeste was born, they kept women in hospital for five days after vaginal births, ten days after Caesareans. But with budget cuts, Cate and Dana are only in the hospital two days before they are discharged. John belts Dana safely into the new car seat he's had installed, beside Celeste in the back seat.

Dr. Cote has assured Cate that she no longer has diabetes, and the first thing on her list is to eat a burger and fries. On the way home from the hospital, John stops at Peter's Drive-In.

"Nothing has ever tasted better in my life," Cate says as she munches away on her greasy burger. "If I ever eat another salad, it will be too soon."

John is back to work and Celeste is in school. Cate can barely find the energy to get dressed, she's so tired. She feels like she's burning up, and her head is fuzzy. When she goes to the bathroom, a mucus blood clot the size of a chicken egg plops into the toilet bowl.

"Ew, how gross," Cate murmurs under her breath.

She decides to call Dr. Cote's office and explains her symptoms to the nurse, who recommends Cate come in for a follow-up. Cate feels too loopy to drive so she gives her parents a call. William answers on the second ring.

"Daddy, it's me, I'm not feeling so good. I need to go to the clinic and I'm too weak to drive."

"What?" William says, an edge of concern in his voice. "I'll be there right away, Caty. You just hold on tight."

William arrives at Cate's house in record time. He holds Cate steady and buckles her into the passenger side, then secures Dana in her car seat and drives them to the clinic. The nurse at the desk jumps up and ushers Cate into an examination room right away. William rocks Dana in her seat and sings to her quietly while he waits.

"You have a fever of 40.2," Dr. Cote says as she checks the screen of the thermometer. "And from how you described that blood clot, I'm concerned that not all your placenta came out. I'm going to treat you for an infection with oral antibiotics, and I want you on total bedrest. Will your father be able to stay with you, to take care of you and Dana?"

"Yes, I know he will, and my mom will come and help out too, I'm sure," Cate says. "I feel so weak and faint, even my eyes are sweating."

"Where's Dana?" Cate says, having a lucid moment inside of her brain fog. She's been asleep for several hours.

"Shh, now," William says. He is sitting vigil by Cate's side, on John's side of their bed. "Don't worry, your baby girl is safe with your mom and me. You need to rest."

"Dad, I feel so weak, I'm not sure I can feed her. We bought some formula, just in case, it's—"

"Shh, Caty-bug." He runs his hand up and down Cate's arm. "Everything is under control."

Cate closes her eyes and falls asleep.

When John gets home from work, he's barely in the door when Celeste runs over in tears.

"Daddy, Mommy is really sick," she cries, throwing herself against John's leg. Cate's parents are seated in the living room, her mom holding Dana and feeding her a bottle.

"What the hell? What's going on?" John asks. He strides over to join them.

"Cate has a high fever, an infection, and needs to be on bedrest, so we came over to look after her and the girls," William says.

"Why on earth didn't you call me at work right away?" John spits the words.

He turns on his heels and takes the stairs two at a time. From the doorway of their room, he sees Cate, looking deathly still. He approaches the bed and shakes her, gently, but Cate doesn't stir.

"Cate, for God's sake, answer me!" John says in a frantic voice.

"What is the matter?" Donna asks, entering the room. William and Celeste follow and they all crowd around John, who is bent over Cate's side of the bed.

"She's not responding, I, I, can't wake her." John lets out a sob. "I think she's unconscious."

William picks up the phone on the nightstand and dials 911, his hand trembling.

"Hello, operator? I need an ambulance. My daughter is unconscious."

William cradles the phone against his ear, then tells John to take Cate's pulse, as the operator instructs him.

"It's pretty weak, but I've found it," John says. He counts how many times Cate's heart beats while watching the second hand of his watch. "It's forty-two. That's low, isn't it?"

Minutes later they hear the sound of an ambulance turning into the cul-de-sac. The paramedics arrive and Donna meets them at the door, then shows them to the bedroom. She runs to the nursery, the sound of the siren having woken baby Dana. One of the paramedics gently taps Cate's cheek.

"Cate, can you answer me?" he asks. "The patient is unresponsive," the paramedic says to his partner. They transfer Cate's limp body onto a stretcher and strap her in. He slips the needle of an IV into the faint cerulean vein at Cate's wrist.

"Can I go with her?" John asks.

"Yes, of course," the paramedic says as he struggles with his partner to navigate the gurney down the narrow, curved stairway of their home. When they get to the bottom of the stairs and are heading to the door, John turns to William.

"Take good care of my girls," John says.

"You take good care of ours too," William says, looking as overwhelmed with worry as John.

"Is Mommy going to be okay?" Celeste asks, her bottom lip trembling, her hand in Grandpa's.

"Don't worry," John says as he follows the paramedics out their front door to the ambulance parked in the driveway. "Your Mommy is going to be better and back home before you know it, I promise."

Cate is in the hospital for five days. She is given a D & C, to remove the infected placenta tissue. Intravenous antibiotics are pumped into her 24-7. With Cate's persistence, the hospital staff allow Dana to be admitted too, but they aren't willing to provide care for her. Cate's parents help John to look after Celeste, and the three of them take shifts at the hospital to help bedridden Cate take care of Dana.

When Cate returns home with Dana a week later, she is back to her old self and ready to get into a routine, but all of the disruption and drama seem to have knocked Dana off course. She wakes up crying after only two hours of sleep and will only drink from one breast at each feeding, resulting in a crazy twenty-four hour cycle of constant feeding and power naps. She wants to be held all the time. Cate ends up strapping her into a cloth sling that fits over her shoulders and tummy like a reverse backpack. She totes Dana around while she attempts to cook and clean around the house. It isn't long before exhaustion sets in again.

One morning during one of Dana's rare, peaceful naps, Cate gets out her journal. She notices the date. She hasn't made an entry in weeks, and a tear slips from her cheek onto the blank page.

So much has happened since I wrote last. The past few weeks feel almost too crazy to be true. I remember Dad tucking me into bed when we got back from the clinic. Then everything goes blank, until the moment I realized my spirit was no longer residing in my body. It was hovering somewhere up by the ceiling. I could see my limp body on our bed, drenched in sweat. I could see John sobbing beside me. I wanted to whisper some words of reassurance to my husband, but my lips remained motionless. It was all so surreal. Some part of me felt I should be upset, that I was likely on the way to my death, yet I couldn't manage to feel anything except an incredibly deep sense of peace. I had a flash of memory from when I was a child, when I was with the Magician. I remembered God holding me then, and suddenly I could feel God close by. Somehow, I seem to have lost my connection with God the last few years. Then I heard Dad on the phone to an emergency operator. I wanted to call out to my father, that I was okay, he looked so terrified, but I still couldn't connect with my lips. I heard the siren of the ambulance. The piercing noise woke up Dana. I could hear her crying. I wanted so badly to go and get her from her crib, to comfort my baby girl and tell her everything was going to be okay. But I couldn't move a muscle. Mom left to tend to her. I watched helplessly as John and Dad tried to hold it together. Then I saw Celeste at the door, crying and shaking like a leaf. I no longer felt at peace. I knew I wasn't ready to leave the land of the living.

The sensation of floating began to dissipate and I could feel the pain returning. The peacefulness that had been enveloping me evaporated. The feeling of lightness left me completely as my spirit returned to my body. By then I was inside the ambulance, the noise of the siren deafening. I turned my head to look at John, who was sitting beside me, holding my hand. I tried to reassure him, but all I could manage was a weak half smile. It must have been enough, because he beamed like a lantern and called out to the paramedic that I was coming around.

The noise and the bright lights of the emergency room startled me. There was quite a commotion of people hustling about my stretcher. I fell back asleep, and when I awoke it was quiet. I opened my eyes to see John at my side. I knew in my heart that everything was going to be okay. And it is.

In the hospital, I found out that I'm a bit of an unusual case. I still have diabetes. Apparently, it is very rare, but occasionally women diagnosed with gestational turn out to have type 1 diabetes triggered by the pregnancy, a late onset form of the disease. Dr. Cote told me I tested positive for thyroid disease too. So now I'm taking medication every morning and injecting insulin five times a day. I've read everything I can get my hands on about it, in my limited free time. It's an autoimmune disease. Like rheumatoid arthritis. Like my father.

It's a lot to take on. Two new health problems and a baby suffering with colic. But at least I have John's support, and my mom and dad's too. Michael and Ashley announced they are going to move back to Calgary this summer. That's something to look forward to. Michael was so amazing with Celeste, I'm excited for him to meet Dana.

I don't know what the future has in store for me, but one thing I know for sure, I am blessed. I'm so in love with my two precious girls. My family feels complete and I know I've got this.

Chapter 14

*D*ANA IS ONLY A few months old when John breaks his promise to never have more than three drinks. He goes out with some friends to watch a hockey game at the pub near his work and calls Cate several hours into it.

"The Flames won," he slurs into the phone. "I'm going to stay a bit longer to celebrate. Don't bother waiting up for me."

"Seriously?" Cate says. "You promised you'd be home in good time. You've made a commitment to clean out the garage tomorrow. And it sounds like you've already broken your three-drink rule."

"Do you always have to be such an uptight bitch? It's suffocating to live with such a fucking control freak. I just want to let loose and have a little fun for a change."

"Wow," Cate says. She has to hold back tears. "So that's how it's going to be? Your promise means nothing? You're going to make this about me?"

"It's just this one time, it's no big deal. Go on to bed, I'll catch a taxi home."

Cate slams down the receiver then goes upstairs to check on her girls. They are both fast asleep. She knows that she should go to bed and catch up on some much-needed sleep too, but she's too wound up. She goes back downstairs. She pours cleaning liquid into a plastic bucket, then goes a little crazy, scouring the kitchen backsplash and counters with an old toothbrush like a madwoman. When her arm feels about to break off, she puts away her supplies. She gets into her pajamas and brushes her teeth, then checks in on Celeste and Dana once more before climbing into bed.

Dana wakes her up twice before midnight. Cate feels like she's just fallen back asleep when there's a crash and a bang downstairs. She hears John swear loudly as he stumbles into the house. She looks over at her alarm clock. It's three a.m.

John lets out a belch as he walks into their room, past their bed and into the ensuite. Cate hears him vomiting into the toilet. She wants to cry but keeps it pushed down, afraid if she starts, she will release a flood of pent-up feelings. When John crawls in beside her, she feigns being asleep, her back to him.

It isn't much later when Dana cries out, waking Cate for the fourth time that night. She throws on her terry robe, slides into her slippers, and tiptoes quietly from the room.

"Hush, now, little one," Cate coos. She takes Dana in her arms and sits in the rocking chair in the nursery, then opens her robe and undoes the clasp of her nursing bra. Dana nestles in and gulps hungrily. After only a few minutes, Dana pulls her head back and starts to cry. Cate offers her breast, but Dana refuses. She tries the other breast, but Dana arches her back and tilts her head back. Cate puts Dana over her shoulder and pats her back, hoping a big burp might relieve her, but Dana just cries harder.

"Shh, little one, you'll wake the whole house," Cate says as she rocks her.

On a night like this, Cate would normally put Dana into her car seat and take her for a drive, but with John passed out, she doesn't feel comfortable leaving Celeste. She takes Dana downstairs and places her in her windup swing, then turns on the classical station on the radio. The movement and music calm Dana and soon she is asleep. Cate goes upstairs, quietly retrieves her journal, then returns. She puts on a pot of coffee and curls up on the couch, the sun just starting to rise, the sky tinted a soft pinky-grey.

> *I'm writhing with anger. I can't believe John broke his promise. I'm grateful that he didn't try to make any moves with me when he got home, although I must admit, it hurts that he suddenly seems uninterested in sex. He was counting the days, having marked off six weeks after Dana was born on the calendar with a green marker when Dr. Cote said it would take me that long to heal properly after the extensive episiotomy. Drinking usually encourages him, but something has shifted ever since I was in the hospital. Or maybe it wasn't then. Maybe it started later, when Dana developed colic? I can't remember, my memory is a blur. All I know is there's been a shift.*
>
> *Oprah's guest the other afternoon was sharing his battle with bipolar disorder. It gave me pause, listening to him describe his experience. I wonder if John has a mental illness? I remember when I took psychology in university, the list of mental health disorders outlined in my textbook was extensive. If John does have a*

*physiological imbalance, then maybe going on
medication could help him, like it turned around that
guy's life. He told Oprah that medication, along with
a healthy exercise routine and regular therapy with
a counsellor, changed his life. He wrote a book about it,
but I've forgotten the title. If it comes to me, I'll be sure
to pick up a copy.*

*I'm scared to even mention my theory to John,
in case he gets angry. But I have to think about the long
term. And about my girls. I need to find the courage.
It sucks, this feeling of walking on eggshells. I'm
overwhelmed. It's hard enough to manage my own
health challenges with diabetes on top of the no-sleep
exhaustion of having a newborn.*

God, if you're listening, I could use a lifeline here.

*Maybe going to church as a family could be
helpful? John was raised in the United Church, same as
me. He might be more open to that than to counselling
or seeing a doctor. That's it, that will be my new
strategy. I'm going to broach the subject with him
later today.*

"I wonder when Daddy is going to get up?" Celeste is still in
her pajamas, entertaining herself with her puzzle collection,
even though it's approaching noon.

"I don't know, angel," Cate says. "I'm sorry I can't play
with you, but Dana is having such a go of it today. If you
want to invite Gillian over after lunch, I'm more than happy
to go pick her up."

"Really? I would love that. Thanks, Mom. I'll call her
right now."

A can of vegetable soup is heating up on the stove and Cate is slicing carrots when John walks into the kitchen, his hair sticking straight up. His skin looks clammy and grey.

"Is there any coffee left I can heat up? I've got one hell of a headache."

"No," Cate says with a sigh. "I had the last cup hours ago. And I doubt your headache is from a lack of caffeine. What time did you get home anyway?"

"It wasn't long after midnight," John lies. "And I didn't have that much to drink."

"Yeah, okay, whatever." Cate turns her back to him and gives the soup a stir.

"Are you going to stay mad at me all day?" John asks. He edges up behind Cate and caresses her bottom.

"Stop that," Cate hisses. She slaps his hand away.

"Geez, Cate. I haven't been out with the guys in so long. Aren't I allowed to have any fun anymore, without facing the wrath of Cate?"

"It's not about you going out. It's about not keeping your word. But I don't have time to squabble with you. I've got to get lunch finished for Celeste, and I promised her I would pick up Gillian for a play date."

"I can drive over to Gillian's."

"No. You smell like a brewery. And besides, you promised me you'd clean out the garage today. Or are you going to break that promise too?"

"God, woman," John says, his voice rising. "You can be such a fucking martyr."

Just then Celeste appears on the stairway landing, dressed and ready, her long hair pulled back in a tidy ponytail. She looks from John to Cate, her eyes wide.

"Sorry, Celeste," John says. He looks ashamed. "I can't seem to do anything right."

John sulks out of the kitchen and back up the stairs to their room.

"Are you and Daddy getting a divorce?" Celeste asks. She takes a seat on a bar stool at the kitchen island.

"What?" Cate says. "No, angel, we were just having a fight. I'm sorry you had to witness that, but it's normal for moms and dads to fight sometimes."

"Are you sure?" Celeste asks. "My friend Patricia's parents are getting a divorce. She told me they fight all the time and her mom said they'd be better off without him."

"Yeah, well, you're right, divorces do happen sometimes. It's upsetting to think about, but try not to worry, my angel. It won't help."

Celeste gives Cate a hug, Dana asleep and sandwiched in her sling between them. Then she stoops down to take out a pad of coloured construction paper and her scented markers from the craft cupboard and takes a seat at the dining table.

"Is lunch going to be ready soon?" she asks after she finishes her drawing.

"It will be served in three minutes," Cate says. She comes over to look at Celeste's picture and frowns. She's made a family portrait, with a scowling daddy, a stressed-out-looking-mommy, and a crying baby in a stroller. A little girl is off by herself, to the side.

"Do you like my drawing?" Celeste asks, looking up.

Cate quickly transforms her face into a smile.

"Yes, it's very well done. I like all your attention to detail and your happy-faced sun. As for lunch, all I need to do is put out some crackers and pour you a glass of milk, so please put away your things and go wash up."

Cate takes out her insulin and dials up her lunchtime dose, then injects into the loose flesh under her arm. She sighs. The weight of the world feels heavy on her shoulders.

She has her hands full the rest of the day, with Dana and the never-ending list of housework. She puts on a load of diapers and cleans two of their four bathrooms. John spends the entire afternoon out in the garage, but when Cate peeks her nose in to check in on his progress, things look just as untidy and disorganized as always.

To cement her unhappiness with John, Cate chooses to sleep on the couch that night, Dana in her bassinet beside her on the floor. Cate sleeps fitfully and wakes up with a crick in her neck, but by morning she has worked through her resentment and is ready to make up with John.

Celeste is watching morning cartoons, and John is reading the morning newspaper, spread open on the glass coffee table. Cate pours herself and John steaming cups of coffee and takes a seat on the couch.

"I'm sorry I've been in such a sulk," Cate says.

Dana utters a mewing sound, and John winds up her motorized swing.

"I'm ready to let it all go and start over, if you are," John says.

"I agree that's best." Cate places her coffee on a coaster. "It's too late to start today, but I was wondering how you feel about us going to church, maybe next Sunday?"

"I would love that!" Celeste pipes up before John can answer. "Gillian's family goes to the church in her neighbourhood. She's in the junior choir, and she says in Sunday school you get to make crafts. She says the minister there is really nice too."

"Well, if you two are both keen, I suppose it's not a bad idea," John says. He scratches his chin, dark with stubble after only one day without shaving. "I seem to remember I used to enjoy going with my parents."

"Perfect, it sounds like we're all on board to start next week," Cate says.

"I can hardly wait to tell Gillian tomorrow," Celeste says.

The decision turns out to be a positive one for the whole family. Celeste thrives in Sunday school and joins the choir with Gillian. Dana seems lulled by the serenity of the sermon and falls asleep. She wakes up during the hymns but is content. John's moods seem to steady a little too.

A few weeks before Christmas, John approaches Cate about surprising Celeste with a puppy from Santa.

"There's an ad here for silky terrier pups for sale." He's circled the address in the newspaper with a green highlighter. "It looks like it's way out by the airport, but I did some reading about this breed of dog. They don't shed, their fur is hypoallergenic, and they're smart too." He produces a book he's signed out from the library and shows Cate a photo of an adorable little dog with black and tan fur streaked with silver.

"They are certainly exotic looking, gorgeous really," Cate says. "And you know how much I love dogs. But really, John, don't you think our hands are full enough?"

"I know, we're crazy busy," he admits. "But I think it would be good for Celeste to have a companion, you're so occupied with Dana. And she would benefit from taking on more responsibility."

"Good point. Although my parents ended up doing most of the work with our dogs."

"Yes, well," John says, "we won't be as indulgent and spoil Celeste like they spoiled you."

Cate is hurt by John's criticism of her parents, but she chooses not to engage in an argument.

"Why don't you go have a look," she says. "I trust you to choose the right one for our family."

"Really?" John's eyes brighten. "I thought for sure you'd fight me on this one. Thank you, Cate. I think a little puppy is going to be just what the doctor ordered."

John chooses the runt of the litter, the last puppy born. She is so tiny, at only eight weeks old, she is barely the size of a tissue box. John's parents agree to keep her at their house until Christmas Eve.

On Christmas morning, John and Cate are up early with Dana. When they hear Celeste coming down the stairs, John takes the sleeping puppy and places her carefully in Celeste's stocking.

"Merry Christmas!" John beams as Celeste turns the corner into the living room and spots the ball of fur.

Celeste squeals with delight. "What's this! I never even asked Santa for a puppy!" She runs over and scoops the puppy out and into her arms, then showers kisses all over the top of her head. The puppy shakes awake and looks about, then squirms free and totters across the floor. She squats and pees in the middle of the area rug.

"Oh, oh!" Celeste says. "Sorry!"

"It's not your fault," Cate says. "And it's to be expected with a new puppy."

"Yes, potty training her will be your first job," John says. "First things first, you need to give your new dog a name."

"Can we name her Lady, like in the *Lady and the Tramp* movie?" asks Celeste, the consummate Disney fan.

"That's a great name," Cate says.

"Should we call her Lady Downing or Lady Henderson?" Celeste asks.

"Dogs don't need last names," Cate says. She doesn't want to bring up the subject of their differing last names, still a bone of contention with John, who has said he wants to adopt Celeste and for all of them to be Downings. But it's too late, John's happy face has turned upside down.

"Actually Cate, dogs do need last names for their registration forms and vaccination paperwork," John says, his voice suddenly sounding sour.

"Well, we can sort that out later," Cate says. "Celeste, why don't you look in your stocking and see what else Santa brought you?"

Cate was right to suspect that a new puppy would be more work than anyone bargained for. Lady chews on the heels of all Cate's shoes and on the corners of the wood furniture. She pees on the carpet every day, despite Cate taking her outside at regular intervals and Celeste taking over when she gets home from school.

One evening a week, John looks after the kids so Cate can have some time for herself. On one of these evenings, she drives to Chapters and settles into a chair with a soy latte and her journal.

> *Who knew my life would become such a rollercoaster of emotional ups and downs? Back when it was just Celeste and me, things were so calm and steady. We had such a lovely flow, just the two of us. It feels like John's polar energy has taken over. Celeste is sensitive to his mood swings, and baby Dana is already picking up on his shifts in temperament. Even Lady seems uncertain. She will bark excitedly when he comes home from work and sometimes be greeted by a cheery pet, then other times by a grouchy command to get down.*
>
> *It feels as though the two of us are in a constant battle over what little free time there is. I had to practically beg for these two hours a week. And I can*

*be certain not a single chore will get checked off the list
when I get back, even though John has a freak attack
if the house isn't spotless and dinner isn't ready the
minute he gets in the door from work.*

*Church has been a literal godsend. It's a few hours
of sanctuary every week. Although when I tried to drop
Dana off in the nursery, it was a total fail. She wailed
the entire time. The whole congregation could hear her,
and I couldn't just sit there, despite John telling me I
should just let her cry it out, that she'll get used to it
eventually. I don't mind having her with me, and I
don't feel comfortable asking complete strangers to look
after a crying baby.*

*John asked me the other day if I'm going back to
work in the fall. I would love to, but I'm not sure about
leaving Dana. She's so attached to me. Her happiness
has to come first. I told him it was too early to tell, and
he seemed content enough.*

*The good news is that Michael is back home. It's so
good to have him around again, even though he's super
busy with his new job and setting up house with
Ashley. They got engaged, with plans for a big wedding.
I'm so happy for him.*

*The bad news is Dad has to have another
operation. On his left hand this time. Even though his
right hand has started to cripple-up again, it's a huge
difference compared to how it was before. The surgeon
is hopeful. It's just so heart-wrenching to witness my
dad struggle.*

*With my crazy busy life, I hardly see any of my
family anymore. I haven't gotten together with Diane
for months now. The last time I saw Rose was at Dana's
baby shower. And Tripti moved to the US. I feel so
alone. I'm exhausted to the bone. I have to remind*

*myself to take one step at a time, that this too
shall pass.*

Cate is barely in the door when she hears Dana howling and Lady going berserk, barking. She can hear her skidding in circles on the hardwood floor.

"Where the hell have you been?" John screams.

Cate comes through the laundry room and into the living room to find him pacing with Dana over his shoulder, bawling, her face bright red. Celeste is nowhere to be seen.

"What do you mean, 'where the hell have I been'?" She walks over quickly to retrieve Dana from him. "I told you I was going to Chapters."

"Yeah, well, you're only supposed to take two hours," John huffs. He looks over at the wall clock. "It's ten after nine."

"Seriously? You're blowing a gasket over me being ten minutes late? It was bloody slippery on the roads and I had to take it slow, for God's sake."

"When you've got a crying baby in your ear, ten minutes feels like an eternity," John says. He walks over to the liquor cabinet, gets out a bottle of whiskey, and pours himself a generous glass.

"You think you're telling me something I don't know?" Cate says, her voice soft. She kisses Dana on the head while opening her blouse to feed her. "I'm the one who is home all day."

"What, am I supposed to be grateful I get to work my ass off in the office all day? It's no picnic for me either."

"I never said it was," Cate says with a sigh. "It isn't a competition. We're both in the thick of things, John, but this difficult time will pass."

Dana pops off Cate's nipple to gaze up at her with a smile, then nuzzles back in for more.

"When, Cate?" John asks. "When will it pass? Because I'm feeling done, now."

"I don't know. But I set up an appointment with the nurse at the community clinic next week, for a consultation. Maybe she'll have some suggestions for how I can bring some calm for Dana. Isn't that right, my little love?" Cate coos to Dana while stroking her thick mass of dark blonde hair, already at least two inches long.

"That is good news," John says. "I hope so."

"Is Celeste in bed?" Cate puts Dana over her shoulder and pats her back.

"I can't say for sure, I was so distracted," John says. "I'll go see."

John peeks in Celeste's room. She's built a fortress of stuffed animals all around her in bed and is curled in a ball. He can tell she's been crying.

"What's the matter?" He moves into her room.

"Nothing," Celeste says. "I'm fine, you can go."

"Okay." He doesn't bother to press her. "Sleep tight."

Cate's appointment with the nurse goes even better than she'd hoped. She explains to Cate how a small percent of babies, usually intellectually gifted ones, have difficulty settling into a routine. She agrees with Cate's suspicion, that the early trauma of Cate's hospitalization likely contributed. But she has a bag of tricks, including a book, *Solve Your Child's Sleep Problems*, by Richard Ferber. She summarizes his position, that some babies need to be put on a strict schedule. She tells Cate it will take willpower to let Dana cry for periods of time until she learns how to self-soothe, but in the end, she feels confident Dana and the rest of the family will feel happier. Cate feels hopeful again, for the first time in ages.

Two days into Dana's new feeding and sleeping routine, John doesn't get up for work in the morning. He calls in sick, then crawls back into bed, to sleep the entire day. He doesn't have a fever, or a cough. Cate worries, but she doesn't have much time to devote to John, her hands full with Dana, Celeste, Lady, and running their home.

When John doesn't get out of bed again the next day, Cate goes into their room after she tucks Celeste and Dana in for the night.

"John?" She sits on the edge of their bed and shakes his shoulder gently. She wrinkles her nose; the room smells stale. "John, wake up."

"What?" John says sleepily. He looks over at Cate, his face drawn and pale.

"I'm worried about you. You haven't gotten out of bed in over twenty-four hours, except to use the washroom. You haven't eaten, or showered…"

"I didn't think you cared or noticed," John says. He rolls onto his side, his back to her.

"Of course I care, you're my husband. I know, we've been having a few struggles lately, but I love you."

"You do?" He turns over. "I thought perhaps you'd fallen out of love with me."

"John, when I said my vows, I meant them. In sickness and in health, remember? Please, don't shut me out. Tell me what's going on."

"I think I'm depressed," John says. "I don't know that much about it, but I've done a little reading. I signed a few books out from the library, I guess it was over a year ago now, when I first started having these dark feelings. It feels like I'm in a deep, black hole, and I can't see my way to climb out of it. I have no energy. I've totally lost my appetite. And I'm sure you noticed I have no interest in sex."

"Yes, I have," Cate says. "I guess I've had my head in the sand, not wanting to face reality. But that won't help, will it? What can I do?"

"I honestly don't know." His voice quivers. "But it means so much to know you care, that you still love me. I'll call and make an appointment with Dr. Cote tomorrow morning and see what she has to say."

"That sounds like a good place to start." She leans over to kiss him on his cheek. It is clammy and cool. "I know it's still crazy around here, but this Ferber thing does seem to be doing wonders for Dana already. She woke up from her nap this morning all smiles and finished her whole bottle."

"You fed her a bottle?"

"Yes, I've decided to wean her too. I'm going to do it slowly. That way I'll have more freedom and you'll have more opportunity to bond with her. And you know your mom blames my milk as part of the problem."

"I hope you're right, that things are changing," John says.

"Let's just take it all one step at a time."

Cate feels a little lighter. She brushes her teeth and crawls into her side of the bed. She even treats herself to five minutes of reading.

John goes to see Dr. Cote the next day. When he gets home, he heads straight upstairs to their room, not even saying hello to Cate, who is scrubbing the area rug vigorously with carpet cleaner for pet odour. Lady scampers over to say hello, but she's ignored too.

When Cate goes up to check on him, she sees that he's thrown his clothes in a pile on the floor and put on the same pajama bottoms and T-shirt he's been wearing all week. He's crawled back into their bed, the blinds drawn.

"Do you want to talk about it?" she asks, coming around to his side of the bed and taking a seat beside him.

"Where's Dana?" John asks. "I haven't adjusted to seeing you without her strapped to you."

"She's having her nap. I can't get over what a difference this Ferber thing has made. It's like she's a whole new person, back to the little one I first met in the hospital."

"Maybe we should Ferberize me," John says sullenly.

"What did Dr. Cote say?"

"She said my symptoms all point conclusively to clinical depression." He points to his dresser where there is white paper bag from the pharmacy with his thirty-day trial prescription of Prozac inside. "I'm so embarrassed. I don't know what excuse I'm going to give my boss for not being in all week, but I'm sure as hell not going to tell her I'm mentally ill."

"It's your right to tell who you want," Cate says. She strokes his forearm affectionately. "But you have nothing to be embarrassed about. I've read about depression a little in school. And my aunt Winfred suffers from it. It's not your fault. It's an illness, just like I have diabetes."

"Well, say what you want," John says with a yawn. "But I feel like a total fuck-up, like I'm letting you and the girls, everybody, down."

"That's your illness talking," Cate says. "I bet once your medication kicks in, you'll have a whole new perspective."

Cate is right. After a week, John's cloud of doom starts to lift. He's able to motivate himself enough to go back to work. After two weeks, he's almost back to his old self, the side of

John that Cate is in love with. He gets up early to go to the pool to swim laps every second day. He tries two different therapists. He doesn't click with either and lets therapy slide, but he's back on track. Cate is feeling hopeful, again.

When Dana turns one the following March, Cate lets her principal know she's considering coming back to work in the fall, and when a colleague goes on maternity leave the last three weeks of June, Cate accepts the temporary position.

When Cate picks up Dana from daycare at the end of her first day, she finds her sitting in the exact same spot at the window she was in when Cate drove away. When Cate walks into the room, Dana crawls over as fast as she can and climbs up Cate's leg, tears streaming down her chubby little cheeks.

"Up, up, Mama," she says with the saddest voice Cate has ever heard.

"Come on up, my love," Cate says as she reaches down. She hugs her in close, then moves her onto her hip. "Don't tell me she didn't move from the window all day," Cate says to Salma, the daycare worker in charge.

"No, she didn't, I'm sorry to say. All of us tried our best to coax her with offers of food and toys, but she refused, just sat there and stared out the window. I tried to change her diaper for her, but she wouldn't let me, just cried for you, 'Mama, Mama,' over and over. It was the hardest day I've ever had."

"Oh my, that's so horrible, I'm so sorry," Cate says, as tears form in her own eyes. She kisses Dana on top of the head. "Mommy's here, my love."

"I noticed Dana is scheduled to come in every day for the next three weeks," Salma says. "I must say, I'm a little worried."

"Me too," Cate says. "I don't know if I can get out of my work commitment."

"Well, sometimes even the stubborn ones come around after a few days," Salma says. "Although I must admit, I've never seen one as wilful as Dana."

"I can't leave her to sit by the window all day, day after day for three weeks," Cate says. "Even one more seems like too much. I'll call my dad and see if he might be able to take her, although he's recovering from surgery."

She thanks Salma, goes downstairs to pick up Celeste from the after-school program, then loads her girls in the van. Her mind is a whirl of anxious thoughts on the drive home. When she takes Dana inside and sets her on the floor, she crawls over and attaches herself to Cate's leg and refuses to let go.

"Oh, my sweet girl," Cate says with a sigh. "Mommy has traumatized you. I'm so sorry."

"Daycare is fun," Celeste says to Dana. "I started when I was your age, and I loved it, right, Mommy?"

"Yes, you did. It's sweet of you to try and cheer up your little sister, but you know everyone is different. You're so much more extroverted than her."

"What does 'extroverted' mean?" Celeste takes her backpack off the floor and retrieves her lunch kit, then rinses her containers and puts them in the dishwasher.

"It means you are more at ease with other people," Cate says. "In fact, sometimes you were a little too much the other way, willing to go to any old stranger. But try not to worry, Celeste. I'll figure out what to do."

"I know you will, Mommy," Celeste says with a smile. "I'm going to get my homework done and out of the way before dinner."

Cate makes dinner and loads the dishwasher, makes lunches for the next day, and then irons her blouse, with Dana stuck to her side like glue. After she tucks her girls into bed, Cate feels the exhaustion. Even though she can barely keep her eyes open, she knows that writing out her feelings in her journal is a healthy coping practice, so she takes the time to jot down a few lines before she sets the alarm and turns out the light.

It was so distressing to arrive at the daycare after a long day at work to find Dana at the window crying for me. When Salma said that Dana remained vigilant at the window all day, it broke my heart. I can't imagine going back to work full-time in the fall, but I suppose that's a long way off. I need to take this one day at a time, starting with contacting the school's human resources department to find someone else to take on this temporary gig. I've set my alarm for a bit earlier than usual, so I can meet with the principal to explain the situation. And I called Dad, just in case. He said it was no problem, but I'm worried it will be too much for him to take on Dana all day. But Mom might be able to clear up her schedule a bit by juggling a few things around and help too.

I'm so stressed out. My blood sugars were through the roof when I checked them before supper, and even after a huge correction bolus, they were still up before bed. I'm such an emotional creature.

John looked so heartbroken to see Dana so clearly traumatized. All night she crawled around following me everywhere I went. Even to the bathroom. She refused to let me out of her sight until she conked into bed. And it wasn't easy to get her to settle in.

It would seem my life is just a series of new and different challenges. When one starts to resolve, another one manifests. Perhaps this is how all mothers of young children feel. It sucks, because it's such a brief, precious time when they're young. It wasn't like this with Celeste. I never felt this overwhelmed with worry or this kind of heaviness, even during busy exam weeks. I'm yearning again for those easier, simpler days. But deep down, I know I wouldn't change a thing. I love Dana so much. We'll figure out how to get through this challenge. This too shall pass, just like I said to John.

Chapter 15

*C*ATE FINALLY MAKES IT to the phone on the seventh ring.

"Hello." She's a little out of breath.

"Hello," Donna says. "I was beginning to think you and Dana were out and about."

"Nope, just a little slower than my usual slow."

"Is everything okay?"

"As good as can be expected, six months pregnant and as big as a barn already," Cate says. "Ashley said I looked ready to deliver when you guys were all over here last Sunday, but what does she know?" She chuckles half-heartedly. "Anyway, Dana is creating more of her amazing artwork down in the basement, and I shouldn't leave her unattended."

"Oh my, she is a budding artist already, isn't she?" Donna says. "Tell her Grandma says 'I love you.'"

"Okay, Mom. Are you all right? You sound off."

"It's all good, darling, just having one of those niggling feelings that usually ends up being nothing," Donna says. "Maybe I'll give your father a ring and see how's he faring. He's been so sick all week with that nasty flu bug."

"Okay, well, let me know if anything is amiss," Cate says. "I love you, Mom."

Cate listens to the messages on her answering machine after returning from grocery shopping with the girls later that afternoon. There's one from her mother.

"I hightailed out of work, the niggling feeling suddenly in overdrive," the recording begins. "There was no question something was wrong when your father didn't answer my calls. I drove home like a bat out of hell, and as it turns out, it was a good thing. I found him lying on our bed unconscious, drenched in sweat. The heat emanating from his body was so intense, I called 911 immediately. When the paramedics arrived, his temperature was forty-four. Of course, I couldn't help but think of when you got so sick right after Dana was born. I'm sure you can imagine what a state I was in. Anyway, I suppose I should cut short this lengthy diatribe before your answering machine runs out of space. Please, Cate, come and be with me as soon as you can. I'm in the Foothills Emergency waiting room."

Cate is about to call John at work when a second message begins.

"Oh, and Cate, I forgot to tell you," there is a momentary pause and Cate hears her mother stifling back a sob, "the doctor said to notify your father's next of kin right away, that his situation is critical."

Cate almost drops the phone. Her heart thumps like a machine gun in her chest as she dials John's office with a trembling hand.

"Mr. Downing is in a meeting and can't be disturbed," John's secretary says.

"This is a family emergency," Cate says, trying her best to stay calm.

"Emergency?" the secretary repeats. "Well, if you're sure—"

"I'm bloody well sure," Cate says, seething. "My father has been taken to Emergency and I know John would want you to interrupt him, so please, just do as I ask."

A few seconds later John comes on the line and tells Cate he will be home as soon as he can. Cate hangs up and goes off in search of Dana and Celeste. She finds them in the playroom in the unfinished walkout basement, the contents of the large blue Rubbermaid container labelled *Barbies* dumped out on the floor between them.

"It's lovely to see you two playing so nicely together," Cate says as she enters the room. Celeste looks up and smiles. Dana jumps up, knocking a half-dressed Barbie from her lap, and runs over to wrap herself around Cate's leg.

"Who left the long-winded message?" Celeste asks. "Oh, let me guess, was it Grandma Henderson?" Celeste laughs.

"As a matter of fact, it was. She has some very bad news, I'm afraid."

Cate lowers her bulky pregnant body onto the floor and Dana scrambles into her lap, popping a thumb into her mouth and snuggling in.

"Grandpa William is really sick," Cate continues once she's seated. "He's in the hospital."

"Is he going to have another operation?" Celeste asks, an expression of concern replacing her earlier bemusement.

"No, it's not like that," Cate says. "That was a scheduled surgery. Grandpa went to the hospital in an ambulance, it was an emergency."

"An ambulance? Like you did after Dana was born?"

"Yes, angel, I suppose it is just like that. I don't know the details yet, only that he has a high fever and the doctor thinks it could be critical."

"What's tridital?" Dana asks, popping her thumb out of her mouth temporarily.

"It means Grandpa is very, very sick," Cate says. "Daddy is on his way home from work now. As soon as he gets here, I'm going to the hospital. I don't know how long I'll be gone."

"Will you be bat in time to tut me in?" Dana asks, a worried look on her face.

"I can't promise," Cate says. "But I'll try."

They hear the sound of the garage door opening. Lady starts to bark like crazy.

"Sounds like Daddy's home," Celeste says.

Both girls race up the stairs to greet their father. Cate waddles slowly behind them. When she enters the main landing, John is holding Dana in his arms.

"Hi," John says. He leans in and kisses Cate. "I'm sorry I took so long to get home, but things were crazy at the office and then traffic with all the construction downtown was nuts."

"That's okay, I understand. I'm just glad you're here."

"Mommy wants to do to the hospital to see Drampa. Did you know he's tridital?" Dana says.

"Yes, I did," John says. "When will you be home, do you think?" he asks, turning to Cate.

"I don't know. I told Dana I'd try to be home to tuck her in for her bedtime, but—"

"Are you kidding?" John interrupts. "It's already four thirty. That's pretty unrealistic to expect."

"You're probably right, but—"

"I want Mommy to tut me in!" Dana starts to wail.

"I know you do," John says in a firm voice. "But we can't always get everything we want. What would you say if I said you can watch a movie after your bath?"

"Hooray!" Dana says. "And Cela said she would read to me." She stops crying as quickly as she started.

"Sounds like everything is all settled," Cate says. She gives the three of them big hugs and lots of kisses, then grabs her purse, throws in her blood meter kit, grabs the car keys, and heads through the laundry room to the garage.

Cate walks into Emergency and spots her mother and Michael right away, engrossed in conversation. They both get up from their seats to give her a hug.

"How's Dad?"

"He's had a few fleeting moments of consciousness," Donna says. "We still don't have any updates, but he's been asking for you."

"He has?" Cate says. Her hand goes to her heart. "Can I go and see him?"

"You have to check in at the triage desk," her mother says.

Cate goes immediately to check with the triage nurse, who buzzes the electronic door to allow Cate entrance into the emergency department case rooms. She follows the rows of curtained cubicles until she finds her father's. She pulls back the curtain.

"Daddy? It's me."

There is no answer. Her father is snoring quietly, dressed in a blue hospital gown, his hair soaked in sweat and plastered to his skin. He doesn't look good. Cate spots a small metal stool beside the bed and takes a seat. She takes in his shockingly pale face, the stubble of his beard only highlighting the whiteness of his skin. She reaches out to touch his hand, his arm by his side, his fingers curled over. His skin is so hot, she pulls her hand back involuntarily, then returns it to gingerly trace her fingers along the vein travelling up his arm, the one with the IV needle protruding from it. Her gaze follows the lines to the stand beside his bed where there are three plastic bags hanging from steel poles.

"Daddy, I don't know if you can hear me," Cate begins tentatively. "But I'm here, rooting for you. I need you, Daddy. I'm not ready to lose you, you can't give up."

Cate senses a change in her father's breathing and looks up from his hand to his face. His eyes are open, staring back at her.

"Hi," Cate says, a huge smile erupting.

"I've been waiting for you." He coughs, his voice croaky and faint.

"I know, Mom told me. I'm sorry I wasn't here earlier."

"How are my precious little granddaughters?"

"They're great, Dad," Cate assures him, with a gentle squeeze of his hand.

"And how's the little one you've got in the oven?" He glances toward Cate's belly.

"Cooperating nicely at the moment. You're the one I'm worried about."

"Try not to worry, Caty-bug." He pats her hand. "I'm not ready to give up yet." He closes his eyes and falls back to sleep.

Cate drifts in and out, uncomfortable on the stool with her head leaning against the wall. Her neck and shoulders are sore and stiff. She looks at her watch. It is eight fifteen. Her father appears to be in a deep sleep so she goes back out to the waiting room to join her mother and brother. Ashley is sitting beside Michael, leafing through a magazine.

"I'm so glad you're here," Cate says, taking a seat across from her.

"How are you holding up?" Ashley asks.

"I'm doing okay, I guess, considering the circumstances. I was just going to go and grab something from the vending machines. Do any of you want anything?" She rummages around the bottom of her purse, looking for loose change but the rest of her family isn't hungry.

Cate chooses a Snickers bar, then returns to her seat. She takes out a vial of insulin and a syringe and dials up a small dose, then lifts her maternity blouse and injects it into her tummy.

"There's no change in Dad's condition," Cate informs them. "He was conked out most of the time I was in there, although he was lucid for a few fleeting moments."

An older man, perhaps in his late fifties and dressed in blue hospital scrubs, walks over to where they are seated.

"Excuse me, are you the Hendersons?"

"Yes, we are," Donna says.

"Hello, I'm Dr. Evans." He gives each of them a cursory handshake.

"Do you have any updates on my father's situation?" Cate asks.

"Yes, I do," Dr. Evans says. "I have conducted a thorough examination. William is fighting a very aggressive infection. I noticed he has several lesions on arthritic nodes on his elbow, knee, and right knuckle. That could have been where the infection entered. I think it most likely that the infection is bacterial—a staphylococcal, streptococcal, or pneumococcal—but we have to wait for the results of his blood work to come back from the lab. I've started an

IV infusion of a combination of antibiotics, hoping that one of them will be the right one to fight this thing off."

"Do you still consider my husband to be in critical condition?"

"It's still too early to say which way this will go," the doctor replies. "But we will let you know as soon as we have any new information."

"Thank you, Dr. Evans," Michael says.

When the doctor leaves, there is a heavy pall that lingers behind him. The four of them lean in for a group hug.

"I think we should go in for one more visit and then head out," Ashley says to Michael, pulling away from the embrace. "I've got another busy day at work tomorrow."

"That's probably wise," Michael says. "We've left our phone numbers at the desk, so if there's any news, I'm sure they'll call us. We might as well at least try and catch a few winks."

"Okay," Cate says. She crumples up her chocolate bar wrapper and attempts to toss it in the garbage can, but misses. "I should probably do the same, but I hate to go."

Michael and Ashley say goodbye to William then leave for home. Donna and Cate wait around a bit longer, hoping the lab work might come back, engaged in small talk. A man comes barging through the Emergency doors with a wooden stake that looks like a fence post protruding from his right shoulder, a towel with congealed blood wrapped around the end. The woman sitting a few seats down from them cries hysterically, then starts laughing like a maniac while talking animatedly to the empty space beside her.

Cate and her mother stay until almost midnight, but there is still no news. They decide to go home and meet back at the hospital in the morning.

By the time Cate gets home and ready for bed, it is almost one. Anxiety dreams punctuate her sleep. She wakes often, in a sweat, her heart beating wildly in her chest.

When her alarm goes off the next day, she still feels exhausted. Her first thought is of her dad. She's anxious to return to the hospital as soon as possible, but she decides to jot down a few lines in her journal.

> *I can't believe this is happening. My father is in the hospital, fighting for his life. Apparently, he has some kind of crazy-assed infection. It's hard to believe it was just last Sunday we were all gathered together here for a family dinner. He was playing animatedly with my girls, just like he used to with me, when I was little. He has such a knack for relating to children on their level, in a way that has them feeling seen and loved. He must have watched Celeste perform dance routines for over an hour. And it was hilarious listening to him be the voice of Little Red Riding Hood, reading to Dana.*
>
> *I can't accept that it's his time to go. I need him, so much. If you're listening, God, please hear my prayer. Please give my father the strength he needs to fight whatever this is.*

John is still fast asleep when Cate slips quietly into their ensuite to take a shower. The hot streams of water invigorate her tired bones. She closes her eyes and her mind drifts as the stress and anxiety seem to wash off her and down the drain.

"Mommy!" Dana sounds affronted. She is standing on the bath mat with her blanket dragging on the floor. "I was talling you and talling you!"

"I'm sorry, I didn't hear you, my love," Cate says. "Just give me a minute to dry off and I'll be right with you."

"Otay," Dana says. She seats herself on the floor and waits. She looks over at Cate's transforming body. "Mommy, why are your boobies detting so bid if the baby is drowing in your tummy?"

"Well, sweetheart, that's because they are getting full of milk for me to feed the baby," Cate says with a chuckle.

"Dere's milt in dem?" Dana says. Her eyes widen into huge saucers. "I tawt babies drint milt from bottles?"

"Well, you're right, some babies drink from bottles. It depends on what the mommy chooses. But your mommy plans to breastfeed. I breastfed both you and Celeste, you know."

Dana looks astonished. "I had milt from your boobies?"

"Yes, you did. It's perfectly natural."

"Tan I have some now?" Dana asks.

Cate laughs again. "I'm afraid not. You're a big girl now, and big girls drink milk from a cup. Only newborn babies need breast milk. It's very special, and helps them to develop their immune systems to grow big and strong. Besides, my milk won't actually be ready until the baby's born."

"How many more sleeps until the baby tums?"

"I don't know for sure. Babies don't always come exactly when you think. You were a few days late and Celeste was more than two weeks overdue. But the baby is supposed to come near the beginning of July, so there's still lots more sleeps to wait." Cate ties her robe and reaches for Dana's hand. "Come along then, Miss Curious. Let's go get some apple juice for you and coffee for me. And try not to wake up Daddy."

Downstairs in the open living area, Dana plunks herself down in her toddler-size *Beauty and the Beast* plush chair in front of the TV, and Cate pops *Alice in Wonderland* into the VCR. She puts on a pot of coffee and fills a sippy cup with apple juice for Dana before going back upstairs to wake Celeste for school.

By nine thirty Cate has dropped off Celeste at the bus stop and left Dana at her neighbour's house, with the promise to pick her up in time for lunch. She drives back to the hospital and goes directly to Emergency. She finds out that a bed became available for her father on unit eleven some time during the night. She walks down the hall that connects the emergency department to the main hospital and catches the elevator to the eleventh floor.

After checking in at the nurse's station, Cate walks to her father's room, almost at the end of the hall. The door is slightly ajar. The cubicle to the right is curtained off, but as Cate peers around, she sees her dad sitting up slightly in bed talking with her mom, who is sitting in the visitor's chair in the corner next to the window.

"Good morning," Cate says. "What a lovely surprise to see you awake and sitting up in bed, Dad."

"Good morning, darling." Donna stands up to give Cate a hug. "I didn't expect to see you so soon, after our late night."

"I'm so glad they found Dad a room. How are you feeling?" she asks her father.

"Like I've been hit by a truck," William croaks. His laugh breaks into a succession of coughs.

"The doctor is supposed to be making rounds this morning," her mother says.

Right on cue, Dr. Evans enters the room.

"Well, how nice to see your family here," he says to his patient. "But I'm ready to examine you. Would you ladies please wait in the visitor lounge at the end of the hall? I'll come out and speak to you when I'm done."

Dr. Evans enters the visitor lounge, thumbing through a stack of papers on his clipboard.

"Let's see now, where to start?" He consults his notes briefly for a moment before continuing. "The first round of blood work came back this morning and we can confirm that this infection is staphylococcal."

"What does that mean?" Cate asks.

"Staph bacteria live on the skin of up to 20 percent of healthy adults and can be present without causing any illness," Dr. Evans says. "They need to find a portal to enter the bloodstream to be dangerous. In your father's case, he has several arthritic nodules with lesions where I suspect the infection entered. The bacteria were then able to multiply so quickly and vastly without being detected because of the immunosuppressants, steroids, and corticosteroids your father is taking for rheumatoid arthritis."

"What do you mean, so advanced?" Donna asks.

"I say advanced because of how serious William presented upon arrival," Dr. Evans explains. "He is looking much better than he was then. The antibiotic infusion we are administering intravenously is an aggressive combination of penicillin, vancomycin, and rifampin, and it does seem to be working to slow the rapid rate at which this infection is multiplying. That said, these things tend to progress in waves. We're not out of the woods yet."

"Is there anything else you can do, besides give him medications?" Cate asks.

"We're also draining the infection, which has formed a clump on his knee. He's scheduled for an MRI today and then we should be better able to determine how widespread the infection is. If there are internal clumps such as the one on his knee, which I suspect there are, we may have to surgically remove them. Like I said, we still have a long way to go."

"Do you have an estimate on how long William will need to be in hospital?" Donna asks.

"To be honest, no," Dr. Evans admits. "I'm still not certain which direction this thing will go."

"Direction?" Cate asks.

"What I'm trying to say is that at this point I don't know whether we've caught the infection in time, whether the treatment can contain it faster than it can multiply."

"I'm sorry, I'm confused." Cate's mom shakes her head. "Are you saying there's still a possibility that William won't make it?"

"Yes, I'm afraid that is exactly what I'm saying," Dr. Evans says. "I'm sorry to have to share this dire possibility with you, but I feel being forthright is the best way in these situations."

Dr. Evans excuses himself, leaving Cate and her mother to digest the news.

"It's so hard to believe," Cate says. "Dad looks so much better."

"I know," her mother agrees. She takes Cate by the hand and begins a prayer. "God, please give us strength. Please bring wisdom to the doctors. Be with all of us and give us the courage and faith we need to support William and each other."

The two women are locked in an embrace when Michael enters the room.

"There you are," he says. "I was just in visiting Dad. He said you two were in here, that the doctor had an update?"

Their mother summarizes what Dr. Evans just told them.

"We should probably reach out to Grandma Henderson," Michael says.

"Yes, she needs to know," Donna agrees. "I'll call her later. For now, let's go and be with your father."

They all head down the hall to William's room and, opening the curtain, they discover William covered in sweat, unconscious, his body convulsing.

"Call the doctor!" Donna screams.

Michael pushes the button labelled Press in Case of Emergency at the head of his father's bed. Cate heads for the door. "I'm going to the nursing station." She steps into the hallway, yelling out for help. A group of medical staff appear a few feet down the hall, pushing a huge machine and rushing toward her. Cate follows them back to the room.

"Code blue, Unit 11. Code blue, Unit 11," blares over the hospital PA system.

The team of medical personnel enter William's room in a frenzy of activity. Cate looks over at the heart monitor next to his bed. There is a straight line on the screen and an eerie flat tone. She's seen enough TV dramas to know that her father's heart has stopped. Two technicians are setting up the machine they wheeled in. They rip open William's gown and put a series of paddles on his chest. One of them calls out "Clear" and a volt of electricity surges through William's body, sending him several inches into the air. The line on the monitor is still flat. Donna looks ready to faint. Michael and Cate go over to steady her as the doctor shouts "Clear" again. This time, the monitor resumes its rhythmic tone. The screen shows the flat line is now a series of small hills and valleys.

"Good work, team. Now let's get him to the ICU, stat," the doctor says.

"Mom, you stay with him," Cate says. "Michael and I will find the ICU and meet you there."

"Pray for him!" her mother says as she runs to keep up with the stretcher, the team rushing him to the elevators.

By the time Cate and Michael join their mother in the ICU waiting room, William is stable. Cate calls her neighbour to tell her she will be late then leaves a message for John at work. It is late afternoon when a doctor enters the room.

"William is currently stable but in critical condition," the ICU doctor begins. His name tag reads, Dr. Foster. He stops to take a breath. The three of them hold one another's hands, their faces drawn in worry.

"The MRI shows staphylococcal infection clumped in more than one area of his body," he continues. "There is a significant mass growing on his heart. That's what caused his heart to stop temporarily this morning. On top of that, William has bacteremia, an infection of the bloodstream; endocarditis, an infection of the heart valves; and meningitis, an infection of the brain fluid. I'm so sorry."

Cate takes a deep breath and swallows her tears.

Over the course of the next several weeks William's condition stabilizes, then deteriorates again, in a cycle of ups and downs. He moves in and out of consciousness. The family meets with infections specialists, surgeons, and heart specialists, all with conflicting opinions. One heart specialist insists William needs open-heart surgery, to remove the clump of infection on his heart valve. But an infection specialist feels it's too risky, that the drugs need more time to break the clump down. New medications and combinations of medications are introduced.

Almost three weeks from the day Cate's father is admitted, they get the good news that the infection on William's heart and brain stem have almost completely dissolved. William's condition is upgraded to serious but stable, and he is moved from the ICU to the neurological ward.

Just as William turns a corner, John slides into another deep depression that has him unable to get out of bed. Cate can hardly believe the shitty hand she's been dealt. She's angry with John, even though she knows it isn't totally his fault. During one of her rare peaceful moments at home, when Dana is down for her afternoon nap and Celeste is at school, Cate gets out her journal and vents her frustrations.

> *I don't know what on earth possessed John to think now was a good time to try going off his medications. I doubt he even bothered to check in with Dr. Cote first. I've been so distracted with Dad in the hospital that I haven't been paying much attention to him. Maybe that's what this all amounts to, an attention grab. But that's rather unkind of me. I should try and be more understanding and supportive. It's just that it's been such a challenging time. I needed John to step up to the plate, and he let me down, hard. Instead of helping me with the girls, he's been totally incapacitated and unable to work for almost a week now. On top of everything else, I'm stressed out about our finances, worried that his boss might end up letting him go if it keeps on like this. And with me about to give birth, I'm not exactly in a position to go back to work.*
>
> *Mom came over to help with the girls the other day, bringing over a bucket of KFC and staying to help Celeste with her homework while I bathed Dana, John hiding out in our room all the while. She asked me if I'd thought about getting a divorce. I almost fell over. It seemed to come out of nowhere, but I suppose now that I think about it, it isn't that surprising, with how up and down our relationship is. But with baby number three on the way, I can't imagine for one moment even considering a divorce. I just hope John*

*can get back on track, like he has before. I hope my
baby isn't feeling all the negative energy. I read
somewhere that even in utero, babies can pick up on
the mother's emotional and mental state. I'm so heavy,
literally and figuratively. I just have to keep going, one
step at a time, and pray that I won't crumble under
the weight of these burdens.*

"It's been almost three months," Cate says as she enters her
father's room. "I think you're going to get discharged just
before this baby is born, Dad."

"You might be right," he says. He reaches over to touch
Cate's stomach.

"I'm carrying so much like I did with Dana. All out in
front. I wonder, do you think it's a girl or a boy?"

"I had a dream last night that you had another little girl,"
William says, his eyes watering. "She was a preemie, just like
you. I half expected you wouldn't be in to see me today."

"Well, that dream was off the mark," Cate says with a
laugh. "It's only three more days until our due date, and at
the last ultrasound they said this one already weighs over
nine pounds."

An older lady in blue hospital gear pushes a cart of
lunch trays through the doorway.

"Thank you," Cate says as she walks over and picks out
the plastic-covered tray labelled Henderson, William. "I'll
take that."

She sets the tray down on the table at the end of her
father's bed and takes off the lid.

"Let's see, what do we have here? Jell-O, chicken broth,
orange juice, and tapioca pudding. Yum, yum, I bet your
mouth is watering now, eh, Dad?"

Cate helps her father with his lunch, combs his hair, and brushes his teeth. She is applying some Vaseline to his chapped, dry lips when his neurologist arrives.

"Hello, William, nice to see you enjoying a visit with Cate," he says. "Are you ready for your daily memory quiz?"

"I suppose so." William doesn't sound very enthusiastic.

"Do you know what day it is today?"

"I think it's Monday," William says.

"Very good," the doctor replies. "Do you know what month it is?"

"It's June." William scratches his chin. "No, actually, now that I think about, it just turned July."

"Good, good," the doctor continues. "Do you know the date?"

William hesitates for a moment. He looks up at the ceiling, as if the answer may be hidden in the fluorescent hospital lights. "Hmm, I can't quite remember. I know it's near the beginning of the month…"

"It's okay, Mr. Henderson. It's the fifth of July."

"The fifth already, eh? I still can't get over how long I've been in here."

"Now, can you tell me how many fingers I'm holding up?" the doctor asks as he holds up four.

"Five?" William guesses, squinting his eyes.

The neurologist jots a few notes on his clipboard, then excuses himself, promising to be back the next day around the same time.

"Well, I suppose I should be getting home," Cate says. She leans over and kisses her father on the top of his forehead. "I'll be back after supper to visit with you for a few hours, when John's home with the girls."

At the hospital the following day, Cate finds her mother and Michael visiting too. Dr. Foster comes in and shares the wonderful news that William is going to be discharged from the hospital on Thursday.

"That reminds me, I have some news too," Cate says. She places her hand on the top of her belly. "I went for an ultrasound yesterday and they say this little guy is around ten pounds already. They've scheduled me to induce labour tomorrow."

"That's great news," Michael says. "And did I hear you say 'this little guy'?"

"Yes, you did. The technician kept asking me if I wanted to know the sex. I said no, but he was so persistent. He said it was really obvious and I put two and two together."

"That's great news," her mother says. "It will be so nice to add a grandson to the mix."

"And I was so certain it was a girl," William says. "When are you scheduled to be induced?"

"Tomorrow night, after supper, around seven," Cate says. "They warned me it could take a while."

"Well, I guess Dad's going to be going home just as you're being admitted," Michael says. "I'm so happy how everything is unfolding."

"Me too," Donna says, a huge smile on her face. "Only I suppose it will be a little tricky for me to watch the girls as we planned, since I'll be bringing your father home."

"Oh, not to worry, Mom. John has already made arrangements with his parents to come look after the girls at our house."

"Oh, how perfect," Donna says.

"Yes, but I hope you are recovered soon and well enough to bring the whole clan over to our house so your mom and I can meet our new grandson," William says.

"Don't worry," Cate says as she leans over to kiss him on the forehead. "We'll all be there as soon as we can. I'm just so happy you're finally going home."

The next evening after dinner John's parents show up with a packed carry-on suitcase and a grocery bag full of chips, Cheezies, and pop for the girls. Once Cate goes over the schedule she's written out on the whiteboard, John grabs her overnight bag and they load into the van to head to the hospital.

Dr. Cote inserts a Foley bulb into Cate's vagina, a catheter-like device that will soften her cervix to induce labour. By midnight, Cate is still only two centimetres dilated, so Dr. Cote makes the decision to break Cate's water.

"This worked pretty well with Dana, if I recall," Dr. Cote says. She reaches an instrument gently inside Cate until she sees birth water trickling down Cate's thigh.

"Yes, except it did take thirty-three hours," Cate says. "Let's hope we aren't in for such a long haul this time."

"That would be unlikely, since this is now your second vaginal delivery," Dr. Cote says. "But you never know what's going to happen."

Cate sleeps on and off, her contractions mild, John conked out in the chair beside her. In the morning, things start to progress. She requests an enema, remembering a story from one of her friends about pushing out more than just a baby during delivery. She stands naked in the shower off her birthing room, the pulsing water providing some relief, while John rubs her lower back. When the shower no longer helps ease her pain, Cate climbs onto the bed. She positions herself on her hands and knees and sways and moans through each contraction. She pushes her face into the pillow like a trowel, entangling her fine hair into a massive bird's nest. Just when she thinks she's at her wits' end and is ready to get an epidural, Dr. Cote does an internal exam.

"You're ten centimetres," she says. "It's time to push."

Dr. Cote adjusts the bed so Cate is almost sitting up and cranks it to raise her bottom higher. She places Cate's feet into the steel stirrups. John rubs Cate's shoulders as she pushes.

"I'm sorry, guys," Cate says. "I think I'm going to poo!"

"It's the baby's head crowning," Dr. Cote says with a laugh. "I've never met anyone more paranoid of losing their bowels in labour as you. Come on now, a few more good pushes should do it."

Cate summons all her strength and pushes hard. She hears a soft mew, like a kitten, and then suddenly her baby boy is being placed on her stomach as Dr. Cote cuts the cord.

"Oh, my goodness, he's so big and bald and gorgeous," Cate cries out. "Hello, my sweet son. Oh look, what's that white stuff on his eyelids?" Cate brushes the thick, white cheese-like goo away gently with her finger, then bends down to kiss him, once on each eyelid.

"The technical term is *vernix caseosa*," Dr. Cote says. "It's nothing to worry about, just a natural lubricant that eases delivery and moisturizes the baby's skin."

"Oh, I could just gobble him up," Cate says. "Are you still happy with our choice to call him Taylor Michael?" Cate asks John.

Before John can answer, Dr. Cote scoops up Taylor.

"I'm sorry, Cate, but your son is a little blue. I need to take him to the newborn ICU for some oxygen, immediately."

"What?" Cate says. "But he looks so big and healthy."

"I know, and he is. He'll likely only need to be on oxygen a few hours, it's nothing for you to worry about."

Dr. Cote whisks Taylor away.

"Don't worry, I'll stay with him," John says, following Dr. Cote out the door.

Cate is still elevated on the delivery table. She scoots her bottom right to the edge and reaches her bare feet the few inches to the ground, then hobbles, naked, to a stack of plastic-wrapped gowns on the cupboard at the side. The nurse is busy typing up her report on the computer when Cate traipses off down the hallway as fast as she can, her body still in shock from the delivery. She's running on pure adrenalin as she shuffles along. She gets lost a few times, taking the wrong turn, but eventually she spots John standing outside the newborn ICU, gazing through the window at their son.

"He looks so out of place amongst all the tiny preemies in there," he says with a wistful sigh. "I wish I could hold him."

"Me too," Cate says, sliding her arm around John's waist.

"I can hardly believe what an oaf I've been these past few weeks." John turns to face her. "But I'm back on my meds, ready to be the man you deserve and the father our children deserve too."

"That's the third bit of good news I've received today," Cate says with a grin.

"Third?" John says.

"Yes, third. First, Dad was discharged. Second, Taylor was born. And third, my husband is back. I think things are moving into a huge upward curve, and I'm so incredibly grateful."

Chapter 16

CATE'S PREDICTION DOESN'T COME true. At least as far as her marriage to John is concerned. Little more than a year after Taylor's birth, things have begun to disintegrate, again.

Cate is throwing on a load of laundry, checking through everyone's pockets for stray tissues or discarded gum wrappers, when she finds a piece of paper in John's trouser pocket with a phone number scratched on it. It's clearly his handwriting—block letters, tight and precise. Her intuition is ignited into overdrive and her heart starts to beat wildly as thoughts start to spin. She picks up the piece of paper and holds it under her nose, then breathes in deeply. She detects a faint scent, of something sharp yet flowery, a hint of carnation, rose, and spice. A woman's fragrance. Cate tucks the slip of paper into her jeans pocket and finishes sorting the load. As she closes the door of the washer, the room starts to spin. She closes her eyes and grips the edge of the machine.

"Mom, there you are," Celeste says, peeking her head into the laundry room. "I've been calling out and looking all over for you. Hillary just called and asked if I can come over to practice our lyrical duet. Can you drive me?"

"Huh, what?" Cate gives her head a shake.

"Are you okay? You look like you just saw a ghost."

"I do?" Cate says, blinking her eyes. "No, I'm fine, just low blood sugar, I suspect." Cate doesn't know why she feels the need to make up some stupid lie, but she does. "Let me grab a snack. Your brother is going to be getting up from his nap any minute, and I'll go tell Dana. We should be able to leave in about fifteen minutes. Will that suit you?"

"Yeah, sure, that'd be great. Thanks, Mom. I'll go change."

Cate is still thinking of the scrap of paper as she climbs the stairs. It feels like it's burning a hole in her pocket, into her flesh. She's dying to dial up the number and see who answers, but she doesn't want to be that kind of wife, and besides, she doesn't have time. Instead, she opens the door to the nursery and peers into Taylor's crib. He is wide awake, contentedly staring up at his zoo animal mobile. Both girls would have woken up and bellowed it to the world, Cate thinks as she walks into the room.

"How's my big, handsome boy?" she asks, reaching in to pick Taylor up. "Did you have a good nap?"

At just over one, Taylor isn't saying too many words yet, but the huge toothy smile and bright eyes speak volumes.

"Let's give your diaper a quick change before we go for a car ride," Cate coos as she sets her son down on the change table and undoes the safety pins. She sets his wet cloth diaper to the side, to be tossed in the diaper pail in the bathroom when she's done. As she's reaching for a fresh diaper on the shelf below, Dana tramps into the room.

"Mommy, Cela says you're driving her over to Hillary's for a dance practice, is that true?"

"Yes, my love, I was just going to change Taylor and come find you to tell you to get ready to go."

"Do I have to come? I'm learning my new sight words, and I don't want to go for a car ride."

"Now Dana, you're far too young to stay at home alone," Cate says with a chuckle. "Don't worry, we'll only be gone about half an hour, the time will fly by."

"No, it won't." Dana pouts. "I won't get into any trouble. I'll just stay in my room and do my flash cards, just the same as if you were here. Please, Mom."

"There's no use arguing," Cate says as she pulls up Taylor's sweatpants, "it's out of the question. Go on now, get on your sandals and grab two Fruit Roll-Ups from the pantry for you and your sister to munch on in the car. For that matter, why don't you bring along a few packs of your flash cards too?"

"Okay," Dana says with a pout and a shrug of her shoulders as she turns to go to her room.

Just before supper, John calls to say he has to work late, to go ahead and have dinner without him. Cate's hand goes to the note, still in her pocket, but she leaves it to prepare the meal. While dinner is cooking, she feeds Taylor Pablum and puréed peaches, then fills Lady's bowl with a scoop of kibbles. She doesn't have a minute to think more about the note.

Dinner is finished, the children all bathed and tucked into bed, when the phone rings.

"How's it going?" John asks. "Did you manage okay without me?"

Cate sighs. "You know well enough how challenging it is to get all three kids sorted with only two hands. But yes, I managed. Are you going to be home soon?"

"Unfortunately, no. I have a Skype conference call with the overseas team. I'll probably be at least two more hours. Go ahead and go to bed without me."

"Yeah, okay, whatever."

"I don't appreciate your tone," John says. "It's not like I enjoy working so hard, but someone's got to pay the bills. Celeste's dance costs are through the roof and she just keeps taking on more."

"I know," Cate mumbles. "It's just that…"

"It's just what?"

"Nothing, nothing at all, I'm just tired," Cate says.

After she hangs up, Cate takes out the piece of paper and dials the number.

"Good evening, this is the Palliser Hotel, Aaron speaking. How can I direct your call?"

"I, oh, I'm sorry, I seem to have dialled the wrong number," Cate stutters.

"Okay, well, have a great day," the cheery receptionist says before hanging up.

Cate stares at the receiver.

"Mom, can you tuck me in?" Celeste yells from her new room downstairs that John finished not long before Taylor was born.

"I'll be right there, angel," Cate yells back. She rips the paper into tiny shreds, then tosses them in the garbage.

When the house is quiet, Cate makes herself a cup of tea and takes it up to her room. She sets it on a coaster on her nightstand and gets her journal out of the drawer.

I'm certain now. John's having an affair. I've been suspecting as much. There have been too many signs to ignore, and now today I found a phone number in the pocket of his pants for a hotel downtown. I can think of no other reason for him to have the number for a hotel. And besides, the scent of a woman was unmistakable. I think it's his secretary. Classic. Now the only question is, what to do about it? Should I confront him? All that will likely do is cause a fight. It won't change our crumbling marriage or make him faithful. It won't make him want me. And I don't think I'm prepared to leave him. There are just so many ties that bind me to my marriage. I haven't gone back to work yet. I was planning to start back part-time this fall, but Taylor is still so little, and with three children, the daycare costs outweigh the financial benefits of working part-time. Money is tight already, but if I leave John, there will be two households to run on one salary. And money isn't the only issue. I have to think about our children. Who would they live with? It should be me, but I'm not certain John wouldn't fight that, just to spite me.

Taylor only turned one a few weeks ago. All my children need a father, even if he is absent a lot. Not to mention in a foul mood half the time. I need John, too. If I'm honest, it's more than that. I want John. I took my marriage vows seriously. But it takes two to tango.

Cate stops to wipe a tear from her eye. She holds back a sob, her hand to her throat. She takes a sip of tea, then continues.

Maybe I can suggest marriage counselling? John might be willing to try it, although he hasn't had much

*success with therapy to help him with depression.
Maybe this affair is just an offshoot of his mental
illness? I don't know. I don't have the answers. And the
truth is, when would we find the time to go for
counselling anyway? We don't even make time for our
weekly date nights anymore. I never realized how busy
it would be with three kids. You can't know what you
don't know. And I love them all, so much. I wouldn't
change that.*

Lady barks, wagging her tail to come up.

"Come on then," Cate says, lifting her and setting her at the foot of the bed with a tousle of her ears. Cate puts away her journal, then pulls up the covers tight, right up to her chin, and cries herself to sleep.

She is awakened early the next morning by the sound of Taylor calling out, "Mama, Mama." She slips quietly out of bed, but it isn't necessary as John is out cold.

"Come on, my little man." Cate hefts him from his crib, takes him down to the kitchen, and straps him into his high chair. She puts on the kettle to boil some water for his bottle and puts on a pot of coffee. She peels a ripe banana and mashes it in a small glass bowl. While the coffee drips, she prepares Taylor's formula then takes him over to the couch to feed him his bottle. He gulps enthusiastically, popping off the rubber nipple to smile up at her now and again, and Cate's heart is gripped with the fierce, protective love of mothers.

Both girls get up a few hours later. It's still six weeks until school starts back for Celeste and Dana starts preschool part-time, yet they are both already restless, the long days stretched out before them like the horizon at sunset. The girls are sitting at the table, eating a light breakfast of fruit and cereal, discussing what they might get up to later.

"Mommy, why is Daddy still sleeping?" Celeste asks as she brings over her bowl and glass to put in the dishwasher. "Doesn't he have to work today?"

"Yes, he does, but he was at work late last night, so he'll likely sleep in a bit longer," Cate says.

"How come he's working so many nights anyway?" Dana asks.

"Because he's working on a new project with a team overseas and with the time difference, they are up when he's sleeping and vice versa."

"What's a 'time difference' mean?" Dana asks.

"Oh, I know about that," Celeste answers. "Come on in the office and I'll show you on the world map we have on the wall."

Celeste takes Dana by the hand, eager to teach her little sister about time zones. Taylor has drifted off in his baby chair. Cate takes the opportunity to clean up the kitchen. As she is wiping all the counters down with a dishcloth, John descends the stairs, dressed and ready for work.

"Good morning, gorgeous," he says, coming up behind Cate. He reaches around and tweaks her nipple through her blouse, a suggestive grin on his face. "Maybe tonight I'll get home in decent time, before you're asleep—"

"I wouldn't assume anything," Cate interrupts, smacking his arm away.

"What's with the attitude?" John says, a dark cloud descending over his scowling face.

"You haven't said two words to me in days, and the only thing you can think of is sex," Cate says, her hands on her hips.

Deep down, she knows it's more about her suspicions of him having an affair than the lack of attention she's been getting, but she isn't about to open that drawer of dirty laundry. She hears the door of the office close and pastes on a smile as Dana and Celeste walk into the kitchen.

"Daddy!" Dana squeals. "You're up! Will you come into the office so I can show you what Cela taught me about time zones?"

"Sorry, princess," John says. He is pouring himself a coffee in a large travel mug. "I've got to get a move on. No summer holidays for me."

"But, Daddy, please!" Dana says. "Can't you just wait five minutes more?"

"Okay," John says with a strained smile. "But only five minutes."

Dana and John disappear and Celeste puts on the television. Five minutes later, to the dot, John emerges and calls out goodbye. Celeste doesn't even look up from her show. Only Dana walks him to the door to say goodbye.

On Friday, Cate is looking forward to family pizza and games night, but John calls just before six. He leaves a message saying the gang is all going out for beers at the pub on the corner across from his office to celebrate finishing phase one of the design for a new steel mill.

"When's Daddy going to be home?" Dana asks when the pizza arrives. "Are we going to wait for him?"

"He's going out with his work buddies tonight, my love."

"But it's supposed to be family night," Dana pouts.

"I know, but Daddy's been working so hard, he needs a break," Cate says, in an effort to defend him.

"Isn't spending time with us a break?" Dana asks.

"Are you two getting a divorce?" Celeste asks.

"Celeste, really," Cate says with a frown. "I don't know why you always think with every fight or problem that your father and I will get a divorce. It doesn't work like that. At least not in this family. We've made a commitment to each other, and to you three."

Cate can't help but think Celeste almost looks disappointed, but she convinces herself she is only imagining it.

"After I tuck Taylor in for the night, us girls can play dress-up and do makeovers, maybe even have a spa," Cate suggests as she sets three plates on the table. "What do you think?"

"Okay, that sounds fun," Celeste says. "Can we paint our toes red and put glitter on our eyes?"

"Can I wear my Princess Jasmine pajamas?" Dana asks.

The atmosphere changes from dark and gloomy to light and cheery as the girls chatter on. They end up staying up way past their bedtimes, but it's summer holidays, and Cate is glad to have the company. When she turns out her light after reading a book by her new favourite author, Miriam Toews, John still isn't home.

Mid-August, Cate discovers just the opportunity she has been hoping for. A position opens up at a new private preschool, only a ten-minute drive from their home. Cate is overqualified, but the director and owner seems so kind-hearted and committed to positive early experiences with education for children, Cate can't resist. It seals the deal when Cate finds out the position is only part-time, four mornings a week.

When she gets home from the interview, she finds her father seated on the couch with hair curlers sticking out from the top of his head, Dana holding a comb and inserting a bobby pin, playing hairdresser. Taylor, who isn't walking yet, is sitting in his activity centre, contentedly turning the steering wheel in circles and beeping the horn. Celeste is over at her friend Gillian's for the afternoon.

"You're back early," her father says, looking over. "How did it go?

"It turns out that it's a perfect fit and I was hired on the spot," Cate says. "I hope you're still up for looking after these two for me? It's four mornings a week."

"Absolutely," he says with a grin. "It's not like I've got anything else on the go. Since this old cripple-father of yours is on permanent disability, I might as well be of use to someone."

"Now, Dad," Cate begins.

"Hooray!" Dana whoops. "I love it when Grandpa looks after us!"

"Yes, well, you'll be starting preschool yourself when I go back to work," Cate says. "But maybe Grandpa will agree to stay and have lunch with us after I pick you up and we're all back at home, once in a while at least."

"Will you, please, Grandpa?" Dana says earnestly. "I want you to stay with us every day!"

"Well, how can I say no to the offer of your mother's delicious cooking and spending more time with you and your brother?" He gives her ponytail an affectionate tug. "But I can't stay every day. Grandma needs someone to fuss over."

"It sounds like it's settled then," Cate says. "Let's plan for a family dinner here this Sunday to celebrate. Will you check with Mom and see if your schedule is open?"

"I already know your mother's answer will be yes, even if she does have something else planned," William says. "She's always willing to reschedule her other commitments around family."

"It's done then." Cate's smile reaches her eyes. She can hardly wait to tell John her good news. She calls Michael to invite him and Ashley over to join them for Sunday family dinner too, to celebrate her new job and the completion of the new home he and Ashley just finished building.

The day of the party, Cate gets to work on her task list early, juggling looking after her children with cleaning the house and preparing the meal. John sleeps in until past ten, then heads out to the garage to tinker on one of his ongoing projects.

A half-hour before everyone is supposed to arrive, Cate still hasn't changed out of her scrubs and is peeling hard-boiled eggs for potato salad when the doorbell rings. Lady runs to the door, wagging her tail and barking with excitement.

"Can somebody please get that?" Cate calls out. "I'm up to my elbows in here!"

"I'll get it," Celeste says, appearing at the top of the stairs, all smiles.

"It's Grandma and Grandpa," Celeste calls back. She greets her grandparents with big hugs.

"You're here early," Cate says, looking over at the clock on the microwave.

"Yes, well, better early than late, I say," her mother says with a wink. "I thought maybe you'd appreciate some help. Where's John?" She looks around, taking in the immaculately set table, fresh flowers in a vase.

"Oh, he went for a bike ride about half an hour ago," Cate says. "He should be back any minute."

"You'd think he could pitch in once in a while," William says.

"It's important for him to exercise." Cate sounds a bit defensive but isn't fooling anyone. They'd fought over his decision to go, and he left in a huff and a cloud of dark energy. "It's part of his strategy for managing depression."

"Yes, well, that's all well and good," snorts her father. "But surely he could have chosen a better time?"

"Let's not get into it, please," says Cate as she stirs all the salad ingredients together in a large glass bowl. "I'm going to put this in the fridge until dinner and run up for a quick shower."

"Okay, dear," her mother says. "I brought over a loaf of oregano rye bread I just made this morning and some hummus. Shall I slice some up and put it in a basket?"

"Thanks, Mom, but I think it's still a little early for that," Cate says, wiping her hands on a tea towel. "But if you wouldn't mind taking the skewers out of the fridge and basting them with the marinade, that'd be a huge help."

"Okay, off you go then."

"Grandpa, will you come outside with me?" Celeste says. "I've perfected my cartwheels since you were here last."

Fifteen minutes later, Cate is dressed, freshened up, and ready. She wakes Taylor from his nap and changes him into the outfit that Michael and Ashley bought him for his birthday, then perches him on her hip and goes downstairs to join the guests. John still isn't home, but Michael has arrived bearing a bottle of expensive-looking Australian red wine.

"Hey, Sis, hi, little man," Michael says, his smile lighting up his eyes as they crinkle.

"Thank you for the wine, we'll serve it with dinner," Cate says, pulling her brother to her in an embrace. She sets the wine on the kitchen table. "Where's Ashley?"

"She called to say she's running a little late. She had a hair appointment so we took separate cars."

"Oh, that's no problem, John is late too. Mom and Dad are out back watching the girls perform gymnastics. Why don't you grab us both a cooler from the fridge and we'll head on out to join in on the fun?"

Everyone is having a great time enjoying the sunshine in the backyard when John rides up on the ravine path just outside their steel-wire fence, drenched in sweat.

"Did you have a good ride?" Michael asks, coming over to open the gate.

"Yeah, kind of lost track of time, though, sorry," John says.

"It's all good," Cate pipes in. "Ashley is late too and it's still early. Go on up and shower. We'll start up the barbeque when Ashley gets here."

When everyone is gathered around the table, Cate takes out a bottle of champagne that she's had chilling in the fridge. She pours white grape juice for the girls.

"To new beginnings," Cate says. Everyone raises their glasses and clinks them together to toast the occasion.

That night Cate wakes up drenched in sweat, her heart palpitating wildly in her chest. She's having difficulty breathing, dreaming about the wolf. The clock radio shows just past three. She shivers and takes a drink of water from the glass on her nightstand. She's wide awake but her brain feels fuzzy so she checks her blood sugars. They are crazy high, 22.4. She grabs her journal and tiptoes from the room.

Downstairs, Cate opens the fridge and grabs an insulin pen, thinking how much handier they are than the old vial-and-syringe method. She dials up her correction dose and injects it into the soft flesh of her tummy. She puts on the kettle to make a cup of tea, then settles on the couch to write.

*In my dream the wolf was watching me from
a thicket of forest trees while I stooped to take a drink
from a waterfall spilling into a tiny creek. As soon as
I felt his presence, I tried to scream for help, but I'd lost
my voice. The wolf grinned as he advanced toward me
from the shadows, showing his sharp teeth. He tilted his
head back and let out a sinister sound, a cross between
a laugh and a howl. I tried to run, but my legs were like
blocks of cement. I just stood there, terrified, as he got
closer and closer, and then, just as he was about to
grab my arm, I woke up. It all unfolded in the way my
dreams often do, as if I was watching a movie, seeing
myself from a camera lens instead of from inside
my body.*

*I haven't dreamed about the wolf for so long.
I wonder what it means, if anything? I hope it isn't
a premonition. But that's all a bunch of hogwash, as
my father would say. Just my overactive imagination.
Maybe in my subconscious I'm connecting my suspicion
that John is having an affair with past abuse? Maybe
the wolf symbolizes betrayal? Who knows. It won't
change anything to waste my time worrying about it,
so I might as well just forget about it.*

*I'm so tired of making excuses for John's bad
behaviour. It was embarrassing, defending him to my
parents for being such an entitled oaf, like somehow
because he works hard at his job he doesn't have to
follow through with any responsibilities at home, that
he can just show up to events we're hosting as if he's a
guest. Of course, after tossing back a few beers, a glass
of champagne, and more glasses of wine than I could
count, totally ignoring his three-drink rule, he became
the life of the party, making jokes and speaking in
different accents, as he thinks he does so well when he's*

inebriated. I saw Celeste watching him with a worried expression, and then she disappeared downstairs to her room without saying goodbye to everyone, so out of character. At least Dana and Taylor were both fast asleep by then.

God, my life is such a mess. I feel like I'm wandering, lost in the wilderness.

Cate sets down her journal, gets the Yellow Pages from the kitchen drawer, and looks in the index for marriage counsellors. She thumbs through the long list of therapists. Most have a short description following their title. She chooses someone who uses Cognitive Behaviour Therapy, and one who has been practicing for over twenty years. She writes down the contact information and sets her list by the telephone. She stands up tall and squares her shoulders. When John gets up, she's going to inform him of her decision. In her mind, it isn't up for discussion. Either he agrees to try counselling or she starts the proceedings for a divorce.

Chapter 17

THE MORNING OF DANA'S ninth birthday party, Cate wakes up with her head pounding, but she doesn't have time to nurse a headache, or for any other distractions. She has a massive to-do list with corresponding boxes beside each item, waiting for the tick that signifies its completion. She heads straight into her ensuite bathroom, opens the medicine cabinet, spills out two Tylenol into the palm of her hand, and fills a glass of water from the tap. She looks in the mirror. For the briefest of moments, she sees a vision of her little girl self. She senses something, but thinks of her list and swallows the nagging feeling down with the pills.

A half-hour before the party, Cate is frantic, her list of tasks still incomplete. She is tying balloons to the dining room chandelier when the phone starts to ring.

"Could someone please get that?" she calls out.

On the third ring she jumps down off the chair she is standing on, cursing every member in her family under her breath. The answering machine kicks on just as she picks up the phone. She can hear Michael, but his words are drowned out by her recording.

Hi, you've reached the home of John, Cate, Celeste, Dana, and Taylor. We can't come to the phone right now, but if you leave a message, we'll get back to you as soon we can.

"Sorry about that, Michael," Cate says once the recording ends.

"Thank God you picked up," Michael says. "I don't want to alarm you, but—"

"Alarm me?" Cate's heart starts banging against her rib cage, her intuition in overdrive. "What do you mean, 'alarm me'?"

"I'm at Mom and Dad's place. I've found Dad unconscious."

Cate's knees start to buckle. She grabs the edge of the kitchen counter with her free hand to steady herself.

"Unconscious?" she says in a high-pitched, child-like voice she recognizes all too well.

"Yeah, unconscious. I came over to drop off his prescription and found him sprawled on his bedroom floor with a bloody gash on his forehead. Oh, they're here! I've got to go!"

Michael hangs up, leaving Cate in a state of sheer, uninformed panic, wondering who the hell *they* are. She conjures a ghastly vision of her father lying rigid, blood seeping from a deep and devastating wound, coagulating in the turquoise fibres of the carpet. She can't concentrate on anything. She feels like throwing up. Waiting is unbearable. She paces. She peers out the office window, looking for Dana's guests, but there's no one in sight. She goes back into the dining room and starts setting out the purple paper party plates, her hands trembling so hard she can barely separate the thin cardboard. She accidentally pops a balloon and the sound almost stops her heart. Hand at her throat, Cate watches as the embossed, metallic *Happy Birthday* transforms from thick and jovial to thin and shrunken. The balloon swirls in a series of circles then lies forlorn in the middle of the floor, all shrunken and limp, a shadow of its once festive self. Cate can't help but think of her father's hands, before arthritis crippled them. She shudders. When the phone rings, it startles her so thoroughly she jumps.

"Michael?" Cate's voice is tight with the strain.

"Hey, sorry about that, Sis. That was the paramedics. They just finished transferring Dad onto a gurney. I'm going to follow the ambulance to the hospital and I'll call you when I get there, okay?"

"What the hell is going on? What's wrong with him?"

"I'm not sure. It looks like he hit his head on something. I'm thinking maybe he was a bit out of it from the drugs he's on for his ankle infection, got up to use the bathroom or get a drink or something and then stumbled in the dark and fell. Anyhow, somehow he banged his head and must have got a concussion or something."

"Do you think it's serious?"

"Like I said, I really don't know. It all feels kinda surreal."

"Well, serious or not, I have to be there," Cate says.

"Yeah, I know. But what about Dana? Isn't it her birthday party today?"

"Yeah. In fact, I'm surprised none of her guests are here yet."

"Well, if you need to be there, I can handle things on this end," Michael says.

"I know, and I really appreciate that. But I won't be able to concentrate on throwing a party, knowing Dad is lying unconscious in the hospital. I have to be there, but damn,

I do hate to disappoint Dana. It really sucks that Mom is in Banff. Have you tried to call her?"

"No, not yet; I don't even know what hotel she's staying at," Michael says.

"I guess we can figure that out later, once we know more. I'll meet up with you at the hospital as soon as I can."

Cate hangs up the phone and goes downstairs. She says a prayer under her breath, that her father is going to be fine. She finds Celeste is in her room, listening to music and doing homework on her bed. It is covered in a chaotic mess of clothes, teen magazines, towels, and even a few dirty dishes. Cate bites her tongue, reminding herself of her recent decision to pick her battles.

"Can I come in?" she asks, knocking on the half-open door.

"Sure, Mom, what's up?"

"I just got off the phone with Uncle Michael. Grandpa William has been taken in an ambulance to the hospital. I hate to abandon Dana on her special day and leave managing her party all to your father. You know how stressed out he can get with these things."

"It sounds like you're trying to ask me if I'll pitch in," Celeste says. "I'm happy to help out, Mom. I just hope Grandpa is okay, that he isn't in the hospital for months, like last time."

"Thank you so much, my angel, I'm sure it's nothing serious," Cate says with a smile. "In fact, I'll likely be back before things really get under way, but just in case."

Cate leaves to look for John. She spots him and Taylor through the window of the still-unfinished basement family room, playing soccer out on the back lawn. She goes outside and repeats everything she just told Celeste.

"Off you go then," John says. He seems totally unruffled. "I've got the party covered. Hell, you're so organized, it could probably run all by itself. And, like you said, by the time you get there your dad will likely already be coming around, ready to be discharged."

Cate thanks John and gives him a hug. She kisses Taylor, once on each eyelid. She goes back inside and writes out a detailed checklist for John on the whiteboard in the kitchen. After scribbling out instructions, she steels herself for the hardest task of all—telling Dana.

Dana is standing in front of the floor-length mirror in her room, brushing her thick ash-blonde hair that is almost to her waist. Cate sits on Dana's bed and pats the space beside her.

"Come, sit beside me."

"What's up?" Dana asks. "You look upset."

"Yes, well, you're very perceptive, as usual. I just got off the phone with Uncle Michael. Grandpa William was rushed to the hospital, in an ambulance. Uncle Michael found him unconscious. I know it's your special day, and it's probably nothing, but—"

"But you need to be there," Dana finishes for her. "It's okay, Maman, I understand."

"Thank you. That is very mature of you. Celeste has offered to help Dad, and I've left instructions on the whiteboard. Your guests should be here any minute, but I want to get a move on right away."

"*D'accord*, Maman," Dana says, reverting to French, her habit from being enrolled in French immersion.

"Make sure your dad takes tons of photos." Cate leans in and kisses Dana on the top of her head. "I love you so much. I hope you have an absolutely amazing time, celebrating the gift that is you."

Cate heads back downstairs, stuffs her blood testing meter in her oversized purse, then takes the keys for the van from the hook by the door. Dana's best friend, Ella, is

walking up the sidewalk just as Cate turns to go through
the laundry room to the garage and Dana enters the foyer.

En route, Cate's mind wanders to the many trips she's made
over the years to Foothills Hospital. All three of her children
were born there. Her father had all of his surgeries there too.
She remembers, with a stab of pain, the time, almost seven
years ago now, that her father came close to dying. It was a
long time ago, but not long enough.

Cate scans the waiting room and spots Michael slumped
over in one of the faded red vinyl chairs. His thick, dark hair
is dishevelled. Cate imagines him raking his fingers through
it with worry, a habit he inherited from their dad.

"Hey, Sis." Michael's cobalt-blue eyes, red-rimmed and
squinting into the fluorescent lights above, manage to
twinkle and his mouth slips into a smile as he stands up.
"Come, give me a hug."

Cate rests her head against Michael's shoulder in a warm
embrace, the scent of Drakkar Noir drifting into her nostrils.

"They are running some tests right now, so we can't see
him," Michael says. "They suspect he has a staphylococcus
infection again."

Acid creeps up from her stomach to her throat. "I hope
they're wrong. It was such a fucking nightmare last time.
We almost lost him. I, I…."

"I know, Sis. Try not to jump to any conclusions until
we can speak to a doctor."

"I'm going to go ask if I can see him." Cate goes over to
stand in line at the triage desk. When it's her turn, the nurse
behind the plastic window looks disinterested as she scans
the computer screen in front of her.

"Ah, here we are, William Henderson. He's in bed twenty-one, but it's off limit for visitors. You'll just have to be patient and take a seat."

Cate paces the room, watching the entrance to the emergency ward like a hawk. When she sees an attendant pushing a tall cart of supplies key in the access code, she ducks in behind him.

She walks past beds one to twenty and then stops to mentally prepare herself. She takes a deep breath and pulls back the curtain, but the cubicle is empty. Confused and uncertain of what to do, Cate wanders the corridors in a daze.

"Cate?" a familiar voice says. "What are you doing?" Denise, a friend of their family, has been working as a nurse at the Foothills for some time.

"I, I was looking for my dad, is he, do you know where he is, if he's okay?" Cate stutters. Her bones and muscles feel like they've dissolved, her body ready to crumble to the floor.

"I have seen your dad's chart," Denise says. "But I'm not at liberty to go into the details, as I'm sure you can appreciate. They've taken him to get a CAT scan. He's still unconscious, Cate. It's going to be a while before we know anything, but I promise, I will personally come and find you in the waiting room the minute the doctors have news of any sort, okay?"

Cate thanks Denise and makes her way back to the waiting room, her thoughts spinning like a washing machine on rinse cycle. She feels a bit sheepish as she walks past the admissions station. The nurse who told her to wait glares at her, and Cate lowers her gaze to the floor, picking up her pace.

Ashley has joined Michael, and Cate gives her a hug before giving them the update.

"What a crazy coincidence, that Denise happens to be working today and literally bumped into you," Michael says.

"I know, right? I feel better, knowing she'll let us know what's going on."

They sit together in strained silence, sipping from vending machine sodas while they wait. They engage in small talk and steal furtive glances at the clock on the wall.

It seems an incredibly long span of time, but eventually Denise approaches them. It is clear by the expression on her face that it's not good news.

"I so hate to have to tell you this, but your father's situation is very serious," she begins. "He is being transferred to the ICU. They need to run more tests in order to get the most comprehensive diagnosis, but the CAT scan revealed extensive infection that needs to be treated immediately. To be quite honest, it could be some time before you can see him."

Cate's world starts to spin off its axis. The headache she'd had that morning shifts into a migraine. She has to squint her eyes against the bright lights as Denise leads them down the hallway to the ICU waiting room.

The threesome chooses a table in the corner by the window to wait. Cate harasses the nursing station continuously for an update, but nothing is forthcoming. She picks up a well-leafed-through magazine from the piles strewn across the laminate table and stares at the images without seeing, then tosses it aside. She fixates on the details of her surroundings. The sage-green paint on the walls is peeling. A young mother holds her baby in her arms and rocks it back and forth, making soft shushing noises. She feels like she's entered a twilight zone. She rummages in her purse to locate her pocket-sized, out-and-about journal and a ballpoint pen that is missing its cap.

If I were superstitious, believed in omens, or possessed some level of spirit-body awareness, I might have anticipated that my life was about to be irrevocably altered when I woke up this morning with that niggling feeling. As it was, I was numb to my intuition, detached from my experience and focused on tasks. It's clear now my headache was my spiritual self, the part of me that is deeply connected with my dad. We can see into one another's souls, we sense things before we know them. My senses were past tingling. They were vibrating at a high voltage, trying to send me a signal that something was terribly wrong with my father, but I chose not to listen.

I've ignored my spiritual self so often these past years. I still go to church regularly, but that's different. Church is a haven, but not a place where I am still, where I listen to the wisdom of the universe. God has provided amazing opportunities for my spiritual self to blossom, but, like the seeds Jesus mentions in the parable, they landed on dry, parched ground. I planted my seeds of love in my marriage to John, and despite all the watering and sunshine I've showered upon him, the seeds haven't been able to take hold. When I first threatened him with a divorce, he agreed to go for marriage counselling, but he never followed through on the promises he made during therapy. I know I'm living a lie, but most of the time I suppress that knowledge. It's so much work to sustain the image.

All of a sudden, as I write, a memory comes to mind, of when I was eight or nine, sitting at the piano. The lesson book is propped open. I'm near the end of a piece when I hit an incorrect note. I start over. I play it incorrectly, again. In a fit of frustration, I pound the ebony and ivory keys with a vengeance. My hands are mid-air when I feel the warm presence of my father. He sits next to me on the piano bench. A tear slips down my cheek. Dad gently picks up both my hands and places them on top of his, finger to finger. He doesn't know the first thing about playing a piano, but it doesn't matter. In silence, we sit there, him and I. Then he lifts his hands away and places mine back on the keys. He doesn't utter one word, but he doesn't need to. I turn my head toward him. Reflected in his eyes is such a depth of emotion. My heart knows it perfectly. Dad smiles his crooked grin and wipes the tears from my cheek, even though they are almost dry. He kisses my forehead before rising and leaves me to conquer the song.

I wonder if my children feel as treasured as I felt growing up, if I've been able to pass on the love that was showered upon me by both my parents?

I'm not ready to let my father go. I still need him so much. Please, God, if you're listening, answer my prayers.

Cate sets down her journal and sighs. Her mind is still playing over old memories when Denise comes into the room.

"Dr. Leyden is ready to talk with you in a family conference room," Denise says, then leads the three of them down the hallway.

The meeting room is small, furnished with red vinyl chairs like the ones in the rest of the hospital. Cate notices a solitary piece of artwork hanging on one wall that looks like a knock-off Monet. She wishes Michael's calls had been successful in locating their mom, knowing how much she would want to be with them.

"Hello, I'm Dr. Leyden," the doctor says as he strolls into the room. He shakes their hands and beckons for them to take a seat. Cate thinks he looks remarkably like a stereotypical doctor from television. He could be starring in any one of the popular hospital dramas currently on TV. Dressed in wrinkled khaki pants with a pale blue smock over top, he's wearing white sport socks with worn Birkenstocks. He has classically handsome features— a rugged five o'clock stubble, a mop of thick black hair streaked with grey at the temples, and blue eyes the shade of the sea and likely as easy to drown in. He could easily give George Clooney a run for his money. Cate's cheeks redden. She's self-conscious of her inappropriate attraction and at such an inconceivable time.

"I've examined William and reviewed the tests that have come back from the lab and CAT scan," Dr. Leyden says. "But it would be helpful if you could fill me in on the events leading up to his admission."

Michael clears his throat. "Dad called me early yesterday morning because his ankle was very sore and he didn't think he would be able to drive himself to his family doctor's clinic. He asked me to take him, but when I arrived and saw the pain he was in, I decided to bring him here, to Emergency."

"So, you were at this hospital, just yesterday?" Dr. Leyden says.

"Yes, I brought him here. Dad never complains, but he was limping and grimacing pretty badly. The triage nurse sent us to rheumatology to see the specialist there. I can't remember his name now. I filled him in on Dad's history, including the illness that had him in this hospital for three months back in '93."

"Three months? Could you elaborate on that?" Dr. Leyden asks.

"Dad was here for three months, fighting a staphylococcus infection, apparently the same infection he's fighting right now," Michael snaps. "I thought you said you read his records?"

"I'm sorry if I've offended you. I'm trying to be absolutely clear on every detail, for your dad's sake. I have to tell you straight, this is a very grave situation. In the interest of time, can we please continue?"

Michael swallows hard and mumbles an apology before continuing where he left off.

"The rheumatologist examined Dad's ankle and diagnosed it as an arthritic flare-up. He prescribed a higher dose of prednisone, upping Dad's usual dose from one milligram to three, and also gave him a prescription for Tylenol 3 to manage the pain. Dad and I stopped at the pharmacy on the way back to his house, but they were out of prednisone. The pharmacist said a new order would be in today and asked if I could come back to pick it up. Once we arrived back at Mom and Dad's, he took his pain medication and I made us some dinner, but he didn't have much of an appetite. We sat around for a bit, watching TV, but Dad said he just wanted to go to bed. I asked him if he'd like me to stay overnight, but he assured me he was fine, so I left, with the promise of coming back this morning. When I arrived today, he was unconscious, with a massive gash on his forehead, so I called an ambulance. I guess you know the rest."

"I called Dad last night around eight thirty," Cate says. "He sounded groggy and told me I'd woken him up. He wasn't making a heck of a lot of sense, and I was having trouble understanding him because he was slurring his words. I was a bit concerned, but then I knew from Michael that he was on a heavy dose of medication, so I ignored it."

Tears begin to well up in Cate's eyes, the guilt heavy.

"This isn't your fault," Michael says, as though reading his sister's mind. "If you're to blame, you might just as well blame me for leaving Dad, or better yet, the incompetent doctor who sent him home yesterday in his condition."

"Trying to lay the blame on someone isn't going to help," Dr. Leyden says rather abruptly. "I'm not sure what caused William to lose consciousness. The CAT scans aren't conclusive, but they show a pervasive staphylococcal infection in his blood and clumps on his organs. Likely there is a clump on his brain that caused a stroke, but we need to do an MRI. It is possible that we can't fight this aggressive infection quickly enough. William's situation is critical, potentially fatal. I recommend you notify your family immediately. Myself, or a member of the team, will update you as new information becomes available."

Dr. Leyden leaves, the three of them stunned into silence. They file out like walking zombies, back to the ICU waiting room.

"What should we do? Who should we call? We need to figure out how to get a hold of Mom," Cate says. She is still trying to process the word *fatal* but has already slipped into take-care-of-business mode.

"We can't use cellphones inside the hospital," Michael says, pointing to one of the many signs taped to the wall with an image of a cellphone and a large red X going through it. "Ashley, will you please keep vigil in here in case there are any updates? Cate and I will go outside and make calls."

"Too bad I don't have a cellphone," Cate says as she walks hand in hand with her brother. "Your sister can be a bit of a dinosaur when it comes to technology, but I can use the pay phone at the entrance."

Instead of stopping at the pay phone, Cate follows Michael outside. It is a typical chilly spring day, but she welcomes the chafing wind against her cheeks, a contrast to the numbness encircling her heart. She shoves her hands into the deep pockets of her fleece-lined denim jacket after pulling her collar up around her neck.

Michael calls directory assistance to get the number of the curling rink his mother is playing at, but when he calls the rink there is no answer. The wind picks up, nipping at their ears.

"Do you have Sharon's number in your contacts?" Cate asks. "Her husband might know what hotel they're staying at."

"No, unfortunately, I don't. This is so frustrating. We have to get a hold of Mom, but I honestly don't know how, short of getting in the car and driving to Banff."

"I'll call John," Cate says. "He should be back from Pizza Hut with takeout for the girls by now, and I'm sure we have Sharon's number in our address book."

"Okay," Michael says. He passes Cate his Blackberry and she dials home.

"Hi, John, I'm so glad you are home. It's more serious than I thought. Dad has another staph infection. We need to get a hold of Mom in Banff. Would you mind looking in our address book for Sharon's number?"

"Wow, that's horrible news. Just a minute while I grab it."

Cate scribbles the number messily on the back of a grocery receipt she finds at the bottom of her purse. "Please, don't tell the kids anything just yet," she says.

"I know you don't want to wreck Dana's party," John says. "But it will be worse if anything happens and you didn't tell them."

"Nothing is going to happen." Her voice catches. "John, don't you dare give up on my father. We can wait to tell the kids when we get the news that he's turned the corner."

Cate gives Michael the number and hands him back his phone. He calls Sharon's house, but it goes straight to voice mail.

"What a total failure," Cate says. "Should we call Grandma Henderson?"

"Let's delay that, just for a bit. I want to let Mom know first."

Cate and Michael head back inside. Ashley has bought a coffee and is absently peeling the edges off the cardboard wrap designed to protect you from burning your fingers on the thin paper cup. The discarded coils nestle together on the table, reminding Cate of the worms inside her dad's fishing tackle box. She remembers how much she used to dread watching him thread the squishy worms through the hook. Everything seems to be dredging up old memories.

"Any news?" Cate asks quietly as she and Michael sit down.

"No, nothing."

Cate is reaching into her purse for her meter to check her blood sugar when Denise comes into the waiting room.

"They've got more results in," Denise says, her face sombre. "The MRI shows the infection has formed a large clump on William's heart. He's going to need open-heart surgery, immediately."

Chapter 18

*C*ATE KNOWS NOTHING ABOUT open-heart surgery or what it entails, but she knows it is a serious operation that will be complicated by her father's infection. As she mulls statistics over in her mind, she is overcome with the sensation that her tears have reversed direction and are flowing backward, drowning her from the inside out. She feels faint. She sees Michael's lips moving, in conversation with Ashley, but can't hear what he is saying over the buzzing in her ears. The room starts to spin. She gets out her meter and checks her blood sugar. Sure enough, she's going low, the number on the screen 3.8, so she fishes out a pack of Life Savers from her purse and crunches on a few.

"You okay, Sis?" Michael says as Cate tucks the rest of the candy back into her purse.

"Yeah, just needed a bit of sugar, it's all good."

"Alright then, I'm going to go back outside to try Sharon again." Michael stands and smooths the crinkles in his trousers.

"I'll come with you and call John," Cate says.

"I'll stay here in case there are any updates," Ashley says.

Cate presses the silver buttons on the pay phone. Her trembling fingers dial the wrong number twice. She takes a deep breath and wills herself to relax, but her heart feels like a loose cannon booming in her chest.

"Hi, Mom." Taylor answers the phone on her third attempt. "How's Grandpa?"

"Not well," Cate says. "I need to talk with your father."

"Okay, he's right here. We're watching TV in your room while the girls watch movies. And Mom, please tell Grandpa I love him."

"I will." She chooses not to tell Taylor that his grandfather is unconscious, that no one has been able to see him. "I love you."

"What's up?" John sounds distracted. The television blares in the background.

"Can you turn the volume down?"

"Sorry, just a second," John says.

Cate tries to pull herself together. She takes a deep breath.

"Dad needs emergency open-heart surgery," she says, rushing the words together. "It's really dangerous, because of the infection I told you about, but they said if they don't do the surgery immediately, he might die."

"What?" John says, suddenly at full attention. "I'm so sorry, Cate. I wish I could be there with you, but I've got my hands full."

"I know, the timing sucks. Not that there's a good time for such things." She laughs the hollow laugh that is becoming a habit. "I wonder if you could do me a huge favour and call Grandma Henderson? She'll likely want to fly out, regardless of…" Cate stops, unable to say the rest.

"Geez, Cate, is that really necessary?" John says. "You know how uncomfortable I feel around your grandma at the best of times. And I've got my hands full with six girls here for a sleepover. Can't someone else call her?"

"Really, John? You're going to pull your woe-is-me act now?"

"That's not fair—"

"Just fucking forget I asked," Cate says. "Michael and I will handle everything. I hope taking care of our children isn't too much of a struggle."

Cate hangs up the phone with a slam, without saying goodbye. She leans against the wall. She feels about to collapse when she sees Michael walking back into the hospital, brushing off the light skim of snow that has accumulated on his jacket and stamping his shoes on the runner. She goes over to her brother and puts her arms around him, then buries her face into his chilly neck. She takes a few deep breaths.

"I told John," she says as she pulls away. "I asked him to call Grandma, but he's too stressed out with the responsibility of Dana's party."

"No problem, Sis. I'll call her right away. But first, I want to share my great news. I got a hold of Sharon's husband and he gave me the name and number of the hotel Mom's staying at." He pulls out a crumpled sheet of paper from his pocket. "They're at the Inns of Banff. I was able to get a hold of Mom."

"That is great news. I'm so relieved. What did she say?"

"She pretty much went hysterical and is upset that she isn't here. I tried to console her, told her no one could have predicted this, but I don't think it sunk in. I'm just glad she's with friends. Sharon is going to drive back with her. I hope she can get here before Dad's surgery."

"Me too. Let's go back and tell Ashley."

When they walk into the waiting room, Ashley jumps up and comes over.

"Finally, you're back. I was just going to come look for you. Dr. Leyden is requesting we meet again, immediately."

"Let's go then," Michael says.

They have to stop to check in at the nursing station. Cate feels a cramping sensation as acrid bile rises up from her stomach into her throat. She runs down the hall to the washroom as fast as she can, throws open the stall, and vomits into the toilet. Sweat trickles down her back in rivulets as her stomach heaves.

"Cate? Are you okay?" Ashley calls out, having followed her in.

"I'm fine," Cate manages to say, which is ridiculous. She's far from fine. She wipes her mouth with some toilet paper, then gets up and goes to the sink to wash her hands and rinse her mouth with tap water.

"Sorry," Cate says. "I'm so stressed, my stomach is in knots."

"It's okay," Ashley says, putting her arm around Cate's shoulder. "Are you sure your blood sugars are level? I know when you're low you often get nauseated."

"Yeah, I'm sure, I checked just a while ago and ate some candy. Let's go."

When the three of them walk into the meeting room, Dr. Leyden is already there.

"Were you able to get a hold of your mother?" he asks.

"Yes, thank God," Michael says. "She's on her way from Banff as we speak. She should be here in a few hours."

"That's good news." Dr. Leyden takes his reading glasses from the pocket of his blue smock and sets them on the bridge of his nose, then consults his clipboard.

"Unfortunately, William's vitals have continued to decline. His heart rate and blood pressure are both very low. We need to get the surgery under way as soon as possible. I need you to sign the consent forms, on behalf of your father, as the closest next of kin."

They've been waiting for over half an hour with no updates when Cate starts to feel impatient and restless.

"I'm going to check in at the nursing station," she says. "I'll be right back."

She wanders down the hall and asks the nurse at the desk if there is any news on her father's surgery, but she is told no, they are still prepping him. On the way back, Cate detours to the lobby and out the front entrance where a group of smokers are all huddled together. The wind cuts her cheeks like the edge of a sharp knife, so she shifts gears again and heads back inside. She can't seem to make decisions or sit still. She sees the pay phone and decides to call home again. As she waits for an answer, she rifles through her purse for a stick of gum. After several rings, Celeste answers.

"Hello, my angel. How are you?"

"I'm good," Celeste says. "But what about Grandpa? How is he? How are you?"

Cate feels torn between saying all is well and telling her daughter the truth. She decides the truth is always best.

"Grandpa isn't well at all, I'm afraid. He's about to have open-heart surgery."

"Heart surgery?" Celeste says. "That sounds serious."

"It is. The doctor isn't confident the surgery will be successful. He's let us know there is a chance Grandpa won't make it."

Celeste starts to cry. A gut-wrenching feeling of protectiveness comes over Cate. She wishes she could be there to hold and comfort her daughter.

"I love you so much," Cate says. "I'm sorry I can't be there, but my place is here, with my dad."

"I know," Celeste says with a huge sob. "I'm glad you're there, Mom. I just, I wish…"

"I know," Cate says with a sigh. "We all wish. Try to stay positive and say a prayer. I'm blowing you a kiss. Now, can you please go and get your father?"

"Yeah, good night, Mom. Try to take care of yourself. I love you."

Cate waits while Celeste goes to find John. She twirls the long silver cord of the phone and stares at the ceiling, unseeing.

"Hi, Cate, how are you holding up?" John asks.

"I'm feeling as fucking shitty as I've ever felt in my life, to tell the truth," Cate says. "But I'm sorry I hung up on you earlier. I'm just such a wreck. I'm so scared I'm going to lose my dad. The surgery is so risky and the doctor hasn't been at all encouraging."

There is a moment of silence.

"I have to be there, with you," John says. "I'm going to call my mom and dad and see if they can come look after the kids."

"Are you sure? It's so late and with the party and—"

"I'm sure. I need to do this, for you and for me too. I love your dad too, you know."

"Thank you," Cate says. "I didn't realize I was hoping you would say that until you did. We're in the ICU waiting room."

"Okay, I'll be there as soon as I can."

Cate hangs up, numb and lost in thought. Her gaze is caught by a shiny speck of paper being propelled along by a gust of wind just outside the glass doors. As the paper dances and dips along the pavement, two magpies dive down from a lamppost and make chase. Cate thinks of all the times her father has complained over the years about the sound of a magpie's squawk and wonders if her dad will ever have the opportunity to be annoyed by them again. She shakes herself from her reverie and walks back to the waiting room.

Michael and Ashley are seated side by side, holding hands and engaged in an intense discussion when Cate returns. She doesn't want to interrupt them, so she quietly takes a seat opposite them and closes her eyes. She has no idea how much time has passed when she feels a gentle squeeze on her shoulder. She lifts her head and opens her eyes to see John.

"I got here as soon as I could. I'm sorry it took so long, but everything seemed to take longer than it should have and I couldn't find—"

Cate interrupts. "It's okay. You're here now and that's all that matters."

"Is there any news?"

"No, no news."

"Well, I'm glad I got here before the surgery," John says.

"Me too," Michael says, getting up from his chair and embracing John in a rugged man-hug.

A hospital staff member they haven't seen before comes into the room. "Are you the family of William Henderson?"

"Yes," Michael says. "Have they started the operation?"

"Yes, Mr. Henderson has been prepped and the surgery will begin any moment now," the young man replies.

"Rats, Mom's still not here," Cate says. "Can we see him… What did you say your name is?"

"No, I'm sorry, you can't see him until after the surgery. My name is Charlie. I'm here to show you to a different waiting room, on the ninth floor, where the surgery is taking place."

Everyone gathers up their belongings and follows him to the elevator. Charlie leads them to the new waiting room. It is as sparsely furnished and uninviting as the ICU room, sterile and functional.

Michael is riding a caffeine-induced high, full of energy, after downing three extra-large coffees since they arrived. He is researching open-heart surgery statistics on Ashley's laptop. Ashley attempts to listen, but her head bobs intermittently and her eyelids flutter closed. John and Cate sit in the comfortable silence of long-married couples.

"Oh, thank God, I've found you!" Donna says as she walks into the room. "I've been trying, to no avail, to get some kind of an update regarding William's surgery, and no one has been able to offer me a single strand of information."

"It's okay, Mom," Michael says as he sets the laptop on a coffee table. He gets up and wraps his arms around his mother. "You're here now, that's all that matters."

"I'm just so upset that I was in Banff, that I wasn't here…" she says, then falters.

"None of us have been able to see him since we brought him in," Michael says. "It's just fortunate that you got here before he comes out of surgery. We'll all be able to see Dad once he's in recovery."

"I can't help thinking that if I hadn't gone to Banff, your father wouldn't have been alone. Maybe none of this would have happened."

"I understand how you feel," Cate says. "Michael and I have felt it too. But you go for the ladies' bonspiel every year. You couldn't have possibly known."

"Thank you for saying that," their mother says. She pats Cate's arm, then takes a seat beside Michael on the couch.

They take turns filling her in on the few details they know. After a half-hour or so, a stranger walks in.

"Are you the family of William Henderson?" she asks. She has long blonde hair, thick black glasses, and is wearing jeans and T-shirt.

"Yes," all five of them say in unison.

"Hi, I'm Susan, a family counsellor here at the hospital. I'm here to answer your questions and prepare you for the hours ahead."

Susan takes a seat and asks everyone to introduce themselves.

"I appreciate you meeting with us," Cate says when it's her turn. "It's been very hard, receiving so little communication. We haven't even been able to see my father once since he was admitted."

"Yes, I know, it isn't the best situation," Susan admits. "We are very understaffed, and the night shift and Emergency are the busiest. But, I'm here now. First, let's start with any questions you have."

"I have a question," Michael says. "I've been doing some online research, and I'd like some clarification. I read that the surgery involves replacing blood vessels in Dad's heart, but I didn't think clogged blood vessels were an issue in his case. Is that correct?"

"Hmm, sorry, but I can't say I know the answer to that one for sure. In your father's case, I think a clump of infection needs to be removed. Likely the infection is clogging his blood vessels."

"Do you know how long the surgery will take?" Cate asks.

"Usually anywhere from three to six hours," Susan says. "Every surgery and each situation is different. If you're able to rest at all, I would highly recommend it. The surgery is just the beginning. It will take William several days, if not weeks, to recover enough to go home."

"I also read he'll have several catheters inserted, in his wrist, heart, nose, and bladder," Michael says. "Will they still be in when we see him in recovery?"

"That's a good question," Susan says. "They will probably leave all the catheters in until he is out of the recovery room. And while you're on the topic of how your father will look after the surgery, there are some things I should prepare you for. He will have a temporary pacemaker attached to take over his heart functioning. They will have sawed his breastbone in half with an electric saw, and the incision will be closed with large stainless-steel wires, then liberally dosed with a bright orange antiseptic. They have to keep the area exposed, and it is quite a shocking sight. He will be pale, and his face, hands, and feet may be extremely bloated."

"That's a damn vivid description," Cate says. She can feel the blood draining from her face.

"There is no point in me playing it down," Susan says as she reaches out her hand to rest it on Cate's. "This is a major operation. Your father's heart is going to be stopped while a heart and lung machine bypasses his heart's functioning. His entire body will be in a state of shock and trauma, and you need to be prepared. That said, this procedure is more and more common, and the success rate is very high."

"Well, that's good news at least," Michael says. "Will Dad be conscious when we see him?"

"That depends," Susan says. "Heart patients are given a general anesthetic, and how quickly it wears off varies with the individual. But according to your father's chart, he was already unconscious before the surgery, so it is highly unlikely he will have regained consciousness when you see him. However, many patients report that even while unconscious they feel the presence of their loved ones."

"Can we all go in together?" Donna asks.

"Actually, the protocol is one person at a time," Susan says. "There may be other patients in recovery, and keeping the environment quiet and sterile is important."

"I don't know if I can do it alone," Michael says. "I almost faint just from the sight of blood."

"I'm sorry, but those are the rules. Are there any more questions before I go?" Susan says as she half smiles and stands up.

No one has anything left to say. Susan leaves the room and a deathly quiet descends.

Cate drifts into a fitful sleep, punctuated with anxiety dreams, only to be shaken gently awake by John whispering, "You can go and see your dad now."

Startled into instant recollection, a strange sensation of dread and excitement returns to Cate as she contemplates seeing her father. She is frightened and looks into John's eyes, trying to find strength in their steely grey depths, but there is nothing for her to hold onto. John takes Cate's hand and walks with her to the recovery room where her mother has just emerged, her face contorted in agony.

"Oh, Cate," Donna says, grasping her hand. "I don't know what to tell you, except what Susan said doesn't even begin to, I mean, he's so—"

"Don't discourage her," John interrupts, more brusquely than necessary. He puts his arm around Cate and turns to face her. "You can do this. You are a strong woman." He prods Cate gently toward the door. She takes a deep breath, then enters.

The room is so dim, Cate has to take a moment for her eyes to adjust. A staff member appears and instructs her to wash her hands, pointing to a sink.

Cate leans over the white enamel basin and scrubs each finger and in between with the pink antibacterial soap provided. When she finishes, she's led past several beds to the foot of her father's. Cate feels like a character in a slow-motion movie as she turns to face her father. When she sees him, she gasps. She tries to calm herself down by reversing her gaze from her father's bloated face, which looks twice its normal size, to his hands, but they are puffed up just as much, if not more, and are a horrendous pale yellow-grey. Cate exhales. A deep groan escapes from her lips, traitorous to her desire to provide strength and reassurance to her father. She can't stop herself, despite her greatest effort. She turns abruptly and walks briskly back toward the exit. In her mind, she tries to send a heartfelt message. *I'm so sorry, Daddy, I love you, but I can't do this.*

Cate staggers through the recovery room doors like a drunkard, weaving erratically. She stumbles, then falls into a lump on the floor, like a rag doll. John, who had been waiting for her just outside the doors, kneels down beside her and helps her to her feet, mumbling words of condolence. He half carries her back to the waiting room where he lowers her onto a chair.

"God in heaven, have you forgotten him?" Cate sobs, her head in her hands. Her body heaves and convulses. The family does their best to console one another, but it is of no use.

Several hours later, William is moved from recovery back to the ICU, and the family reclaims the same spot they'd been in before. Cate is waiting anxiously to see her father again when her mother, who is the first to go and see him, returns.

"I have the best news," Donna says as she walks in, grinning like she just won the lotto.

"Please share, we could use some good news for a change," Cate says.

"While I was in with your father, he regained consciousness."

"Oh my God!" Cate yells as she jumps up from her seat and wraps her arms around her mother. "That is better than good news. It's incredible, amazing, fantastic news!"

"What a miracle," Michael says. "I can hardly wait to see him. What did he say?"

"He can't speak," Donna says as sits down between her children. "There is a tube going down his throat. I'd so wanted to ask him what happened, but the doctor I spoke with says it's possible he doesn't remember anything, even if he could talk."

"I don't care about the tube or that Dad can't speak," Cate says. "I'm just so frikkin elated that he's conscious! That's got to be a good sign!" She gathers her mother into a huge hug. Everyone starts babbling at the same time.

"Enough of this prattling on," Cate says. "Michael, do you mind if I go and see Dad next?"

"Not at all," Michael says.

Cate approaches her father's bedside practically on tiptoe. Cascades of tubing snake out from his bed to various machines with digital green, red, and amber numbers and graphs blinking on their screens. Stiff white hospital sheets are draped over her father and suspended to create a tent enshrouding his body. They hide his face. Cate veers around to the left. Her knee grazes the mattress, causing her to startle. She takes a deep breath, then looks up, hoping she is prepared for the unimaginable. Her father turns his head toward her. His face is not nearly as swollen as it was earlier, and he is gazing at her with eyes that are brimming over with love. He has a tube down his throat, as her mother said, and there is plastic tubing inserted into his nostrils as well. He can't talk, but words aren't necessary. She feels his soul connecting with hers, and she is able to stay calm.

Cate walks to the top of the bed and bends over to kiss her father's forehead, feeling stronger than she thought possible just a few hours before. His skin is salty, clammy against her lips. She pushes back his cowlick that is covering his eyelid and rests her fingers in his fine hair at his neck. She shifts her gaze to her father's left hand, which is peeking out from under the covers. She reaches to grasp it when she notices his fingertips have changed colour, no longer pale yellow-grey but an unsettling shade of charcoal, like the ashes in the fireplace the day after a fire. She swallows and somehow finds the willpower to keep a poker face.

"I love you, Daddy," Cate whispers into her father's ear. She caresses her fingers along the soft hair on his forearm. "We're all here for you. I know you saw Mom already, but Michael and Ashley and John, they're all here too."

Her father opens his eyes a crack and looks at her with an expression that seems to say so much. She senses his love, understanding, acceptance, and protectiveness in their brief exchange.

"You are an incredible man," Cate says. "Do you realize how amazing you are? I feel so lucky to have you as my father. You're going to be okay. You're going to beat this infection, just like you did before."

Cate glances over at the glass window of the cubicle and sees Michael on the other side.

"Michael's here, Dad. I'm going to go now, but I'll be back again, soon." She places her hand gently on top of his, careful to avoid the ends of his fingers. "I love you."

As Cate walks away, she makes a mental note to ask the doctor the cause of the discolouration in her father's fingers. She stops to give Michael a quick peck on the cheek and then goes back to join the others.

Michael is able to get in touch with Grandma Henderson and she makes the long thirteen-hour drive from Winnipeg with William's sister, Anne. They arrive at the hospital to find Cate and the rest of her family still camped out in the ICU waiting room, just in time to attend a family meeting with Dr. Leyden.

Once everyone is seated at the table in the centre of the private meeting room, Cate offers to take notes, having her ever-present journal tucked inside her purse. She is doodling down the margins when the handsome Dr. Leyden joins them.

"Mrs. Henderson, I presume?" Dr. Leyden says. He walks over to Cate's mother and offers a firm handshake in greeting. "And you must be William's mother," he says, turning to greet Elizabeth, who in turn introduces Anne. Elizabeth looks to have aged more than the five years since Cate last saw her, and Anne looks so much like William, the same ash-blonde hair and small, expressive eyes, Cate finds it both unsettling and comforting at the same time.

"I'm so glad everyone is here," the doctor continues. "I'm sure you all have a lot of questions, but as I'm scheduled to perform another surgery, I would appreciate it if you allowed me to present my summary without interruption. If you have any questions once I'm finished, I will certainly try and stay as long as possible to answer them for you."

There is a silent nodding of heads.

"Well then," Dr. Leyden says. "I'd like to share the good news first. I feel the surgery was very successful. We were able to remove the clump of infection on William's heart. There wasn't a human donor valve available, so we replaced the tissue we removed with a pig's valve."

Cate feels queasy at the thought of a pig's valve. She imagines a curly tail.

"Using a pig's valve is a perfectly appropriate option," Dr. Leyden continues, as though reading her mind. "They typically will last around ten years."

Ten years, Cate thinks to herself. Her father will only be seventy-one when he might need another surgery.

"At that time, we will do an MRI to determine how the valve is holding up and schedule a replacement with a human valve, if necessary," Dr. Leyden says. "But that will depend on if the valve holds."

"If?" Cate says out loud. She feels heat rising into her cheeks and her headache returning. "Excuse me, Dr. Leyden, but did you just say *if* it holds? I thought you just said the surgery was successful."

"Yes, I did. But I want to be totally honest with you and not leave you with any false optimism. Despite the surgery's success, there are still so many hurdles for William to overcome. We've had to give him anti-rejection drugs so that his body won't reject the foreign tissue, and with his immune system already so compromised, it is even more challenging than usual. Furthermore, the infection is still multiplying more quickly than we have been able to diminish it, despite administering the most aggressive course of IV antibiotics. We are draining the infection from various sites on his body, but his kidneys went into failure and we had to put him on dialysis. Unless something changes, his overall trend seems to be worsening rather than improving. I'm afraid the prognosis for a partial recovery is poor, but a full recovery, back to how he was before, is impossible."

Dr. Leyden pulls a handkerchief from his pocket and blows his nose.

"I'm sorry to be the bearer of such unfortunate news," he says. "The next twenty-four hours will likely determine whether William will pull through or not."

The hope and optimism Cate had felt during her visit with her father evaporate into thin air like the smoke from a snuffed-out candle. The room is silent with the heavy news.

"Well, Dr. Leyden, we all appreciate your compassion at this difficult time," Michael says, pulling out his chair to stand up. "As you said, you're a busy man, so why waste words or beat around the bush with—what was your term?—oh yeah, false optimism. If you're quite finished, please get the hell out."

Donna begins to apologize for Michaels's outburst, but mid-sentence she breaks into tears. Dr. Leyden mumbles his regrets and leaves the room.

"Where do we go from here?" Cate asks, her bottom lip trembling.

"You should likely go home and get some rest," Michael says. "You haven't set foot out of this hospital once since this all started. You need to take care of yourself."

"There's no way in hell I'm leaving him," Cate says. "Even though it breaks my heart that I haven't been home, to be with my children. I just can't."

Michael and Ashley go home, Elizabeth and Anne following in their car to get settled in their guest room. John goes home too, to be with the kids and update his parents. Cate and her mother return to the ICU waiting room, where Cate rolls into an uncomfortable ball, two chairs pulled together, and falls asleep. She's been out cold for a few hours when she hears her mother's voice.

"Wake up." Donna shakes her by the shoulder.

Cate squints open her eyes to the bright light of the ICU waiting room and shakes her head, her mind in a fog.

"What time is it?" she asks, rubbing the sleep from her crusty eyes.

"It's just past ten."

Cate looks around and sees Elizabeth, Anne, and Michael have returned. Susan Morgan is there, too, introducing herself to Elizabeth and Anne.

"It's wonderful to see so many loved ones here to offer support and prayer to William," Susan says. "I just dropped by to let you all know that the team of surgeons have been discussing William's case with Dr. Leyden, as he will be off for the next couple of days. His replacement will be Dr. Fitzgerald, and he has asked that I arrange a family meeting to discuss a plan of action and share the latest updates. They will be available at eight thirty tomorrow morning."

"Does the doctor want us all there?" Elizabeth asks. "I'm sure if there are any important decisions to be made, it would suffice for Donna and I to attend."

"Every family is unique in how they choose to handle these situations," Susan replies. "I always suggest that it is easier to include everyone, so let's leave it that anyone who wants to attend the meeting tomorrow is welcome. The main issue is whether or not to resuscitate in the event of a life-threatening incident."

Everyone in the family chooses to attend the meeting the next morning. Donna and Cate have been too stubborn to leave the hospital and have spent another night camped out in the waiting room. Their clothes are wrinkled, and with no showers to freshen up, they don't smell their best either. Cate wrote out an itemized list of things for John to bring back with him before he left, but when Michael arrives with Elizabeth and Anne in tow, John is still nowhere to be seen. There is only five minutes until the meeting is scheduled to begin when John walks in, carting a duffel bag, out of breath and a ball cap thrown over his own unwashed hair.

"Sorry I'm late," John says. "I was late getting the kids to the bus and they missed it so I had to drive them to school."

"Thank you," Cate says, and turns away. She takes the bag and leaves for the nearest bathroom to change. She takes off her wrinkled, slept-in clothes and rolls them into a ball, then takes out a fresh pair of jeans and the black V-neck top she requested, but discovers John forgot to pack clean underwear. Cate sighs. *I guess I'll just have to go commando,* she thinks to herself. She slicks her oily hair into a low ponytail, gives her teeth a once-over, and walks back to join the family.

"Well, as far as I'm concerned, there's nothing to talk about," Cate's grandmother is saying when she returns. Elizabeth is dressed in turquoise polyester slacks with a white turtleneck and a cardigan of pink, purple, and turquoise wool that she knitted herself. "At least it seems to me, someone as young as William, ordering full resuscitation regardless of the situation is the only possible decision we can come to."

"I agree with you, Grandma," Michael says. "But I could use some more information about Dad's quality of life." He thrusts his hands into the pockets of his khakis as he paces the floor.

"I think we all need to put aside our own wishes and try to think about what Dad would want," Cate says, taking the empty seat beside her mother. "After all, he is a very proud, independent man, and if resuscitating him left him permanently incapacitated, I'm not certain he would want that. On the other hand, he is a fighter. If he could recover to a mostly independent state, he could probably deal with that, even if it meant a struggle. He's had to reinvent himself more than once in his lifetime."

"It's so unfortunate that Dad can't tell us what his wishes are," Michael says.

"Sorry we're running a bit late," Susan says as she enters the room. She escorts them to a meeting room that is more like a classroom. There is a long rectangular table running down the middle, with wooden chairs tucked in neatly all around it. A projection screen is rolled up in its casing, and a projector sits on top of a black steel stand. Everyone takes a seat along the sides, the head of the table claimed by an intimidating pile of notes and a take-away coffee cup. An uncharacteristic silence, punctuated only by the hum of the furnace, falls over the room.

After fifteen minutes or so a tall, gangly man with white fly-away hair and Coke-bottle glasses strides in. Cate thinks of the scientist in the *Back to the Future* movies.

"Good morning, everyone, I'm Dr. Fitzgerald. I'm sorry I'm late. I know we have a great deal to discuss, but first tell me who we have here, please."

Everyone introduces themselves and their relationship to William. Then Dr. Fitzgerald takes the floor.

"I'd like to start by re-emphasizing what Dr. Leyden told you, that the last twenty-four hours were significant," Dr. Fitzgerald says. "I am encouraged by what has transpired. As you already know, William's heart surgery was successful."

Cate suddenly remembers that she wanted to ask about her father's discoloured hands and puts up her hand.

"Did you have a question, um, Cate, is it?" Dr. Fitzgerald says.

"Yes, sorry to interrupt," Cate says. "But when I was visiting Dad, I noticed that some of his fingers look almost black at the tips. Is that from the surgery?"

"I was about to get to that," Dr. Fitzgerald says with a slight frown. "William's blood flow has been seriously restricted, and his hands and feet have been compromised. The tissue is dead in several fingers and toes. We will likely need to amputate them sometime down the road, but right now that is the least of our concerns. Our priority is to diminish the infection faster than it can multiply. It is such an aggressive strain that we have been unable to accomplish this goal. Furthermore, the infection has spread to William's stomach and kidneys. We are feeding him through a tube directly into his gut, and I believe you were already informed he is on kidney dialysis. This brings us to the question for today, of resuscitation. With his inability to communicate, that decision is left to the family, unless William has expressed his wishes to anyone prior to his hospitalization."

Dr. Fitzgerald pauses to let this new information take hold and to see if anyone can answer his question about William's thoughts on the issue. It takes everyone a few moments to digest what he has said.

"Well, regardless of what he may have said before, I feel that with William being so young, we need to have an order for resuscitation, no matter what the circumstances or complications," Elizabeth says.

"I don't feel the same," Cate says. "When I imagine my dad stuck in a wheelchair or hospital bed with part of or all of his hands and feet amputated, I'm not sure he would want to live like that."

"I just want William to be as comfortable as possible," Donna says. "He's suffered so much already." She lets out a long, ragged sigh. "It's so unfortunate, but we never did get around to discussing these matters, we thought we had more time…"

"I'm sorry to have to pressure you," Dr. Fitzgerald says. "But I need you to form a unanimous consensus or appoint someone to make the decision. I will leave you to discuss this together. I'll be back in half an hour and you can let me know what you've decided."

Dr. Fitzgerald pushes back his chair, gathers up his things, and leaves the room.

"I hope as much as anyone that William can overcome this," Donna says, choking back tears. "But as I've said, I can't condone his suffering. If it is God's will, and his time, who are we to keep him alive? Just because we have the modern science to do so doesn't make it right. In my mind, it isn't about living over dying, it's about living with dignity and quality of life."

"Well, Donna, that is just like you to give up," Elizabeth says, with a little more venom than necessary. "I didn't raise a quitter. When William was sick back in '93, the doctors were ready to give up on him and look how he rallied. Would anyone here deny him these last seven years of his life?"

"Of course not," Cate says. "But you didn't see him right after the surgery. It was absolutely awful. You can't compare what was then to now."

The minutes tick by, but the family comes no closer to reaching a consensus. In the end, everyone agrees that as his wife, Donna should make the decision. When Dr. Fitzgerald returns, Donna instructs him that no resuscitative procedures should be performed. Elizabeth rocks back and forth in her chair, clutching her arm to her chest, and releases a guttural wail of despair.

Chapter 19

T HE MEETING FORCES CATE to face the reality that it's going to be a long time before her father is discharged from the hospital, if ever. She comes to grips with the fact that it isn't feasible to continue sleeping at the hospital. With her family's blessing, she organizes them into groups of two to take shifts so that someone is always at the hospital. She schedules Elizabeth and Anne to take the first shift, beginning that morning after the meeting. Donna's sister, Winfred, has driven in from Peachland, and Cate slots them in for the afternoon, followed by Ashley and John that evening. She and Michael have agreed to take the first night shift.

"Well, that's the first twenty-four hours organized," Cate says. She drops her pen and journal back in her purse with a sigh and stands up. "I really appreciate that we all agree someone needs to be with him at all times. I couldn't possibly relax and go home for some proper rest and connection with my kids without your support."

Winfred gets up and pulls Cate to her ample bosom, her stocky frame a comfort for Cate, who has always had a soft spot for her. Winfred's expressive eyes, so like Donna's, say more than mere words.

"It is a good plan," Michael says. "And I suggest we keep it simple by rotating through the time slots, taking one shift earlier each day."

"Yes, and let's hope that William recovers quickly, and very soon it won't be necessary," Elizabeth adds.

On the way home, Cate's heart races as John speeds on snow-covered roads. She works hard to push down her anxiety. She closes her eyes and takes a few deep breaths. She is falling asleep from sheer exhaustion when John opens a conversation.

"I must admit, I'm a bit surprised at your unwillingness to resuscitate your dad. I would have thought you, of anyone, would do anything to keep him around."

Cate jolts wide awake.

"You're right. From a totally selfish perspective, I would do anything possible to keep my dad alive," she says, with an edge of irritation. She swallows, but the tears catch in her throat. "I'm trying to picture myself in Dad's situation. I don't think I would want to be resuscitated. I believe there comes a time when you have to accept what is. And even though Dad and I are different in a lot of ways, I think he would agree with me on that. We're both crazy stubborn, independent and proud. I feel certain that if Dad had to spend the rest of his life lying in a hospital bed, hooked up to a dialysis machine, with no hands or feet, unable to go to the bathroom by himself or feed himself, he would hate it."

"You're probably right, but you've never been in that situation, so it's hard to say how you would feel, or how he feels. They say the survival instinct kicks in."

"I have heard that." Cate tries to fight back her annoyance. "I may not understand Dad's situation, but remember when I had that out-of-body experience, just after Dana was born? I know how peaceful it felt."

"How could I forget?" John says, and Cate senses him shiver.

She folds her arms across her chest and stares vacantly out the window. Soon John is pulling into the garage.

Cate is barely through the back door when Lady comes running over, all three kids right behind her.

"Mom!" Taylor says. "You're finally home!" He throws himself against her.

"How's Grandpa?" Celeste asks, her question quickly followed by a barrage from all three of them.

"Please, slow down, and one at a time," Cate says. "I'm exhausted to the bone, but I know you all have questions, so let's go have a family conference in the living room. I can give a quick update before I go lie down."

Everyone files into the living room. Dana and Taylor squish in beside Cate on the couch. Celeste sits down on the loveseat while John puts on the kettle to make tea and Lady curls up in a ball on the area rug by Cate's feet. John has turned their propane fireplace on, and the cozy warmth has Cate yawning only minutes later.

"You look ready to fall asleep sitting up," Celeste says as Cate's head bobs for the third time.

"Yes, well," Cate says. "It's been a gruelling few days. As much as I would love to reconnect with you all, I'm going to run a bath and then crawl into bed."

When she wakes from her nap a few hours later, she feels re-energized, even though all her worries are stowed just below the surface. She puts on some sweatpants and a cozy sweatshirt and heads downstairs.

John is sitting at the island breakfast bar, munching on some peanut butter on toast, when Cate enters the kitchen.

"I'm going into the office," John informs her between mouthfuls. "I need to get in at least a half day of work before my shift at the hospital."

"Well, I suppose one of us needs to," Cate says, disappointed, but not surprised. "I'm just grateful my boss has been so supportive."

"You can hardly compare your gig as a kindergarten teacher with my work," John says. "But yes, I appreciate her too."

"Where are the kids?" Cate asks, looking around.

"They took Lady for a walk. But that was a while ago now. I imagine they'll be back soon, but I'm going to get a move on."

When he leaves, Cate goes upstairs and gathers a load of laundry, then takes the overflowing basket downstairs to the laundry room. As she is loading clothes into the washer, her tummy rumbles. She decides to make some lunch for herself and the kids, but when she enters the kitchen, she is overwhelmed by the mess that has accumulated over the last few days. There are dirty dishes piled high in the sink, and the counter is littered with crumbs and cereal, crackers and takeout cartons. She tidies up and washes the counters with a soapy dishcloth, then heats up the electric fry pan to prepare grilled cheese sandwiches. As she peels the cellophane wrappers off the processed cheese slices, the kids come barging through the front door, a loud and rambunctious trio.

Taylor is the first to spot Cate. "Mom, you're up!" He runs over and throws his arms around her in a huge bear hug. "Do you feel better, after your nap?"

"Yes, I do, thank you. And I'm also almost finished preparing us some lunch, so go wash up, please."

Over lunch, the conversation returns to Grandpa William.

"Dad said Grandpa's heart surgery went well, but he's still in critical condition," Celeste says. "I've been praying so hard, every night. How does he look to you?"

"Grandpa is still fighting for his life," Cate says. "I think I already mentioned that Great-Grandma Henderson and Great-Aunt Anne arrived here from Winnipeg, that they're staying with Uncle Michael and Aunt Ashley? Anyway, between them and the rest of our family, we're taking shifts at the hospital until Grandpa's out of the woods."

"Out of the woods?" Taylor says. "What does that mean?"

"She means when they're sure Grandpa's not going to die," Dana says.

"That's right," Cate says, doing her best to present a brave face. "But Grandpa has so much courage, I'm confident he will fight this and pull through."

"Celeste told me Grandpa was really sick before, when I was still in your tummy," Taylor says. "She said it took, like, three months or something, but he got better. I think he will now too."

"That's true, he was and he did," Cate says. "Let's all agree to only have positive thoughts."

"Did Grandpa remember it was my birthday?" Dana asks.

"Grandpa can't talk," Cate says. "But I'm sure he remembers."

"Why can't he talk?" Dana asks.

"He has a feeding tube down his throat." Cate puts her hand on Dana's head and strokes her shiny hair.

"That sounds horrible," Taylor says. "Does it hurt?"

354 *Lynda Faye Schmidt*

"I don't know, I hope not," Cate says. "He seems comfortable enough. He's managed to smile, with his eyes, a few times now."

"I love how Grandpa's eyes twinkle when he chuckles," Taylor says.

"When is it your turn to go back to the hospital?" Celeste asks.

"Not until after midnight, when you're all fast asleep," Cate says. "So, should we play a board game or go up to Blockbuster and rent a movie?"

"Let's do both!" Taylor says. "Starting with Monopoly."

"I get to be the shoe," Dana says as she gets down from her stool. She goes to the game cupboard and retrieves the much used, taped-at-the-corners box, and the three of them get it all set up at the kitchen table. Cate puts together a few bowls of munchies and pours them all drinks. After a two-hour battle, Dana emerges victorious, having covered the board in houses and hotels.

"It looks like Dana has earned a new nickname, Ms. Real Estate Mogul," Cate says with a laugh as they all tidy the pieces away.

"What's a 'real estate mogul'?" asks Taylor.

"An entrepreneur who builds a massive empire of properties," Cate says.

Taylor laughs. "Well, that fits Dana, that's for sure. Are we going to go rent movies now?"

"Okay," Cate says. "Let's go."

"Can I drive?" Celeste asks, still thrilled to have a new driver's license.

"Absolutely," Cate says with a grin as she passes her daughter the keys.

At Blockbuster, Cate allows each of her children to choose a movie, and they draw straws for which one they will watch first. She treats them to Slurpees and a stash of junk food from 7-Eleven, and then they return home to settle in. John calls to say he's going to grab a bite to eat and head straight to the hospital. Cate decides to ditch making dinner. Celeste offers to drive back up to the shops to pick up subs. They watch another movie and take Lady for a walk along the ravine, Taylor running off ahead, the girls holding hands. Cate feels nourished, her fuel tank back at full gauge.

Dana and Taylor are both tucked into bed and Celeste is in the family room on the phone with one of her friends, when it's time for Cate to head back to the hospital.

"Sorry to interrupt, I'm about to head out," Cate says as she peeks her head around the corner. "I had a wonderful day." She kisses Celeste on the top of the head. "And thank you for staying up to keep an ear out for your brother and sister. Your dad should be back soon."

"Mom, it's okay, I am sixteen and perfectly capable," Celeste says. "Don't worry about us."

"I know. But I still appreciate you."

"Thanks, Mom. Give Grandpa a kiss from me."

"I will, see you in the morning." Cate leaves Celeste to her phone conversation and tiptoes past Dana and Taylor's rooms, down the stairs. She checks the list she made for herself earlier on the whiteboard by the phone so she wouldn't forget anything, grabs all of her diabetic supplies, and heads out.

At the hospital she looks around for John and Ashley, but they're nowhere to be seen. She's just about to go check in at the nursing station to see if she can visit her dad, when John and Ashley walk in together.

"What's wrong now?" It's clear from their expressions that something is amiss.

"I think you should sit down," John says.

"I don't know if I can take any more bad news," Cate says as she takes a seat. She remembers the birthday balloon and thinks she's running out of air herself.

"We were just talking with the head nurse, and some more tests have come back," Ashley says.

"The tests confirm your dad had a stroke," John says. "On top of that, they've discovered a clump of infection growing on his brain stem. They said he's at risk to develop meningitis. If the clump dislodges, it could cause an aneurism."

"You've got to be kidding me!" Cate rises from her seat and starts walking toward the door, then turns back around. "What more can he take? Hasn't he got enough to cope with already? I, I've got to go and talk with them myself, this just can't be true, you must have it wrong…" she trails off as her legs crumble. She falls to her knees on the linoleum floor.

"It's okay, you're going to be okay," John mumbles unconvincingly. He helps Cate to her feet, and Ashley takes Cate's other arm. They lead her back to her seat.

"You're wrong, John," Cate says, tears streaming down her face. "I'm not going to be okay. This isn't okay. I, I…"

Cate drops her head into her hands and sobs.

Minutes later, Michael walks in for his shift with Cate. When he sees his sister slumped over on a chair, he goes over and gives her a big hug.

"What's wrong?" he asks, rubbing Cate's shoulders.

"It's Dad, he's, they've. . ." Cate can't find the words, so John gives Michael the news.

"Man, this really sucks," Michael says with a huge sigh. "But you two have been here long enough, you need to get some rest. Cate and I and have got this."

"Are you sure?" John asks.

"Yeah, I'm sure," Michael says.

"I can call the family to update them, if you want," Ashley says.

"No, it's past midnight, there's no point waking everybody up," Michael says. "There's nothing they can do. I'll call Mom and Grandma first thing in the morning."

After John and Ashley leave, Cate looks around the waiting room. Even the plastic bouquet of flowers on the table across from them seems depressing.

"Let's go visit Dad," Cate says. "I don't think I can tolerate this goddamn room one minute longer."

Michael puts his arm around Cate and they walk to the nursing station together.

"Is our father able to have visitors?" Cate asks the nurse behind the desk.

"Henderson, right? Just a minute while I check." The nurse looks at her computer screen. "Yes, you can go on back."

It is quiet outside William's room. Cate looks through the glass windows. A nurse is monitoring his vitals. Michael knocks tentatively on the glass door.

The nurse looks up and motions for them to come in. Cate recognizes Abeena, a pleasant and friendly nurse whom she's become fond of. Abeena acknowledges them with a smile and nod of her head.

Not having seen her father since she'd left early that morning, it is quite a shock. He looks so small and frail, lying there on his massive bed. He turns his gaze toward them, his eyes glassy.

"Hi, Daddy," Cate says. She wipes away the tears on her cheeks with the back of her hand.

"Hey, Dad," Michael says.

Neither one of them seems to know what to say. Their father looks at them and blinks. Cate bends down. She gently raises her father's gnarled, decaying hand to her lips and places a kiss on his soft, wrinkled skin, just below his knuckles. She raises her head and looks into his eyes.

"I can't bear seeing you struggle like this," Cate says in a soft voice, barely more than a whisper. "I hope you're not in too much pain, but I'm guessing you probably are. You are so stoic. Even if you could talk, you'd never complain. I've been wishing you could talk to me, but maybe it's a blessing in disguise, to not know the truth of your suffering."

"I wish I knew what you're thinking too," Michael says. "I so want you to recover. I really want to give you a chance to get better, but I don't know if that's what you want, and you can't tell us. I, we, all want the best for you, Dad, but we can't seem to agree on what that is."

"You are so loved," Cate says. The tears reappear in the corners of her eyes. She doesn't bother to wipe them away; her father has drifted off to sleep. Cate lays her head down on his shoulder. She inhales, the mustiness of his unwashed hair, the scent of hospital chemicals and sweat somehow comforting. She closes her eyes. Michael leans in and takes Cate's hand in his and they stand together in silent communion. After a few moments, their father starts to snore.

"Remember how Dad used to fall asleep while watching a football or baseball game, only to deny it vehemently?" Cate says.

"Yeah, I think he used to claim he was only resting his eyes," Michael says with a slight chuckle. "I don't know why he didn't just admit he was tired and took a nap."

Cate pushes back her sleeve to check the time.

"Wow, it's already two o'clock. Shall we leave him to rest?"

"Yeah, I could use a stretch," Michael says.

Cate bends over and kisses her father's forehead, then she and Michael walk hand in hand down the dark corridors. They are approaching the ICU waiting room when Cate turns to Michael.

"Why don't we find someplace different to hang out for a while?"

"I would welcome that," Michael says.

They go back to the nursing station and tell them they're going outside for a bit. The air is crisp, the sky ink black, a heavy cloud cover over the stars. Cate and Michael stroll down the street toward a large green space. Huddled together, heads down against the biting wind, they walk in comfortable sibling silence.

After a while Cate's feet start to ache, cramped inside her pointy-toed, high-heeled boots. They return to the hospital waiting room where they doze on and off in the uncomfortable chairs, without incident, until their shift is through.

Late-morning sunlight is filtering through the sides of the closed blinds, illuminating the bedroom with a gentle glow. Cate stirs. She checks the alarm clock. The neon-green numbers read 11:11. It feels like an omen, four ones in a row, but of what, Cate has no idea. Four hours of sleep doesn't feel very satisfying, but she's wide awake, so she takes her journal from her bedside drawer, throws on her robe, and makes her way downstairs.

The house is quiet, with the kids in school and John at work. Lady is curled up in a ball on her bed near the fireplace, but when Cate steps onto the wood flooring with a slight creak, her ears perk up and she hobbles over. At eleven years old, she's not as frisky as she used to be. Cate bends over and gives Lady's head and ears a good scratch. She washes her hands, puts on a pot of coffee, and checks her blood sugars. They are sky high, 19.7, but it's no surprise with the stress she's been under, not to mention her routine knocked totally off kilter. She sighs and gives herself a correction bolus, then tidies up the dishes in the sink until the coffee is ready. She chooses her favourite handmade ceramic mug and adds a generous dollop of cream, then takes her journal and curls up on the couch to write, wrapped up in a blanket.

> *When I saw my dad last night, it was like I had on a new pair of glasses. I realized that after the trauma of his heart surgery, I created a false image in my mind of what my father looks like. Sort of like when I've put on a mask to hide the truth of my ongoing challenges with John, but in reverse. I suppose it was a healthy coping mechanism. It allowed me to show up for my father with the strength and integrity I desired. But somehow leaving the hospital and spending time with the kids, living a normal day, broke the spell. The veil was lifted, and the truth of what I saw hit me, hard. It is clear to me, beyond any doubt, that my father is slipping from this world. I don't know how long his time to transition will be, but his aura appeared to me as a different colour than the azure blue it has always been before, more of a silver grey. It made me think of ghosts and spirits.*

Cate closes her journal, the words on paper too painful. Her next official shift at the hospital isn't until after dinner, but with everyone gone, being alone in the house feels oppressive. She goes up to her room, the heavy emotions making each step up the stairs an effort.

Cate's barely out of the shower, wondering what she's going to get up to next, when the phone rings. She picks up the receiver on her bedside phone.

"Hi, Cate?"

"Hi, Mom. How are you?"

"I've been better." Donna's voice catches. "After the news from your brother this morning, that there is a clump of infection growing on your father's brain stem, Winfred and I came to the hospital right away. I asked to meet with a doctor, but I've had no luck hearing from anyone. Anyway, I decided I'd like it if we could all meet up here, for another family meeting. Are you okay with that?"

"Yes, of course, Mom, I'll be right there."

When Cate enters the waiting room, no one from her family is there so she sits down and flips through to the entertainment section of a newspaper someone left on the coffee table. As she is reading, a flash of light catches her eye. She lowers the paper to watch the assortment of tropical fish darting in and out of the green plastic foliage and brown Styrofoam rocks of the waiting room aquarium. The clear, crystal water looks so tranquil, but then Cate sees a dead fish, floating on its back, bobbing along the surface of the tank. She feels queasy as she stares at the still little creature. She thinks how all living things, big or small, fish or father, are bound by the laws of mortality. She feels strangely comforted. A whoosh of air blows across her as the door opens and her mother and Aunt Winfred walk over to join her.

"Cate, you're here," her mother says. "I forgot to tell you I booked one of the family conference rooms. Everyone is waiting."

"Oh, I'm sorry." Cate stands and gathers up her things, then follows her mother and aunt down the hallway. Her aunt, always one with a tender heart, gives Cate a squeeze of her hand.

"Would anyone like a cookie?" Elizabeth is asking when Donna and Winfred return with Cate in tow. Elizabeth pulls a large Tupperware container out of a fabric bag and pops the lid. "I made a few dozen oatmeal and date cookies last night. They're William's favourite, and Michael, aren't they yours too?" Not waiting for a reply, Elizabeth continues to offer the container of cookies to the gathered assembly.

"I don't know about anyone else," Michael says between mouthfuls, "but I'm fed up with the lack of communication around here."

"I know, right?" Cate says. "How sad is it that we have to nag and plead to get any updates, and when the bloody surgeons finally get around to meeting with us, they drill us for information and come off all doom and gloom."

"Well, let's not get sidetracked," Donna says. "I called this meeting to discuss the latest news about William's stroke and the new clump of this goddamned infection sitting at the base of his brain. I don't think it could get much worse."

"I'm so sorry, Mom. I know you're frustrated," Michael says. "I wish we could do something, but I just don't know what."

"I think we need to ask for better, more timely communication," Cate says.

"That's all well and good," Michael says. "But remember what Susan said from the very beginning—they are way understaffed and overworked. Personally, I think they should focus their energy on treating Dad."

"I know," Cate says. She crosses her arms over her chest. "I'm just frustrated. It feels like all we do is go around in circles, and with each update, Dad's getting worse." She stops as the words catch in her throat. "I'm sorry, but I just can't handle another family meeting right now."

Cate stands up and grabs her purse, then exits the room.

"Hey, Sis, wait up!" Michael calls out, following her down the hallway. "I didn't mean to upset you."

"I know you didn't," Cate says with a sigh as she turns around. "I just want to be alone, okay?"

"No, it's not okay," Michael says. "I know you and your inclination to disappear down your rabbit hole when there is conflict. I think the last thing you need right now is to be alone, whether you want to admit it or not."

"You know me too well," Cate says. She laughs weakly and punches Michael lightly on the shoulder. She puts her arm around his waist. "I don't really want to be alone, I'm just so sick of this bloody hospital, of all of it. I feel like a ball of yarn unravelling."

"Why don't we go for a drive?"

"Seriously?"

"Yeah, totally seriously."

Michael and Cate leave the hospital together on an impulse, totally out of character for either of them, and walk through the parking lot to Michael's BMW. Cate climbs into the passenger seat and fastens her seat belt. Michael calls Ashley on his cell phone so the family won't worry, starts the ignition, and backs out of his stall. He exits onto the road out front and then turns off onto 16th Avenue, heading west.

"Where should we go?" Michael yells over the din, the soft-top of his convertible down and the wind blasting.

"Straight toward the mountains," Cate yells back. She laughs, a crazy, stress-filled, slightly psychotic sound.

The mountains loom before them as Michael zooms along. For Cate, the craggy rocks look even more majestic than usual, with almost a spiritual quality about them. Seated beside her brother with the wind gusting through her cotton-candy hair, Cate questions her belief in God. The snow-capped mountain range seems to attest to the existence of a supreme being, of an immortal creator, yet Cate feels so abandoned. As she gazes at the granite peaks, each rock and stone seems to whisper of God's eternity and the cycle of life and death. A few fluffy white clouds loll across the mountain peaks, apparently in no rush to get anywhere, and Cate allows her thoughts to drift along too.

Michael drives all the way to Banff without either one of them saying a word. He takes the turnoff into town and is driving slowly, on the lookout for stray elk or other wildlife, when Cate spots the sign for one of her favourite restaurants.

"I'm starving," Cate says. "Some delicious Mexican food sounds divine, what do you think?"

"That does sound like a great idea." Michael pulls onto a back street and parks the car at a meter. Cate holds Michael's hand as they enter the dimly lit restaurant, the tempting aroma of refried beans and hot green chilies permeating the air. Cate's stomach growls as the hostess leads them to a cozy corner table. The restaurant is almost completely empty, mid-afternoon on a weekday, with only two other tables occupied.

"Would you like anything from the bar?" the waitress asks as she places the menus in front of them on the table.

"You know what, I think a lime margarita is exactly what I want right now," Cate says, acting completely out of character again. "What do you think, Michael? Will you join me?"

"What the heck," Michael says. "I can drive us back safely if I only have one."

Cate is looking over the menu options, having difficulty deciding what to order, when Michael clears his throat.

"Are you ready to talk?" He pushes back his dangling cowlick in exactly the same manner as their father. Cate smiles, only to break into tears.

"I don't know what there is to say. I feel like my heart and my head are at a war with one another."

"Yeah, there is often a pretty deep chasm between our hearts and our brains. What's eating me up is, if Dad dies, will everyone, including me, blame me?"

"What on earth are you talking about?"

"Well, it was me who took him home from the hospital." Michael rakes his hand through his hair again. "It didn't feel right, but I ignored my instincts and just blindly followed what the doctor told me to do. If there's one thing I've figured out since Dad was admitted, it's that doctors are only people with a lot of education, that they make mistakes too, and they certainly don't know everything."

"Michael, there is no one to blame, not you, not me, not the doctors." Cate puts her hand on her brother's. "You said as much to me, that first meeting with Dr. Leyden, when I was the one feeling guilty. Sure, with hindsight, we can all see things we could have done differently. But you couldn't possibly have known at the time. And how fortunate that you did return that morning, that you found Dad when you did. What matters is that we love Dad and we'd do anything for him, and he knows that, without question."

"I just can't help but wonder, does Dad know I let him down?" Michael asks, his shoulders slumped forward.

"You didn't let him down, Michael. You were amazing. You called for an ambulance right away. You called me. It was you who finally got a hold of Mom. You've been a rock star, and I know with certainty that Dad is nothing but proud of you."

"I guess all we can really do is support and love one another through this," Michael concedes.

Cate gets up and moves to the vacant chair beside her brother. She takes both his hands in hers and squeezes them.

"I love you, Michael, so much. You are a magnificent man. Cut from the same cloth as Dad. Believe in that one true thing."

Michael turns quietly inward as he lets go all of his guilt. He slumps his head to rest on Cate's shoulder, and she holds him until their server returns with their meals.

When they get back into Michael's car, they are ready to drive back to Calgary, both at peace with themselves, at least for a few precious moments.

As the week progresses, the Henderson family is met with more challenges, but a few successes as well. Cate's dad squeezes her hand, ever so slightly, one afternoon while she is reading the sports section to him. He communicates a little, blinking once for no, twice for yes. But a follow-up MRI shows a lump of infection growing back on his heart. In seeming reaction to the news, he relapses into unconsciousness.

Chapter 20

CATE TOSSES AND TURNS, overwhelmed with worry. She can't stop thinking about her father. She wonders if he will pass away when she isn't there. She can't stand the thought of not being there. Eventually she falls asleep, but peace eludes her, with nightmares occurring, one after another.

After a particularly vivid and disturbing dream, Cate wakes up flushed, the sheets twisted around her like a rope. She touches her mattress, as if to confirm she is indeed in her own bed. She glances at the alarm clock. It is 1:11 a.m. Three illuminated numeral ones, similar to the other day, when there were four. She shivers. She tries to drift off again but lies in bed wide awake, staring at the ceiling. After an hour, she abandons all hope of sleep. She lifts the covers, drops her feet soundlessly to the floor, then slips quietly out of bed. She walks stealthily into her closet and throws on some jeans and an old T-shirt. She sweeps her hair back into a low ponytail, grabs her book from her nightstand, and makes her way downstairs, careful not to wake her sleeping husband.

The house is still pitch black and a chill has settled in overnight. She plugs in the kettle and turns up the furnace thermostat. She takes her steaming cup of black currant tea over to the couch and curls up with her book, *The Mammoth Hunters*, by Jean Auel. It is a masterfully written saga, but even the vivid scenes describing passionate encounters between Ayla and Jondalar are unable to hold her attention. She sets her book down and considers writing in her journal, but it feels like too much effort, so she busies herself with the mindless tasks of cleaning out the pantry and scrubbing down the inside of all the cupboards.

Hours later, Taylor comes bounding down the stairs, two at a time, then sails across the wood flooring in his sock feet.

"Good morning, Mom!" He stands on his tiptoes to give Cate a hug, still damp from his shower. She kisses his eyelids.

"Good morning. Did you sleep well?"

"Not really. I've been having scary dreams about Grandpa dying every night since he was admitted to the hospital."

"Me too," Cate says with a frown. "I'm sorry you're like me that way. But speaking of the hospital, I've decided it's time I brought you and your sisters to see your grandpa."

"Really?" Taylor says, his face a picture of surprise. "I would love that. But you do know it's a school day?"

"Yes, I know," Cate says, stroking his damp hair. "I'm not that out of it. But I think in this case, you're allowed to play hooky."

"Play hooky?" Dana says as she walks into the kitchen to join them, all groggy-eyed.

"Yeah, Mom said we can skip school and go and see Grandpa today."

"Seriously?" Dana is suddenly wide awake. "That's awesome news." She comes over and gives Cate a big hug. "Do I have time for a quick shower?"

"Yes, my love, there's no rush. I'll go see what Celeste is up to, and we'll leave whenever everyone is ready."

Cate finds Celeste blow-drying her hair in her room downstairs and shares the news.

"I have to admit, I'm a little nervous," Celeste confides. "I never have liked hospitals, and you know how even the sight of your needles makes me queasy."

"Yes, you are a sensitive one," Cate says. She strokes Celeste's long auburn hair. "You don't have to go in to see him, but why don't you come to the hospital with us anyway? You can decide later what feels right for you."

"That's a great idea. Thanks, Mom," Celeste says, but despite her words, she has an apprehensive look on her face.

When all three kids are at the island eating their breakfast, Cate decides to try and prepare them, like Susan Morgan did.

"Before we go, I think we should have a little talk, about how things are at the hospital, how your grandpa looks—"

Taylor interrupts. "Oh, I know what the hospital will be like. I went to the children's hospital for the teddy bear program, remember, Mom? You volunteered."

"Yes, I do recall that field trip," Cate says, "but this is going to be quite different. Grandpa is in an adult hospital, in a special unit called the ICU, for very sick people."

"ICU, what does that stand for?" Dana asks.

"Intensive care unit," Cate says. "It is a very busy place, very sterile. Grandpa is hooked up to several high-tech life support machines."

"I've seen ICUs on TV," Celeste says. "They looked very stressful."

"Well, television tends to overdramatize things," Cate says. "It's intense, but I wouldn't say stressful. In fact, your grandpa's room is quite quiet and peaceful. You can each have your own special time with your grandpa, but I'm requesting that you all be quiet at the hospital, no running or goofing off, no fighting or fooling around. On your best behaviour. I also want to warn you that Grandpa looks a bit scary."

"Scary?" Taylor asks, his eyes wide.

"Yeah, scary. His colouring is off and he's lost a lot of weight. You know how skinny he was already. There are bandages all over his chest. He has tubes inserted in his nostrils and throat. And some of his fingers and toes have turned black."

There is a moment of silence, the air heavy.

"I don't know about anyone else," Dana says quietly. "But nothing can stop me from going to see Grandpa. I don't care how scary he looks, he's my grandpa and I love him and I need to tell him that."

Taylor and Celeste agree, although Cate still thinks she detects a look of hesitation on Celeste's face.

"Okay, all of you, off you go then and brush your teeth," Cate says. "We'll leave in ten minutes."

Everyone goes off in different directions while Cate tidies up the kitchen. She is just jotting down a note for John when she hears footsteps on the stairs. She looks up, expecting Dana or Taylor, but it's John, dressed and ready for work.

"How come the kids are still home?" John asks as he makes his way into the kitchen.

"I gave them permission to skip school today," Cate tells him. "I'm taking them to visit Dad."

"Oh?" John says as he pours himself a cup of coffee. "That is a big surprise."

"Yes, well, I was just going to write you a note," Cate says. "But now there's no need." She crumples the yellow sticky note and throws it in the wastepaper basket just as Taylor comes down the stairs.

"Mom says you're off to the hospital this morning," John says. "Be a good boy and say hi to your grandpa from me."

At the hospital, Cate leads her troupe to the ICU waiting room. Elizabeth and Anne are seated together, as it is their shift. Elizabeth is knitting something with a beautiful buttery yellow wool, and Anne is filling in the crossword in the *Herald*.

"Hello, young fella!" Elizabeth says as she squishes Taylor's cheeks between her hands. "Isn't this a nice surprise to see all the kids here? I was beginning to wonder if your mother would ever bring you by for a visit with your grandpa."

Cate chooses to ignore her grandmother's passive-aggressive remark.

"I hope you brought the kids some activities to keep them occupied," Anne says. "You know how dull it can get waiting around in here."

"I brought my Pokémon cards and travel Sorry, plus some books and Lego," Taylor replies, holding up his stuffed school backpack for emphasis. "Do you want to play something with me, Great-Grandma?"

"I'm busy knitting right now," Elizabeth says. "Why don't you ask one of the girls?"

"I'll play with you," Anne says, setting her newspaper down on the table beside her. "How about Sorry?"

Taylor beams. "Okay, I'll set it up. What colour do you want to be?"

Celeste has decided she wants to go and visit her grandfather first, so she doesn't have to hear second-hand news from her brother and sister, and also so she doesn't lose her nerve. Once Dana and Taylor are settled, Cate leads Celeste down the hallway to William's room.

Celeste's big brown eyes look around the room at the intricate arrangement of life-saving equipment. She gulps and turns to look at Cate, an unspoken question in her raised eyebrow.

"It's all right, go on, I'll be right here," Cate says from the doorway.

Celeste walks slowly around the end of her grandpa's imposing bed and up the side. His face peers out from the thin white flannel blankets pulled up to his chin. It is chalk white, his cheeks sunken, but he has the best facsimile of a smile he can manage.

"Grandpa, it's so good to see you," Celeste says. She hesitates, then looks over at Cate. "Can I hug him?"

"You sure can," Cate says.

Celeste hugs her grandpa and buries her face into his neck. She whispers into his ear. Cate waits patiently by the door, but it isn't long before Celeste is saying her goodbyes.

"I love you, Grandpa," Celeste says as she kisses his cheek. She walks over to join her mother and they leave together.

"Wow, that was tough, to see Grandpa looking so sick," Celeste says, turning to look at Cate. "I'm glad you prepared me before I came so I wasn't too shocked, but it was still hard. He looks like he really could die."

"Unfortunately, that is a reality. That's part of why I chose to bring you and your brother and sister in, so you'd have the chance to say goodbye, just in case. I'm sure seeing you was some of the best medicine your grandpa has received yet."

"Do you really think so?" Celeste asks, obviously pleased.

"Yeah, I really do."

Back in the waiting room, Celeste joins the assembled family members. It is Dana's turn to visit. She walks beside Cate in silence. When they arrive at the room, Cate is about to walk in when Dana stops her.

"Do you mind if I go in alone?" Dana asks.

"Of course, my love, that's fine. I'll just wait here."

After a half-hour or so, Dana emerges, red-eyed and solemn. She doesn't say a word. Cate and Dana walk together to the ICU waiting room in silence.

Celeste is doing homework at a table and Taylor is engrossed in Dana's Game Boy.

"Can I please have it back?" Dana asks.

"In a minute," Taylor says, not looking up from the screen. "I'm almost done."

Taylor finishes his game and hands the console back to Dana. He gets up off his chair and goes to Cate, then takes her hand so tightly he almost cuts off her circulation.

When Taylor and Cate arrive, William's eyes are closed and his breathing rhythmical, but as soon as Taylor approaches the bed, he opens his eyes. When he sees Taylor, his eyes mist over. He looks as though he wants to speak. He lifts his hand in a weak gesture to motion him to come closer. Taylor starts to cry. He reaches out to hold his grandpa's blackened, deformed hand but when he sees it, he hesitates. He looks over at Cate.

"Go ahead, it's okay, you won't hurt him."

Taylor takes his grandfather's hand gently in his own. Tears stream more heavily down his cheeks, and his nose runs. Cate rummages in her purse for a Kleenex and hands it to him.

"Didn't you have something you wanted to tell your grandpa?" Cate prompts.

"Did I?" Taylor says. Then, suddenly remembering, he turns back. "I wanted to tell you you're the best grandpa in the whole wide world!"

Taylor relaxes when his grandfather smiles back with his eyes—the ice is broken. Soon Taylor is talking a mile a minute. He tells stories of all the relevant things going on in his young life, about how he got a certificate of achievement in math and rode his bike all the way to 7-Eleven without stopping. He talks about playing street hockey with the boys on their block. The list seems endless. As Taylor shares his stories, it's clear to Cate their conversation is therapeutic for all of them. Taylor is the only visitor who has been able to act like nothing at all is different, to talk with his grandfather exactly the same as he would have before. In just a few moments, Taylor has somehow, magically, transported all three of them out of the hospital. It is a place that Cate recognizes, but it feels like such a long time ago.

Taylor and Cate make their way back to the waiting room, walking the quiet halls of the ICU. Cate stops and turns to face her son.

"Listening to you talk with your grandpa in there, I realized, I haven't been a very good listener lately. I'm sorry I haven't been there for you."

"Aw, Momma, you don't need to apologize," Taylor says with a grin and a squeeze of her hand. "I'm glad you've been here for Grandpa. It's one of the things I love about you."

"Thank you," Cate says, a tear in the corner of her eye. "You have so much empathy for a six-year-old, sometimes it kinda blows me away."

"What's 'empathy'?"

"It's an ability to relate to and understand how others feel. And trust me, there are many people far older than you that just don't have it. They can only have compassion for things they've experienced."

"Well, I'm glad I didn't need to have you or Dad in the hospital to imagine how it must feel for you, Momma," Taylor says. "If it were you in there, I'd be way more of a basket case than you have been."

"Yeah, well, let's hope that isn't something you have to figure out, for both our sakes," Cate says with a half-hearted laugh.

The next day Cate decides to do some more housecleaning. She starts in the kitchen. She pours a generous dollop of dish soap into the sink and adds hot water, then gets out a fresh sponge and starts in scrubbing down the counters and stovetop. She's just getting into a groove when the phone rings.

"Hello," Cate answers, the phone wedged against her cheek and chin as she dries off her soapy hands with a dish towel.

"Hi, Cate, I'm glad I caught you at home."

It's John's mom, Darlene. Cate sighs. She's not up for her meddling.

"Yeah, I haven't been around much, I'm mostly at the hospital these days," Cate says. "What can I do for you?"

"Well, your mom called a few nights ago to give us an update on your dad. I did appreciate it, not having heard a single thing from you, but I must admit I was shocked to hear how much William has deteriorated, that he's still in the ICU. Cliff and I were hoping to go to the hospital to see him, but I just wanted to check in with you first."

"That's very thoughtful of you. As it is, the visitor list is limited to immediate family. But I'm happy to let him know you're thinking of him when I go in later."

"Okay, I understand," Darlene says. "Just tell your father that Cliff and I send our love. And try to take care of yourself, dear."

Cate hangs up and stands staring at the phone, paralyzed. Every time she tells someone about her dad, it seems to cement the reality. She shakes her head and gets back to scouring, but she can't concentrate even on a mundane task. It strikes her that the hospital seems to be the only place she feels comfortable. She sighs and puts her cleaning supplies away, then checks the wall calendar. She sees that Celeste has a ballet exam the next day. Another item she forgot. She wonders if she might be getting early Alzheimer's, her mind has been so scattered, but she knows deep down it's because she's living in a constant state of anxiety. It isn't healthy, and yet she doesn't know how to do it differently. She doesn't have a playbook for how to manage this.

After dinner she spends a few hours chilling out with the kids, watching television while John stays late at work again. By nine o'clock she can barely hold her eyes open. She decides to tuck into bed early as she's on the early shift at the hospital. When she's completed Taylor's goodnight routine, she says good night to Celeste and Dana and crawls into her pajamas. She rummages in her nightstand and retrieves her journal.

It would seem my world is falling apart. I can feel it in my bones. In the eleven days since Dad was admitted to the hospital, I have created many different endings to this story. To say I have felt confused is an understatement. As I sift through all of the information

I've been given by the doctors and reflect on my experiences with Dad, I try to make sense of it, but I can't. Words like amputations, permanently hospitalized, daily dialysis, stroke, they all float into my mind. They are emotionally charged words. I hate these words. I hate all the statistics I've been quoted, about his chances of survival, about his chances of living some kind of normal life if he gets through this. If.

I've looked to my father for the answers I seek, but he cannot speak. I've tried listening by watching him as he lies, unmoving, on his hospital bed, a mere shadow of his once vibrant self. I imagine empty space where his blackened toes and fingers are. I imagine him confined to a bed, for always. I picture what his life would be like. I can't bear to look upon these visions in my mind. I don't know what his destiny is. But I don't think it is supposed to be a life of dependency, pain, and constant struggle.

When I close my eyes, I see my father running after me, playing tag. I remember him running around the bases at countless ball games, when I was a little girl. But my father hasn't been able to run for a such long time now.

Machines have given me the precious gift of time with my father, the opportunity to say goodbye. But at what cost? Dad has had to endure so much pain. It doesn't seem fair. We're delaying the inevitable, sentencing my father to this suffering, because we don't want to let him go. The words of a song by Simon and Garfunkel keep repeating themselves over and over inside my head. "When you're weary, feeling small, when pain is all around, like a bridge over troubled water, I will lay me down."

Cate sets down her pen and closes her journal. She lets the tears fall. When she can't cry anymore, she realizes she still isn't ready to lay her father down. Not yet.

Cate wakes at midnight with a jolt, gasping for air, her sheets in a knot. Her hair is tangled and sweat glistens on her brow, under her arms, and in the crease where her panties meet her thighs. She's had the same terrifying dream, again. She stares at the ceiling, unable to stop shaking. John snores softly beside her. She takes her journal from the drawer and creeps quietly downstairs.

I'm walking down a series of long corridors, shaking the locked steel doors at the end of each one. I pound on the doors until my wrists ache. Despite my banging, no sound reverberates in my dream world, it is silent. I know I need to go through the doors. The sense of foreboding is pervasive. A cloaked form appears. I can't see his face, but as one hand emerges from the folds of the cloak and points, I recognize it as the Magician's. My eyes follow the finger's focus, to another set of steel doors with a sign: Morgue. Suddenly everything starts to spin. My feet lose their footing and I'm crying out, "No!" but the doors open as I stumble closer. I'm willing them to close, to lock like all the others. I'm in my nightgown, barefoot, when I feel air gusting gently against the back of my bare legs, encircling them like tendrils of long hair, caressing them gently but pushing me forward, insistent. The chilly wind blows me through the doors, into the cold, damp room. I cry out "No!" but my voice is enveloped in a cloud of vapour, like when you exhale outside in the

*winter. The invisible force continues to pull me
along, past rows upon rows of mortuary cubicles.*

   *Then, as suddenly as the wind appeared, it
vanishes. My feet are no longer being propelled along
but settle into the cement floor like bare feet on sand.
Trembling, I look up to see the name on the cupboard
directly in front of me. The letters stick to the top of my
mouth as I attempt to say them out loud, my tongue is
so dry, my throat parched, like a survivor lost in the
desert. W, I, L…they spell my father's name. "Stop!"
I yell. Then creepy laughter that sounds like Vincent
Price in the video "Thriller," permeates the room. It
changes to a howl, and the cloaked figure transforms
into a hairy, black wolf. My plea is ignored. My feet
are still rooted to the floor. The cubicle flies open, the
shrouded body a mystery, but I know. One by one, all
of the cubicles begin flying open and closed, but still
there is no sound. I feel dizzy. Then all the cubicles
stop and close tight, except for the one in front of me.
A hand appears out of nowhere and lifts the covers to
reveal an arm, which reaches out to grasp me by the
wrist. I'm afraid to look, but as I turn my gaze to the
hand encompassing mine, I discover it isn't attached
to a body—it's a bloody severed paw, dangling in the
crisp air.*

Cate ends up falling asleep on the couch, her journal splayed
out on the floor, only to wake up with a stiff neck just as the
sun is beginning to rise. The house is silent. She looks at her
watch. It is just after five. She has just enough time to take
a quick shower before she needs to leave for her shift at the

hospital. She starts a pot of coffee and heads back upstairs
to get ready. She tiptoes past John, still in a deep sleep.

After her shower Cate gets dressed and does a quick
makeover, applying the basics. She blow-dries her fine, thin
hair so it won't freeze in the frigid air, then goes downstairs.
She writes a note to John and the kids, then grabs her
oversized handbag and stuffs it with a scarf, her leather
gloves, and all her diabetic supplies. She fills a stainless steel
travel mug with fresh coffee, pulls on her boots, and
grabs her keys.

She parks in her usual spot at the hospital. When she
opens the car door she is instantly struck by the crisp air of
early spring. The newspaper she'd tossed in her bag from the
front doorstep tips out and onto the cold pavement.
Grumbling under her breath, Cate stoops to retrieve it, the
melted sludge of mud-brown snow smudging the words on
the front page. She wipes the paper hastily down the front
of her jeans, then stuffs it inside her jacket. She crosses her
fingers, feeling a pervading sense of doom, a premonition
or omen of some sort.

Inside the hospital, Cate decides to skip conversation
with her family members who might be in the ICU waiting
room and heads straight for the nursing station. The nurses
behind the counter are busy, on the phone, working at the
computer, or consulting stacks of files. Cate tries to wait
patiently. She hears a male voice from behind her and turns
to discover Dr. Leyden.

"Hello, Cate," he says, extending his hand. Cate is
surprised he remembers her name. She hasn't seen him for
almost a week.

"Uh, hi," Cate replies a bit awkwardly, shaking hands
with him.

"I've just been reviewing your father's case,"
Dr. Leyden says.

"You have? Is there anything new?" She wishes he wasn't so damn good-looking. It makes it hard to hate him, but she does anyway.

"I know I haven't been the bearer of great news," Dr. Leyden says. He lets go her hand.

"That's an understatement," Cate says.

"Yes, well, I am sorry that I haven't been more positive. I wish it were different, you know." He places his hand on Cate's forearm, sending a tingling sensation up to her shoulder. "But there's no point avoiding the truth, either."

"Maybe as a surgeon you think you know what the truth is," Cate says. She takes a step back and his hand falls away. "You think that what you observe and how you interpret your observations is the only reality. But I believe there are more ways than one to see things. I believe in things you can't measure, like love, and the power of faith."

"That must be comforting for you," Dr. Leyden says. He looks down at the floor.

"Do you not believe in miracles, then? Or in God for that matter?"

"I truly don't know what I believe anymore. All I know is when I lose one patient, even if I've saved ten others, it just doesn't feel good enough."

"Maybe these souls aren't yours to lose or save," Cate says.

"You could be right about that. I'm an atheist, so I can't speak about souls. But I took an oath to save lives, and I mean to do that if I can."

Dr. Leyden mumbles goodbye and disappears down the hall. Cate turns around. One of the nurses gives her the go-ahead to visit her dad.

On her way to her father's room, her mind is abuzz. She realizes Dr. Leyden never did tell her any news.

The sheets are tented around her father's feet as usual. Cate inspects them. Four of five toes, all but his baby toe on his right foot, are completely black. So are the middle three on his left. They are dry and flaky, like papier mâché. Cate walks around the foot of his bed, past the machines. She stares at the numbers on the screens. His blood pressure is low, his heart rate normal. When she turns to look at her father, his heavily bandaged chest rises and falls with each breath. He is asleep. She can hear a gurgling, rattling sound and worries he might be developing pneumonia. She sees how old and tired he seems. He's aged years in less than a week. She looks down at his right hand, propped up on a small pillow. His hands have always been a sign of strength for her, even when arthritis deformed them, but now they look so frail. His fingers seem as surreal as his toes, all five black and obviously in a state of decay. Cate wonders if he has the strength, somewhere deep inside, for one last triumph, one last hit into the stands, one final home run.

Cate leaves the ICU, dreading having to deal with her family even more. She doesn't want to leave the hospital, but also doesn't feel like being there. She decides to walk over to the Tim Hortons across the street. She walks past the smokers congregated outside the doors, the fumes of their cigarette smoke acrid in her nostrils. The wind pulses, almost blinding her. She pulls the hood of her jacket up over her head, frost already clinging to the tendrils of hair that frame her face, transforming them from dark blonde to white.

At the coffee shop, Cate takes her bagel and extra-large coffee to a booth as far from other people as possible. She retrieves her newspaper, still stuffed down the front of her coat, and opens it randomly. She discovers she's opened it to the obituaries. Goosebumps appear on her arms. Another omen. She decides to read each name and offer silent tribute to them and their families. She notes the charities mentioned, to give donations to in lieu of flowers. Most are for the Heart and Stroke Foundation or the Cancer Society. No mention of mysterious infections.

Cate dials up a dose of insulin to cover her bagel. She finishes reading the paper while sipping her coffee. When she's done, she sits for a few moments in silence. She summons her strength. She is ready to return to the hospital, to her family, to the drama.

Her mother rushes forward as soon as Cate walks through the door of the ICU waiting room.

"Cate, where have you been?" She reaches for Cate's arm and guides her down the hall. "We've all been worried sick."

"What are you talking about?"

"When Michael went in to see your dad, the gal at the nursing station said he was sleeping, then said you'd just been in to see him."

"Oh, uh…" Cate sighs. "I'm sorry, I didn't mean to worry anyone. I just needed a bit of fresh air, to clear my head."

"Are you okay?" Her mother puts her arm around Cate's shoulder.

"I'm fine." She pauses. "No, actually, I'm far from fine. I'm having a particularly bad day."

Cate looks over her mom's shoulder. Behind her, Elizabeth and Anne are in their usual places.

"Where's Aunt Winfred?" Cate asks.

"She's caught a cold and decided she shouldn't come in." Donna shrugs and gestures to the waiting room chairs. "Are you going to come and join us?"

"Ah, no, actually. I thought I would, but I still don't feel like socializing. I think I'll head down to the hospital chapel for bit. I'll be back soon."

"Do you want company?"

"No, thanks for the offer, Mom, but I'd rather be alone."

She leaves the suffocating confines of the waiting room and walks half-blindly through a veil of tears, past the maze and buzz of people. It takes her a good fifteen minutes, but then she spots the sign. She pauses outside the closed wooden doors, listening to the faint chords of an organ. When it is quiet, she opens the door slightly, trying to be as inconspicuous as possible, and slides into a pew at the very back.

The pastor, a short, thick man, with long grey hair receding and pulled into a ponytail, is reading to the small gathering. He nudges his round metal glasses into place without stopping. Although the sounds she hears resemble words, Cate seems to have lost her ability to comprehend language. She picks up the large, black-leather Bible on the pew beside her and flips through the delicate pages. The scent of a hundred different hands lingers amongst them. She stops at the book of Psalms and scrolls her finger across the words of prayer. She reads "A Prayer for Help," then reads it again, over and over.

"Lord, hear my prayer. In your righteousness listen to my plea. I am ready to give up; I am in deep despair. I lift up my hands to you in prayer; like dry ground my soul is thirsty for you."

She lowers her head and says a prayer of her own. With each word a feeling of peacefulness spreads through her. She feels the most grounded she's felt since she first heard from Michael that their father was on the way to the hospital. She looks around the room to discover she is alone, the chapel deserted. The sun, which had been filtering through the stained-glass windows, has lowered, and the room is bathed in a late afternoon glow. She checks her watch, it's a quarter past three. She is stunned at how much time has elapsed,

how the world kept turning while she seemed to stop. She
hates to leave, but the blissful serenity is already evaporating
as her senses return her to the world. Cate gathers her coat
and gloves, slings her bag over her shoulder, and walks back
to the waiting room, ready to make peace with her family.

When Cate returns to the hospital the next day she is
bombarded as soon as she crosses the threshold. Every
member of her family is gathered together in the
waiting room.

"Cate!" her mother says. "We've all been waiting for you
for almost an hour. When I called your house, John said
you'd left already and then when you didn't show up here,
well, I was beginning to picture you in a ditch, in a car
accident or something."

"I'm sorry, I didn't mean to worry you." Cate doesn't
want to get into why she's late in front of everyone. She has
a killer hangover after drinking too much wine the night
before, a futile attempt to drown herself in her sorrows.
On the drive over her stomach cramped up. She'd had to
stop at a disgustingly dirty gas station bathroom.

"Dad's kidneys went into failure," Michael informs her,
rising from his chair. "They've requested another
family meeting."

"Oh my God." An all too familiar feeling sends a deep
chill down Cate's spine. She starts to shake involuntarily. Her
knees buckle. The room goes black as she loses consciousness.

"What happened?"

"You went out like a light," Donna says, cradling Cate's head in her lap. "You'll be fine, dear. Here, have a sip of water and a few SweeTarts."

Cate wonders why people always offer a glass of water in a crisis. She pulls herself up on her elbows and takes a sip, then crunches back some sour candy, not bothering to confirm her low blood sugar with her meter.

"Thank you," she whispers. "I'm sorry to cause so much drama all the time. When is the meeting supposed to begin?"

"As soon as you feel able to," her mother says. "Everyone else has moved to the conference room."

"Okay, let's go then."

She takes a granola bar from her purse and eats a few bites on the way, Michael supporting her by an elbow. Not long after they've taken their seats, Dr. Leyden enters the room.

"Thank you all for coming in on such short notice," he begins. He riffles through a stack of papers in front of him. "I'm told you were advised that William's kidneys went into failure. Now, we can try and put him on another dialysis machine, but—"

"What do you mean, try?" Elizabeth interrupts.

"Well, it's not as easy as it might sound," Dr. Leyden says. "We don't know what caused William's kidneys to fail while on dialysis. It is very puzzling. We could run some tests, but to be honest, I think it's rather futile, in light of everything else."

"Everything else?" Michael says.

"William's condition has markedly degenerated in just a few hours," Dr. Leyden replies. "His blood pressure is extremely low. His heart rate is erratic. Worse, his latest MRI indicates that the infection on his heart has multiplied to the point that he needs to have another surgery, and frankly, his body isn't strong enough to tolerate it. I wouldn't even consider operating on a man in his condition." He stops to take a sip from his water bottle before continuing. "The infection on his brain stem has grown as well, and there is a high risk it will dislodge. The bottom line is, we just haven't been successful in stopping this infection." He pauses again, looking down at his notes. "William has put in a good fight. We've done everything we can medically do, but I'm afraid the fight is over."

"No! You're wrong!" Elizabeth cries out. "This fight is not over. You must perform the surgery. You must try to save my son's life!"

"I'm so sorry, Elizabeth," Dr. Leyden says. "I've consulted with every specialist here at the hospital and they all concur. The best we can do is to make William as comfortable as possible. We'll move his bed into a special family room, where you can have unrestricted visitation. We can disconnect as many machines as possible. Unfortunately, we'll have to keep the tube in that's draining his lungs or he'll drown in his own bodily fluids. But we'll keep his pain medications maxed."

Cate can't believe what she's hearing, how Dr. Leyden is able to recite everything so coolly, so matter-of-factly. She wishes he would just shut up.

"I don't know what to tell you in terms of a timeline, it's hard to judge these things," Dr. Leyden continues. "It could be an hour, or as many as three or four days before he goes."

Elizabeth starts rocking back and forth, moaning "No, no, no." Cate and her mother cry silent tears. Michael shakes his head in disbelief, clenching and unclenching his fists.

Cate had known this moment was imminent. She'd thought she was prepared, after her time in the chapel just the day before, but she was wrong.

Dr. Leyden takes off his glasses and puts them in the pocket of his smock. He stops beside Cate's mother on his way out.

"I'll need you to sign the necessary papers, Donna, to get started on the arrangements," he says. "As soon as you feel able, please stop in at the nursing station. I'll leave all the paperwork there."

He pats her shoulder. His familiarity, calling everyone by their first names, annoys Cate. She knows it's not his fault, that he tried everything he could. But it is easier to hate him, to blame him, than some intangible concept like fate.

Chapter 21

"SO, THIS IS IT?" Elizabeth says. Her voice rises an entire octave with each syllable.

Cate's heart goes out to her grandmother. She thinks about Celeste, Dana, and Taylor, and how horrific it would be to lose a child, even if that child was a sixty-one-year-old adult. She knows she would be as devastated. You aren't supposed to outlive your children.

"I'm sure your being here has been a huge comfort to him," Cate says as she puts her arm around her grandmother's frail shoulders. Elizabeth lifts her wrinkled, thin-skinned hand, speckled with age spots, to pat Cate's arm.

"Thank you for saying so, Cate, but I just can't accept this, that they're giving up," Elizabeth says.

"I don't think it's a matter of giving up, Grandma," Cate says. "It's more about accepting what is and letting go of what we want it to be. We've all been in conflict, wondering what to do, but in the end, it wasn't our decision to make."

"I'm grateful, that Dad isn't going to die alone, that we all get this chance to say goodbye," Michael says. "We'll be able to be with him, right to the very end. I'm certain that will be very comforting, for everyone." He pauses to choke back tears. "I'm sorry, Grandma, I don't mean to fall apart."

"Don't ever apologize to me for expressing your grief," Elizabeth says. "But I'm not going to sit around in some cold hospital room and watch my son die. I won't do it."

"You don't want to be at his side?" Donna asks.

"I was there when Philip passed," Elizabeth says. "I witnessed all his suffering at the end. He was in so much pain, practically gasping for his last breath. The terror in his eyes, well, it was just too much for me. If I couldn't bear to watch my husband go, I couldn't possibly endure witnessing my son die. I just can't do it. It's too much."

Cate is struck by this uncharacteristic sharing of feelings. She realizes she's never seen anyone die before. She'd gone to see her grandfather when he was near death, but he'd held on for several months. Her experience of funerals is limited too. She's never seen a dead body, other than on TV or in the movies. She wonders what it will be like, to see a dead person. Not just any person. Her father. She is terrified, but she knows no matter what, she will stay with her father as long as they'll let her.

"Maybe this will be different, Grandma," Michael says. "Grandpa died from cancer and I've heard that's one of the worst ways to go."

"It makes no difference to me," Elizabeth says. "Cancer, an infection, it's all the same. Besides, I don't condone what these doctors are doing, just giving up. I won't hear another word about it. I will go collect my things from your place after I go and say goodbye to my son, if you don't mind."

When Elizabeth leaves, the room is quiet for a few moments.

"I'm going to call John and let him know," Cate says. "Do you want me to call Ashley too?"

"No, I can tell her in person when I drop Grandma off," Michael says. "I'll come back as soon as possible."

"I suppose I should go and sign those forms," Donna says.

"If you wait until I call John, I'll go with you."

"I would appreciate that." Donna takes Cate's hand lovingly in her own and squeezes it gently. "But I want you to do whatever you feel you need to do, without worrying about what anyone else thinks, including me. Do you think you can do that?"

"Thanks, Mom," Cate says, the words catching in her throat. She coughs. "I really appreciate your encouragement. I hope you can take your own good advice."

When Donna and Cate arrive at the nursing station to sign the papers, the preparations for William's transfer to a family room have already begun. There are personnel of every description drifting past the nursing station, relocating machines and pushing trolleys laden with bed linens, disinfectants, and other cleaning supplies.

"Excuse me," Donna says. "I think there are some forms here for me to sign?"

An unfamiliar nurse glances up from her computer screen.

"And your name would be?" she asks.

"Oh, sorry. Most people here know me. I'm Donna, Donna Henderson. The documents are for my husband, William."

The nurse thumbs through a stack of files. "Ah, here we are, Henderson." She hands Donna the thick folder and a pen, then quickly turns back to her computer.

"Why don't you pass me half that pile?" Cate says.

"That would be great." Donna separates the stack into two piles, pushing one across the counter toward Cate. The page on top of Cate's pile is titled *Deceased's Organs to be Donated*. Bile rises up into Cate's throat. She swallows. This is not going to be an easy task.

It is almost half an hour later when Donna writes her last signature on the final piece of paper, which outlines the hospital's commitment to store *the body* in the hospital's morgue for a maximum of one week, or until arrangements can be made for *its* removal by a funeral home. She sets the pen on the counter and takes Cate's hand. They look into one another's eyes, no need for words, both feeling the heaviness. Legs like lead bars, they walk together in silence to the family room.

William's room is dimly lit. Cate's eyes take a moment to adjust. The multitudes of machines are gone, other than a solitary unit that is draining her father's lungs and recording his vitals. Cate sees the pattern of his heartbeat flowing like a green river across the screen. The room feels barren, cold, and sterile, not like a family room at all. Cate and her mother approach William from either side of the bed. His eyes are closed. There is no place to sit, so they stand, still in silence, neither of them knowing what, if anything, there is to say.

After a while two attendants enter the room carrying chairs like the ones in all the other hospital waiting rooms. They set the chairs down along the left wall.

"There's a room with lockers and a vending machine for the families," one of them says. "If you go back toward the nursing station, hang a left down the corridor just before it, it's the third door on the right."

"Thank you," Donna says. She pulls one of the chairs over near the bed and Cate does the same.

Cate pulls off her boots and rubs her right foot. She notices the waist of her jeans isn't as tight as she bends over. She isn't surprised. She's had no appetite for the last two weeks. She's quiet as she imagines her life without her father. She has an overwhelming urge to snuggle up with him. She thinks of her mother's words, to do whatever she feels she needs, and on an impulse, she climbs into the bed beside her father. She rests her head as gently as she can on his shoulder. Her father's heavy breathing stops momentarily, but then resumes its steady rhythm. Cate lets out a sigh of relief, lays her arm across her father's stomach and closes her eyes. Within minutes she drifts off.

She startles awake. Another dream. The side of her face she's been lying on is damp with sweat, her hair plastered against her head. She runs her hand across her cheek and feels thin indentations from her hair, like the lifelines on your hands. She looks around the room, disoriented. Her mother is resting her head on the other side of her father's bed, and Michael has taken a seat in one of the other chairs by the wall, his eyes closed too. Cate takes her purse and discarded boots and goes over, sock-footed, to join her brother.

"How are you holding up, Broski?"

"Hanging in. You looked awfully cozy, snuggled up with Dad."

"Yeah, I was. But I had a bad dream."

"You and your dreams." Michael laughs half-heartedly. "You must hold the world's record for the least time needed to be asleep before dreaming commences. You couldn't have been asleep more than half an hour."

"I know, right?" Cate looks around the room. "I guess Ashley decided not to come back with you?"

"Yeah, no, I think it's all too much for her. Plus, she felt it should be just us. I guess John felt the same?"

"Yeah, he's going to stay home with the kids. If you don't mind, I want to jot down my dream quickly in my journal, while it's still fresh. I want to record as much of these last moments with Dad as I can."

In my dream, Dad and I are in a canoe, fishing lazily on the smooth surface of a still, black lake. I'm sitting on the bench and Dad is kneeling behind me, his arms like extensions of my own as he attempts to teach me that exact flick of the wrist that casts a perfect line. I'm using all of my willpower for my wrists to cooperate, staring at them in deep concentration. I want to please my father, so badly. Time passes slowly. I cast my line through the air, such a pale blue that it appears almost white. The line lands with a soft dip into the murky water and disappears beneath the surface. More time passes. I feel a sharp tug. My rod bends. I am thrilled. I turn to announce my triumph to Dad, but he has disappeared and I am all alone. I start to panic, feeling an urgency to reel in my catch. Whatever I've caught is really putting up a fight. I figure I must have caught a real whopper. Then all of sudden, with one mighty heave, the surface of the water breaks and the biggest fish I've ever seen arcs upward, its silver scales shimmering like a beacon in the early morning sun. It seems as if the fish actually desires to be captured as it catapults though the sky and lands with a flop on the floor of the canoe. It's writhing horribly, the end of my hook piercing the skin of its mouth. I look into its eyes and realize with horror, this fish has the same eyes as my dad. He's looking at me with a sad, questioning expression. Then I'm crying and my tears are falling across the lake, like raindrops, rippling the water.

Cate tucks her journal back in her purse and looks over at her father with misty eyes to see his are open. She is so happy to see her father's blue eyes staring back at her. She walks over to her father's bed, bends over, and kisses his forehead, all smiles. Donna and Michael come over to join her. Her mother kisses William's sallow cheeks, and the three of them hold hands. Her father blinks once, then twice, then drifts into unconsciousness again.

"Well, that was short but sweet," Cate says. She feels restless. "What time is it?"

"Just past two thirty," Michael says, looking at his watch. "Dr. Leyden said it could be a few hours, or even several days. Not knowing is so hard."

"I can't help but wonder, now that all those machines aren't hooked up to him, if his soul hasn't already started to disconnect," their mother says.

"He sure looks peaceful," Michael says. "His face has the most serene expression I've seen since he was admitted."

"Yes," Cate agrees. "There's no sign of that anxious look he's had so often."

"That is a small blessing," their mother says.

After an hour or so, Michael suggests they all head down to the cafeteria to grab some sandwiches to go, but Cate has no appetite. Shortly after, they return, their hands full with food and drinks, including some snacks for Cate in case she's changed her mind. They take a seat in the chairs along the wall. Michael pops open a can of Diet Coke and takes a long sip.

"Wow, I was so thirsty. Are you sure you don't want at least a little something, Cate?"

"No, not right now, thanks." She is content to remain seated by her father's side, and besides, her stomach feels queasy.

When Donna finishes eating, she goes over to join Cate, on the other side of the bed.

"Would you mind if I had some alone time with your father?" she asks, sitting down.

Cate isn't at all happy to comply with her mother's request. She worries that her father could pass any minute, while she's out of the room. But she looks at her mom and sees her need etched into the very lines on her face.

"Yeah, sure, Mom."

Michael and Cate walk down the hall to the tiny kitchenette. Cate decides to brew up a pot of coffee. She checks her blood sugar while she waits. Her screen reads 5.4, a perfect number. It feels ironic, considering the stress she's feeling. She hasn't had a good number in days.

She taps her toes restlessly and disappears down the hall every five minutes to try and peer in through the frosted glass rectangle in the door to her father's room. She sips her hot coffee. It seems like an eternity, but after ten or fifteen minutes, their mother ushers them back in.

"Thank you so much," she says as Cate and Michael re-enter the room. "I really needed some private time with your dad."

Cate goes immediately to her father's side. She whispers, "I'm back," in his ear. She thinks she sees a look of awareness pass over his face, although she knows it is probably just her imagination. She plops back down in her chair to keep vigil, placing her hand over top of her father's.

Over the next several hours, William regains consciousness for a few minutes here and there, but for the most part he's in a deep sleep. Cate whispers to him about anything and everything that comes into her mind. She tells him about her grand ideas of going back to school, to become a psychologist. She talks about taking a creative writing course, writing a novel, or finding a publisher for the children's books she wrote for Celeste, Dana, and Taylor. She confides ideas she hasn't shared with anyone. She opens her heart about her hopes and dreams. She confesses the mistakes she's made as a parent. She tells him how much she loves him.

Time ticks by, slowly. Hospital staff drift in and out of the room. Her father sleeps. His lungs rattle and gurgle noisily with each breath.

There's a soft knock on the door. "Hi, you guys," Abeena says as she enters. She goes over and puts her hand on Donna's forearm. "I came by as soon as I could. I heard they'd moved William here when I started my shift, and I wanted to come and offer my condolences." She makes eye contact with each one of them.

"Thank you, Abeena," Donna says. "It means a lot. You've been one of the angels amongst us these past two weeks."

"I never had the privilege of knowing William," Abeena says. "But I've come to appreciate by watching all of you who love him so dearly, how special he is." Abeena swallows and takes a deep breath. "I'm sorry to say, I also have some difficult news. I thought it would be better if you heard it from a friend."

All three of them slip into alert mode. Donna sits up straighter. "Well, go on then."

"The doctor who was in to check on William last observed that despite our attempts to drain his lungs, they are starting to fill with fluid. We have to change his tubing out, but the procedure can be very painful. To be honest, we were hoping he'd be gone before it came to this, but as it is, well, it would be worse not to do it."

"How soon does the replacement need to be done?" Michael asks.

"It can wait maybe an hour, at the most," Abeena replies. "I'm going to get everything prepared now, so it's all ready for the doctor to go ahead. I'm so sorry to burden you with this." She squeezes Cate's shoulder and leaves the room.

Michael reaches his arms out to support his mother just as she teeters forward, almost collapsing. He lowers her into her chair and retrieves her bottle of water. Once her mother seems steady, Cate chooses to keep the resolve she'd made earlier, to always follow her heart, and crawls back into the bed beside her father. Donna does the same on the other side. Michael stands at the head of the bed and lowers his cheek to his father's, the three of them forming a shrine of love.

Cate closes her eyes. She blocks out the hospital room and listens. She hears the beating of her father's heart. She feels the warmth of his skin and the rise and fall of his chest. She hears her mother whispering a prayer. A tear drops from Michael's eye and lands on Cate's cheek.

With sudden clarity, Cate knows that her father is still holding on for them. She doesn't want him to make any more sacrifices for his family. She moves in closer and whispers into his ear.

"It's okay to let go now, Daddy. Did you hear Abeena? If you don't go, they're going to have to replace the tubing that is draining your lungs and it will hurt, a lot. You don't have to have any more pain, Daddy. You can let go now. God is waiting for you."

There is a strained silence. Her father's raspy breathing alters, as if he is listening and considering. His energy shifts. The silence is shattered as he inhales, another laboured breath. Cate lifts her tear-stained face from her father's cheek, watching his chest. She can sense something different. Her skin tingles. Her heart beats faster. Her father inhales once more, but when he exhales, it is his last.

Cate stares at her father in disbelief, despite everything. She waits to see his chest rise again, to hear the raspy sound of his breath, but there is only silence. She lets go a heart-wrenching sob and buries her face into his chest.

Time passes, likely only minutes, but for Cate, it's all so surreal, it feels an eternity. She continues to cling to her father.

"Cate, it's time, we need to let go," Michael says softly.

She doesn't move. She doesn't want to accept this. She's not ready to let her father go.

"Goodbye, Daddy," Cate sobs into his neck. She lifts her head and looks around the room, then into the faces of her mother and brother, then back at her father's still body. She shakes her head and gets up off his bed. Her entire body feels so heavy. She wills her legs to move, one step in front of the other. Michael has gathered up her things. He takes Cate by the elbow with his free hand and her mother takes the other.

As they leave the room, Abeena comes in and gives them all big hugs before ushering them out of the room to begin the necessary procedures. All three of them are numb, unable to speak, as they leave the hospital room and make their way down the hallway to the main entrance. They stop at the doors. Cate feels lost. She feels as though she is in a dream. She pinches herself, hoping to wake up, but it's of no use. This is her new reality, her life without her father in it.

Outside, Cate braces herself, taking a deep breath of fresh air, then turns to face her mother and brother. Their faces mirror back to her the loss and emptiness she is feeling.

"Are you okay to drive?" Michael asks, breaking the trance they are all under.

"I, yeah, I guess so."

Out in the parking lot, there is only a scattering of cars, the sky above them dark with clouds, a sliver of moonlight. Michael and her mother walk Cate to her van. There's nothing to do but go home.

Cate walks into a quiet house. Lady hears her and comes padding out to greet her, tail wagging. She seems to sense Cate's heaviness as she presses her muzzle against Cate's shin. Cate bends down to pat her and Lady licks her hand. The simple gesture brings a flood of fresh tears. Cate throws herself on the couch. She doesn't know how to do this. She retrieves her journal, still in her purse. She looks out the window at the sky. The stars twinkle. Cate hopes to spot her father's spirit ascending to heaven, but all she sees is space. She turns to a fresh page and begins to write.

> *Looking out the window into the dark night sky,*
> *I glimpse the beginning of a new and spectacular dawn.*
> *The sky in the east transforms from inky black to*
> *rusty indigo, to majestic magenta, to a soft cherry pink.*
> *It seems to speak to me of promises and dreams, of*
> *someplace I recognize but feels like so long ago.*
>
> *I don't see my father's spirit out there, but I picture*
> *him in my mind, playing baseball. I see him standing*
> *at the plate, legs planted firmly, his expression deadpan.*
> *I see him looking over at me, sitting in the bleachers—*
> *a conspiratorial wink. The pitcher releases the ball.*
> *It sails through the air. Dad swings the bat. Crack.*
> *It makes contact. Dad drops the bat in the dirt and*
> *starts running.*
>
> *I pray that somewhere in that forever sky my father*
> *is running free, watching over me, proud of who I've*

*become. I pray he will always be with me, bonded
in spirit, in our hearts, for eternity.*

*I don't know how I'm going to do this, how to carry
on without him. God knows I've endured one hell of
a lot of hardships in my lifetime, but this feels like too
much. My father was my rock, the one true thing I
always could rely on. He was a simple man. He didn't
change the world, but he changed mine. I felt witnessed,
accepted, perfect. His hands have always held me as
I laughed and cried. My father's hands, they were my
refuge. I always felt safe in his arms, with him only
a phone call away. Where will my strength come from
now? How will I manage, stuck in an unhealthy,
unhappy marriage? How will I be the good mother
my children need me to be, deserve me to be?*

*I don't have the answers. All I have left are the
memories, of the holding. I suppose it will have to
be enough.*

Cate is crying so hard by this time, she can't write
anymore. Her tears fall onto the page, smudging her words.
She closes her eyes. She sits in silence, for how long she
doesn't know. After a while she stirs, as if aroused by divine
inspiration. She has the strongest urge to write a poem for
her father. She goes into the office and sits down at the
computer to write. The words flow out of her with lightning
speed, her fingers on the keyboard barely able to keep up.

> *When I was born
> My father's hands were young hands.
> They held me when I cried
> And patted my back to sleep.
> They tickled me on my tiny toes
> And held my bottle while he fed me.*

My father's hands were perfect
For encompassing a baby girl.

When I was small
My father's hands were busy hands.
They taught me the grip for swinging a baseball bat
And threaded bait onto fishing lines.
They pierced marshmallows onto campfire sticks
And steadied my bicycle when I learned to ride.
My father's hands were perfect
For playing with his little girl.

When I was a teenager
My father's hands became sick hands.
Rheumatoid arthritis bent them, giving him pain.
They wrung themselves together when I started
to rebel,
When I wore too much makeup, tight shirts,
and high heels.
They gripped me by my shoulders when I lied
Then held me close when I said sorry and cried.
My father's hands were perfect
For loving me unconditionally.

When I became a mother, too young,
My father's hands were helping hands.
They rocked my daughter with his magic touch
When I needed to rest, four hours' sleep
not enough.
They tucked her in her crib for me
While I took night classes to earn my degree.
My father's hands were perfect
For supporting me.

When I got married,
My father's hands were relieved hands.
They held my hand as I walked down the aisle
And comforted me when my marriage had trials.
They let go a little, almost tentatively,
While still remaining strong for me.
My father's hands were perfect
For setting me free.

When I was pregnant the second time,
My father's hands were worried hands.
Diagnosed with diabetes, I got very sick;
He opened his expanding support tool kit,
Then held me throughout the thin and the thick.
My father's hands were perfect
For nurturing me.

When I was pregnant yet again,
My father's hands became crippled hands.
He became critically ill,
Spending three months in the hospital.
The day my son was born
Was the day my father finally went home.
My father's hands were perfect
For beholding me.

Two weeks ago
My father's hands became ravaged hands.
Infection spread into them as I stood helplessly by,
His fingers ash-black; blood tears I cried.
My father gifted his love and reassurance
Even in the midst of his struggle to live.
My father's hands were perfect
For comforting me.

Today my father's hands are gone,
They are in God's hands.
They cannot encompass me, play with me,
Love me unconditionally, support me, or
set me free.
They cannot nurture me, behold me, or
comfort me.
They cannot give him any more pain.
My father's hands are perfect,
Forever in my memory.

Author

Lynda Faye Schmidt

LYNDA BELIEVES THAT CREATING is her life purpose. Whether that manifests in building meaningful relationships, writing, or simply preparing gorgeous food, she loves to be fully engaged in the process of life.

Lynda pens emotionally impacting, character-driven novels based on real-life experiences. Her novel, *The Healing*, was published on April 23, 2021. She also posts regularly on her blog, *Musings of an Emotional Creature*.

Lynda earned a Bachelor of Education and worked as a teacher in a variety of different educational settings. She has attended writing workshops and completed several creative writing courses during her years as a teacher in public, private, and special needs settings. She was also a contributor for *DQ Living Magazine*.

Solid routines balanced by open spaces that allow for opportunities contribute to Lynda's happiness, all within the foundation of her incredible partnership with her husband, David. They live a peaceful existence in Riyadh, Saudi Arabia, where her days are filled with time spent on her computer writing, practicing yoga and meditation, and connecting with the people she loves. She is passionate about mindfulness, spirituality, equality, human rights, and honouring the planet.

To find out more, visit her website at *www.lyndafayeschmidt.com.*

With Gratitude

DAVID SCHMIDT, YOU ARE my rock, our loving partnership the foundation of everything. My treasured relationship with my father, Kenneth Smith, was the inspiration for *The Holding*. Carol Kujala, your friendship, support, and love provide me with my compass. Anne Marie Horne, thank you for breaking your rule about befriending clients and being open to transforming friendship to family. Christina Forgeron, I cherish our bimonthly, open, and honest conversations about anything and everything. Julia Crouch, your consistent support, no matter how busy your life gets, blows me away.

The Holding wouldn't be what it is without the incredible talent and editing advice from my co-publisher and dear friend, Anne O'Connell. Thank you also to the rest of the team: Grace Laemmler, interior design; David Edelstein, cover design and e-book conversion; Marianne Ward, copy editing; Sarah MacFarlane, proofreading; Danielle O'Brien, cover photograph.

I'm also indebted to all my advance readers, who graciously agreed to plow through the unedited manuscript, provide valued feedback and most-appreciated reviews: Elizabeth Kingsman, Christina Forgeron, Linda Smith, Michelle Moran, and Alison DeLory.

CPSIA information can be obtained
at www.ICGtesting.com
Printed in the USA
BVHW080713040322
630365BV00001B/8

9 781989 833162